NAPOLEON'S BLACKGUARDS

NAPOLEON'S BLACKGUARDS

A story of adventure and courage,
sacrifice and loss

by

Stephen McGarry

Napoleon's Blackguards by Stephen McGarry
Copyright © 2019 Stephen McGarry

ISBN-13: 978-1-946409-62-1(Paperback)
ISBN:-978-1-946409-63-8 (e-book)

BISAC Subject Headings:
FIC014000FICTION / Historical
FIC032000FICTION / War & Military
FIC031020FICTION / Thrillers / Historical

The Book Cover Whisperer:
ProfessionalBookCoverDesign.com

Address all correspondence to:

Penmore Press LLC
920 N Javelina Pl
Tucson AZ 85748

Reviews

"McGarry tells a great revenge story set among the Irish soldiers who fought for Napoleon. Compelling characters, exciting scenes and a fascinating fictional ride through a refreshingly different aspect of the Napoleonic Wars."
—Tim Newark, author of *The Fighting Irish*.

"At long last! A novel that focuses on the significant Irish contribution to the extraordinary success of Napoleon's army, set against the backdrop of The Peninsular War. *Napoleon's Blackguards* is a pacy, sharp-shooting, vengeance-fuelled ode to an age of deadly duels, cavalry charges, cocked hats and musketry."
—Turtle Bunbury, best-selling author and historian.

'Whiskey in the Jar'
(17ᵗʰ Century traditional Irish ballad)

As I was going over
The Cork and Kerry mountains
I saw Captain Farrell
And his money he was countin'
I first produced my pistol
And then produced my rapier
I said "Stand and deliver
Or the devil he may take you"

(Chorus)
Musha ring dum a doo dum a da
Whack for my daddy'o
Whack for my daddy'o, there's
Whisky in the jar,

O Being drunk and weary
I went to Molly's chamber
Taking my Molly with me
And I never knew the danger
For about six or maybe seven
In walked Captain Farrell
I jumped up, fired off my pistols
And I shot him with both barrels.

PROLOGUE

The Field of Mars, Paris 1805

Sous-lieutenant James Ryan of Napoleon's Irish Legion had been standing at attention for an hour and breathed a sigh of relief when he could finally stand at ease. He removed his shako, wiped sweat from his brow, and jammed the helmet back on as he waited to receive the Irish battalion's Imperial Eagle.

The great city of Paris had shaken off the drabness of a cold December morning and bustled with activity. The route along the parade ground to the Champs de Mars fluttered with red, white and blue tricolours festooned onto railings and windows, as thousands slowly made their way to the Imperial Pavilion where Emperor Napoleon was to bestow his new bronze-cast Eagle battle-standards on the army.

The regimental representatives from the entire Grande Armée had been mobilised weeks in advance for the event, and the roads into Paris had been choked with traffic for days as dusty, cloaked detachments arrived from Italy, the Rhine and the Low Countries, including the units posted along the Spanish border and the German towns of Mainz and Strasburg.

The sight of the multi-coloured troops from the far-flung garrisons of the French Empire was simply magnificent; for their flamboyant uniforms comprised gaudy pastels ranging from blues, oranges and yellows to scarlet, with long plumes in various colours protruding out of shakos. The officers' tunics glittered with silver buttons and gold-laced epaulettes, while their braided cocked hats sported silken tricolour cockades and ostrich feathers trimmed with lace. The finery extended down to their polished, silver-spurred jackboots.

Napoleon's cavalrymen sat on sleek mares and stallions of various hues of black, dun, brown and chestnut. Everywhere the smell of oil and polish and the acrid, ammonia-like sweat of man and horse, tinged with musty eau de cologne, wafted the air. A troop of cuirassiers in polished breastplates and curved silver helmets trailing two-feet-long black manes sat proudly on their magnificent chargers. The green-coated dragoons and the Polish lancers of the guard soothed their horses as two chasseurs à cheval of the Imperial Guard in their enormous bearskins struggled to control them as their forelegs rose up and stomped loudly on the cobbles. Napoleon's elite light cavalry arm of hussars leered heavily under their busby hats and strange, loose-fitting, velvet pelisses. The exotic mounted bodyguard of Oriental cavalry, the Mamelukes, who'd followed Napoleon home from the Egyptian expedition, were also there. They too were resplendent in outlandish Oriental garb and strange white-plumed turbans, ivory-handled, curved daggers tucked menacingly in their belts.

The backbone of the Imperial Army, the Regiments of the Line, the Light Infantry, the Horse and Foot Artillery, the Gendarmes and the National Guard were also present, including fierce-looking, axe-carrying bearded sappers. The officers of the Marine stood behind them, in swallow-tailed navy tunics with golden epaulettes, followed by sailors in blue jackets and tricolour breeches.

Everything was in place as contingents from the entire army paraded in full dress uniform and took post in front of the Imperial Pavilion. They stood frozen at attention with fixed bayonets and puffed up chests studded with hard-won medals, the very epitome of martial dignity.

They dipped their colours as musicians of Napoleon's personal bodyguard, the Imperial Guard, belted out 'La Marseillaise,'—that great patriotic marching song from the early days of the Revolution—followed by the unofficial anthem of the French republic, 'Veillons au Salut de l'Empire.' The assembled crowds applauded fervently. The rolling din of artillery fired out a bombastic one-hundred and one Imperial salute. The mesmerised crowds gasped in awe.

On the Champs de Mars an elaborate twenty-foot-high wooden pavilion, with porticos painted gold, had been constructed where the many hundreds of invited dignitaries, senators, royals, and ambassadors drawn from all over Europe had been seated. Raised high behind the Imperial Pavilion were proudly displayed two-hundred captured enemy flags taken by the French army in Italy and Egypt, and, of course, at the crowning triumph over the Austrians at the battle of Marengo.

A galaxy of Marshals of France, exquisitely tailored in high-collared ceremonial navy tailcoats embellished with garlands, completed the spectacle. They haughtily carried their cylindrical navy batons studded with golden Eagles. Richly gilded swords and scabbards hung around their waists. Many wore the red ribbon and white enamel cross of the Légion d'honneur and the silver-starred Grand Eagle.

Two heavily embossed, gilt-framed thrones with crowned Eagle motifs took pride of place in the centre of the pavilion where Emperor Napoleon, his wife, the Empress Josephine, and the Imperial princesses were to receive the homage of the army. Josephine looked radiant in a white silk dress in the Empire style, wearing a crown of pearls, but all eyes were on the star of the show himself. Emperor Napoleon, wearing a crown and a full imperial garb of crimson velvet, stood up from his chair holding the imperial silver wand. The Army shouted the formal greeting to the Emperor on parade three times, 'Vive l'Empereur!'

Drummers began to play with choreographed precision as columns of men marked time, wheeled about, and converged at the foot of the staircase to have their trophies blessed. The colonels of the different regiments passed in file along the Imperial Pavilion, each tipping his Eagle at the required forty-five-degree angle as he passed. The Emperor then touched the Eagle with his ungloved right hand while the colonels saluted. The colonel then handed the new battle-standard to his designated Eagle bearer.

The last unit to receive its battle-standard was the Eagle escort of Napoleon's Irish Legion, newly raised to lead an anticipated invasion of Ireland. The Irish light infantrymen wore a full parade dress of emerald green faced in parchment yellow on their cuffs and collar. They carried their green flag with embroidered golden harps bearing the inscription; *l'Indépendence de l'Irlande.'* Ryan felt the hair stand up on the back of his neck as he received the sculpted battle-standard after the Emperor had blessed it.

'Soldiers!' addressed the Emperor with outstretched hand, gesturing towards the Eagles. 'These Eagles shall be your rallying-point. Do you swear to sacrifice your lives in their defence and to keep them always? Do you swear it?'

A vast chorus arose from the army.

'We swear it!' they repeated fervently, while drummers began a frantic beat amid exulted volleys of *'Vive l'Empereur! Vive Napoleon!'*

Napoleon then turned to the adoring crowds and raised his hands. The electrifying spectacle resembled a religious experience and the soldiers of the Imperial Army responded by throwing their shakos and bicorns in the air, some dangling their headgear on top of sabres and bayonets.

'Vive l'Empereur! Vive la France!' they shouted hoarsely, as the crowds became ecstatic and could hardly control themselves. Even the battle-hardened veterans of the Imperial Guard choked with emotion and wept.

CHAPTER 1

August 1808. Three years had passed since the Day of the Eagles in Paris. Crickets trilled furiously in the long grass as the sun beamed out of a clear azure sky, warming the lush green countryside of northern Spain.

The twelve-man infantry patrol slowly sifted through the countryside.

'Get a move on, lads!' exclaimed Captain James Ryan, now raised from sous-lieutenant. He paused to uncork his canteen to take a swig of water and laid out his compass in the palm of his hand to check their position. The taste of the earthy, lukewarm water lingered unpleasantly in his throat.

'How far now, Cap'n?' asked Corporal McGowan.

'Not too far—the monastery should be just three hours' march.' The Cistercian monastery of Santa Maria was where they were to procure food and supplies, their destination that day.

Ryan's men were a foraging patrol of the 2nd battalion's voltigeur company of Napoleon's Irish Legion who formed part of the advance guard of VIII Army Corps that had invaded Spain. They were a motley crew if ever there was one; a strange mix of blackguards, cutthroats, deserters, and others escaping the long hand of the law, all led by a band of former Irish rebels.

Ryan let the men pass and checked O'Brien's cantina for liquor. A quick sniff assured him that it contained just water. He shoved the flask back to the voltigeur. 'Carry on!'

They passed over a ridge and saw the monastery in the

distance. The men wore the standard French light infantry uniform in green faced in yellow. Their sun-bleached jackets, once emerald green, had turned olive from exposure to the sun, but the faded olive hues were ideal for looking for cover when skirmishing. Their standard bell-shaped French shakos retained a dull brass echelon plate, pressed onto it was the 'Maid of Erin' harp motif surmounted with the words '*Légion Irlandaise.*' As an elite company of voltigeurs, they carried the Charleville dragoon-musket, with a light infantryman's *épée* sword hooked to the belt. Their battered boots were the same ones that had marched one-thousand miles over rough ground from their regimental depot in northern France.

As James Ryan walked, he knew something bad was going to happen—he felt it in his bones. He didn't know when and didn't know where, but he knew things would not end well.

A sputter of coughs interrupted Ryan's thoughts, as boots kicked up dry dirt suspending it briefly in the still air before smutting into the faces of those behind. Ryan raised his eyes and saw his forward scout running towards him trailing his musket.

'Enemy cavalry, sir!' Vandam blurted breathlessly
Ryan looked at him hard. 'How many?'
He hurriedly opened his battered brass telescope.
'A handful, sir,' Vandam replied.
The lens jolted him forward as he scoured the horizon, then Ryan pushed it back and saw five or six horsemen dressed in blue. *They don't look like Spanish*—he thought to himself as he adjusted the telescope's focus. Then he saw from their uniforms that they were British!

The horsemen climbed down the hill. When they were a hundred yards away, he watched with apprehension as their curved sabres extended out in the 'engage' as they clattered down the slope. He heard the command, '*Charge!*' He knew that infantry were at the mercy of horsemen, caught in the open, where one firm downward stroke delivered by a strong sword arm could literally slice a man's head to the eyeballs.

Snapping the telescope shut, he turned to his file. 'Follow me and make for the wooded area at the foot of the hill. *Quick!* Those bastards can't get us in there!'

'*Hell's bells!*' McGowan exclaimed.

The squad knew things were looking bad when McGowan shouted this. They began to run.

Ryan had already noted the nearby wood for such an eventuality when he'd stepped out of line to let the men pass earlier. *Always think two or three steps ahead*, he thought to himself. That was a sign of a good officer.

He peered over his shoulder and saw the horsemen gathering pace. He hadn't seen any British since he had arrived in Spain. Until now, the enemy had always been the poorly equipped Spanish army who had increasingly melted into the ranks of the guerrillas.

When the squad were two-hundred paces from the safety of the wood, in the tail of his eye Ryan glimpsed Kaminski squat down on one knee, load his musket and fire at the leading rider, who had a half a furlong lead on the others.

'You stupid bastard, Kaminski!' he shouted.

It was a recklessly brave manoeuvre, as it was difficult enough to hit a moving target coming at you at speed. Ryan was impressed with the man's *sangfroid*, but he'd seen stupid bravery result in men getting killed many times before. If Kaminski missed, the horseman would catch him in the open, and he would be no match against cavalry. Ryan turned his head back to look. Kaminski had fired too low. Luckily, the shot hit the horse on an upper thigh, causing the horse to buckle and throw his rider, who pitched headfirst to the ground. It looked as though his neck had snapped. Kaminski raised himself up and sprinted towards the woods.

'Get a move on, Kaminski!' Ryan bellowed as he pulled one of his men by his epaulettes, causing him to stumble head first into the wood. Relieved, Ryan knew he and his men were now safe.

Ryan watched as a cavalry officer, breathless after his gallop, cautiously reined his horse to a halt a short distance away, outside musket range. '*Messieurs—*' the officer began in French.

Ryan saw now that the horsemen were dragoons, for he knew the blue-coated light cavalrymen well, as they had served in Ireland. He made a speaking trumpet with his hands. 'You can forget that froggy language for a start. You've just run into Napoleon's Irish Legion—we're not French, we're Irish!'

A chorus of sniggering and wolf-whistles followed. The abashed officer swallowed slowly, froze in amazement, and self-consciously straightened the sheepskin liner under his saddle before pulling his horse to the side. Corporal McGowan loaded his musket and skirted the wood to be closer to the dragoons, and, obscured from view, aimed and discharged his musket, hitting a dragoon squarely in the shoulder. The spherical leaden ball lodged deep in the flesh with a dull thud and caused the trooper to wrench back and grimace in agony in his saddle.

McGowan removed the fiddle strapped to his back and loudly rattled '*rum-dum-rum-dum-rummadum-dum*' with his fingers on the fiddle's neck. 'Get used to the sound of old trousers,' he bawled. 'Old Trousers' was the name the British gave to the drumroll rhythm of Napoleon's feared *pas de charge* attack drumbeat.

The dragoons were furious and unleashed a fruitless

volley from their carbines into the darkness of the wood. Further away, Ryan heard the rumble of French cavalry approaching, which caused the dragoons to quickly disperse.

The French light cavalry troopers were Ryan's mounted support, who had abandoned the infantry patrol when they'd galloped ahead to look for food for their horses. They were the black knights of the French army called the Hussars of Death dressed in black dolman jackets with fur-edged black pelisses slung jauntily over their shoulders. A silver skull and crossbones deadhead *totenkopf* insignia on their shakos was carried onto their *sabretache,* the leather pouches hanging from their belts. They were the most dastardly cavalry regiment in the French army. They famously never gave quarter.

By the time the hussars arrived, Ryan saw that the British horsemen had gained too much ground and the hussars soon gave up the chase.

'We just made it to the wood, boys! If you'd been ten seconds later we would've been dead men,' said Ryan as he watched the Black Hussars approach cautiously. 'Where the hell were you? You left us stranded!' he shouted in French to Captain Lejeune, a tall, sallow-faced, moustachioed young officer. His braided hair *cadenettes* dangled from his temples to his ears and were tied with musket balls to ensure a good vertical hang. This was the fashion at the time.

Ryan sniffed deeply. 'I've a good mind to pull you down from your saddle and show you cold steel—we were nearly cut down by those bloody dragoons! You know very well we stand no chance against cavalry caught in the open.'

Lejeune's horse edged sideways. 'We were collecting food for our horses, *M'sieu'*, he answered curtly, as he soothed his buckskin gelding with a series of little slaps to the horse's neck.

Ryan took out his cavalry pistol from under his belt and continued to load it as he walked towards the hussar.

Lejeune placed a hand on his carbine.

Ryan ratcheted the pistol's hammer back, ordering in English, 'Take your hand off that carbine, laddie!'

Although Lejeune's command of English was poor, he had learned his lesson about scrapping with these wild Irishmen before. Ryan turned towards the wounded horse shot by Kaminski. The animal was on its haunches, grunting and whining in pain.

'May I remind you that we are on the same side!' He placed the pistol to the horse's temple and fired the coup de grâce. The horse's head dropped to the ground with a dull, heavy thud.

Captain Lejeune sniffed indolently but said nothing.

Ryan pulled Kaminsky to one side. 'You disobeyed my order! That was just plain stupid! Out there in the open field, you nearly had half a dozen horsemen on you and you would have been cut to pieces with cold steel. This is no place for showing off to the other men. Those tactics only get men killed! And besides, it's a bad example in front of the others.'

Kaminski feigned a smile. 'I still made it, sir, didn't I?'

'You did, but just about! I thought you were the best shot in the company!'

Kaminski remained silent.

'For you missed that bloody dragoon and hit the bloody horse instead.' Ryan spat.

'I *am* the best shot in your company and I didn't miss. I knew by the way the dragoon was riding—galloping at speed with his body high up over the horse's neck—that if I hit the horse on the thigh it would throw the rider. It was too easy to shoot him out of the saddle.'

'You're a mad bastard, Kaminski! You're no better than

McGowan!' Ryan pulled back his shako in disbelief. 'Don't disobey my orders again!'

Their scrap with the British dragoons had prevented them from making it to the monastery in time, and with the fading light, Ryan thought it was too dangerous to remain in the countryside because of the risk of guerrilla attacks.

The twelve-man squad swished through the long grass and snaked their way back to their garrison, followed by the Hussars of Death, sauntering in the rear.

Birds whistled noisily from one end of the valley to the other as the platoon marched on. The crunches of plodding boots on dry soil and the jangle of the horses in the rear were the only sounds until Corporal McGowan broke wind.

'Vive l'Empereur!' he blurted with a broad smile. His mouth framed an incomplete set of teeth, for one was missing in front, the others were tinged yellow. Tufts of brown hair, stiff with dirt, stuck out under his battered shako. A large gold earring hung from his left ear.

A low hubbub of laughter ran through the men. The warm air quickly carried the foul odour up the noses of the men in the front.

'Pipe down!' Captain Ryan snarled angrily.

'Sorry, sir!' McGowan grinned proudly as he spat hard on the ground. 'It was last night's onion soup.

The squad later approached the summit of a ridge. Ryan took out his telescope and scanned the countryside for miles around, looking for any enemy. There was no one. 'Rest here for ten minutes,' he ordered. 'Sergeant Hoffman!'

'Sir?'

'What's the name of that marching tune the Imperial Guard sings before an attack?' The Imperial Guard were Napoleon's elite bodyguard.

'Oh, it's called "Le *Chant de l'Oignon*", the song of the onion.'

The men chuckled.

'Tray beans!' said Ryan. 'Tray beans!' The term was a running joke in the Irish regiment due to the poor quality of spoken French and was a play on the French term *Trés bien* —Very good. 'And furthermore, McGowan,' continued Ryan, 'I very well may put you on report for disrespecting our dear Napoleon Bonaparte.'

McGowan grumbled a sailor's oath and muttered quietly, under his breath. 'May the lamb of God stir his hoof through the roof of heaven and kick you in the arse down to hell.'

'You need to say something to me, corporal?' challenged Ryan mockingly. 'Don't give me any of your auld jaw!'

McGowan smiled contemptuously. 'The Emperor can kiss me royal Irish arse!'

'You're intelligent, McGowan, I give ye that, but you're a fool! I don't know why Sergeant Conway gave you liberty. You're a ne'er do well, a bad sort and a blaggard!' Ryan sneered, rubbing his nose on the back of his hand.

'Well, sir, that may be true, for I've been a thief for most of me life, and I thought I would land myself in a better place here in the Legion with grander opportunities for plunder!'

'Little shite!' Ryan spat dismissively. He stood up and sloped his carbine rifle. 'Now get a move on!'

One hour later, the majestic cut-stone spires of the capital of Old Castile in northern Spain came into view.

'Ain't I glad to see dear old Burgos,' McGowan declared happily.

The tired and weary platoon trundled over the old bridge, through the gates of the city walls, and back into Burgos.

CHAPTER 2

Back in his quarters, Ryan heaved off his heavy boots and unslung his rifle. He sat on his bunk, took hold of his rifle, and read the high copperplate engraving on its lock. '*M're Impériale de Versailles*' denoted the rifle's manufacturer in Paris. It was still in near perfect condition, but the stock had a crack in the burl walnut, caused by a brawl with a cuirassier officer back in Bayonne. Ryan had whacked him across the head, leaving him out cold, but it had split the rifle's stock. He rubbed over it and wondered if the battalion's armourer could repair it.

He thought back about the encounter with the British dragoons. In the 1798 Irish Rebellion he had fought against the British and was on the run when a troop of dragoons arrived at his home. They then murdered his wife and child. The officer responsible, he'd been told, was an albino called Daniel Darkford. His mind drifted back to the brutal manner they were slain when a sharp rasp on the door interrupted his thoughts.

'Beggin' your pardon, sir,' a voice gently called out. It was his *valet de chambre*, a young, pale-faced Scottish orderly. 'Commander Lawless wants to see you in his study, sir.'

'Come in, Ferguson!'

Private Ferguson had served with the 95th Rifles based in the British garrison in the Channel Islands. After taking part in a raid along the French coast he'd been captured and held for three months in a French prison when two of the Irish Legion's recruiting sergeants had visited him. They'd harped on incessantly with tales of the comforts and bonhomie of life in Napoleon's Army and consequently, for better or for worse, he'd taken up the offer to join the Irish Legion.

'How long did you serve in the Rifles, son?'

'Four months, sir.'

'Just four months?'

'Aye, sir,' said the orderly as he brushed down Ryan's jacket.

'You a good shot with a rifle, lad?'

'Aye, not too bad, sir, I've seen worse shots than me, aye, I have, sir.'

'Do you know a dragoon officer called Darkford? If you saw him you would know, as he's an albino.'

'Captain Dark-f-ford?' stuttered Ferguson as he paused in thought. 'No, sir, can't say I have, sir.'

Ryan rubbed the sole of his aching foot. 'No matter. That'll be all.' He sighed heavily as he routed around under his bunk for his wooden clogs, he put them on and tossed his forage cap onto his head and made his way out towards the battalion commander's quarters.

Ryan knew that *Chef de battalion* William Lawless was finding the stress of leading the Irish battalion in a difficult war too much to bear. Lawless sat behind his desk, furtively massaging his temples. Lawless had served in Clare's Regiment of the Irish Brigade of France under the *ancien régime*. He was now getting on, and appeared to Ryan to be somewhere in his mid-fifties, overweight and a little too fond of drink. Lawless had been without leave for two years and the strain was beginning to show. Ryan couldn't stop himself staring at Lawless's limp right arm. It had received a sabre-cut from a Mameluke horseman while he'd been serving in Egypt, which had rendered the limb nearly useless.

'I heard that you ran into some British dragoons on your foraging patrol, Ryan.'

'Yes, sir, and we were lucky to escape as the Hussars of Death had left us high and dry.'

'Hussars of Death,' repeated Lawless mockingly. 'Any hussar who is not dead by the age of thirty is a murdering blackguard!'

Ryan nodded and looked at Lawless hard with a set of steely grey eyes.

'I will pass this onto General Junot's staff. We've received rumours that Lieutenant-General Sir Arthur Wellesley commands a 50,000—strong British Army that has shipped into Lisbon to assist the Spanish and Portuguese in ousting Napoleon. The bloody dragoons must have been on a reconnaissance patrol, assisting the local guerrillas. I've ordered a mounted patrol out to make sure they are not part of a larger force, but our intelligence confirms that there are no significant British troops this far north.'

Lawless coughed and cleared his throat. 'There's something else I wanted to talk to you about, Ryan. We have a fresh batch of recruits. Sailors! Irish sailors from the Royal Navy!'

'Deserters?'

'Naval prisoners of war who arrived from some god forsaken hole up north and were sent down to us.'

Ryan frowned. 'Ships' boys and gunners who can't march. Can't you send them to the Artillery?'

Lawless shook his head, his brow furrowed. 'You know that's not possible, Ryan. They're Irish, and, besides, they don't speak French. The Irish Legion is the only place for them.'

NAPOLEON'S BLACKGUARDS

Lawless offered a cigar to Ryan and placed one in his own mouth. He removed a lighted taper from his desk and paused to light it. 'Besides,' he continued, pursing his lips and slowly exhaled the sweet tobacco smoke, 'you should feel lucky to have them! Don't' forget those aul' salties can bloody well fight! And they're an agile lot too. They can shimmy up ropes like rats and aren't afraid of the smell of gunpowder either,' he affirmed. 'They can live on a sup o' water and a chomp of bread; throw in a daily ration of brandy grog and they'll follow you to the gates of hell! I was thinking of sending them to your company, as you're gaining a reputation.'

Lawless passed the flickering taper to Ryan.

'Well, I'm glad to hear that, sir. They might decorate me with the Legion of honour yet, Commander.'

Ryan curled his upper lip disdainfully as he lit his cigar.

'Don't smirk, Ryan,' Lawless replied brusquely, as he picked up a sheaf of papers from his desk, 'for I have bad news. The battalion inspection report is in and it doesn't make for good reading. It doesn't make good reading at all!' Lawless placed his pince-nez on his nose and began to read.

'*The Inspector General congratulates the men of the 2nd Irish battalion on their bravery and esprit de corps—*'

'But this is fine, sir! We are commended.'

'Hold on, Ryan, it gets worse,' Lawless said, then continued.

'*In general, the men are well maintained and clean but their hair is too long and not tied at the back in a queue. Their collars are dirty and many have grown non-regulation beards under their chins.*'

Lawless sighed heavily and adjusted his glasses.

'*The battalion talk loudly when formed up on the square. Their firearm training also leads much to be desired, as many wear their cross-belts too loosely, making access to their cartridge boxes difficult. Additionally, the men have carved their initials into the stocks of their Charlevilles, while the regulation clearly specifies that the stocks are to be numbered only. Furthermore, the battalion is urinating against the barracks instead of using the buckets provided making a terrible stench. Many of the officers wear non-regulation headgear and habitually wear them tilted over one eyebrow.*

'Worst of all are the instances of infighting and dueling among the corps. Indeed, fighting is not just restricted to the rank and file in the Irish battalion but many of the officers have also been brawling with each other.'

The battalion commander exhaled loudly and looked up at Ryan from under his reading glasses. 'This will just not do! It will not do.' He slumped down like a sack of potatoes behind his desk. 'I need to tell you, Ryan,' he went on, 'that some of the staff officers have been complaining about the lack of discipline in the Irish battalion for some time now. They have voiced concerns about some of the dubious characters in your *voltigeur* company in particular.'

'I can't do much about that, sir. They're a rough, uncouth lot alright.'

'Yes! yes! We know all that, Ryan, but it reflects badly on me and on the Irish Legion as a whole. I've heard that these complaints have reached General Junot's ear.'

Ryan lounged in an armchair as he puffed hungrily on his cigar.

Lawless tapped hard on the report. 'They say that the men in your company comprise the worst blackguards in Napoleon's army. They fail to show respect and are found brawling and thieving, and they typically wear non-regulation uniform—this last inspection confirms it! The men have even removed the plumes from their shakos for

God's sake!' Lawless scratched his head and grimaced. 'There's also talk that you are setting a bad example to the men.'

Ryan stared at an imaginary spot on the ceiling and puffed out plumes of smoke circles. 'Napoleon's blaggards!' he said, smiling, 'I like the ring of that.'

'You're trouble, Ryan,' Lawless said. 'You'll be the end of me yet!' He threw his arms up in the air in frustration and raised his voice. 'I'm trying to run the battalion in this vile little war, cooped up here in the arsehole of Spain. If our dear Emperor, Ol' Boney, hears that his Irish Legion is found wanting he may simply disband us and we'll all be out of a job.'

'Found wanting? Have no fear. If Boney disbands us, we'll be sorely needed elsewhere in another regiment. You know that.'

'Yes, of course, but if another invasion of Ireland is planned, where will we be then?' Lawless whacked the report on his desk. 'High and bloody dry! That's where we'll be, high and dry!' With that the battalion commander, his face now red and swelling with rage, collapsed back into his seat with a long, laboured sigh.

It was all getting to be too much.

'I don't bloody care what those froggy officers think,' said Ryan. 'They should feel lucky they have us on their side. Nobody can dispute we're one of the best fighting units in the bloody French army. What do they expect from deserters, cutthroats, marauders and thieves? We're not the typical genteel conscripts, the well-born sons of mannerly artisans or respectable school teachers from decent French villages!'

'Yes, I agree, but don't be so bloody cynical, James! We're a thorn in England's side as they've lost too many men to desertions.' Lawless flicked his fingers as an orderly briskly decanted a bottle of cognac and poured it into a pair of crystal-fluted glasses.

'We just need to be seen to conform a little, just keep our heads down,' Lawless replied, consoling himself as he swirled the amber coloured liquid in his glass.

The two men held their glasses and paused in silence

'*Sláinte!*' toasted Lawless in Gaelic before they eagerly gulped down their drams in one.

'Ah!' Lawless sighed with satisfaction, 'now that lifts the fog of the heart!'

He shot a look at Ryan, gesturing impatiently to his valet for another refill.

'Will that be all, Commander?' said Ryan.

Commander Lawless held his glass out as his valet filled it. 'You should grow a moustache, for it's most becoming. If it's good enough for the veterans of the Imperial Guard it sure as hell is good enough for us.'

Ryan raised his eyes to heaven as he turned to leave.

Ryan made his way across the parade ground towards the officers' mess, his head spinning from the effects of the cognac. He saw the Irish battalion's canteen mistress alight from her covered wagon. 'La Belle Marie' was one of the civilian sutlers who dispensed brandy to the men in battle, tended the wounded, and sometimes even fought alongside them.

'Captain Ryan, glad to see you again,' she said in a low, husky voice, as Ryan lifted her infant son off the wagon.

He patted the boy on the head. 'The little fella is getting big, isn't he?

Marie nodded and smiled, displaying a perfect set of white teeth.

'Give me a double dram, will you?' Ryan stood and

admired her as she opened the little brass tap of her *tonnelet* and dispensed it into Ryan's own pewter tankard. Marie's complexion was fair and she had light blue eyes, and her face was framed with a long mane of curly blonde hair. She wore a wide-brimmed black mariner's hat, surmounted with the harp crest on the front, trimmed with ribbon and a tricolour cockade. She had tailored her Irish Legion's green tunic to fit her slender frame, and wore it over a white blouse and red tricolour skirt. The brandy doled out by Marie was better than the rotgut served out in other units in the French army. The goodness of the brandy corresponded directly to the beauty of the *cantiniére*, an old soldier once laid it down, and, as her name suggested, La Belle Marie was as beauteous as they came.

He remembered the story told often around the campfires, for all new recruits who joined the Irish battalion were infatuated with her. Marie was the daughter of a wealthy family in Paris. She'd fallen for a servant boy and when he was called up for army service, she followed the drum and secretly ran away with him. The only way women could join the army overseas was to serve as regimental *cantiniéres*. The story went that she had accompanied Napoleon's army to Egypt, and her sweetheart had died of fever on the voyage over. During the Battle of the Pyramids, Mameluke cavalry captured her and held her for months before she was rescued. She didn't speak for a year after her release, such was the suffering she had endured, and she later hid her wounds beneath a veneer of gaiety. She'd fallen in love with an Irishman serving with the Army of the Orient before he transferred to the Irish Legion where Marie had followed him, serving as the Irish battalion's *cantiniére*. He'd been killed the previous year.

Ryan beamed a smile at Marie as he handed her two sous

and thanked her, then returned to his quarters.

That night Ryan was troubled. He couldn't stop thinking about the encounter with the British dragoons. He finally fell asleep but awoke abruptly a little time later drenched in sweat. The night sweats and the nightmares had begun again. His daughter had appeared to him in a recurring dream, asking him why he hadn't saved them. Tortured and riddled with guilt. he couldn't stop thinking about their deaths, their terrible deaths at the hands of Darkford. He tried to put these thoughts behind him, but he couldn't, and he was still wide awake, staring at the ceiling unable to sleep, when the buglers beat reveille in the morning.

CHAPTER 3

The 15th of August was Napoleon's birthday. The garrison were celebrating with copious rations of cognac as a score of bedraggled Irish sailors, held as prisoners of war by the French, heavy-footed it into Burgos. The sailors shuffled wearily onto the parade ground, where the battalion commander and Ryan stood waiting.

Commander Lawless ordered the parade to attention. 'Gentlemen! I want to welcome you to the Irish Legion. Although we form part of the French Army, we fight for Ireland! Ireland has a proud tradition of military service in France, spanning over one-hundred years, and we recall the achievements of the illustrious regiments of Dillon, Clare and Fitzjames of the grand old Irish Brigade of France. The Irish Brigade scored numerous victories for France, most notably defeating the British at Fontenoy, leading the charge that crashed through the British Foot. We strive to emulate their glories in the Irish battalion. Remember! The battalion is Ireland. When you are serving under our green flag you are serving Ireland.'

Lawless paused and turned towards Ryan. 'Captain, they're all yours!'

'Thank you, Commander!' Ryan looked keenly into the rough, hard-bitten faces, glistening with sweat and grime. He strutted forth, paced up and down the line of men several times, throwing his feet forward in a martial swagger, but he said nothing. He surveyed the scatty lines of battered and barefoot recruits, drawn up double as he walked in front and behind them. *If this is the best we can do,* he thought, *God help us.*

'I have never seen such ragged lines!' he bawled as he held his hands firmly clasped behind him. He stopped in front of a teenager whose pasty face was marked with smallpox scars. 'Name?'

'O'Callaghan, sir.'

Where are you from, son?'

'Fermoy, County Cork.

'Ah, a garrison town. And how long did his Britannic Majesty have the pleasure of your service?' Ryan asked, mimicking the fellow's Cork accent.

The sailor looked perplexed. 'I'm sorry, sir, I don't understand the question,' came the answer.

A spattering of laughter carried down the lines.

'Quiet in the ranks!' Ryan snarled, and turned again towards the young men. 'Do ye not speak English, laddie? What I meant was, how long were you in the Navy?'

'Two years, sir.'

'Were you pressed or did you volunteer?'

'I volunteered, sir.'

'Hmm!' Ryan murmured as he turned to the next man. 'What's your name?'

'Seaman Doyle,' the sailor blurted before checking himself. 'I mean, my name's John Doyle... sir,' he added belatedly. Doyle's mean and icy eyes squinted in the sun as he stared at Ryan. He was barefoot, like the others, and still wore the British sailor's garb of red and white striped cotton trousers rolled up at the ankles and the typical sailor's Monmouth cap from when he'd deserted the fleet.

'Where were you serving?'

'I was a top man, the cream of seamen on a man o' war. I was on blockade service for six months in the Channel and then served on Admiral Kingsmill's Irish squadron, the Irish Watch, based in Cork.'

Ryan considered him closely. 'A good officer?'

The seaman pulled back his shirt to reveal deep lacerations on his upper back. 'May the curse of Mary Malone and her nine illegitimate children chase him so far over the hills of damnation that the Lord Himself can't find him with a telescope.'

Ryan laughed. 'You have an honest face and not just a way with words—you'll make a good soldier. I'm quite sure of that.'

Ryan's eye caught sight of a grizzle faced man smirking at the back. 'Where did we dig you up from you dirty sea dog? If your mother could see you now...'

Ryan looked the bare-foot sailor up and down. The sailor's heavily matted, dirty hair hung in a ponytail, his jaw was covered with several days' beard growth. Ryan stared into the man's light blue eyes. Ryan knew that long hair was a sign a sailor had served for at least two years, differentiating himself from shorn new recruits and pressed men.

'I don't have a mother!' the sailor said stupidly, before adding 'sir.'

The others sniggered. The man's left ear was missing and an enormous gold ring hung from his right lobe.

'Name?' asked Ryan.

'John Kelly, sir.'

'I would find it hard to believe, Mister Kelly, that you were ever begotten upon a woman. What happened to your ear, mister? Somebody bite it off?

'Lost at Trafalgar, cut off by a froggy's cutlass. That's the

God's truth, sir.'

Ryan glared at him harshly, hooded his eyes and squinted. 'That's the God's truth, sir,' he repeated, mimicking the sailor's accent. 'If it wasn't for you bloody Irishmen taking the King's shilling we would've become a free and happy people long ago! Nelson's victory at Trafalgar put all French invasion plans for Ireland on hold, and that's why we're standing here in bloody Spain instead of being home kicking the bloody English out of our own bloody country! Now *that's* the God's truth!'

'God bless old Ireland,' somebody muttered from the back.

'Amen to that!' said another.

'Quiet!' spat Ryan.

'Here, sir...' Kelly offered, pulling his filthy white shirt down over his shoulder. He proudly revealed the damage the cutlass had made on his scrawny body as it had made a downward swipe after slicing through the ear, leaving a huge gash in the shoulder in its wake. 'That's from the froggy's sword,' he offered.

'You served with Nelson?'

Kelly nodded, as he turned the quid of tobacco from one cheek to the other with his tongue. 'I saw Nelson hit by a *crapaud's* musket ball. I was ship's carpenter on board HMS *Victory*. She's enormous, sir, first rater, of course—over 200 feet from her decks to her masthead—and looking up from the decks, she looks so tall that you'd think she's touching the sky. She carries over a hundred guns. Her anchor cables measure the girth of a large tree, and it takes over 150 men to raise just one of her anchors. She's massive, sir, massive!'

Ryan snorted deeply and hooked his thumbs into his trouser belt. 'Now listen to me, Kelly. We don't go around calling our gallant French allies *"crapauds"*, now do we?'

Kelly stared unflinchingly and smirked.

'We don't call them *crapauds,* or froggys, see? We call them Frenchies! As long as we're in this bloody froggy army we have to be careful what we say, now don't we? Can't be upsetting the grand marshals of France and old Boney,' Ryan stepped back from the line and shot the men a long, hard, slow look. 'A right shower of gentlemen!' he said, cynically. 'A right shower! Welcome to his Imperial Majesty's Army. You'll no doubt be glad to hear there are no floggings here. The Frenchies believe it runs contrary to the ideals of the French Revolution, those of Liberty, Equality, and Fraternity —that means "Brotherhood" to those who don't know.' He looked left and right. 'How many of you've been flogged?'

Well over half of the men sheepishly raised their hands.

Kelly spoke. 'Captain's word is law, sir. To look at an officer the wrong way, or to be caught drunk is cause for a flogging with the cat o' nine tails on the quarter-deck in front of the whole crew, before being thrown in the brig.'

Ryan's lip curled. 'You can forget about the Royal Navy tradition of rum, sodomy and the lash! The French won't flog ye, they won't make ye run the gauntlet or hang ye, but by God what they'll do is shoot ye! So mind your step, gentlemen, and that's fair warning.'

Ryan sniffed deeply and cleared his throat. 'Sergeant Hoffman!'

'Sir?'

'I want these men deloused, washed, shaved and kitted out in regular French infantry uniform as soon as possible. I want the best shots to join my company,. The bigger lads can go into the *carabinier* company, and you can send the dregs into the bloody fusiliers. They're all yours, Sergeant.'

'*Jawohl,* Captain!' shouted the Prussian sergeant as he clicked the back of his heels. Sergeant Hoffman was highly organised and trained. Although he was middle-aged, he still presented a vivid spectacle dressed in his green tunic. His epaulettes gave the impression that his shoulders were even wider. His imposing martial look was finished with a white cross-belt over a pair of loose campaign trousers. Hoffman straightened his enormous bicorn hat, rubbed his moustache through his fingers and curled it before snapping to attention with his back rigidly straight to address the men. 'We're going to make soldiers out of you,' he began whilst motioning over to Corporal McGowan to throw him his musket. Hoffman snapped his right arm forward and keenly snatched the firearm by the stock, presenting it in front of the men at the ready position. 'In the French army we carry the Charleville musket. This piece of expertly engineered iron and wood is the best musket in the world and it will be your only focus from here on in. You need to mind it, love it like a mistress and guard it with your life,' continued Hoffman. 'Remember, a soldier never abandons his musket as by doing so he is no longer a soldier! As Captain Ryan said, the most agile, the fittest, the best shots, the most intelligent will join Captain Ryan's voltigeur company. They are one of the nastiest, roughest, ugliest, most feared companies in the French Army.'

Hoffman went through the various drill movements for loading the Charleville musket.

The wily old sergeant knelt down, cocked his loaded musket and pulled the trigger. The crack of the musket enveloped his copper-coloured, weather-beaten face in thick, sulphurous, white smoke. He sputtered and coughed heavily as he raised himself up from his knees with a little difficulty. His left knee made a clicking sound as he stood up. 'We know the British have landed in Portugal and it won't be long before we face them in the field. As you have served under the British flag, you know they are good fighters. I have seen them in action when I served in the Prussian Army.'

Hoffman handed the musket and cartridge box to O'Callaghan. The former sailor bit open the paper cartridge and poured gunpowder into the musket's priming pan. The musket slipped and fell on the man's bare foot. The others laughed while he mouthed off some incoherent sailor's curse.

'Give me the musket back, you *schweinhund!*' bawled Hoffman angrily. 'I see that you will need a lot of training. French infantry are required to fire three rounds a minute, but those wanting to gain entry into the elite voltigeurs have to fire four rounds. You need to be careful when shouting in English in the field. Voltigeurs are vulnerable when deployed in the field and could be mistaken for enemy troops while calling out to each other in English. We lost a dozen men months ago when our lads were shouting in English. A heavy cavalry regiment of breast-plated cuirassiers thought they had run into a British advance guard and attacked. Only the roars of *'Vive l'Empereur!'* saved the company from being massacred.'

Mustered into their respective companies, there followed a week of drilling. The new recruits had never known such finery in the fleet. Their new green tunics and breeches were spotless, as were their bell-shaped shakos, sporting polished brass plates adorned with enormous green-tipped yellow plumes. They could hardly believe their luck, as previously they'd been disheveled deserters rotting in prison.

Sergeant Frederick Hoffman was named after the famous Prussian general, Frederick the Great. He'd joined the Irish regiment the previous year, when the Irish had deployed from coastal defence duties along the French coast to the German campaign. The French defeated the Prussians at the

Battle of Jena along the Rhine and gave the captured Prussians two options; remain in chains for years as a half-starving prisoner of war or join the Irish Legion. Two-hundred former Irish revolutionaries of the United Irishmen also joined the Irish battalion there. The British Government had sold them to Prussia to labour in her salt mines following the Irish Rebellion.

The sergeant had stared death in the face many times. He was a professional soldier and had followed the drum since he was fourteen-years-old, through six campaigns. He had run the gauntlet many times and suffered drought, famine, exposure, severe wounds and illness but had survived against all the odds. All the deprivation, however, had taken its toll.

Hoffman had grown up in rough environments with few home comforts. From infancy he'd been subjected to frequent famines and hardships, and had suffered a plethora of illnesses. Hoffman had worked the land in daily physical toil, and his lean muscular frame, and his hands roughened at the plough had made him resilient in the face of the privations and vicissitudes of military life. The hard hand of warfare had toughened him up further. He had marched for miles carrying a heavy pack, and slept out in barns or under hedges in constant fear, while hunger, fatigue and exhaustion had also affected him. Hoffman's main ailment was the rheumatoid arthritis in his knees, caused by years of bivouacking in the open and standing for hours on guard duty in wind, snow and torrential rain. He keenly remembered how on many occasions the barrel of his shouldered musket had overflowed with water, as he stood at attention for hours on end, drenched to the skin.

The old sergeant was writing up the company pay in his billet when Ryan entered. 'How are Napoleon's newest invincibles getting on, Sergeant? Lieutenant McCarthy has high hopes for those blackguards.'

'*Mein Gott!* There have been no better men to step foot on a parade ground since the time of Frederick the Great,' Hoffman replied cynically, as he poured two drinks and handed one to Ryan.

Ryan knocked the drink back and raised his eyebrows in mock surprise. 'And the men say you have no sense of humour!'

'It's just not *their* humour, sir,' Hoffman protested curtly, a little annoyed.

'The men at least look well. Their new green uniforms stand out a mile, but the bright green will soon change to a duller tone,' said Ryan.

Hoffman nodded. 'I have already prepared a list of the new recruits. I know what makes a good soldier and what makes a bad one. I recommend we put one half of these *schweinhunde* into the voltigeurs, and there are four heavy-set men who would fit very well into our fusilier company.' Hoffman removed his long-stemmed, clay pipe from his mouth, knocked the ashes out, reached over to his desk, and handed Ryan the list. 'I just hope they can march. Sailors make terrible infantrymen, and a week's drilling does not change that.'

'As long as they can stand and fight,' Ryan said, scanning the list. He folded it and put it in his pocket. 'The Governor of Burgos has already made known to Commander Lawless his displeasure with the fact that three of our lads deserted last night. The bloody fools! They'll more likely get their throats cut when the partisans catch up with them!'

'You Irishmen are too rebellious. You don't obey the rules and you disrespect all authority. The men need hard Prussian discipline!' Hoffman sighed deeply, then added grimly, 'but I fear this would only make them worse.'

Ryan bent down to light a cheroot from the furnace. He felt privileged to have such an experienced soldier in his company, and knew Hoffman had the best interests of his men at heart, unlike many of the other officers and NCOs, who were more concerned with their own glory and wouldn't hesitate to send their men to their deaths at a whim.

Ryan watched as the sergeant carefully shaved some strands from a thick rope of spun Perique tobacco and pressed the strands into the bowl of his pipe.

'One of the men who served with the British told me those Light Dragoons we encountered recently were a newly raised corps of intelligence officers,' said Hoffman.

A worried look spread across Ryan's face.

'Is anything the matter, Captain?' Hoffman asked, concerned.

'The bastards from the same regiment killed my family back in Ireland,' Ryan said.

Hoffman looked at Ryan compassionately. 'I also had a family, but they are all dead now,' he said sadly.

The sergeant filled their glasses with drink, while his mind drifted back. 'My only daughter was just five years old when she'd toppled a candle. It set fire to her nightdress and engulfed her in flames. My wife died of a broken heart shortly afterwards. I brought my two sons, Tobias and Dieter, into my regiment when they were young lads. We served together for years and always watched out for each other.'

Ryan listened intensely.

'During the Battle of Jena our regiment had been attacked by a troop of Polish lancers. We had just formed square to repel an incoming enemy cavalry charge when a round-shot landed on top of us and destroyed our square's corner section. The blast knocked me off my feet. The round caused a gaping hole in the square, permitting the lancers to charge through. I saw my youngest son, Tobias through the smoke. He lay slumped forward, with half his face gone. I watched as a horseman vaulted over the wounded men. One was just about to spear me when my other son, Dieter, bayoneted the rider in the thigh. He was wounded, but still managed to impale his lance through Dieter's ear. I then grabbed a loaded musket and shot at point-blank range through the horseman's jaw and he keeled over dead.'

As Hoffman recalled the events of that day, Ryan heard the tough old sergeant's voice quaver.

'A sad tale, and I mourn your loss, Sergeant,' said Ryan. The details of the deaths of his own wife and daughter were too raw for him to tell. Ryan turned to leave. As he pushed open the door, he looked back and saw Hoffman wipe a tear from his eye. Ryan felt sorry for him. The sergeant had a grave saturnine expression drilled on his bronzed face as he sharpened his goose quill, dipped it into the well, and finished the company's payrolls.

CHAPTER 4

Ryan lay in his quarters, unable to sleep, deep in thought. He had being holed up for weeks in the mountain ranges in northern Spain hunting down guerrillas. He was now enjoying the comforts of garrison life, compared to the constant fatigue and deprivations of campaigning in the mountains. He had endured months of little food and had slept out in the open field under stumps of fallen trees in the wet miserable winter months, sometimes with only his woolen greatcoat for protection. He had witnessed many die of sickness and disease, and had seen that stragglers, who were exhausted and unable to keep up, were brutally murdered by marauding guerrillas.

He knew his men and saw that they were happy, despite all their travails. It was a responsibility looking after their wellbeing and it sometimes weighed heavily on him. His men had few responsibilities, just do what they were told, march, wait to be fed and blow the couple of sous on drink and women. They were far removed from the humdrum daily grind at home, far from the bitter tongues of nagging wives and noisy, pestering children. They were doing something adventurous with their lives, away from the toil of their former unremarkable existence. They were young, courted danger, and savoured the camaraderie, for they never felt more alive than when standing close to the enemy, staring death hard in the face. They didn't fight for the Emperor or for France, not even for Ireland, but for each other.

Garrison life in Burgos trundled on as normal for Ryan's voltigeurs, with the daily tedium of drills, humdrum exercises, inspections and parades. The day always began the same way, with drums and bugles sounding reveille in the parade ground, awakening the soldiery from their slumber. The men's boots stomped heavily about on the floorboards as they prepared their bunks for inspection.

These were the familiar percussion sounds of everyday regimental life.

Corporal McGowan oversaw the company as it filled the morning hours shining the brass hilts of their *épées*, and polishing their cartridge pouches. The men stripped, cleaned and oiled their weapons, washed their clothes, polished their boots and spent hours cleaning their leather kit by rubbing it with unsalted animal fat.

The bugle sounded the signal to fall in as the battalion helter-skeltered in double time on to the parade ground and corporals began roll call.

Ryan stood next to Sergeant Hoffman as he received his orders of the day from Lieutenant McCarthy. He was handed a list of men who were sick and unfit for duty.

Ryan inspected the men, and minutely checked that weapons were clean, uniforms were freshly laundered and trousers had neat seams down each leg.

With inspection complete, Ryan assigned a guard mount to their various guard posts. When Ryan was on duty as the officer of the day, he liked to choose the best-turned-out soldier to run errands. This was a nice handy job as the soldier was excused from monotonous guard duty.

Following exercises and manoeuvres, Ryan checked on the battalion's cobblers while doing his rounds. They stood at their benches and hammered away for hours repairing the poorly manufactured shoes, which had fallen apart and disintegrated on the dirt roads of Spain.

He saw that the camp followers were also busy. The soldiers' wives earned a few extra sous as they soaped and vigorously scrubbed the officers' dirty linen over wooden washboards before wringing them tight and hanging acres of the coarse sheets out to dry.

A light brown cow with a white head, the type seen all over northern Spain, struggled and made low wailing noises as she was pulled by a rope around her neck and brought forward to be slaughtered. Ryan had seen enough blood and quickly moved on before the regimental butchers slit her throat. The carcass would soon be drained and cleaned before the meat was segmented and dressed.

Teams of sweaty bakers kneaded dozens of batches of dough needed to supply the battalion with their daily bread as orderlies washed mountains of vegetables for the daily enormous cauldrons of soup.

Ryan had ordered a work party to be sent out to collect firewood to light the fires. He paused and watched as they now returned.

The garrison was a flurry of activity. Here and there patrols were to-ing and fro-ing. A convoy of covered wagons trundled in. Thirsty messengers, covered in dust arrived on tired, lathered horses, and finely dressed ADC's with their large escorts, brought much needed supplies and orders from France.

Ryan checked his watch. It was nearly noon. He walked towards a messenger as the soldiers' children laughed and skittered back from the school. He shared some friendly banter with the messenger as he took hold of the Government's news sheet, *Le Moniteur,* and scanned it eagerly for news of the war's progress against the Austrians in the north.

Blankets, uniforms, boots, gaiters, thousands of rounds of ammunition, horse equipment for the cavalry, razor blades, soap, tobacco by the ounce and grimy blocks of salt by the hundred-weight, as well as coffee, sugar and caviar also arrived. There were cases upon cases of fine Burgundy and Bordeaux, casks of cognac and panniers of champagne—all for the officers; the rank and file made do with local rotgut.

As he passed the battalion's armourers, he saw that they were flat out inspecting the newly arrived wagonload of new *Charlevilles*, so named after the armoury where they were manufactured in the French town of Charleville.

Sergeant Hoffman oversaw a line of voltigeurs as they sweated profusely and passed cans of chicken between them, and stored them securely in the battalion's quartermaster stores. Ryan handed Hoffman the news sheet and watched as the men eyeballed the tinned chicken greedily, for there was nothing more important to a soldier who has experienced hunger than good quality, regular food.

Bundles of mail also arrived. Ryan checked the addresses and verified that indeed most letters were destined to men of the other regiments as the men of the Irish battalion received few letters due to the war. There was no way of getting correspondence from Ireland. An orderly handed Ryan a sheaf of letters consigned to his battalion. He briefly went through them. As he scanned the names on the front he read that most of them came from family members living in France or were letters sent from Poland to his Polish voltigeurs. He put them under his arm and continued on.

Troopers brought their horses from the stables, and groomed and exercised them in the yard. He heard the farrier's anvil dinging clear as a bell from the hammer blows onto a newly forged horseshoe. He walked closer and saw a handsome bay mare waiting patiently, while another horse was being shod. He stood and watched as the horse's hooves were trimmed and rasped. The farrier removed a red hot metal shoe with his thongs, and placed it onto the horse's hoof for a second or two, to ensure a perfect fit. The horse had to be steadied as the hot steel started to sizzle and the hoof began to burn. It smelt like burnt hair. The farrier then quenched the shoe in water and nailed it into place. Ryan started to walk away, then turned back. He saw the horse prance happily on the cobbles, proud of herself in her new shoes, as she was led away.

In the afternoon Ryan came off duty. There was plenty of time for leisure activities. He liked to play *jeu de paume*, a form of tennis, and sometimes played *boules* using 6-pounder cannon balls. The French soldiers looked on curiously as he and some of the other Irish lads played a game of hurley with sticks, curved and flattened, cut from local olive trees.

While on patrol in the countryside, Ryan honed his wits and his fitness level. This relieved some of the boredom of garrison life. Earlier in the week, he and his men had climbed several hundred metres and admired the Spanish countryside laid out before them. Their muskets were lazily slung over their shoulders but they were always on the alert for guerrilla attack. He had even hunted for wild boars. It was all one big adventure.

He had always enjoyed growing his own vegetables, and he liked to tend the potato patches in the garden outside Burgos. He ate well on a diet of soup, dried beef and bread. He also joined the regimental clubhouses and spent hours in the library. He particularly enjoyed reading the dog-eared copy of Voltaire's French satire *Candide* and Maria Edgeworth's well-thumbed popular novel *Castle Rackrent* about life in Ireland before the rebellion.

Ryan also attended the regimental Freemason military lodges. And drank heavily, oftentimes too heavily, in the local cafes where fortunes were won—but mostly lost—over ceaseless games of billiards.

In the evenings he practiced the skills of the sword in the battalion's fencing school. Or he relaxed in the canteen, purchasing tots of brandy from the *cantinières,* playing cards, usually games of *vingt-et-un*, and smoking his pipe to his heart's content.

McGowan and Hoffman conjured up several kegs of strong porter beer using hops, grain, sugar and salt and downed it heartily by the gallon. It reminded Ryan of the porter he drank back home in Ireland.

He knew that McGowan and some of the others smoked marijuana, if they could get hold of it, although it was forbidden. He turned a blind eye to this. The drug was smuggled back by Napoleon's soldiers from Egypt. Smoking it helped blot out the hardships of the war.

The Irish were popular and there were opportunities aplenty to flirt with the sultry, dark-eyed local beauties in the nightly dances held in the city's square.

It was at one of these dances that Ryan met Carmen. It was a warm and humid evening in September when a large group of curious spectators congregated around the Plaza de Santa Maria fronting Burgos's majestic Gothic cathedral. The soft, gleaming moon lit up the old playa, throwing its reflective, eerie light onto the cobblestones. Ryan and McGowan approached the plaza, as local men played guitars and girls clicked their castanets and filled cups with copious amounts of the local hooch. Wisps of plaintive music floated through the square. An old man dressed in a dirty, heavy brown overcoat and wide-brimmed hat plucked heartily on a guitar. He raised his eyes to them as they passed. Ryan could just make out his huge, grey, curled moustache through the shadows, but otherwise everyone ignored the two Irishmen. The Spanish flavour of the dance changed, and all heads turned when Ryan took out his rosewood whistle and played along to the rhythm. The pitched, chattering clacks of the castanets echoed loudly from the plaza as the women perspired and danced. McGowan had already turned his charms to a blushing local girl; the two lovers leaned over the plaza's elaborately carved stone fountain as water cascaded loudly behind them.

Ryan turned to McGowan and called out, 'Come on, now, you didn't bring that fiddle with you for nothing!'

The corporal gulped down his wine, smiled at the raven-haired girl and shyly removed the fiddle hanging from a cord around his back. Then the mood took him and he whipped the fiddle's bow from his belt, raised it under his chin and began to play.

A broad smile of approval spread across the face of the old Spanish guitar player.

The three musicians went hell for leather. The Spaniard increased the rhythm and tried to outdo the Irishmen. Ryan kept pace with his whistle, and McGowan did likewise with the fiddle as the crescendo increased. McGowan sawed like mad on the gut strings. The dancers manipulated the castanets with such speed that they clicked with shrillness in the warm Castilian air, and onlookers clapped furiously.

A couple of Irishmen approached, their heads swelled by drink. They whooped and laughed as they swung girls about with ease. 'Hurrah for the boys of Connaught! Hurrah for the girls of Spain!' they shouted, before the crescendo finally died down and the old Spaniard playing the guitar finished the medley with a vigorous flourish over the strings.

The old man exhaled heavily as he caught his breath. '*Juegas muy bien, señor.*'

The dancer mopped the sweat from her brow with her sleeve. 'You play very well,' she translated, panting heavily, as she took out her elaborately painted fan and waved it furiously before her face.'

'*Gracias, amigo.*' Ryan bowed to the guitar player and smiled. He turned to the dancer and stared into her warm brown eyes as she smiled shyly. Her face glowed in the dim moonlight. She was young and pretty, and as she'd danced he'd eyed her lustfully, as a famished wolf would a sprightly spring lamb. He admired her long, chestnut hair and her perfectly slim frame, visible like a shadow through her white dress.

She had caught his eye earlier. He'd stood captivated as she waved her hands and hips while clicking the castanets. At one point, he'd thought she batted her eyes in his direction. He wasn't sure, as he'd been too focussed on the drink and on the music.

'Glad to meet you. My name is James Ryan, at your service, *señorita.*' Ryan took another mouthful of wine.

'My name is Carmen de Santa Cruz.' She blushed slightly, and flirtatiously curled her hair above her ear.

Ryan felt a mutual attraction. He turned to McGowan, who had the plump, raven-haired girl sitting on his knee. 'Let's show them a little Irish reel. You know the "The Blackbird" don't you, McGowan?'

McGowan nodded, lifted the girl off, patting her on the bottom as he did so, then grabbed the fiddle's neck. Together they played "The Blackbird", then belted out the '*The Wild*

Rover,' followed by several melancholic ballads, which made them dewy-eyed with thoughts of home.

An old Spaniard ensconced on a chair, chewing a cigar, asked in Spanish why the Irish were fighting for Napoleon here in Spain.

Carmen intervened. 'Señor, the reason the Irish are here in Spain is because the French emperor wanted to take over Ireland to invade England. He formed an Irish regiment in his army, but lost interest in Ireland and sent them to fight in Spain instead.'

Ryan looked at her and smiled, impressed. 'Now we're going to play you another song,' he said. 'It's about an Irish highwayman from long ago who holds up and robs an English officer, but is then betrayed by his sweetheart! Now you wouldn't do that, would you, guapa?'

Carmen's face blushed.

Ryan started in on the rollicking tune 'Whiskey in the Jar' and McGowan joined in on the fiddle a heartbeat later.

Later that evening, he walked her home and the war was forgotten in a passionate kiss. The couple met every night thereafter. Ryan learned that she was an orphan. Her father had been a doctor, but he had died when Carmen was young. Her mother had died the previous year. Although she didn't have a chaperone, she was respectable and earned her living by tutoring the children of a wealthy family. Ryan in turn told her of his time on the run from the British in the Wicklow Mountains, following the Irish rebellion.

'You ask so many questions. For all I know you could be a guerrilla spy,' teased Ryan.

Carmen pouted. 'I am a patriot, not one of those liberal afrancesados, those Spanish who love the French and support their occupation of Spain, like the parents of the children I tutor. I hate the French because they have invaded my country, and yes, it is my heartfelt wish to see them leave, but I do not tell secrets!'

'Amen to that!' he sighed. 'The sooner we are out of Spain the better. It's a difficult country to make war in, for the Spanish have put up stiff resistance.'

Carmen was in love. Several weeks later, late one night, she sneaked Ryan into her little room. He took hold of her and she melted into his arms, breathing heavily. He swirled her around to give her a passionate kiss, nearly losing his footing as he carried her to bed.

CHAPTER 5

Early next morning, Carmen lay in bed smoking a cheroot as she watched Ryan sleeping. He opened his eyes and sat up. He pulled her close to him and kissed her. He leaned over to look at his pocket watch. *'Jesus!'* he exclaimed as he flipped it open. 'You should have woken me! The battalion will think I've deserted.' He struggled to put on his jackboots and hurriedly grabbed his tunic before bolting towards the stairs.

'Oh, James!' grinned Carmen seductively.

Ryan's face peered into the room behind the door. 'There is always time for a kiss!' She pulled him to the bed by his collar and kissed him salaciously. 'I'll wait for you until you return, *mi corazón, Adios.*'

Ryan felt an immense sense of relief. He had slept well, the best sleep he'd had in weeks. Meeting Carmen was a good omen, he thought to himself, for he was getting fond of her. It was the first time he'd spent the night with a woman since his wife had died, although when he'd first arrived in Paris, he'd been was so lonely that he had sometimes paid ladies of pleasure for their company.

He walked toward the parade ground and saw that the garrison was already lined up. He discreetly took his place beside Lawless. As an off-duty officer; he wasn't required to be back in his billet like the rank and file.

Commander Lawless gave the order to fall out. 'You were

late, Ryan.'

'Sorry, sir,' replied Ryan.

'Orders have just arrived that we are to attack General Don Julián's guerrillas in the mountains. The Hussars of Death are providing mounted support to your company.'

Ryan threw Lawless a pained sideways glance. 'Damn it!' he cursed. His heart sank to learn that his archenemy Captain Carpentier of the Death Hussars was due to rejoin his regiment in Burgos. Regimental loyalties supported Carpentier in his vendetta against Ryan, and men were keen to show their support for their fellow officer.

Lawless's eyes glowered. 'The whole camp is waiting for a duel between yourself and Carpentier over the death of that girl in Madrid. They are even taking bets, Ryan! You're not the favourite! I must warn you, news has reached General Junot and no one knows more than you about the rules against dueling. If he finds you dueling he'll have your hide!'

Ryan's head turned in the direction of Lieutenant McCarthy as he approached. McCarthy saluted and handed Ryan the *feuille de route*, detailing the route they were to march. 'We have fifty men, able bodied and fit, and ten sick men unfit for duty, sir,' McCarthy reported.

'Thank you, Lieutenant,' said Ryan, as he folded the sheet and put it in his pocket. He saluted Lawless and returned to his company.

Within the hour, the column, numbering around 1,200 men, trooped out of the walled city of Burgos. An advance guard comprising Ryan's voltigeur company and a squadron drawn from the black-garbed Death Hussars led the march. Two regiments of the line plodded sullenly behind. Ryan was told that they could only bring a couple of 4-pounder field guns with them. They had to leave the battery of 6-pounders and ammunition caissons from the Imperial Horse Artillery behind in Burgos as the roads were too narrow.

As he marched, Ryan could not stop remembering his encounter with Carpentier, because it haunted him. When Napoleon's army arrived in Madrid, the proud Madrileño's were incensed by the sight of French troops, and the hated Egyptian Mameluke cavalry revived memories of the Moorish conquest. The Madrileños rose up. As the Irish battalion were one of the first troops to arrive in Madrid, they were tasked with putting down the revolt. Ryan remembered seeing hundreds of bloated bodies in the *Puerta del Sol* under the searing midday heat, left there to serve as a warning to others. The putrid tinge of death lingered in the sultry, stale air. The French had continued their killing spree. Ryan's company tried to calm the chaos, but the Madrileños were running pell-mell for their lives as marauding French troops went on the rampage. The streets had filled with the dead and the dying as a cacophony of triumphal cheers and screams echoed loudly throughout the city. They were the cries of men being pursued and killed and of women being raped, together with the intermittent crack of musket fire. It brought back memories, horrible memories, of Ireland. Captain Carpentier's light cavalry troop of Death Hussars had clattered down in full gallop, and had drawn their sabres to slash the backs of the terrified people running for cover. Ryan had heard the tramp of horses and shouts from the rear.

'Make way for the hussars!'

The infantry opened up to let the cavalry through. There was no need for this cruelty, he'd thought at the time. Ryan spied a Spanish girl running through the streets. Carpentier had seen her, too. Ryan thought she should have remained in hiding somewhere, but perhaps there was no where left to hide. She mustn't have been a day older than sixteen, and she was running for her life. She glanced over her shoulder in terror as the hussar drew alongside her. He whooshed her up over his saddle by her slim waist and laughed loudly, happy with his prize. The captain reined in his horse and pulled his bridle to steer his mare down a cobbled lane.

Ryan saw the girl struggle and he followed them. Carpentier dismounted, dragging the girl with him, and ripped open her blouse.

'Let her go!' Ryan demanded as his hand hovered above the brass hilt of his sword.

'What is it to you, voltigeur?' Carpentier snorted contemptuously. 'She's part of the spoils of war! Do not interfere!' Carpentier's face was hideous. He had only one seeing eye, as his other one was false. It was made of white glass and was stencilled with the Black Hussar's skull and crossbones regimental insignia.

'Leave her be!' Ryan repeated firmly as he drew his sword.

Carpentier flung the girl down so that she fell on the hard cobblestones. He drew his sword, lunged forward and stabbed her through the heart with a skill honed by many kills, both on and off the battlefield. He withdrew the blade with a flick of his wrist to ease its removal. A trickle of blood streamed down the girl's neck, and she turned her head and breathed her last.

'Well, *m'sieu, you* will never have her,' he drawled as he wiped the bloodied blade off her shoulder.

'*En garde!*' Ryan spat angrily. He bolted forward and took a lunging swipe at the hussar, who coolly sidestepped away with precision and grinned. He swished and parried Ryan's next attack and cut him across the wrist with the riposte. Ryan bent his knee, stretched forward in a lunge and caught his adversary in the belly, drawing blood, but the blade hadn't travel deep enough and the Frenchman had nimbly sprung back, only slightly wounded.

The two men's faces were taut with anger. Ryan gritted his teeth so hard that they hurt and used his full force in a swipe on the hussar's sword arm, but his adversary stepped inwards to Ryan's chest and pushed him to the ground. Carpentier pulled out his loaded flintlock pistol. Lying on the ground, Ryan waited for the deadly shot. The hussar pulled the trigger, but it fizzled out with hardly a spark, misfiring.

'*Putain!*' cursed Carpentier, and he threw the pistol at Ryan, who deflected it with his arm.

'You should take greater care and keep your powder dry!' shouted Ryan, gripping his sword and surging to his feet. Carpentier scuttled for his horse.

'We will meet again, voltigeur!' Carpentier spat over his shoulder as he placed his foot in the stirrup.

'Yes, we will! I will seek you out, you coward! My name is Captain James Ryan, 2nd battalion, Voltigeur Company, Irish Legion.'

The hussar lifted his hat in mocked reverence and laughed loudly.

'Enjoy the girl! She's still warm, you know!' Carpentier dug spurs into his mare's sides, and galloped away.

Ryan checked himself for injuries. In the heat of the fight when adrenaline kicked in, even a severe wound could go unnoticed. He knelt down to the girl and gently swept the black glossy hair off her face. Her dark, sad eyes stared out upwards in an expression of surprise and fear. He had seen this look many times in battle, but those were men's faces, hardened by weather and tough living. This was different. This was the face of an angel. Although inanimate in death her face reminded him of a painting he had seen, Raphael's *Madonna of the Rose,* in a Madrid church. He had a vision of a weeping father and mother frantically searching for their daughter's body.

Ryan picked up Carpentier's cavalry pistol, shoved it in his belt, sheathed his sword, and sadly walked away.

That encounter had taken place three months ago, but it might well have happened yesterday, it was so vivid. Ryan had relived the incident many times in his mind, for it had seared into his soul. Racked with guilt, he kept getting flashbacks, sometimes waking up with his heart racing, shouting in a cold sweat. He sometimes mixed his two nightmares up. Sometimes, instead of the girl, it was the face of his wife that appeared in the nightmare, being killed by Carpentier in Madrid, other times it was his daughter.

CHAPTER 6

Ryan was still thinking about what had happened in Madrid as the column marched along the Camino de Santiago, the medieval pilgrim road known as the Way of Saint James.

'You know, Captain,' said Lieutenant McCarthy, walking next to him. 'Since the middle-ages, the rich and the poor, the lame and the blind, popes and paupers, have all followed this pilgrimage route. It leads to the tomb of St. James the Apostle in Santiago de Compostela. The pilgrims believed that walking this sacred route absolved them from sin.'

Ryan turned to McCarthy. 'How come you know so much, Lieutenant?'

'I read a lot, Captain,' replied McCarthy.

They didn't encounter any pilgrims on the Camino that day, Ryan thought, because of the war.

A low winter sun peeked through the dreary, grey sky and shone mercilessly into his eyes as he hiked over the steep mountain passes. The brown patchwork pastures became smaller and turned into wild valleys with various hues of green, awash with fresh, pure springs. He marvelled at the beauty of the countryside, which was one of tranquillity but was also one of desolation.

After marching for five miles, Ryan and his men sought shade and rested in one of the many ancient chapels dotted along the Camino, which had being built to shelter pilgrims. The gradient increased. It was now an uphill climb as they delved deep into the Cantabrian Mountains.

The road narrowed to a series of hairpin goat paths. The hussars led their mounts cautiously by the bridle along the steep gorges as they climbed into the mountains. At times they descended into deep and narrow gorges, or followed rushing streams. The paths were sometimes so narrow that the gunners, armed with picks and shovels, had to widen the road before the caissons could pass and push their unlimbered field guns through. On other occasions, they had to dismantle their guns completely, harness them to ropes and haul them up separately.

These delays caused frustration. Ryan passed sombre, grey-stone mountain villages shrouded in white swirls of mist. The local population had abandoned their villages and followed the age-old scorched earth policy of burning their crops, fleeing ahead of the vanguard of the French army.

Ryan was cautiously approaching a village when a stork suddenly took flight from a roof and startled the men. McGowan kicked open a farmhouse door but found neither food nor livestock in the deserted space. The villagers had either hidden their belongings or taken them higher up the mountains, as look outs had warned them well in advance that the French were coming. The Spanish had invented quite ingenious methods of hiding their provisions, but Ryan had become an expert in foraging. He viewed the disturbed ground under the carcass of a dog with suspicion and told Kaminski to prod the ground with his bayonet. Kaminski braved the horrendous stench to discover a hoard lay hidden under the rotting carcass: wooden barrels of wine buried upright, along with sides of salted meat wrapped in cotton.

At another village, Ryan ran into a local priest with a dozen women and children, caught unawares by the advancing French troops.

'We mean you no harm, *Padre*,' Ryan reassured the priest. He cut two metal buttons from his tunic with his épée and handed them as gifts to the blubbering children.

Ryan turned to McGowan. 'Take two men, secure the north of the village and let no one pass,' he ordered.

McGowan tipped his peak, and he and two others quickly made their way to the other side of the village in double quick time.

'Vandam! Scale up the church steeple like a good man and keep watch. Kami, take a boy as a guide and send the villagers to the adjudants in the rear.'

'Yes, sir,' replied the Polish voltigeur automatically.

Kaminski grabbed a boy by the nape of his neck. His hysterical mother protested loudly, then began pleading with the terrified boy to give the men what they wanted.

'Tell her no harm will come to her son,' Ryan told Kaminski.

Kami translated and explained that the boy would be brought back unharmed. The mother continued to scream uncontrollably. The other village women held her back as the voltigeurs continued their ascent. Ryan cast an eye over his shoulder and saw the frantic woman on her knees with her hands clasped together, imploring one of the officers regarding her son's plight. The officer pushed her aside and she keeled over in the mud, distraught. She lifted her stricken face and spat at a passing hussar; he swiftly pulled out his blunderbuss, pulled back the hammer and discharged a fatal shot which nearly blew the woman's head clean off. Her son screamed and tried to run to his mother, but McGowan held him back.

They marched onwards.

Seeing the violent attack on the boy's mother, the image of Ryan's murdered wife and daughter flashed before his eyes. He was lost in thought, remembering.

Back in 1798, Ryan had received word that British dragoons had come to his house and he had rushed home, but he had been too late. His wife and daughter lay dead, and he'd had to chase the pigs away from their bodies, as they were lapping their blood up from the flagstone floor. This image alone haunted him.

One of the neighbouring children told him what had happened. His wife had been stripped to the waist, strung up and half-hanged three times, but still she would not tell the whereabouts of her husband. Darkford unsheathed his sabre and cut her throat. He found Ryan's daughter hiding under a bed and ran a noose around the blubbering child's neck. He held the rope over his shoulder and hanged the child over his back.

Ryan, guilt-ridden at not having saved them, had made a solemn promise that he would hunt down and kill Darkford. He would follow him to the ends of the earth, and beyond, if necessary.

His left hand was shaking. He reached inside his shirt and took hold of his lucky charm, made from Irish black bog oak, which hung from a thin strip of leather around his neck. His mother had given it to him before he left to join the Irish rebel army.

The mercury dipped as Ryan climbed a magnificent ridge. Fires burnt brightly high above the ridges and the shrill sounds of the guerrilla's hunting horns echoed into the darkness, warning that the French were coming. McGowan swore that he could see shadows between the pine trees, watching. Ryan told him it was just his imagination, but he himself wasn't sure. Occasional cracks of musket fire reverberated, along with the faint, familiar guttural cry of '¡Muertes a los franceses!—'Death to the French!'—carried on the wind. The battle cry seemed to resonate throughout Spain, so much so that Ryan thought he heard it in his sleep, and he wondered if the other men felt the same.

Ryan's company continued in single-file over the heavily rutted, narrow paths, littered with the guerrillas' abandoned possessions. They encountered a score of lame horses and mules, together with several carcasses, saddles, chests, clothes and broken cartwheels, which proved to Ryan that they were fast gaining ground on the enemy.

God was not always on the side of the big battalions, Ryan mused, for, as Napoleon argued, they would never defeat guerrillas. The ferocious Moors themselves had failed to subjugate this part of Spain. He knew well that a patriot's resolve could withstand great adversity. Armed with simple weapons and a knowledge of the local ground, they could prevail against the best battalions. A guerrilla campaign always favoured irregular forces. A peasant army could never withstand a 12-pound battery in the open field, but in the mountains, living off the land, and helped by locals, they could prevail. He recalled the winters that he had spent on the run in the Wicklow Mountains, how his little band caused great havoc ambushing the redcoats. These hit-and-run tactics had been a favourite Irish battle strategy since ancient times, for they took a heavy mental toll on the enemy and could tie up thousands of troops for many months.

He was relieved when the order was given for the column to stop and rest.

Ryan took off his backpack, stretched, and lay down on the damp grass. He felt happy as he chewed some bread, and a smile spread across his face when he broke wind. He got up to go to the toilet, walked from the others and grabbed some leaves. He removed his tunic, unbuckled his sword belt, unbuttoned his breeches and crouched down. While he tidied himself and pulled up his breeches, he surveyed the muted auburn fields below, covered in wildflowers, and stone walls sparkling with rain.

As he walked back, the wind whispered through the leaves of the trees and rattled branches. All was still except for the occasional bird call and the gentle murmur of a mountain stream. The sweet aroma of rosemary, fennel and thyme filled the air. The sun appeared. Shards of bright sunlight broke through the pine trees. A rainbow stretched across the wide valley. The scenery looked melancholic and tinged with sadness, even in the sunshine, and it reminded him of the lush hills of Ireland. He imagined he inhaled the sweet, musky scent of pine trees, of heather and of corn: barley and wheat.

The clouds gathered again and a light rain began to fall. He momentarily shut his eyes and paused to feel the cold rain on his face. His mind's eye recalled the landscape of home: its yellow gorse bushes and purple heather bogs; its mountains abundant with wild stags and lakes teeming with trout, salmon, and oily shad; its strange fairy mounds with hawthorn trees left undisturbed where, some believed, fairies dwelt.

He was momentarily home in Ireland, when his family were still alive during those happier times before the rebellion. He thought he smelt the sweet cool mountain heather and heard the rasping *krek krek* mating sound of the corncrake, so abundant in Ireland in springtime. He recalled the endless green rolling hills peppered with round towers, the roofless abbeys and monasteries laid bare in the time of Cromwell, the crumbling keeps and castles smothered with ivy from the dispossessed Gaelic aristocracy, home now only to bats, daws, and owls. A countryside of thatched cottages emitting thin wisps of smoke from turf fires, dominated by 'the big house' of the local Protestant landlords, the spawn of Cromwell's soldiers.

The loud crack of a guerrilla's musket thumped him back to reality as a bullet-whizzed close by, startling a flock of circling vultures, who noisily took flight. He looked up and viewed the vultures with suspicion; there must be dead prey ahead.

They continued on cautiously.

Voltigeur Kaminski ran down to Ryan waving his musket in the air, his haversack bobbing up and down on his back. 'Captain! Captain!'

'What's wrong, Kami?'

Ryan saw that Kaminski's eyes were filled with panic. 'You'll see sir,' he began, catching his breath. 'There are terrible things further up on the road, mutilated bodies hanging in trees, sir.'

The guerrillas knew the French were coming and had strewn the bodies of captured French soldiers along the path. As Ryan and his men drew closer, they saw that it was a scene of horror. The tales of torture were true! Ryan gazed around wildly. There were several charred bodies, with body parts cut off, and swarms of flies circling around. Severed heads were tied by the ends of their hair onto a nearby tree. The contorted expressions on their faces indicated that these soldiers had died in agony. Putrid bodies crawled with maggots and were covered with a black fur of flies.

A sign hung nearby. Ryan took hold of it. 'What does it say, Kami?'

'*Frutos franceses!*' he gulped. 'It means "French fruit".'

Several men collapsed on their knees and made the sign of the cross. Others stood white as sheets or dry heaved, overcome by the gruesome sight and the terrible stench.

Ryan put on a brave face and gave the order to move on.

He overheard a hussar coming up behind making some lewd joke or another about the bodies, which was followed by laughter.

'Those murdering hussars!' Ryan spat. He turned to his men. 'Move along now! If we are to avenge our mates we much overtake the men that killed them. We'll get these lads buried on our way back.'

They weaved slowly up the mountain. The mountain of death.

An hour passed, and they approached a sharp hairpin bend; it was a likely spot for guerrillas to lie in wait. As Ryan drew closer to the turn in the path, a bird call resonated. The Spanish boy held captive as a guide knew it for a signal and bolted past Ryan.

'*¡Vive el Rey Fernando de España!*' he bawled as he raised his hat high above his head, and in an instant the guerrillas broke cover.

'*¡Venganza!*' they cried, as they unleashed a staggered volley from blunderbusses and rusty *Española* firelocks.

Ryan and the other voltigeurs dived for cover, but several guerrillas opened fire on them from hideouts overlooking the path. The hussars who had been sauntering behind quickly mounted their horses and rushed forward. '*En avant!*' they shouted, and hacked their way through the melee with their sabres, but there were too many partisans and not enough space to attack with horses on the mountain track.

The main body of troops in the rear were too far away to help. Ryan looked around in a momentary panic. Youths armed with knives slashed the French horses' bellies, pulled hussars out of their saddles and bludgeoned them with hatchets, sickles, knives and sticks. The remaining half-troop made a run for it. The guerrilla tactic of leaving the mutilated bodies had caused the French forward sentries to abandon their positions, exposing the column to attack.

Ryan was scared, but he held his ground. 'Move forward!' he shouted to his men as he surged ahead and slashed a guerrilla across the chest with his sword. The guerrilla stumbled, but shot Ryan in the arm. Then a musket stock knocked Ryan to the ground, and a second blow knocked him out cold.

He came to as guerrillas ripped off his fringed epaulettes from his shoulders as a prize. His arms were lashed together and a rope was slipped around his neck and secured around a saddle's pommel. The rope tightened, forcing him to run behind the guerrilla's horse. When Ryan stumbled the rider jerked the rope, and a string of oaths were hurled at him. He fell again, and felt a sharp stab of pain in his ankle. He struggled to bring himself to his feet, the agony of his twisted ankle momentarily masking the pain in his arm and the dull ache in his head. Then he heard screams.

He looked around vaguely and saw wounded men being bayoneted. As he was dragged forward, he spied one of his scouts, naked and bloodied and laid out on the path. It was Hogan. A wound resembling a red ribbon lay under his chin where his throat had been cut. Ryan's heart sank. He recalled that Hogan wore a large gold ear-ring—it was gone now, along with the ear. A mangled bloody mess remained on the side of Hogan's head where the ear had been. Ryan didn't pity Hogan, he envied him.

Before sunset, the partisans and their prisoners arrived in the camp of the guerrilla leader, General Julián Sánchez. Although he was not a nobleman, he was respectfully called Don Julián by his men.

There must have been twenty or so captured Frenchmen corralled in cattle pens secured together with a network of tree branches. The prisoners, stripped to their underwear, stood shivering in the cold night air. Ryan recognised one of them as a courier who'd been captured while carrying despatches from France.

The twanging of guitars accompanied loud, jubilant shouts and musket fire as the cruelties began. The guerrillas were elated with their successful ambush of the French patrol. They puffed furiously on cigars and filled their cups from large flagons of wine in hearty celebration.

Ryan looked on, terrified.

The ecstasy of blood and the excitement of capturing the Frenchmen had annihilated all their feelings of human compassion, charity and honour. A mad frenzy took over the mob. They taunted the hapless prisoners, and as they got more and more inebriated, the unfettered violence only escalated.

A handful of guerrillas entered the pen, dragged the Frenchmen out, two at a time, and beat them to death with clubs and sticks. The mob screamed incessantly for vengeance against one atrocity or another committed by the French.

The cruelty increased as the evening progressed.

Ryan spied a cast-iron cauldron glistening against the fire. It brimmed with human ears and fingers, each one sporting a gold band, and was closely guarded by Sánchez's henchmen.

The mob hauled out a red-headed, buck-toothed young conscript from Brittany. *'Maman! Maman!'* the young grenadier blubbered, between high-pitched shrieks of pain and terror, before he, too, was bludgeoned to death.

'That's for murdering my mother and sister!' someone shouted. The mob chanted the war cry of *'¡Muerte a los franceses!'*

A *maréchal des logis* from the 2nd *Chasseurs à Cheval* was beaten, bound by his hands and feet. He screamed loudly before a drunken brigand ran his knife through his stomach, gutting him like a pig. A sergeant major from the Imperial Horse Artillery struggled violently and screamed as several men held him down and sawed him in half between two planks of wood. Ryan held his eyes tightly shut and hummed loudly to himself to try and blot out the noise.

Outside the holding pen, Ryan could make out the partial skeletal remains of what must have been French soldiers captured in a previous ambush. They were in varying degrees of decomposition, having been left to rot in the open. The familiar, sickening, heavy stench of death wafted up his nose. He mouthed the line he'd read in *The Tempest* back in the battalion's library in Burgos. *'Hell is empty and all the devils are here.'*

The guerrillas dragged Ryan out next. He felt a string of blows all over his body. He tried to land a few punches on his attackers, but there were too many and he was overcome. His body went numb. He was thumped again, kicked, and beaten with sticks. A heavy blow to his head left him unconscious. He was covered in blood and had barely come to when he was dragged back to his holding pen, his ears still ringing from the blow. His arms and legs were tied.

The tortured cries, the shrieks, the drunken laughter, and the relentless guttural cries of *'¡Muertes a los franceses!'* filled his ears. Ryan closed his eyes, cursed his life and wished he were dead.

CHAPTER 7

By the time dawn broke, the mob had become so inebriated that the torture and killing had stopped. Many of the tormentors lay keeled over in a drunken slumber. Most of the other French captives were dead, save for a cuirassier's colonel and a lieutenant of fusiliers. Ryan wondered why they were still alive, then realized the guerrilla commander may have given orders to keep officers alive for interrogating. They'd shivered all night on the cold ground, bound by their hands and feet. Ryan could not see out of his swollen eye, and the right side of his face was caked in dried blood. He tasted blood in his mouth and his lip was badly swollen.

Two guerrillas approached and cut the ropes around his arms and feet, then dragged him from his pen and into a cave. He squinted through his good eye and saw the cavern was filled with oil paintings, chandeliers, and an elaborate suite of furniture. In a corner, a Spaniard sat with clasped hands on a heavily carved armchair. His fingertips were poised to his lips as if he was in prayer. Ryan assumed this was General Don Julián Sánchez, the notorious guerrilla leader. The dim, flickering candlelight cast long shadows throughout the cave, but Ryan could still make out the swarthy rebel leader's square-set features. His shiny black hair, drooping moustache and enormous side-burns framed a pair of dark, hooded eyes under thick tufts of eyebrows that met in the middle. Ryan thought the general was dressed very strangely, very strangely indeed. Don Julián was flaunting a French hussar's dolmen; over this was a blue braided pelisse. He wore a pair of heavily scuffed, dirty blue trousers, with a double red stripe down the side. On his head was a French shako, with a long black vulture feather jutting out of the top, surmounted with a brass Eagle plate placed upside down. He knew this was a badge of honour among the guerrillas, signifying the capture and killing of French soldiers.

Don Julián stood up slowly from his chair, approached Ryan and peered at him closely. His breath reeked of wine and stale cigars. He began in passable French. 'I am General Don Julián Sánchez, leader of the Spanish army in Galicia, but tell me, *señor*, what your name is?'

'My name...' Ryan began, trying to relieve the pressure on his foot, for he could hardly stand from the pain, 'is Captain James Ryan of Napoleon's Irish Legion.'

'*Irlandés?* You are Irish?'

'Yes.'

'Very well, we shall, then, continue in English, as I detest speaking the language of the invader.' He spat on the ground and raised his eyebrows. 'But you must forgive my poor English. I hoped you slept well, *señor Irlandés*. You enjoyed the *fiesta* last night?' Don Julián sat back down and reached for his wine.

Ryan knew that sometimes the guerrillas held Frenchmen for ransom, or used them in exchange for captured guerrillas. In any case, he didn't care if he was killed. He had been through too much already, and he resolved to stand up to the guerrilla leader.

'You call yourselves a Patriot's Army, but you are simply a mob of murdering brigands. If I ever get out of this place alive, all of Europe will hear about the butchery and dishonor of the Spanish, and especially of you, *señor!*'

The guerrilla leader leapt to his feet, furious. 'Do not talk of butchery and savagery! The French slaughtered my family! We are—' he hesitated and closed his lips tightly. 'We *were* farmers from the Asturian Mountains until the invaders came. Frenchmen murdered my father and mother. My brother and I were forced to look on as our sister was dishonoured by French soldiers, then brutally mutilated.' His face reddened as he gritted his teeth. 'We were held hostage without food and water. They gagged us, clapped us in irons and force-marched us over twenty leagues. The French passed a watering well and wished to poison the water so the Spanish could not use it. To conserve their stock of poison, they called for two prisoners to be brought forward. The colonel unsheathed his sword. Boasting that he'd been taught by the best *maître d'armes* in Paris, he swiped its tip through the throat of one of the prisoners, just deep enough to cause blood to spurt, then he showed off to his men how his blade was clean, not even a drop of Spanish blood had stained it. The second prisoner he murdered the same way. I saw them writhing on the ground, gurgling and bleeding to death.'

Don Julián took a long draught of wine and stared, transfixed, at an oil painting of a simple agricultural scene. 'That man was my brother,' he rasped. 'The colonel ordered that their bodies be thrown into the well so that their rotting corpses would spoil the water. I vowed revenge to kill as many Frenchmen as I could until the last one left my country.'

Don Julián pursed his lips shut.

Ryan wondered if the guerrilla leader had revealed so much to a total stranger because he had drunk too much, or if he simply wanted at least one of his enemy to *know,* to understand. 'Cruelty begets cruelty, and mercy begets mercy. That is the way of man,' he said, then added, "And I am not French.'

'*Sí! Sí!* That is true!' the guerrilla leader conceded. 'You are a clever man, *señor*. Violence breeds violence and blood calls for blood; an eye for an eye and a tooth for a tooth, that's what it says in the great book.'

Ryan nodded. 'But it does not justify what happened to my men last night.'

'My men are cut-throats and freebooters, thieves, murderers and smugglers, and I have little control over them, for I can only maintain a certain level of discipline. They must have their rewards and their fun. We fight in the tradition of our great Castilian hero, El Cid, who claimed many victories against the Moors, and we will do the same with the hated French, mark my words, *señor*.'

'Fun? Mutilating men with bill hooks? Cutting them in two? Tying them to trees to be devoured alive by packs of wolves?'

Don Julián looked to be deep in thought. 'It is cruel, *señor*. War brings out the worst in man.' Don Julián pointed his finger. 'But sometimes the best!' he said forcibly.

'There are many who think Spain is one-hundred years behind the rest of Europe. Now I know why.' Ryan looked hard at the guerrilla leader.

Don Julian sniffed deeply. 'We have our own problems here in Spain. There has always been much lawlessness, and the nobility find their domains difficult to govern. They became corrupt and lazy because of all the gold brought into Spain from the New World. We are priest-ridden and the people are superstitious. When I was a child, I witnessed a monk being arrested for refusing to believe in the Resurrection. The authorities tried him at the *auto-de-fe*.

They challenged him, repeatedly, to repent but he stubbornly refused. The flames were lit to first tickle his feet and ankles, and rose ever so slowly so as to give the heretic an opportunity to repent his sin. Still he would not repent, and the soles of his feet were slowly broiled. They roasted him alive before my very eyes. I have never heard such screams, and they haunted me for years, until I heard them again when the French came. I remembered, then, an eye for an eye, a tooth for a tooth, the law of retaliation.'

Don Julián relit his cigar, thought for a couple of seconds, and stared into the abyss. 'There are three Irish regiments in the Spanish army, no? The *Brigada Irlanda.*'

'Yes, the regiments of Hibernia, Irlanda and Ultona, who have served Spain bravely in the past.'

'Hmm!' Don Julián grunted. 'I served alongside the blue-coated Regiment of Hibernia against the French. They are brave and honourable men, and many of their officers are Irish. Would you fight your own countrymen here in Spain, as there are many Irishmen who fight with the British? Tell me, why are you fighting in my country?'

'I am doing my duty, for I, too, am a patriot. Napoleon Bonaparte formed our Irish regiment to liberate Ireland from British rule. An invasion was planned from the camp at Boulogne on the French coast, where the *Armée d'Angleterre* were readied. The invasion was cancelled and we were then ordered to fight for France instead. That is why I am here. When Bonaparte defeats the British here in Spain, it will weaken England and the French may reconsider their invasion plans and liberate Ireland—'

'*Bah!*' interrupted the guerrilla leader angrily, 'I have no interest in those politics. I am only interested in removing the French from *my* country.'

Just then a horse reined up outside and a young British

officer dismounted. He tied his horse to a bough of a tree, brushed his blue jacket down, straightened his sabre and greeted Don Julián. 'Well done on your latest success, Field Marshal Wellesley will be very pleased.' The British officer reached for a pouch inside his saddlebag and threw a cotton sack to Don Julián. 'There are two-hundred silver dollar pieces in that bag, payment for the prisoners and rations for your men.'

Don Julián smiled widely. He opened the bag and his eyes sparkled.

'I heard you captured a cuirassier colonel?' The British officer turned to Ryan. 'This must be one of the men your people told me about.'

'*Sí*. I would like to introduce you to Captain Ryan, an Irishman in the Imperial French Service.'

The British officer slowly removed his leather riding gloves, finger by finger. 'I am Cornet John Williams of the 4th Light Dragoons. I believe our paths have crossed before, sir. We intercepted your patrol when you were out foraging a number of weeks ago outside Burgos, am I right?'

'I thought your face looked familiar, but I'm surprised you recognised mine in my current condition.'

The cornet looked closely at Ryan as he gathered his thoughts. 'I have asked about you. And we know who you are —a rebel and a wanted man. It is the gallows for you, sir! I've orders to turn you over to the British garrison in Ciudad Rodrigo, where you'll be questioned and likely hanged. A troop of dragoons has been despatched from Ciudad Rodrigo and they should be here tomorrow.'

Ryan now knew the reason why the guerrillas had kept him alive.

'The Light Dragoons' Ryan rasped, 'served in Ireland, probably before your time, and behaved dishonourably when they butchered men, women and children.'

Cornet Williams remained silent. Ryan sniffed at him defiantly. 'Is there an albino officer called Darkford still serving in the 4th Light Dragoons?'

'There is a Captain Daniel Darkford in the regiment,' replied Williams. 'But he is no concern of yours, rebel.'

Ryan smiled, for he now had the bastard's rank and regiment. He limped towards the cornet and sized him up. 'Well I don't care for your tone much, laddie! That bastard is a murderer, a dishonourable officer and a scoundrel.' Ryan struggled to stand upright as he stared angrily at the young cornet, until Don Julián abruptly ordered Ryan to be taken away.

It was bitterly cold that night as Ryan sat in the holding pen with the others. His heart raced, for he knew with certainty that Darkford was in Spain. He raised his eyes to the heavens. Thousands of bright stars lit up the black, moonless sky. As he watched, a great comet blazed and scudded across the night sky. Ryan nudged the two shivering Frenchmen, urging them to look. 'This is a good omen! We'll get out of here alive, mark my words.'

This proved true, as later that night a woman wearing a cape over her head and shoulders approached. It was Carmen! She stepped over the slumbering bodies of the two drink-sodden sentries guarding the prisoners, and opened the makeshift gate.

'Shush!' she whispered. She cut loose their ropes as Ryan shook the other Frenchmen awake. 'Be very quiet and follow me. 'Vámonos!'

Ryan, Carmen and the two Frenchmen crept silently out of the camp. 'Wait, James!' she whispered. 'I only have three horses. Sergeant Hoffman is waiting with them. The other men will have to make their way on foot.'

Ryan looked around and spied several horses bridled further up outside Don Julián's cave. 'We need horses.'

Carmen saw that Ryan was limping. 'It's too risky. If you wake them, you cannot outrun them.'

The French colonel whispered, 'You go on and we'll steal the horses.'

'Very well, but wait until we're well clear. If they see you, we're all done for,' said Ryan.

The colonel nodded.

Ryan stumbled out of the camp, supported by Carmen, and limped towards a young, badly beaten Frenchman who lay tied to a nearby tree. Ryan loosened the rope and freed him.

A little further down the path, Sergeant Hoffman waited nervously with three bridled bay mares. Hoffman hauled the barely conscious young French lieutenant up onto one horse while Ryan and Carmen mounted theirs. Ryan could barely hold onto the reins, and he winced in pain from the bullet in his arm. They slowly trotted away. A couple of minutes later they heard several shouts and cracks of musket fire. The two other French officers' plan to steal the horses had been foiled, Ryan thought. They must have awoken the entire camp.

Ryan and the others kept moving all night, and were relieved when their horses finally cantered towards the safety of Burgos as the sun rose.

CHAPTER 8

They passed Général de division Jean Junot's VIII Army Corps as it trundled into Burgos. There were two infantry divisions and one of cavalry. Ryan reckoned they numbered anywhere from 20,000 to 30,000 men. They looked impressive. The Imperial Horse Artillery were followed by several companies of engineers, together with at least a hundred wagons drawn by draught horses and mules. The Artillery Park included a score of artillery caissons, forges, farriers, pack mules, medical supplies and field kitchens. The baggage, comprised of the corp's military chest and the officer's personal possessions, together with the *cantinières,* dairy cows and sheep, meandered half a mile behind, escorted by a platoon of tired infantry. Ryan's horse walked slowly by as VIII Corps pitched tents outside the town's walls and constructed barrack huts into neatly arrayed rows.

Ryan suddenly remembered what Lieutenant McCarthy had warned him, that Carpentier's regiment had joined VIII Corps and that he was still baying for Ryan's blood.

The three bay mares cantered through the city's gated wall. Ryan dismounted and limped the last few metres to the Irish battalion's cantonments.

The men came out to meet them. 'It's Captain Ryan!' a voice shouted. 'Hip! Hurrah!' they cheered.

Commander Lawless greeted him. 'You had a very lucky escape. We thought we'd lost you. Carmen took a great risk in going to your rescue and put herself in great danger. She knew you wouldn't make it back alive, so she found out where the guerrilla camp was hidden.'

Ryan looked at Carmen and smiled.

'Yes, sir. If it wasn't for Carmen's bravery, and Sergeant Hoffman's, the British may very well have hanged me in Ciudad Rodrigo. Thanks for your help, Hoffman,' Ryan said weakly.

'*Jawohl!* It was all in the line of duty. Good to see you back safely, sir.'

'It's good to *be* back!'

Hoffman smiled. 'The men missed you.'

Ryan was indebted to Sergeant Hoffman, and his deed of valour cemented their friendship.

Grimly, Ryan told Lawless about General Don Julián and the French prisoners' fate.

'You are indeed lucky,' said the commander, 'and to cap it all, that lieutenant of fusiliers you saved is none other than General Jean Junot's son.'

'*The* General Jean Junot? I saw their cantonments when we arrived.'

Lawless laughed. 'The one and the very same, me boy! How many General Junots do you know?'

'Your return is a great morale boost for the battalion. I wouldn't be surprised if Minister Clarke and Emperor Bonaparte get wind of this. There's talk of giving you leave out of this bloody war!'

Ryan was helped into sickbay and Carmen kept him company. He was glad to be back with his men. He declined the offer of a couple of weeks leave back in France, as he'd no family there. The battalion was now his only home. He needed rest after his ordeal, and the torture he'd witnessed had affected him greatly. He noticed that his left hand was trembling more often. He wondered if he was losing his nerve. The only thing that was keeping him going was the thought of revenge. The anger was building up inside him. He would try to avoid the dueling Carpentier. All he wanted was to complete his quest to find Darkford and to kill him.

He was lying in sickbay when the battalion's surgeon major came to treat his arm. O'Reilly sniffed the wound. 'There's no odor of gangrene, but I'm very sorry to say you may lose the arm... we may be able to save it. We can apply a daily mixture to the wound. It's not always successful, but it's worth a chance. But first we must out with that bullet. The procedure is painful, but so is an amputation, so it's worth a try.'

'I'll try anything,' replied Ryan, as he looked O'Reilly firmly in the eye, 'absolutely anything to save the arm.'

Ryan knew that without his arm he would have to leave the army. He didn't have a trade, as soldiering was the only job he knew. And leaving the army was out of the question, for then he would have no way to catch up with Darkford.

O'Reilly nodded. 'I knew you'd say that, my boy!'

The surgeon examined Ryan's ankle. 'That's a nasty sprain, and it's badly swollen. You'll need to keep off it for a week. Now let's deal with your arm.'

O'Reilly opened his walnut, velvet-lined box of surgery tools, containing his amputation saw, scalpels and knives, and various tourniquets. He took out a pair of long nose pliers.

'Brace yourself now, Ryan! This is going to hurt,' he said, motioning for two medical orderlies to restrain his patient.

Ryan tightly closed his eyes as O'Reilly gouged deep into the wound to retrieve the lead ball lodged near his elbow joint. He never made a sound but bit down sharply on his bottom lip. After what appeared to Ryan to be a lifetime of excruciating pain, the ball was recovered. An orderly poured a small pot of warm wine and sugar into the wound to help prevent gangrene. This procedure proved to be the most painful part.

O'Reilly sighed deeply. 'Well, that's the best we can do for now. Rest a while, then we'll start on the maggot treatment.'

Ryan's face was white from fatigue and strain, and his arm throbbed violently. That night, Ryan caught a fever. He became delirious, talking wildly and loudly, believing he was back home having a meal of dressed potatoes and bacon with his wife and daughter. The surgeon wasn't sure if he would pull through, but two days later he was recovering well when O'Reilly came to check on him.

'How are you feeling, Ryan?'

'I feel I'm getting better,' he replied, 'I'm absolutely famished!'

'That's a relief,' said the doctor, as he removed Ryan's bandage. He opened a jar filled with maggots and, using a pair of fine tongs, placed them one by one into the wound cavity. 'I cover them with cotton because they need to breathe while feeding on the infected flesh, leaving the healthy flesh behind. Don't worry, James. These little critters will do you no harm at all. I once treated a severely wounded soldier with a large flesh wound in his abdomen and scrotum. Apparently, the poor fellow had spent several days wounded in the field. When we removed the man's clothing, we found thousands of maggots feeding on the infected flesh of the wound, and what they left in their wake was beautiful pink healthy tissue. And this man, would you believe— *survived.*'

Ryan grimaced. 'Will the maggots not mate and transform themselves into flies, then?'

'Have no fear. They're still larvae and cannot reproduce

until they become adult flies, and they'll be long gone before that happens.'

Ryan sighed. 'Good to hear I'm in such capable hands. I'm on the pig's back, me, glad to finally get some rest on a comfortable bunk and away from this war.'

The following morning, orderlies arrived at Ryan's bunk, carrying bags of captured British correspondence.

Lawless picked up a sheaf of papers and tossed them to the foot of Ryan's bed. 'Sift through these, Ryan. They were taken from a British regiment's baggage, which they left behind. See if there's any intelligence we may find useful.'

Ryan was happy to while the hours away reading, but he felt saddened because some of the captured correspondence was addressed to Irish soldiers. The domestic economy had collapsed following the Irish Rebellion, so many Irish men had no choice but to join up and 'take the King's shilling'.

He recognised one or two of the names on the correspondences as men he'd fought alongside with against the British, but they had now joined the British Army. There were letters from wives requesting money, while other letters informed soldiers of the deaths of children, from malnutrition, disease, and a score of different accidents. One letter told of how Private Murphy's wife had died during childbirth, the five surviving children having to enter the workhouse.

Not all the news was bad. There were also stories announcing the birth of children, or an impending marriage, and among letters addressed to the officers there was news of debutantes attending their first balls in Dublin Castle, or some other party or engagement in some landed gentry country house. This news from home might have come from a different planet it was so far removed from Ryan's life in

Spain.

As he delved deeper, he read official communications and requisitions, some questioning why an infantry regiment had received several hundred accoutrements of cavalry, or why six-hundred white gaiters were received when the regiment required boots. There were complaints about the poorly sewn British tunics, which lacked sleeve linings and a simple snit frequently served as a buttonhole, about ill-fitting coats made of poor cloth and of poor quality boots that quickly wore out on long marches on the unkempt roads of the Peninsula. Interesting enough, but he found nothing of tactical or strategic consequence.

After a week of being bedridden, he had read most of the books in the battalion's small library and was eager to return to duty. He picked up a battered leather bound copy of Jean Rousseau's *Social Contract*. He'd just re-read the first line. '*Man is born free but is found everywhere in chains*', when Lawless entered the room.

'How are you faring up, Ryan? O'Reilly tells me your wound is healing and the maggots have performed well.'

'I bloody well hope so, as they itch and tickle like hell.'

'You'll no doubt be delighted to know that General Junot wants to see you.'

'See me? Why?'

'Well, for one, he told me he was very much indebted to you for saving his son's life. It was a great deed, Ryan! You did the battalion proud, man.'

Ryan scrunched his face in pain as he winched himself up on his bunk by his good arm. 'I did my duty, Commander, that is all,' he replied raggedly. A medical orderly arrived and began to unravel the bandages on his arm. 'Me little beauties!' he crooned to the burrowing, wriggling larvae. Just as the doctor had said, the maggots had munched through the rotting flesh and left the healthy tissue unscathed. Ryan picked up one of the maggots and examined it.

'If you can make it up to see the general at one o'clock?'

'Don't you worry, Colonel, I'll be there.'

Lawless got up to leave. 'See you in my study, then. I've already told Ferguson to prepare your uniform. By the way, Ryan, as you're still limping, I'm giving you a lend of my shillelagh.'

'Thank you, Commander,' replied Ryan, as he took hold of the blackthorn walking stick.

CHAPTER 9

The medic continued carefully removing each maggot from the wound in his arm to a tin tray, then applied fresh bandages to the wound. Ryan hobbled out of bed, clutching Lawless's blackthorn shillelagh for support, and sat down for his valet to shave him. He glanced across the room and saw that his green trousers had been darned and washed, the tears in the knees repaired. The brass lozenge of his shako was polished and the yellow and green plume was new.

'Kaminski darned the trousers himself, sir, and repaired the boots,' Ferguson informed him.

'He did an excellent job. I'd forgotten he was a cobbler before the war,' said Ryan, as he pulled his trousers up with difficulty. 'And this looks as good as new,' he commented, taking up his green jacket.

'Yes, sir. The epaulettes and buttons were replaced, and the sleeve's braiding repaired.'

Ryan tugged on the heavily polished cavalry boots, and his valet helped him button up his green tunic. He faced the mirror as Ferguson clipped his officer's gorget, with the punched out image of a harp in the centre, around his neck.

Ryan stared back at his reflection in a gilt wood-framed mirror. 'That'll be all.'

The orderly saluted and left the room.

Ryan continued to stare back at his reflection. He was the very picture of a professional soldier. His face wore a look of bitter experience. His skin had turned from a ruddy hue to light brown, and his wavy hair protruded from behind his ears, curling just above his shoulders, while his sideburns gave him a distinguished look. As he stared back at the mirror, he felt like a fraud, a fake; he didn't feel like a soldier. How different his life was now compared to when he was living in Ireland, before he got involved with the Revolutionary Society of United Irishmen, which had led to the Irish rebellion and his forced exile.

The United Irishmen had gambled everything to liberate their shackled country. They'd put lucrative careers on hold as they schemed and plotted in whispered tones in the back rooms of Dublin pubs. Their greatcoat collars pulled up high and their cocked hats pulled down over their eyes, they were always on the lookout for the despicable informer.

If the rebellion had never happened, he would've continued to live a comfortable life with his wife and child, and probably would have had more children. His daughter would have been what age now? *Let me see,* he thought. *It's 1808 now and she was three years old in 1798. That would make her thirteen years old. I'm thirty-five, and Mary would have been thirty-two. Yes, that's right,* he calculated.

A glum expression appeared on his reflection. He'd never had any wish to serve as a soldier. His greatest assets were his agility and his swiftness, not strength or power. What he possessed was the ability to anticipate an opponent's next move in a contest of hand-to-hand combat, which had saved his life on many occasions. He wasn't particularly brave, either. His legs frequently turned to jelly before a battle. The will to fight was always just barely just stronger than the instinct to save his skin and flee in the face of impending death or severe injury—he'd learned to keep his fear under control. He knew of other officers who hadn't been able to hack it, who physically reeled before a battle. That, of course, would never do in front of the men. Such officers were forced to leave the army. Those with the right connections obtained plush desk jobs in regimental headquarters, far away from the battle lines.

Although he'd acquitted himself in battle, he detested the unbridled violence and savagery of hand-to-hand combat. The terror and the excitement of battle gave way to physical and mental exhaustion, and the relentless, monotonous banality of garrison life. He feared death and hated killing, yet frequently told his men that a good soldier kills without thinking of his enemy as a human being at all. He remembered the first man he'd killed, and how sad he'd felt as he stood over the lifeless body, but for a long time after that he hadn't cared. This was changing. Those who died close to him were affecting him. He was beginning to recognise that warfare was taking its toll, not just on his body but also on his mind. But he mustn't let that show.

And he couldn't get Darkford out of his mind.

He examined his front teeth in the mirror, rubbed them clean with his forefinger and cocked his shako jauntily to one side. Then he turned, picked up Lawless's blackthorn shillelagh and limped out to meet General Junot.

As he walked, a troop of Black Hussars trotted past on their horses. Captain Carpentier was among them. He cast a side glance at Ryan, who held his gaze. The hussar snarled, then growled at his horse to giddy up. *'Hue! Hue!'* He jabbed his spurs into the white mare's sides to urger her forward, and spat heavily at Ryan's feet.

A short time later, Ryan arrived at the colonel's door. He knocked, and Lawless let him in.

'I'd like to introduce you to General Jean-Andoche Junot,'

said Lawless.

The highly ambitious and tempestuous general was one of Napoleon's favourites, hard as nails from his spurs to his pompon. Junot was forty years old and retained a thick head of jet black hair. Ryan looked on as Junot sat back on a chair near an open fire for his *valet de chambre* to shave him.

'We have to look well in front of the men,' said the general, 'nothing worse than a poorly kept officer.' He extended his mouth downward, allowing his upper lip to be shaved with ease.

Junot took in Ryan's walking stick. 'Take the weight off your feet, Captain.'

'How is your arm coming along?' Lawless asked.

'Healing nicely, Commander.'

Ryan sat down and keenly studied the general.

An awkward silence followed; nothing but the rasping sound of the razor blade scraping Junot's jaw was heard.

Ryan recalled the story told and retold in the army about Junot's meteoric rise through the ranks, by stealth and guile. Twenty years ago, the republicans had been fighting the royalist supporters of the deposed King Louis during the Siege of Toulon. Napoleon, then a young artillery officer, called for a corporal or sergeant to come forward who could read and write. Junot, a young sergeant of grenadiers at the time, raised his hand and got the job. He was writing a letter for Napoleon when an incoming cannonball whistled loudly and landed close by, kicking up dirt everywhere, including over Junot's letter. All the other officers in the company dived for cover, but not Junot. He remained fearlessly calm and acted as if nothing had happened. He turned to Napoleon and remarked that the cannonball had been a stroke of good fortune, for now he did not need sand to dry the letter's ink. Napoleon, impressed by Junot's *sangfroid,* had promoted him on the spot, and ever since that day the two men had been close friends.

General Junot's valet handed him a towel and he wiped his face, then turned towards Ryan, extending his hand.

'I thank you, Captain, for saving my son's life.'

Ryan felt the roughness of Junot's palm, the sign of a lifetime of hard work, and this raised Ryan's respect for him.

The general stepped forward in front of the mirror and was helped on with his lavishly braided navy-blue tunic. 'You are a brave man, and this is a quality that helps a soldier advance and rise.'

'Thank you, General, but I have little interest in rising through the higher ranks, as I enjoy my rank of captain and like the company of my men.'

'Hmm,' Junot murmured. 'In our army even the common soldier can rise to general, for every French soldier carries a Marshal of France's baton in his knapsack!' The general considered Ryan gravely. 'Where did you learn to speak French, Captain?'

'My uncle was a cleric in the Irish College in Lille before he returned home to Ireland. I was tutored by him.'

Junot's face flashed in recognition and he snapped his fingers.

'You speak like a native of Lille. Your uncle did an excellent job, Captain. It's a pity the other Irishmen, and the other foreigners in our army, are not as proficient in French as *you* are.'

'That's true,' Ryan conceded. 'However, we continue to teach the men French and we should see an improvement as time passes. The Irish have a *esprit de corps* and are proving to be an annoyance to the British. We have many deserters from their army in our ranks.'

Junot looked at him squarely as he nodded approvingly.

NAPOLEON'S BLACKGUARDS

The general straightened his collar, brushing the orderly away. 'What we want in our army are men with vision, men with steely ambition. We want world changers! History makers, like our beloved Napoleon Bonaparte.'

A slight smirk edged Ryan's mouth. Junot stared at the captain and asked solemnly, 'Do you not love the Emperor?'

Junot's fanatical devotion to Napoleon was legendary and it was even known to have bordered on obsessional.

Ryan stared back intensely with dead fish eyes. 'I love my country, General. I have served and will continue to serve Napoleon with the utmost loyalty and believe I can also speak for my other brother officers as well.'

'Well, you are a foreigner, but if a Frenchman indicated that he did not love the Emperor that would indeed be a problem.' Junot paused and thought for a while. 'But I have heard much about you Irishmen. You are an undisciplined lot and are difficult to control but have proven time and again to be good fighters. It may surprise you to hear that I also know about your vendetta against an officer of the hussars. I have many who report in to me what goes on in my corps that may reflect poorly on me. This hussar officer, his name escapes me...'

'If I may be of some assistance,' interposed Lawless, rubbing his hands vigorously, 'his name is Captain Carpentier, a man of supreme dishonour, a blackguard and a murderer to boot! So I am reliably informed.'

'Thank you, Commander.'

'And may I add, General, that Captain Ryan is not the aggressor but has simply defended his honour when he was called out.'

Junot scratched his cheek and looked closely at Ryan. 'A man's honour and his name are his greatest possessions to be valued more than life itself, for the noble trade of soldiering confers the most honour to a man who acquits himself well in battle, and the most dishonour to he who fails to do so. One fault can spell ruin, for a man can lose a reputation he has spent thirty years acquiring in a matter of seconds.' Junot pulled out a silver pocket watch from his waistcoat, flipped it open and read the time. 'As we are, of course, at war, Emperor Napoleon has strictly forbidden dueling between officers and men alike, irrespective of calls for honour, but we must sometimes ignore these things. I fought a duel against an officer while stationed in Egypt in '99 as he had openly criticised Napoleon's leadership.'

Just then, a young *Chef d'Escadron* entered the room and saluted briskly. 'I have an important message from General Massena, sir.'

'Excellent. I've been expecting you,' said Junot, as he keenly cracked open the red wax seal with his thumbs and unfolded the paper. 'Thank you again for saving my son's life, Ryan!' the general said, fluttering the raised letter in his hand. 'I assure you I will not forget what you did.'

Ryan saluted and went out.

CHAPTER 10

After accommodating so many troops belonging to Junot's army, the Old Castilian capital of Burgos was no longer the same sleepy and laid-back city Ryan had known. The once quiet streets, plazas and twisting alleyways now swarmed with hawks and touts peddling their wares. Many private residences, too, had been turned into taverns and places of ill repute. Some of the unscrupulous locals knew that the French would not remain long in Burgos and resolved to make the best of it and make as much money as they could.

After a difficult campaign, Ryan's company were glad to relax and spend their pay and found many willing to relieve them of it in Burgos. In times of war, it is said that inhibitions are often discarded and pushed aside and the city was soon awash with drunkenness, vice, and debauchery of every kind. Some of the camp followers and local Spanish women came down from the outlying villages in the mountains and, spurred on by the French soldiery into drinking to excess, even openly fornicated in the city's medieval alleyways. The respectable city fathers and clergy were appalled. Although the gendarmes patrolled widely and imposed strict discipline on looting it was open season for many of the other vices.

Ryan was surprised how cold it became, as night-time temperatures frequently plummeted below freezing.

Wrapped in his capote with the collar up to keep warm he sauntered through the dark streets before entering a smoky local tavern. He climbed the rickety stairs, and stepped over several drunken couples who lay passed out before he spied Sergeant Hoffman seated on a bench with several Irish voltigeurs. He sat down.

Hoffman swigged wine from a mug. 'How did your meeting go with Junot?

'I thought it went well—he's a good officer.'

Hoffman turned and his face suddenly lost colour. 'Don't look around, Captain, but I just saw Captain Carpentier with several of his hussar cronies in the corner. I don't think he's seen you. If you step away quickly I think you can avoid him.'

Ryan frowned heavily. 'I saw him earlier and I'll have to fight that bastard sometime.' A chill travelled down his spine as he turned in the Black Hussar's direction. He saw Carpentier with a patch over his eye, twisting his moustache and returning Ryan's gaze. A brown mass of hair framed his tanned, weather-beaten face. His thick moustache needed trimming. So did his substantial mutton chops, which extended from his sideburns and ran into his moustache. Ryan's heart pounded in his chest. He sweated heavily but stared back defiantly before turning away. 'Is there no beer in this bloody country? Always this bloody wine,' he snapped angrily.

He reached over, grabbed a bottle, and raised it to his mouth to take a long draught. 'I've no choice but to fight this bastard, but if I could get out of it, I would,' he said drearily.

Ryan felt a tap on his shoulder and turning around he faced Captain Lejeune. 'Good evening. Captain Ryan, I believe?'

Ryan nodded and looked across to the group of hussar officers who were glaring over at him. Carpentier smiled and raised a glass towards Ryan in mock salute. 'Captain Carpentier requires satisfaction for your dishonourable behaviour and the insults which you hurled at him in Madrid during the recent disturbances there.'

Ryan stood up.

'He demands satisfaction, *m'sieu*. He has heard that you are still limping and have not fully recovered from the recent injury you have sustained. Captain Carpentier has very graciously agreed to fight with pistols *á la barrieère*.'

'Oh, did he, indeed,' snorted Ryan angrily.

'We rendezvous tomorrow at dawn, behind the church of the *Iglesia de la Merced* as it's well secluded from patrolling gendarmes.' Lejeune turned and walked away amid loud hooting from the Black Hussars.

Ryan sat and folded his arms in thought.

Hoffman removed his pipe from his mouth. 'What is this type of duel *á la barrieère*?'

'It's the deadliest pistol duel in France,' explained Lieutenant McCarthy. 'It works like this. A field is laid out like an elaborate tennis pitch and a barrier is placed in the centre. This could be a piece of wood or a length of rope. The two opponents stand at opposite sides of the field and are ordered to advance and slowly make their way towards the barrier. The challenged party is permitted to fire first, and if he misses, he's obliged to remain on the spot and let his opponent return fire.'

Lieutenant Séan McCarthy's father had served in Dillon's Regiment of the Irish Brigade before the Revolution. He sported a thick mop of flame-coloured hair and, although born in France and able to speak French perfectly, he was as Irish as they came.

McCarthy slapped Ryan hard on the shoulder. 'Don't worry, James, for I've a superb brace of *Boutet* pistols, the best in all of France.'

Ryan's gaze met McCarthy's. 'Where the devil did you get hold of those? They must have cost a king's ransom.'

Hoffman, impressed, raised his eyebrows. 'Yes, indeed, as they're worth at least a year's wages.'

McCarthy nodded. 'Colonel Armand gave them to me for saving his life during the Spanish rising in Madrid.'

'You're a lucky dog, McCarthy!'

'Well, not really, as I was laid up with a leg wound for my trouble,' returned McCarthy sadly, throwing back his wine. 'Just a thought—is there any way you can get out of this duel with your honour intact?'

Ryan's forehead furrowed. 'I have no choice.' He touched his elbow, as it still ached. 'Luckily the wound I received in my elbow joint wasn't in my pistol arm.'

'Don't worry, I'll sort you out, James,' interposed McCarthy. 'I'll get hold of those pistols this evening.'

Hoffman looked gravely at Ryan. 'This has been building up for a while; I've heard that Carpentier has already killed two sergeants in the foot artillery in duels just two days ago.'

Ryan sighed deeply. 'I'm returning to my billet. I don't feel much like drinking and need to prepare for tomorrow.' He turned to McCarthy. 'Will you stand as my second?'

'I'd be honoured to,' replied McCarthy heartily, but as he got up from the table, he knocked over a bottle of wine, which Ryan saw as a bad omen, the red wine representative of spilt blood.

The two men walked grimly back to their billets. McCarthy retrieved his cased set of flintlock dueling pistols from a padlocked chest under his bed.

'Here you go, James. Now don't you worry, and wake me at cock-crow. Wear dark clothes—don't be wearing a white shirt and present yourself as an easy target.'

Ryan knew he'd get no sleep and, taking the mahogany box under his arms, returned to his quarters.

He propped two pillows against his back and prised open the brass clip on the box's lid, which was made from a thick veneer of Cuban mahogany inlaid with ivory. He sniffed the pleasant pungent smell of oil and gunpowder. *What beautiful pistols,* he thought. The mahogany-handled, octagonal smoothbore brace of barrels was set in head-to-toe position, complete with ramrods and pewter powder flasks in a velvet green padded box. He read the manufacturer's label. *'Nicholas Noel Boutet, Paris,'* was written in elaborate copper plate font, pasted proudly inside the lid.

Ryan uncased one of the pistols, thumbed the hammer back into the cocked position, aimed, and pulled the trigger. He wished he was facing the evil bastard Darkford in the duel instead of Carpentier. He wasn't afraid of dying. He didn't believe in God or in an afterlife, but he held out the hope that if he was killed he would see his family again.

His heart sank as he'd only fought two duels in his life, although he'd acted as second to a principal on four occasions. He'd run a man through with his sword back in Ireland, where dueling was widespread. He was a good enough shot with a pistol but he'd still have preferred to fight Carpentier with swords, as they were less deadly, for he'd already seen what wounds *á la barrieère* had inflicted.

Some years before, when the Irish battalion had garrisoned Quimper at Brittany, he'd acted as second, to a fellow who had recently arrived from Ireland. One summer's afternoon Sous-Lieutenant Manning had been enjoying a drink outside a tavern. There was little else for the Irishmen to do in the sleepy Breton town when off duty. Manning was a great lump of a fellow from the plains of County Kildare and had his legs jauntily sticking out in front of his chair when several officers from the Imperial Horse Artillery passed. One of them stumbled and fell over Manning's foot. The Irishmen laughed. The artilleryman felt humiliated in front of the other officers and whacked Manning with his fist straight across the jaw. Manning rose to his feet and punched the artillery officer on his nose, which began spouting violently with blood. The officer issued a challenge, which Manning instantly accepted, and within the hour, the two men were preparing to fight a duel to the barrier.

Ryan put the pistol back in the box and recalled when the two parties stood their ground and, at a given signal, began to walk towards a white leather scabbard laid out in the middle of the ground to serve as the barrier. Lieutenant Manning was barely twenty years old and his head was still swirling with the effects of wine. He prematurely fired his pistol and missed his opponent. The French officer smiled. 'You are indeed a brave Irishman,' he said with steely seriousness. The Frenchman stepped back two paces and looked hard at Manning. 'I will send my sympathies to your mother,' he concluded before shooting Manning point blank through the heart.

'Affairs of honour, my foot,' Ryan muttered as he traced his index finger across the elaborately engraved stock.

Ryan thought about what McCarthy had said earlier about avoiding the duel without losing face. There were several occasions when a man could graciously decline being called out by bluffing and in so doing not lose honour. He had heard that some men invited their challenger to a meal. This sometimes resulted in both men getting drunk, and more often than not, the two men left each other's company amicably with their honour intact, and the duel was simply called off. Ryan would not and could not—even if he wanted to—entertain this option with a murdering rogue like Carpentier.

Ryan only lightly dozed on his bunk and hadn't even bothered taking off his boots. He took out his pocket watch and saw that it was seven a.m. He reached inside his shirt, took hold of his bog oak amulet, and kissed it.

With a feeling of dread, he threw his capote over his shoulders and knocked heavily on McCarthy's door. 'It's time to go, Séan!'

It was a lovely morning as the two men made their way silently towards the churchyard and birds whistled and twittered the melodic dawn chorus. The sun crept slowly over the nearby Molena Mountain, lighting the sky in a beautiful red-orange hue.

'I want you to send my possessions to my mother if that villain finishes me off. I'm due four month's pay in arrears and she could certainly use the money.' Ryan's widowed mother lived with his two sisters. As his wife and daughter were dead there was nothing in Ireland but sad, dark memories.

The two voltigeurs rounded the church and the sight of a freshly dug grave greeted them. Evidently, Carpentier had had some of his men dig it earlier that night.

'Now remember what I said—aim for the hip,' whispered McCarthy in a low, hushed voice.

The hussar stood prancing up and down in a cocky swagger, beside Captain Lejeune acting as his second. While an elderly, periwigged doctor in a black cloak and cocked hat stood and watched from the side.

McCarthy spoke. 'Duelling etiquette dictates that the two principals should not address each other, so both men are only to communicate through their seconds.'

Carpentier shouted towards his second. 'Tell him, then,

he'll be sleeping in that grave tonight!'

'Tell *your* man,' replied Ryan, 'that he's a dishonourable coward, a blackguard, a violator and a murderer of innocent girls.'

Anger flushed in his adversary's face, because no man likes to lose face in front of his peers.

Ryan shot him an angry look. 'Lieutenant McCarthy? Would you act as a second to a murderer of innocent girls?'

McCarthy smirked and shook his head while the seconds examined each principal's pistols, as both sets had to be similar. Some unscrupulous duellists held pairs of dueling pistols, with one having a rifled barrel. This improved the accuracy of the leaden ball since it spun with greater speed and precision than the pistol held by the opponent who, armed with a less accurate, smooth-bore barrel, was at a disadvantage.

The two seconds approved both pairs of pistols and a greatcoat was laid open in the centre of the graveyard to serve as the barrier. The duellists received their cocked pistols and withdrew fifty paces towards the end of the graveyard.

To prevent any chance of reconciliation, Carpentier glared hard at Ryan shouting wildly, *'No apologies! No apologies!'* while Ryan squinted his eyes and averted his gaze in disgust, much to the hussar's increased annoyance.

'Messieurs,' called Lejeune. *'En avant!'* and at that command, both men started their slow walk towards the grey greatcoat in the centre, with their pistols facing downwards. After taking around ten paces, Ryan raised his pistol arm in the bent position, aimed and fired—but missed. Carpentier hastily returned fire and the ball entered Ryan's tunic, throwing up a puff of dust. Ryan staggered back two steps and swayed heavily but remained on his feet.

'I'm done with that bastard!' shouted the hussar as he turned away towards his second.

'Back on your mark, sir!' ordered McCarthy firmly to Carpentier. 'Back on your mark!' he repeated in a low, agitated voice as both men were handed two freshly loaded pistols by their seconds.

Carpentier displayed a look of fear and surprise and reluctantly returned to his spot. The ball had hit Ryan in the chest but had fortuitously deflected off a tunic button, which broke the balls power and luckily only bruised Ryan's chest. The hussar turned sideways and breathed in, to present a smaller target to his opponent. Ryan steadied himself and levelled his pistol towards his adversary, but the shot rang out and he missed—*again.*

Carpentier levelled his pistol and shot but fired wide. The seconds suddenly called for the men to halt and after consulting briefly, agreed that they should return to their original positions at opposite ends of the graveyard, as according to the rules of the *Code Duello,* the allotted time had elapsed.

'Return to your marks, gentlemen,' instructed McCarthy.

The seconds loaded the pistols for the third time.

Ryan approached his adversary with steely resolve, raised his arm, aimed and fired. The ball lodged high in the hussar's pistol arm and he dropped his pistol in agony as he grasped his wounded arm. Ryan stood his ground, turned sideways and waited for the deadly return shot. Although Carpentier was bleeding profusely, he picked up his pistol and in a blind rage shot at Ryan but missed.

The seconds again consulted with each other before McCarthy announced, 'According to the etiquette of the *Code Duello,* the seconds are in agreement that the duel has been honourably settled.'

'Honour has not been served!' raved Carpentier as the elderly doctor rushed to attend his wound. 'Honour has not been served!' he repeated.

The two Irishmen retrieved their capotes and shakos and hastily made their way back to their lodgings, half-expecting to be shot in the back.

Ryan was clearly relieved. 'That was a close call! I amn't bleeding and it looks like I didn't break any ribs, either. Christ, how many times is it now that I've escaped death by the skin of my teeth?'

McCarthy clapped Ryan firmly on his back. 'You lead a charmed life, my good man, a charmed life indeed.'

They laughed loudly and skipped their way back through Burgos with interlocking arms, which drew several strange looks from the locals going about their business. They laughed again when they narrowly avoided the contents of a chamber pot being chucked out of an upstairs window as they passed underneath.

Ryan turned to his friend as he made his way towards Carmen's lodgings. 'I'm going to enjoy myself,' he said, gesturing towards Carmen's room, 'Have to satisfy the lady, and then will get a good sleep and, after that—who knows?— I may get terribly drunk,' he burst out. 'There's nothing that makes a man feel more alive than when he has stared death in the face and then survived to tell the tale. *Adieu!*' he shouted as he ran towards Carmen's door.

He knew that he'd have to fight the scoundrel Carpentier again sometime in the future but he didn't care. He tried not to laugh, as the pain in his ribs was excruciating, but he couldn't help it, he felt so relieved. He wanted to embrace life. The Grim Reaper had come knocking on his door but he had cheated death yet again.

CHAPTER 11

Ryan awoke, rubbed the sleep from his eyes, pulled his shoulders back and stretched. He exhaled deeply while drawing Carmen close before he spun her swiftly around the bed. They made love again. Carmen afterwards beamed a smile towards him, her large brown eyes glistening adoringly.

'Tomorrow is a very special day in Burgos,' she announced.

Ryan cocked an inquisitive glance. 'Why's that?'

'There is going to be huge spectacle,' she continued as she lit a cheroot and handed it to him. 'Have you ever seen the *corrida*, James?'

'Can't say I have—the *corrida*?'

'It's a bull fight,' she explained matter-of-factly.

Ryan sat up on the bed smoking his cheroot and listened intensely. 'I've heard from some of the officers that it's a very noble art form.'

'Yes, it is. Bullfighting dates way back to the medieval period, some say the Romans brought it with them to Spain. The *corrida* was reserved for the rich who could afford to train and supply the beasts. A bull was released into a closed arena where a single man on horseback armed with a lance stood face to face with it. Over time the horseman had been replaced with the *matador* who fights on foot.' Carmen smiled. 'You want to see? Yes?'

88

'I would love to.'

'*Muy bien, hasta mañana* at seven o' clock.'

'*Hasta mañana,*' he repeated, before he swaggered out of the bedroom, a cheroot dangling from his mouth.

Ryan reported for duty at Commander Lawless's office.

'I have just received an order from a dispatch rider that the Irish battalion, together with a division of VIII Corps, are to march north into the Asturian Mountains to hunt down the guerrillas in the hills,' said Lawless. 'We're to reinforce the small French garrison in León and defeat General Cuesta and his band of guerrillas. Those bastards have controlled much of the region and have made the mountain passes inaccessible. I have heard rumours that Napoleon himself is in Spain to re-establish his grip in the Peninsula.'

Ryan was looking forward to spending time with Carmen and seeing the bullfight but the *corrida* would have to wait.

An hour later, the column waited in line and waited for the order. '*En avant! Marche!*' the commanding officer shouted, and this order was repeated down the lines. Ryan's company stepped off at Sergeant Hoffman's command, as he, too, blared out, '*En avant! Marche!*'

Ryan's voltigeurs were in front and led the march. He was posted behind the battalion's drum major, who sported the most flamboyant uniform in Napoleon's army. Ryan admired how he skillfully threw his staff high up in the air and snatched it on its return as fifers and drummers beat the march. The battalion's bronze cast golden Imperial Eagle glistened in the shimmering sunlight. Ryan had removed it from the battalion's military chest and kissed it for luck. Two light cavalry squadrons joined the Irish battalion. This was the advance guard. Then came Marshal Jean Baptiste Bessières' VIII Corps with the Artillery Park and a limbered troop of the Imperial Horse Artillery. At the rear, a platoon of gendarmes followed to prevent stragglers and deserters. Two leagues behind, four light infantry companies formed the rear guard. Ryan reckoned that the whole column was over a mile long.

Many of the local women and children came out to see them off. They waved and threw flowers at their feet as they marched past; some lunged into the ranks to steal a kiss from a loved one. A soldier held a badger on a leash; others kept rabbits and pet rats in their kit, while scrawny, dirty mongrels kept as regimental mascots followed at the marching men's heels and barked loudly above the din.

The *Grand Armée* could march, Ryan thought. These veterans were the most travelled since the Roman legions had traversed the poorly maintained dust tracks of Spain and Portugal. Precious little had changed since the Roman conquest of Hispania. He'd read that the historian Vegetius claimed that Rome's military pre-eminence was due to the Roman legionnaires ability to march twenty miles in five hours. *That's what Napoleon's Grand Armée emulate and by God they are good at it!* He felt proud being part of it. The convoy resembled a well-oiled, finely tuned machine and trooped off as one cohesive unit. There was just one half metre frontage space between each row of men, each step pushing those in front forwards. Their right arms folded across their chests, their Charlevilles cradled in their left arms in the manner typical of Napoleon's infantry.

The drummers *drmm! drmm! Drmm-a-drm-drmm!* rhythm rang shrill in Ryan's ears, and the heavy sound of thousands of boots thumping loudly on the cobblestones echoed through the city's medieval streets. Ryan and the others had marched for a mile beyond the city's walls, when the column was ordered to break step and march with ease, some hauling their muskets by the barrel with the wooden stock swung leisurely over the shoulder. The men began to roar out the old marching songs. Ryan enjoyed these songs the best. A particular favourite was from the camp at Boulogne. They bellowed at the top of their lungs the part that went, *'From England we'll bring back treasure, that won't have cost us a sou.'*

When they tired of singing, the only noises were the rumbling carts, the heavy snick of metal on metal and the thuds of boots with the odd cough and sneeze mingled in, all permeated with the foul odours of garlic, sweat and the occasional flatulence. Ryan was happy to be alone with his thoughts; others relieved the boredom by telling crude jokes and dirty stories, or engaging in friendly banter. Some bragged about their recent kills or their latest sexual conquests.

Voltigeur Nowak wanted to know how Sergeant Gautier from the 43ème *Ligne* was, as he had been recently struck down with typhus.

'He snuffed it last night, the poor fellow!' a voice answered.

Ryan turned and saw Nowak frown heavily. '*Putain*, Gautier owed me ten francs!'

'Did you see the size of the whore young Pierre went off with?' cried Kami.

'Yes, my God, she was a big girl!' a gruff voice boomed from the back.

'Massive breasts!' another voice piped up.

They all laughed.

'Thank goodness she didn't go on top, as she'd have killed the lad.'

The man was referring to one of the young French conscripts, who'd lost his virginity the previous night. The youth reddened and Ryan observed that he wisely kept his head down.

'I wouldn't talk too loud if I were you, Kaminski,' Ryan teased. 'The last woman I saw you with had no teeth at all.'

'And she had a head on her like a well slapped arse,' McGowan chirped.

Everyone laughed. This remark, followed by more sneering, provoked Kaminski to hold his tongue for the rest of the day. Ryan glanced over and studied him for a while. There were many Poles in the Irish Legion. Voltigeur Piotr Kaminski was the best shot in his company and served as the company's interpreter. He was a cobbler by trade, amiable and intelligent, and had a good sense of humour. Ryan was teaching him English and thought he'd make an excellent sergeant, believing he had potential to rise further up the ranks.

The advance guard had already gained two leagues on Bessières's division of VIII Corps who were marching up slowly in the rear. They paused to rest, removed their heavy backpacks, and adjusted their equipment. Ryan's ankle still hurt and he was glad when he could remove his boot to massage it. He took his heavy knapsack from his sweating back, fumbling through it to find his clay pipe. He took out his biscuit ration, his rosewood whistle, his spare trousers and shoes, sat down, lit his pipe and had his smoke. Afterwards, he took hold of his whistle and played an Irish jig, *O'Sullivan's March*.

They moved on again. Ryan's eyes squinted in the sun as the convoy crossed the wide-open, yellow-brown plains of the monotonous Meseta, with its seemingly unending horizons. His good spirits waned when the weather broke, and he cursed as it became impossible to keep dry either by day or at night through the capricious thunderstorms, pelting rain and blizzards. The men swaddled themselves up in their capotes, pulled up their collars, and plodded on with downcast gloom.

The convoy had covered the guts of 30 miles that day and were relieved to make camp. Ryan and the others collapsed, exhausted, flat on their backs in a wheat field. As there was a shortage of field tents, Ryan's company bivouacked in the open field. A party was sent off to find wood. It wasn't long before huge fires were lit under the metal tripods, to cook the enormous cauldrons of salted fish and meat and boil the great vats of soup so beloved by the French.

At first light, they broke camp.

Spain was a country of exotic, dark-eyed beautiful women, of picturesque stone villages, of sun and wine, of guitars and boleros, but it was also a proud, arrogant land steeped in papist superstition and idolatry, feudalism and cruelty. Ryan often stood mesmerised before the majestic churches and cathedrals he found as the column picked its way through northern Spain. He had always marvelled at the richly decorated pierced stonework of the twin spires of the fifteenth-century Burgos Cathedral with its magnificent vaulted ceilings. Although some of the Spanish villages were picturesque, the houses were simple dwellings without chimneys and appeared mean, reeking of poverty. This was the kind of poverty Ryan knew back home. As he lumbered through decrepit villages, he encountered beautifully built ornate chapels adorned with elaborate Sevillian floral ceramic-tiled floors. On the walls hung paintings and sculptures of the saints, appearing as beacons of culture and civility amongst the grand chaos. Spain was a world power in decline. The wealth generated from her past glories and colonies in the New World had filtered down from the great cathedrals of the main cities in Spain to the smaller churches in some of the larger towns, and even to the chapels in the villages. He remembered how Catholic places of worship were forbidden back home, and so mass was held in a field or in some small dingy back hall.

The landscape changed dramatically from steep mountainous slopes to flat plains and rolling countryside covered in pine forests, stone cut villages and tidy hamlets. They were deserted with few pickings for plunderers. Ryan sighed heavily as a hailstorm lashed out of the heavens.

They trudged on in the rain. He watched as the men's shoulders hunched and their heads bowed while they marched. Morale sank further. Many deserted, including Voltigeur Michael O'Callaghan, the former sailor from Cork in Ryan's company, but he was caught.

A Provost Marshal and a platoon of gendarmes, summoned from Bessières's VIII Corps in the rear, oversaw O'Callaghan's execution. A platoon of drummers stood frozen with their sticks poised to their lips before they were ordered to beat the death march. As the shackled prisoner walked out, the muffled drumbeat kept pace with the condemned man's heavy, slow step. The Provost turned towards the hapless voltigeur. He was barefoot and shirtless save for his green tunic, which hung on his brawny frame; his trousers were soiled, torn, and rolled up at the ankles. His leg irons were unclipped as he was ordered to kneel in front of a shallow grave that had quickly filled with water.

The drums fell silent.

O'Callaghan looked down sadly into the watery hole.

'So long, Mick!' a voice shouted from the rear.

'Silence in the ranks,' growled Sergeant Hoffman viciously as he shot the men a sharp look.

Ryan approached the man. 'Do you have anything to say?'

'No, sir,' O'Callaghan said. 'Nothin'.' He stood and looked

down grimly at his grave. 'For I'll sleep well here tonight,' he added, ashen-faced.

Ryan muttered to himself that he'd warned them that the French shot deserters. *Hopefully,* he thought, *the other men will now learn.*

The Provost tied a blindfold around O'Callaghan's head, took his position at the top of the parade, and turned around to survey the execution. The parade was silent. The silence was shattered when a flock of starlings suddenly took flight. The firing squad stood with firelocks cocked at five paces, ready to discharge them into the man's back. The Provost Marshall silently raised his hand, the volley cracked loudly, and O'Callaghan slumped face down dead into the watery morass.

'Eyes right!' ordered Sergeant Hoffman as the entire company were ordered to file past the corpse.

They moved on. The weather continued to deteriorate. Days passed. Ryan heard reports of at least a dozen men who'd committed suicide rather than go on. He, too, was weary of the march, and of the war. He had once loaded his cavalry pistol, pulled the hammer back, and pointed it to his temple, but thoughts of catching up with Darkford made him reconsider and he had put the pistol down. He took out his whistle and played again the strains of *O'Sullivan's March* to cheer himself and the others up.

The break in the weather was a welcome change as it was cumbersome marching with a heavy kit, and his boots and greatcoat were soaked through. Ryan squinted his eyes, peered over the horizon, and breathed a heavy sigh of relief when he sighted the buttresses of the majestic Gothic masterpiece of Santa Maria cathedral towering above León. He could now finally get out of this awful march, put the shooting of O'Callaghan behind him and get out of the rain, which he thought had entered his bones and begun to eat into his soul.

Two hours passed and the convoy marched through León's gates and made camp for the night.

'Where are we heading to next, Captain?' Voltigeur Ferguson asked.

'We'll camp here and then continue pursuing Cuesta's army—hopefully he'll come out and fight.'

Ryan scooped up a mug of hot coffee from the cauldron. 'It's stopped raining at least,' Fergusson declared happily, as he could now finally remove his greatcoat.

'Just downright bloody uncomfortable,' grumbled Ryan angrily as he adjusted his pack, took off his boots, and massaged his feet with his good arm. He examined the wound in other arm; the wound had healed well but there was stiffness in the elbow, it still ached and he couldn't bend it fully.

'Some of the other lads say that the Spanish lack a fighting spirit,' said Ferguson, as he played with his pet mouse, feeding it with some crumbs before it scuttled up and down his sleeve and dived into his pocket.

'Don't underestimate the Spanish now, Jock,' answered Ryan as he bent down to tip a stone out of his boot. 'Although they're poorly armed and led, they remain a force to be feared. Don't forget that the Spanish defeated a 20,000 strong French flying column at Bailén in the south of the country. We have orders to destroy Blake's Army of Galicia. This is the strongest Spanish army in the north, and that's where we're heading, but don't you fret, Ferguson. When Blake's defeated, we'll control northern Spain. Blake is one of our famed 'Wild Geese', for his father hailed from County Galway.' Ryan thought for a moment. 'You ever seen action, lad?'

Ferguson shook his head. 'No, sir.'

'In the heat of combat your heart races and everything appears in slow motion,' Ryan explained. 'There's no time to be scared. All your senses are heightened and you feel really alive! You can't think and have to fall back on your training. Charging the enemy is one of the few times in life when a man finds how much courage he has and in what quantities. Now heed my advice, son. When we get into a scrap with the Spanish, as we surely will, don't throw your life away for a blaze of glory. I've seen too many brave men lost in that way.'

Ryan sat in his billet and pulled the candle closer as he recorded in his diary. *Following a week of marching, the advance guard of VIII Corps pulled into León. We covered a gruelling thirty miles march per day with no rest days in between.*

CHAPTER 12

The French advance guard pulled out of León shortly after dawn. They marched south for several hours as their spies had confirmed that the Spanish army were forming for battle close to the town of Valladolid. The French soon caught up with the Spanish. Ryan took out his lens and saw that the Spanish Army had taken up position to make battle at a village called Medina de Rioseco. He took out a pencil and drew a field sketch and scribbled down the enemy's strength as he grabbed a horse to report back to Bessière's VIII Corps in the rear.

In less than an hour, Ryan reined his horse to a walk and made his way through the staff officers. They presented a vivid picture, all dressed in their heavy gold braid and plumes, and, seated on beautiful Arab mares. He curved his horse towards Marshal Bessières and dismounted. 'General Joaquin Blake's Army of Galicia have joined forces with General Gregorio Cuesta. Our advance guard have counted twenty to twenty-two thousand men, regulars and militia, six-hundred cavalry and twenty guns. They have split their forces, *Monsieur le Maréchal!*'

The general nodded thoughtfully. 'Well done, Captain Ryan, stand at ease,' he said as an ADC handed him a map. Ryan pointed to where the Spanish grouped their forces. The general's finger hovered over the map spread out over a table, as Ryan showed him where the enemy had taken up position.

Two hours later, VIII Corps reached Medina de Rioseco. From a vantage point above the village, Marshal Bessières trained his spyglass against an aide's shoulder and surveyed the Spanish army below.

'Yes, the Spanish have indeed split their forces, Ryan!' This must be a *ruse de guerre* or perhaps the Spaniards have simply gone mad or are stupid—or both!'

The staff officers laughed.

The French general snapped the brass tube shut and thought deeply for a moment. 'It doesn't make sense that the Spanish have left such a gap between their armies.' He turned to his aides. 'I intend to march our glorious columns through their centre like a massive battering ram and destroy them!'

'Major-General!'

Moulon snapped to attention. 'Sir!'

'I want you to send in fifteen battalions as a screening force to pin down Cuesta in the rear, while you, Merle, will take on General Blake and sweep him from the ridge.'

A flurry of nervous activity followed as aides-de-camp went scurrying down to relay the orders to the various battalion commanders.

Soon afterwards, Ryan and his voltigeurs stood and waited as *cantinières* furtively doled out tots of brandy to the nervous troops. Ryan heard the officers and NCOs shouting, warning them to stand firm in the face of the enemy's volleys as those who didn't would be shot. He guessed that it took a half-hour for the fifteen tightly packed French assault columns to form up; each column of 700 men measured forty ranks wide and 18 deep.

The cannons began to strike up its moaning plaintive

sound as the French Imperial Horse Artillery opened up with a score of heavy 12-pounders, blasting scathing holes in the Spanish ranks. The sound was not unlike thunderclaps. It seemed to Ryan that the very earth itself, braced itself as it prepared to be shattered by the ferocious barrage. He followed the trajectory of the artillery with his telescope. After every blast, the Spanish troops fearfully studied the sky like Coleridge's Ancient Mariner for the black dots hurling through the air. By a strange optical illusion, it appeared that each one was heading directly for them. He had felt the same when under artillery fire and he'd instinctively ducked to avoid the blow. He understood their fear but he felt no pity or compassion.

Ryan closed his telescope and waited as the columns of French infantry prepared to move in. He took out his amulet and rubbed it.

Finally, the order came.'*Bat-t-a-lion! En avant!*'

This order was repeated down the lines, while drummers beat the electrifying *rum-dum-rum-dum-rummadum-dum* of the *pas de charge*. Thousands of voices waited and paused between the drum rolls to unleash their war cry; '*Vive l'Empereur!*'

The earth reverberated under Ryan's boots. Marching at the required 120 paces per minute the ferocious columns soon raised up one of their favourite tunes, *La Marche Consulaire*, commemorating Napoleon's victory at Marengo.

Commander Lawless led the Irish battalion, as hundreds of nimble voltigeurs, including Ryan's voltigeurs were unleashed from the ranks to form skirmish screens in front of the advancing columns.

'Take off those bloody plumes,' Ryan instructed.

McGowan turned to a younger greenhorn as he folded his long plume into the lining of his shako. 'Thank God for that!

Bloody feathers only mark us out as elite troops and give away our position.'

The French pushed forward with two battalions of around one thousand men on Blake's left, as another French force attacked Cuesta a mile further away preventing him from coming to Blake's relief.

'Aim low!' shouted Ryan, 'make every shot count! Keep moving forward! And no skulking!' He ducked and took cover behind a rock as a shot whirled past. The Spanish artillery stopped firing round shot. He suspected that their gunners were lowering the trajectories of their guns and loading up with canister shot. This was more effective at close range. Canister splayed a wide area and was deadly as it was made from chugs of iron and musket balls fired from a tin can. He could differentiate between the sounds and waited for the guns to fire. The cannon made a low heavy thud as it fired and sprayed the area with flying pieces of metal like a giant shotgun. Ryan turned as a sliver of metal sliced into a man's stomach. The voltigeur frantically tried to push his intestines back into the wound cavity, but the slimy mass fell through his fingers as he collapsed.

Another 12-pound cannon ball furrowed gaps in the tightly packed Spanish column and knocked out a file of eight men as it bounded along the ground. Some balls plonked deep into the ground with their long fuses still hissing, but failed to explode.

The familiar dins of *'Vive l'Empereur!'* were carried in the wind through the musket fire and the percussive pounding of artillery charges, accompanied by officers and NCOs shouting orders. The guttural screams of anger and men moaning in agony, were both electrifying and horrific.

Ryan guessed that the attack column were now around one-hundred paces from the ridge but the Spanish had the advantage as they easily directed fire down on the attackers. He pushed himself forwards. He could clearly hear the loud rattle of the French drums below and the mighty columns behind him.

The voltigeurs were deployed in front and this was the real danger faced by skirmishing troops. Ryan knew that they easily got caught on the open ground, the deadly no man's land between their own troops and the enemy. The column's leading battalion were drawn up in line and when they came into enemy musket range the entire section unleashed their thunderous volleys, prompting Ryan and the other voltigeurs to drop for cover.

Ryan's ears rang. He cleared his throat. 'Fall back!' he shouted hoarsely. Alarmed, the bugler, seeing the seriousness of the situation, flatly sounded the signal to retire. Ryan could hardly hear himself through the din.

Ryan just made it beyond the line of fire before the order for the second volley sounded.

The French columns were slowly making ground but they were taking heavy casualties. A battery of canon flashed orange in smoke. He thought the bright, intermittent yellow and orange musket flashes of the smoothbore Charlevilles were beautiful. The thick smoke lingered and limited visibility. A shot ploughed into the first French column, bounced along the ground and cut through a score of grenadiers. Officers serving as 'gap closers' bellowed the order to close ranks. They stepped over the fallen, some lost their footing on the bloodied sludge. They closed up and marched on as drummers continued to beat the charge. Soil rained down on them and plumes of thick white sulphuric smoke filled the battlefield so thickly that Ryan could hardly distinguish the French from Spanish troops.

Ryan looked down at his feet. A drummer boy was

writhing on the ground in the throes of a violent epileptic seizure. Ryan stepped over him when he saw the Irish Legion's *cantinière*. He made his way towards her, quickly drowned a dram, and patted her on the shoulder. 'Thank you, Marie.' He felt the alcohol pleasantly burn his lips and throat.

La Belle Marie turned to a teenage fusilier frozen in terror. 'Quickly,' she motioned. *'Bon Courage!* Here's your dram, but you'll have to drink from your hands for the blast of the cannon shattered all of my glasses.' La Belle Marie opened the brass tap of her elaborately painted brandy barrel. The grateful soldier cupped his hands tightly and heartily supped up the brandy. *'Courage!* she repeated before making her way towards a badly wounded grenadier.

The scene was one of murder and carnage. The French infantry retired in disorder in the face of a ferocious Spanish artillery barrage.

'Sauve qui peut!' a voice screamed out nervously, *'Sauve qui peut!'*—'Save yourselves!'

They tried to hide their fear but the French officers' faces flushed with worry. Their voices now sounded painfully hoarse. The French cavalry reserves would soon save the day, Ryan hoped, as he could just about make out several squadrons of green-coated chasseurs preparing to charge. They trotted, and then cantered as they picked up speed. The horses' heads were down, and their ears were pulled back like greyhounds as they furiously bit at their reins, their hooves thumping the earth, kicking up turf behind. As they entered range, several volleys of canister cut through them but they raced through the exposed flat ground between the two Spanish armies before bounding into the Spanish right.

As the main Spanish fire was now directed towards the French cavalry attack, Ryan saw his opportunity to capture the Spanish guns. 'Come on Napoleon's blaggards! Follow me,' he bawled. 'We're going to boot these bastards off this ridge!'

Ryan's men rallied forward. As the voltigeurs climbed in pairs, Ryan grimaced when he witnessed John Doyle being shot in the throat. Ryan recalled that Doyle had served with the Royal Navy's Irish Watch squadron based in Cork. Doyle dropped his musket, grasped his neck with both hands in a panic, and gurgled loudly on the ground as he spat up blood.

'Poor bastard!' muttered Ryan.

Another soldier yelled in agony as his lower leg was smashed with canister, his face showing more fear than suffering as he crawled, mortally wounded, towards a bush for shelter, just as badly wounded animals or birds do before they die.

Ryan tried to warn the others but his voice was nearly gone from shouting.

He passed a voltigeur hit by an 8-pounder in the neck, which had removed his head and part of his back and shoulders. The headless torso, still on its feet, whirled around in circles and fell into itself. He suspected it may have been Kelly, the former sailor who'd joined his company, but he wasn't sure. He stepped over a youth who lay mangled between the rocks. The lad's head had turned to face his back. His abdomen was torn open and his intestines had spilled out, while his legs lay crumpled up under his torso, back to front. Ryan saw that he still held his brass bugle in his hand. He felt like vomiting but there wasn't time. He turned to check on the other voltigeurs in his company. 'Keep moving forwards!' he shouted hoarsely.

Trumpets sounded over the din and there was chaos coming from the French attack on the other side of the ridge. Ryan could barely make out the sound of the chasseurs' bugles amid officers shouting orders and the mad noises, screams and terrified yells men make when staring death in the face. Ryan knew these blood-curdling sounds, for he'd heard them before. Many times before. His legs were shaking and he needed to push himself on. He kissed his amulet again. The natural fight or flight instincts kicked in. His body pumped with adrenaline. He stood mystified and marvelled at the strange atmospheric energy descending over the battlefield like an invisible fog.

Ryan's voltigeurs continued their staggered climb and had now nearly reached the line of Spanish guns. Through the thick blooms of smoke, Ryan saw McGowan appear from a long tuft of grass. A low heavy thud of canister came overhead, and he saw him fall. Ryan's heart sank as he looked on in shock, but he was relieved as McGowan raised the thumbs up sign. Ryan waved his arm gesturing to him to come over before he dived towards him while nearly under the Spanish cannon.

'Jesus Christ, McGowan!' exclaimed Ryan as a wide smile spread across his face. 'I thought you were a goner!'

'No fear of that—I just lost me footing and slipped, sir.'

Another voltigeur emerged like a ghost through the apocalyptic smoke, and then another, until a half-dozen of Ryan's men had appeared through the hell. Ryan squatted down, still panting from the climb. His men's faces were splattered with mud and gunpowder.

'Has anybody seen Kaminski?'

'I haven't seen him, sir,' replied McGowan raggedly as he opened the top buttons of his tunic and took a swig of water from his canteen. 'Sergeant Hoffman was beside me, but he couldn't keep up.'

Vandam, panting, reached over for McGowan's canteen. 'Kami was with me closer to the column but I saw him fall and then lost him in the smoke, sir.'

Ryan pointed to the battery. 'We're going to storm these guns howling like banshees. The Spanish won't know what hit them. Now fix bayonets.'

'Ready?' Now listen carefully as my voice is going.' Ryan waited until they reloaded their Charlevilles and counted down.

'5-4-3-2-1—*Charge!*'

As expected, the Spanish artillerymen were caught by surprise. The half-dozen Spanish infantrymen protecting the guns and the artillerymen were either shot or bayoneted, and within seconds lay dead, slumped against the wheels of the artillery carriages. The rest surrendered, perhaps sensing that the handful of Ryan's voltigeurs were the advance troops of the by now exhausted French columns who were still half way down the mountain.

They threw their muskets away and went down on their knees, pleading for mercy, crying out pitifully, *'¡Viva el gran Napoleón!'* – 'Long live the great Napoleon!'

'Kill the bastards!' shouted Ryan. He was overcome by anger. No mercy was shown and all were slain, save for two boys. The lads were no more than ten or twelve years old. Their arms were raised, tears had wiped the black smoke off their faces and left them streaked. Vandam laughed madly as he cut their throats. Ryan cursed him, but it had happened too fast—he couldn't save them in time.

They lamed the horses and cut their harnesses and traces before spiking the guns by driving nails into the vent holes with the butts of their muskets to render them useless. Ryan hated laming the horses, but he especially hated witnessing the two young boys being killed. They were only children. He needed to get word to the others and he had to act fast, with the right-flank of the ridge silenced. He removed his green tunic, draped it over his musket and waved it as a signal, relaying the message that the ridge was secured.

Below, he heard the guttural shouts of *'Chargez!'* as the French infantry broke ranks and burst out towards the terrified Spanish infantry, who turned tail and ran. He knew that the French would still have to fight hard for the ridge. A Spanish battalion bravely repelled successive waves of French attacks. It seemed that, despite suffering horrifying losses, the battalion still managed to cover the retreat of Blake's fleeing army.

He watched horror-struck as Cuesta's army in the rear now broke through the French force, and, screened by the thick white smoke, crashed through the French battalions. Several squadrons of blue-coated Spanish cavalry with a detachment of infantry charged up the ridge on the right flank where the Irish battalion had only caught its breath. They were caught off guard.

Ryan watched nervously from the ridge as the Irish battalion began to form square, to protect themselves from cavalry. He knew that they were safe enough in this battle formation, and he smiled when he remembered that an old soldier once put it to him that infantry in square were as safe from cavalry as being snugly tucked up in bed.

It took over two minutes for the Irish to go through the different manoeuvres cohesively to form square. There wasn't enough time and they were too late. He peered through his telescope and saw a squadron of Spanish cavalry cut into the Irish position, and although the Irish managed to lodge their bayonets into a number of the Spanish horses — they were overwhelmed. He could hardly bare to watch through his telescope as the Irish wavered in the onslaught but their officers and NCOs thumped them hard on their backs and shouted at them to remain firm.

Buoyed by the success of their cavalry, the Spanish infantry followed through with a bayonet charge through the Irish ranks. Although weakened, the Irish fell back in good order and rallied around their Eagle.

Ryan peered through the telescope and cursed as he witnessed *Port-Aigle* Murphy hit by a musket ball, dropping to the ground. Sergeant Hoffman, *What is he doing there?* Ryan asked himself, for Hoffman should have stayed with his voltigeurs. He looked on with a worried frown as the big sergeant grabbed the Eagle's staff mid-air and parried several sword thrusts. Hoffman was yelling something, as he and four Irishmen frantically held off the Spanish attacks. With their weapons broken they went on fighting with fists.

The surrounded Irish battalion waved their Eagle up high, signalling that they stood fast but needed help. The Spanish, of course, wanted the Eagle, for it represented the regiment's soul. Its capture brought dishonour and that's why it was a prized battlefield trophy.

Ryan pelted down to French headquarters and reported what was happening to Marshal Bessières. He hurriedly handed the general his telescope. '*Mon Dieu!* I see the Irish appear to be in trouble. Can anyone get word to them? For they'll lose their Eagle and we're running out of time!'

Marshal Bessières turned towards one of his aide de camps. 'I want you to relay the order to the Irish that they are to form square and withdraw in that battle formation, backwards, towards the French position.'

Ryan wanted to volunteer himself instead but he momentarily lost his nerve and couldn't get the words out in time. It was a suicidal mission as swarms of Spanish cavalry stood in their path. The ADC's face was grim as he saluted sharply and swung up onto his horse, galloping towards the hill through the enemy horsemen. The French general followed his progress through the five-hundred yard dash before he lost sight of him. 'I can't see the fellow,' he tutted as his spyglass swept the ground. 'Send in another! Send in another!' he spat as an ADC gulped when he, too, was handed the order.

Ryan found his nerve. 'I can go, *Monsieur le Maréchal!*' he pleaded finally, but the general dismissed him. The aide mounted his horse and digging spurs into his horse, disappeared through the smoke as the general tried to follow his progress with his telescope.

'Go on, young fellow—'said the general excitedly, wishing him on. 'I think he's going to make it...'

The general watched intensely as the ADC warded off a sabre blow from an enemy horseman before two Spanish grenadiers grasped the reins of his black charger, pulled him out of his saddle and hacked him to pieces in a series of downward sabre thrusts.

'*Merde! Merde!*' cursed the French general, plunging his face into his hands not bearing to look. He turned around. 'Take a note of that man's name as I'm recommending him for the *Légion d'honneur.*'

He clenched his mouth shut. '*Putain!*'

Ryan again implored the French general to let him go instead.

'Very well, Captain, God's speed!'

A horse was brought forward, and Ryan observed that its fore and hind legs wore a white stocking. He frowned, as he took this to be a bad omen. He took out his amulet and rubbed it hard. He adjusted the stirrups, removed his tunic and shako, kept his sword firmly in his scabbard, and resolved to race at lightning speed through the enemy position. He dug spurs sharply into the sides of his seasoned battle-charger, grabbed the reins tightly, and sped off with his head down like a jockey. He leapt over the bodies of men with great panache as the Spanish horsemen looked on with bewilderment as Ryan thundered through. He'd nearly reached the Irish battalion, when a drunken Spanish grenadier in a tall mitre hat lunged at him with a bayonet but missed and instead slashed through his horse's shoulder. The horse lunged forward and bit most of the grenadier's cheek and lips off. Ryan's horse then charged through three lines of Spanish infantry before he reached the Irish square.

Hoffman couldn't believe his eyes as the lone horseman galloped up, '*Mein Gott!* It's Captain Ryan! Open the square!' he shouted as a gap permitted Ryan entry.

The Irish appeared exhausted—some sat and supped water as the saltpetre from biting open the cartridges not only blackened and cut their lips but also gave them a terrible thirst. They could hardly breathe through the suffocating, deadly concoction of shells and burnt cartridges. They had just repelled yet another cavalry attack. There was now a welcome lull as the enemy regrouped.

'Commander Lawless!' Ryan panted as he dismounted. 'I've received an order from Marshal Bessières to march in square and make it down the hill to the safety of the French position.'

'It's not possible!' protested Lawless bluntly while he sat on a drum packing his heavily bloodied shoulder with a bandage. 'The enemy are too strong and are preparing for another attack. I'm afraid they'll over-run us,' he added grimly. 'But we'll have to try.'

Ryan saw they were in trouble.

Several minutes later the huddled mass of Spanish cavalry came blazing down towards them. Ryan's body trembled—he was scared but he tried not to show it. He blessed himself. He composed himself in front of the men. They turned their heads towards him for leadership. 'Stand firm!' he ordered as he snatched a musket.

The enemy horses' harnesses were jangling; their long mains were flowing, nostrils flaring, heads low, hooves causing the ground to tremble as they bore down. Four horsemen headed the charge and emerged, Ryan thought, like ghosts through the smoke, like the fabled horsemen of the Apocalypse. A mounted Spanish *carabinier* slashed down forcibly on an infantryman. His sabre sliced the man's head off above the eyes. The *carabinier* was, in turn, bayoneted in the thigh and he wheeled away in agony.

Hoffman still held the eight-foot Eagle oak pole displaying the battalion's green flag and bronze Eagle on top. The flag had been peppered with shot and was full of holes like a sieve. It was stained red with blood, although one could still clearly make out the harp motif.

Ryan's face blanched. 'Sweet God Almighty!' he muttered nervously. 'Come on, comrades!' he rasped while Hoffman waved the flag high to rally the men.

Lawless then stood up in great pain and shouted, *'Remember Fontenoy!'*

The men found fresh courage, reformed from square into line despite the pounding shells and charged the Spanish infantry. This only provided a temporary reprieve. Ryan saw the Spanish cavalry were regrouping to charge again. The Irish frantically changed formation back into square to receive cavalry.

The Spanish charge came but a steady musket volley pushed them back. Hoffman desperately tried to remove the pins holding the bronze Eagle to its pole, to hide it under his tunic and prevent its capture but there wasn't time as he parried yet another blow with the Eagle's staff.

NAPOLEON'S BLACKGUARDS

The Irish had nearly reached their limits and their strength was lost. The Spanish cavalry charged yet again. Two *carabiniers* hacked their way through, entered the Irish square, and were within arm's reach of snatching the Eagle's staff when Hoffman lashed out and hacked the leading *carabinier's* horse's hind legs. The roan gelding toppled forward in agony and fell with a heavy thud, skidding on top of Hoffman. By this time sharpshooters from Ryan's *voltigeurs* had come running up towards them, but it was too late. A *carabinier* snatched the Irish Eagle, dug in his spurs and rode away just as the Spanish sounded the retreat. The French pursued them for a number of leagues before they were ordered to stand down. The guns fell silent.

'We've lost our Eagle!' men cried in tears, holding their heads in their hands, oblivious to their own wounds. Ryan couldn't believe what had happened and knew the news that the Irish battalion's Eagle had been taken as a prize would spread through the army like wildfire.

'How the devil did they make off with our Eagle?' asked Ryan, panting so heavily he thought his chest would burst.

'They came from nowhere,' replied McGowan. *'Hells' bells!'*

Ryan tried to hold the contents of his stomach in, but he couldn't and he bent over and vomited. He wiped his mouth with his sleeve and lay down flat on his back, sweat mixed with gunpowder from his musket trickled down his forehead. He rubbed his face but the powder irritated his eyes and burned. His mouth and throat were dry and he needed water. He got up and walked up to the dying Spanish horse. The Arab gelding was grunting heavily and bleeding profusely from its hindquarters, its eyes protruding widely through its white star markings. The horse tried to stand on its three legs but collapsed; Ryan jabbed it sharply with his sword, piercing the horses' heart and putting the beast out of its misery.

Ryan checked Hoffman's vitals for injuries—he was alive. 'I thought you were dead.'

Hoffman looked at Ryan through his steely blue eyes. 'Yes, I'm alive, but only just. Battles are for young men. I'm getting too old for this, Captain.'

Ryan grinned broadly, relieved Hoffman made it.

Hoffman's face lost colour as Commander Lawless approached.

'I have lost the Eagle—what'll our commander say?' Hoffman gulped as he looked on. 'What'll the Emperor say?'

'Don't you worry about that now—I intend to get it back,' replied Ryan.

'And I am coming with you, Ryan. It is my fault.'

Commander Lawless looked on, crestfallen, and added calmly. 'Take as many men as you want, Ryan, but just get her *back*!'

CHAPTER 13

As the bright orange sun set over the mountains, the work of clearing the field of the wounded and the dead began. Ryan paused and looked around, removed his shako and mopped the sweat from his brow. What a bloody mess. Hundreds of bodies and mangled dead horses, still harnessed to their ammunition caissons, lay strewn over the field. One horse, covered in blood and exposing the milky white stump of its femur bone, had had its hind legs blown off, and crouched, neighing pitifully. The wounded struggled for life or lay between the dead and groaned. The ground itself teemed with so many wounded, twitching men that it appeared to Ryan to be singularly crawling. They lay there and turned to avoid the hooves of loose, shocked horses. Others tried to attend to their own wounds themselves and stumbled to their feet only to fall, but by morning they would lie cold and silent beside their fallen comrades. Deader than Jack McDead.

Even now, the saltpetre and sulphur of the expended gunpowder wafted in the air of the battlefield. It was tinged with the coppery smell of fresh blood and excrement, as in the searing heat of battle men shitted themselves. The sickly, foul-smelling gases and musty odours would soon evaporate as bacteria broke down and putrefied the bodies. This was the distinctive rancid reek of death. It had a strange heavy presence and atmosphere all of its own, and once smelt was hard to forget.

This stole all of the honor and glory from the battlefield.

Ryan swore that the stench could only be sweated out since it entered the pores of the skin, and having entered fabric or leather never fully dissipated.

The scene before him was horrific. There was now nothing left of the pale green olive groves or the apple trees in the orchard. All of the trees were smashed, reduced to stumps, and riddled with shot. The ground around him was littered with arms, legs, heads, the slimy entrails of men, and beasts swimming in ponds of blood. These were mixed with the detritus of battle: broken muskets, sabres, letters from home, shreds of uniform, kettledrums, cannon balls, spent ammunition, helmets, broken spectacles, knapsacks, religious relics, amulets, keepsakes, false teeth, diaries and account books.

A gentle breeze lifted, blowing open a leather-bound copy of Voltaire's *The Age of Louis XIV*, the wind carried sheaves of smouldering writing paper over the gashed landscape, as if recording the carnage and devastation.

Smoke still clung to the battlefield and dozens of fires, lit by the burning musket cartridge papers, were strewn on the dry grass. Those fires would soon reach the hundreds of wounded men who lay in the field and they'd burn alive. It was getting dark. There was a lot to do. The lost Eagle would have to wait, for the men were tired and hungry. The wounded needed to be treated, the dead buried, and lists of the missing compiled.

The sun finally dipped over the horizon as if saluting the fallen. The silhouettes of a wake of bald-headed vultures appeared on a precipice, their heads tucked in tightly, protecting them from the cold as they gaped salaciously down at the battlefield. As he shielded his eyes with his hand

and gazed up at the enormous birds, Ryan, confused, thought at first that it was Cuesta's men lined up for another attack. The birds stood perched, with their sooty black plumage drawn up like cloaks; they had grown fat in the war devouring many thousands of dead men across the Peninsula. Ryan spat hard on the ground. After having acquired a taste for human meat, they bided their time to strike down and gorge their beaked heads into man's mangled flesh. Ryan once saw a wake of them devour a man. They made a raspy, drawn-out slurp—the same noise hungry pigs made. In minutes, the carcass resembled a sucked chicken leg bleaching in the sun. He hated them because they didn't hunt but scavenged carrion.

A full moon appeared but a blanket of cloud smothered its light. It appeared to Ryan that it was trying to hide the brutality of man's inhumanity to his fellow man from the eyes of God. Ryan straightened his shako and walked briskly through the battlefield. It started to rain. The soil turned to mud as glistening red streams ran from the piles of dead. The field appeared to be flooded with blood. Ryan felt the adrenaline flush from his body, and he felt a tremendous sudden exhaustion. This was the void following combat. He rubbed his amulet for comfort.

'When the wounded are brought back I want the dead either burned or buried, I don't want those bastard vermin feeding on my soldiery,' Ryan told his men and pointed to the vultures overhead.

There must have been 400 bodies and it would take the 500-man battalion hours to inter them all

The men set to work grimly to clear the field of the dead. They doused vinegar on cotton, and wrapped it around their mouths to ward off disease, and fortified with free tots of brandy from the *cantinières* gathered up the bodies. Some of the wounded who were covered in blood and in desperate pain, groaned for water, others whimpered for their mothers or crawled on their elbows as far as the campfires to seek help in one of the dressing stations.

A field ambulance battalion fanned out with their litters and loaded some of the wounded men onto spring-load covered wagons to ferry them for treatment. Ryan knew that speed was of the essence, as the wounded stood a great chance of surviving if treated quickly.

It was now the *ambulanciers'* time to line their pockets with ill-gotten rewards. Ryan walked through the battlefield and watched the ambulance crews strip the dead of their blood soaked uniforms and even their soiled underwear. 'Greedy bastards,' muttered Ryan. He knew they were going to wash and sell these things to the other soldiers. Boots were the most valuable item. There was no shortage of eager buyers, as with the constant forced marches and counter-marches, the army wore out its leather, and a half decent pair of boots commanded a king's ransom.

The ambulance battalion was full of thieves whose sole motivation was not to tend the wounded—but to plunder, for they also culled teeth from the dead—and from the dying. He walked closer to an *ambulancier* bent over a body. The *ambulancier* unpinned the chasseur's hard-won *Légion d'honneur* medal from his breast and pocketed it. He prised open the dead man's mouth. The teeth made a sharp cracking sound as each tooth was yanked from the chasseur's mouth. 'There you go, *mon ami,'* he said as he closed the dead man's mouth and patted him on the head, placing the bloodied teeth into a cotton sack, the size of an orange. Molars and incisors clattered loudly in the goody bag, like marbles, as the *ambulancier* moved on to strip the teeth from his next victim.

Ryan had read that real teeth were made into dentures and commanded huge prices in Paris. The *ambulanciers* grew wealthy, and this lucrative trade had become one of the chief perks of the job.

Great pyres, lit from stocks of broken muskets and wagons, were to burn the bodies. The fires would burn for days, fed solely by human fat, like a vast charnel house. The smell was a strange, sickly, musky perfume like roast beef, which made the men hungry, although it was tinged with an odd metallic, coppery smell as blood-filled organs, exploded and burned.

Ryan heard a groan as another naked body was to be thrown into the fire. 'This one's alive!' someone said.

'Bloody hell, it's Kaminski!' another voice shouted. 'I have Kaminski and he's alive!'

'Help me pull him out!' Ryan yanked the man free of the flames. 'Give him some water, lads. You're a lucky man, Kami,' said Ryan, as he routed into the mountain of clothes taken from the dead, pushing back a protesting *ambulancier* until he found a green tunic and blood-stained breeches. 'These'll do. Now get him dressed. I'm bringing you to the surgeon myself.'

Ryan was somewhat relieved to see something good come from all the devastation.

He swung Kami's arm over his shoulder and they hobbled down the road towards the dressing station. He passed dozens of dazed and shocked soldiers, some heavily wounded, as they limped, hobbled and dragged themselves forwards to seek medical attention. A fleet of *ambulancier's* carts, filled with a mangled mess of wounded men, trundled past.

On the road the marching columns had passed down

earlier lay scattered books, playing cards and the like. Before the battle, many of the soldiers had lightened their backpacks and had tossed these items aside. The more superstitious had thrown decks of playing cards over their heads without looking back. They believed these items attracted bullets. Ryan had seen other men on their knees, praying before the battle; some had kissed a talisman such as a wedding ring, pairs of dice, a loved one's lock of hair, or a plug of tobacco. He knew of others who swallowed bullets. They believed that this would protect them from being shot as they already had a bullet in them. Superstition knew no bounds. Men grasped at anything when faced with impending death.

In front of a cow pyre, now serving as a dressing station, scores of wounded men lay under a grove of chestnut trees awaiting medical attention. They groaned and cried out for water as Ryan passed; those with stomach wounds moaned the most because these wounds were the most painful. A fusilier lay with the top of his head blown off; part of his frontal lobe trickled down his face and dried in the sun, giving his face a glazed and coppery hue. He would not survive long, Ryan thought.

'You're not too badly injured, Kami,' Ryan consoled the soldier softly as he carried him into the dressing station, 'only a small head wound and a ball in the upper shoulder— You'll be alright—and besides the head wound, I think your nose is broken.'

'The Eagle!' Kami rasped weakly, 'did they take our Eagle?'

'Yes, they did! The bastards! But I'm getting it back.'

CHAPTER 14

Ryan placed Kami down on the ground of the dressing station. The dull moans of the wounded reverberated throughout. The stench of sweat, excrement and the metallic tang of blood combined with the pungent tinge of vomit was terrible. The smell of death brought Ryan back to his childhood when his father had cut a pig's throat; the blood had cascaded like an open tap as it ran along the stone-flagged floor. It had been his first smell of death. He'd smelt it many times since, hated it, and doubtless would smell it again. He glanced around and quickly recognised the bald patch on the back of Surgeon-Major O'Reilly's head as he crouched over a patient. O'Reilly wouldn't sleep tonight as orderlies hurriedly carried in more wounded to join the hundreds of men already littering the blood-drenched straw floor.

'You'll earn your salary tonight,' said Ryan. O'Reilly threw him a stern look. 'Indeed I will, James. I've already performed well over twenty amputations, in between triaging patients and supervising the orderlies.' He turned his head. 'Hold that candle closer, blast you! I can't see what I'm doing!' he snarled to a blood-soaked orderly.

O'Reilly looked under tremendous strain for the role of surgeon major in a field battalion came with great responsibility. Ryan had fought with O'Reilly in the Irish Rebellion. The doctor had left his wife and children and escaped to France, and later brought his son over and procured a commission for him in the battalion's fusilier company. Amputations were tough work and were a far cry from the tapping of blood and treating patients from smallpox, typhoid or malnutrition at his former practise in Enniscorthy in County Wexford. This was butcher's work.

'Can you take a look at Kaminski?'

O'Reilly glanced down at the wounded voltigeur, pulled back his tunic, and saw the ball in his shoulder. He shook his head. 'Not just now as I have more urgent cases! But hang in there,' he consoled.

O'Reilly was drenched in sweat. His heavily stained butcher's apron was stiff with blood as he examined a grenadier who had a musket ball lodged below the knee. He placed his index finger in the hole, felt the lead ball, and retrieved it with a pair of nose pliers. He felt around in the wound. 'I'm sorry but you'll have to lose the leg as the knee joint has been shattered.' Two medical orderlies held the man down as best they could, for grenadiers were the strongest men in the army. O'Reilly took hold of his curved knife and cut in two sweeps around the grenadier's skin just above the knee. He pulled the flesh back, cut and divided the muscles and rolled them back, exposing the shiny white fibula bone. Being handed his saw by an orderly, he began to saw. The man struggled.

'Ryan, give me a hand!' O'Reilly bawled as he dexterously pulled and pushed the blade back and forth. 'He's a strong bastard.'

Ryan pressed hard on the man's leg, using the full weight of his body to prevent him from moving. The man's face was cold and clammy and his breathing shallow as he went into shock. The surgeon was nearly finished sawing and cursed as the blade caught in the bone. The orderly lowered the leg, enabling it to be freed, and the booted limb finally fell to the ground with a dull thud.

'Amputations are seen as a quick and easy cure, as there's otherwise little chance of saving an injured limb, but time is of the essence. Many believe that when the saw cuts through the bone marrow is the most painful,' O'Reilly explained. 'However, the most painful is when we first cut through the skin and sew up the arteries.'

'Now it's in the hands of God. If fever follows or gangrene sets in, he's a goner.' O'Reilly mopped his brow with his arm, then tied the arteries with a linen ligature using a tenaculum. Momentarily loosening the tourniquet, he checked for bleeding. Satisfied, he nodded to the orderlies as they pulled the soft tissue flap back over the wound face to sew it up. He placed a pad into it, followed by a cross dressing. He had just finished when a flickering candle guttered in its iron plate next to him and a thin trail of smoke appeared.

'You'll have six or eight weeks of severe pain if you are lucky to survive, Citizen,' he told the wounded man, patting his shoulder, 'and then a generous pension and perhaps a place to end your days in *Les Invalides!*'

A frightened bugler approached, cradling his intestines in his hands and inner arms. 'Please help me!' he pleaded. An orderly told him to wait his turn, but O'Reilly intervened.

'It's alright! I'll take a look at him as it won't take long.' He looked down at the intestines and saw they were dry and sticky. He turned to the orderly. 'Fetch me some milk!'

The bugler remained standing, cupping the slimy mass, as O'Reilly poured a pitcher of milk over them.

'We need to keep them moist, lad. Now lie down.' He examined the stomach wound caused by a round shot and fed the intestines with his fingers back into the cavity. An orderly then stitched the wound.

'All done,' O'Reilly said as he wiped his hands on his bloodied apron. 'Just keep off your feet for a couple of days.'

O'Reilly concentrated hard at the task in hand as another man, wounded in the upper arm was lifted onto the table. He cursed as he nearly slipped on a puddle of blood, brains and other gore on the floor. O'Reilly cut the skin and folded back the muscles as he began. His face flushed red. His arms were getting tired and a bead of sweat trailed from his forehead and travelled down the arch of his nose, straight into the patient's wound cavity. The pain was so bad that the wounded man would have preferred to succumb than to suffer it any longer, but he was a brave man, a *very* brave man, and he made no sound as his severed arm fell and was tossed in the corner where a mountain of body parts lay piling up.

Rats scrabbled across the floor and squeaked loudly. Two rats fought a tug of war over a mangled foot, and others dragged body parts away. The surgeon cursed loudly as he kicked one of them aside and wiped his bloodied hands on his apron, throwing a pained glance to Kami. 'Now, then, place this man on the table!' he told an orderly. 'Once that musket ball is out you'll be as right as rain.' The surgeon removed the musket ball from Kaminski's shoulder in seconds. Kaminski groaned, his wound was bandaged and he was placed onto a bed of damp straw.

O'Reilly turned towards an orderly. 'Tighten that bloody tourniquet properly, the man is bleeding to death!' he bawled angrily. The orderly gritted his teeth and turned the leather strap with all his might until the bleeding stopped. The blood-splattered orderly exhaled a gasp of relief. He screwed his eyes up and looked to the surgeon for approval but there was none forthcoming.

A captain of hussars walked in, holding a rag to his face.

O'Reilly asked him to remove the blood-sodden bandage, which he did, revealing a gaping hole where his nose had once been.

'Nothing more to be done, just keep holding the pressure to it, Citizen,' advised O'Reilly compassionately.

An orderly tried to retrieve a musket ball from a young chasseur's shoulder by gouging through the mass of meat using a bayonet, the soldier passed out from the shock.

O'Reilly cursed as yet another artery was carelessly punctured. He rushed over to try and stop the bleeding which was cascading, bright red, from the unfortunate man's leg while he continued to abuse them. He was unable to stop the arterial bleeding. The man bled out. In frustration O'Reilly flung one of the carpenter's saws against a wall and it twanged loudly on impact.

The surgeon wiped his bloodied hands on his apron and momentarily smothered his face in exasperation. 'For the love of God, James,' he continued as he pointed to the orderlies, 'these bloody fools are no good to me at all.'

Ryan saw through the poor shimmering candlelight that several orderlies were inexpertly cutting through arms and legs using rusty old knives and coarse badly tempered carpenters' saws. A corporal with a musket wound above the knee let out a stifled scream and cursed incessantly through gritted teeth as a blunt saw was used to cut through his leg.

'The damned guerrillas have disrupted supply lines resulting in few medical supplies arriving from France. I can't do my job properly without finely tempered and tooled medical knives and drill saws for amputation. Those with head wounds will die if I can't get hold of trephine saws for removing the bones of the skull. The damn things were on their way but were taken by the guerrillas,' O'Reilly said sadly. 'Along with everything else.'

A *sergeant des logis* lay mortally wounded in a corner, his quivering, bloodied fingers clutched a gaudy gilt crucifix tightly as he recited the Lord's Prayer. '*Notre Père qui êtes aux cieux...*'

O'Reilly turned to him. 'Do you believe in God?'

Ryan shook his head.

O'Reilly exhaled wearily. 'I did once, before I came here!'

The nightmare of the wounded continued amid the constant groans for water, the delirium of patients hallucinating with imaginary friends and long dead comrades, and the cacophony of screams, gurgling death rattles and sobbing. Nuns from a nearby convent helped to attend the wounded, some trying to hide their tears, while the army chaplains gave absolution, anointed the dying, and read them the last rites. Those fatally wounded were hauled outside to die; others were laid out in dark corners, overlooked and forgotten.

This is a soldier's lot, Ryan thought.

He stood and watched as orderlies carried bodies out by their arms and legs and threw them into a vast pit that had been dug behind the dressing station. They made a heavy, muted sound as they fell, not unlike sacks of flour. This sound, too, haunted Ryan and added to his nightmares.

Ryan had witnessed similar devastation following the Irish Rebellion but the destruction of human life that day shocked him. The Grim Reaper had been all around when Ryan was growing up. His grandmother had died giving birth to his mother; two of his siblings died in infancy, while many others died from smallpox, typhus, cholera and other natural causes. *But how*, he wondered, *would they view the deaths of thousands of virile young men cut down in their prime in a single day?* He recalled that the Roman poet Horace had written '*Dulce et decorum est pro patria mori*,'—'It is sweet and right to die for one's country,'—but Horace's words rang coldly hollow.

He saw how tuberculosis, dysentery and the great leveller, typhus—caused by the faeces of lice entering the skin—wiped out thousands. He'd witnessed men, women and children burned alive, drowned in metal cages, garrotted, dismembered by round shot, and disembowelled by cannon balls, heads, arms, legs, hands and genitalia blown away. He'd tasted metallic, warm blood as a cannonball smashed the brain of a voltigeur beside him, hurtling the bloodied mash into Ryan's mouth as several molars embedded his cheek.

He traced the ragged scar on his cheek with his index finger.

In battle men were literally blown out of their boots, shitted themselves, vomited from fear and suffered violent seizures. Their hair turned white from shock, and they were hanged and left writhing on the end of a rope, with their bladders and bowels open if their neck didn't snap. He had witnessed badly wounded men unable to move, left for days in the field as rats gnawed at their bloodied limbs and fingers. Others were burnt to death by grass fires lit by burning cartridge papers, or were buried alive under buildings. Skulls were shattered by the pommels of swords or clubbed by the stock of a musket, eye balls jabbed with bayonets or gouged out by thumbs. He'd seen men crushed by falling rocks, wooden beams, stampeding horses or by the heavy wheels of an artillery wagon.

If a soldier was lucky enough to survive these wounds, even a minor injury could cause gangrene or the strange muscle deformity of tetanus, or a simple chill leading to a bout of fever could just as easily kill a man.

There was no glory or honour in war, no glory or honour at all!

Ryan scooped out a quart of murky coloured water from a cauldron and gulped it down before refilling the ladle and handing it to Kaminski. 'I'm going to get our Eagle back tomorrow, Kami.'

As he pulled the door of the dressing station open to leave, he saw scores of bodies heaped onto one of the regimental carts and recognised a bugler from his company. The boy's eyes were rolled sideways and upwards, and his mouth was agape, indicating that he'd died in pain. Ryan felt his blood run cold; he'd promised the lad's father that he'd look after him. He swung his greatcoat over his shoulders and headed back to his company. Ryan couldn't open a door for days afterwards without seeing the boy's contorted face.

The task of burying the dead was far from complete, for there were still many bodies to be burned, when the order was given to stand down until morning. The exhausted battalion lined up for roll call, their coppered faces flecked with powder burns, their uniforms covered in blood and filth. Lieutenant McCarthy had just finished calling out the names when Ryan approached.

'What's the butcher's bill, Séan?'

McCarthy proffered the list. 'Battalion's losses are ninety-five dead and one-hundred and twenty wounded. Your company lost fifteen dead with twenty wounded.'

Ryan grimaced and read the names on the list. 'I passed one of my men with his head blown off. I thought it was Kelly but I wasn't sure.'

'It was Kelly, sir, the former sailor,' affirmed McCarthy, sadly. 'I found his headless body, and came across his head a little further on.'

'Pity!' Ryan said flatly. His finger traced down the list of dead and wounded. They had lost some great characters and some good soldiers. They would be missed for a while, but soon afterwards they would be replaced, and then forgotten.

The paper flittered in Ryan's hand because his hand kept trembling. There were now only around twenty voltigeurs left in his company. *My God,* Ryan thought, *what carnage.* The Irish Legion's recruiting officers would be busy in the floating prisons hulks moored in the French ports. They had gained a notorious reputation trying to persuade Irishmen in the Royal Navy taken as prisoners of war to join the Emperor's Irish Legion. *That is just what we need—more ship's boys and gunner's mates,* Ryan mused cynically to himself. Although the recently recruited sailors had become fine soldiers, most of them were dead now, including Doyle and Kelly.

Ryan planned to leave with just a handful of men at sunrise. He wanted his best men to go into guerrilla-held territory to retrieve their prized possession. He turned to Hoffman but realised he preferred that he not come, as he was slow. He had trouble with his knees.

'I know what you are thinking, Ryan, that I am too old. But I lost the Eagle and, *Mein Gott*, I will get it back. and neither you or anybody else can stop me,' Hoffman protested.

Ryan slapped him amicably on the shoulder and went to address the battalion. 'As many of you know, we have lost our Eagle. Although the battalion bravely defended it, we were overpowered by Spanish cavalry.' He paused and scanned their faces. 'I'm taking a handful of men for a do-or-die mission into the guerrilla-held mountains to get our Eagle back! I feel honoured to have led men like you in battle. Lieutenant McCarthy, I'm bringing you, Sergeant Hoffman, Corporal McGowan and Voltigeur Vandam.'

'God bless ye, sir,' a voice cried out.

Ryan sniffed deeply. 'Sergeant Hoffman!'

'Yes, Captain.'

'I want provisions prepared for five days, as we leave at first light, with muskets fitted with new flints and spares, together with forty rounds of ammunition per man.'

Hoffman sprang to attention stiff as a ramrod even after his heavy ordeal and saluted. Ryan knew that it was wiser to have Spanish speakers in the party to interrogate the local peasants and both McCarthy and Vandam spoke fluent Spanish. It was better to have both of them, because if one of them didn't survive the mission would still stand a good chance of succeeding. He knew Vandam had a mean streak. He'd seen how he enjoyed slitting the throats of the two boys. He didn't like him or trust him, as he appeared unhinged mentally. Ryan had heard him talking to himself several times. He remembered what McCarthy had told him that he had information that Vandam was a murderer on the run from the authorities in his native Belgium, and had slipped across the border into France. *What better place is there for a man escaping the arm of the law*, Ryan thought, *than to lie low for a couple of years in the Irish Legion?*

The battalion slept on the battlefield between the dead. Ryan walked towards one of the bivouac fires, tossed a lump of wood into it and buttoned up his tunic as he stared into the burning flames. The wet log hissed and crackled as it burned. He drew one last puff from his cheroot before flicking it into the fire, pulled over his greatcoat like a blanket, and lay down on the cold, rough ground. He was still alive and uninjured, that was the main thing. There was now only one thing on his mind, to retrieve the lost Eagle; the pursuit of the murdering bastard Darkford would have to wait.

News of the Eagle's loss would soon reach the Emperor in Paris. He'd get it back. The battalion's honour and indeed the very honour of Ireland was at stake.

CHAPTER 15

Ryan slept poorly because of the cold. His body ached and felt stiff from sleeping on the hard ground. Before buglers beat reveille the five men were awake and, following hot coffee and a few mouthfuls of stale bread, prepared to tramp down the road. They unrolled their capotes from their backpacks, and tossed them over their shoulders like ponchos, taking care to protect their meagre one-pound flat oatcakes that hung on cords around their shoulders. Each of these strange square biscuits represented one day's rations. They were each issued with a small chunk of dried horse meat as a bonus, in recognition of the fact that the squad's mission was a very dangerous one—nigh on suicidal—and that they needed as much nutrition as they could get. Ryan also distributed fresh flints to the men and told them to wrap the locks of their muskets in cloth to keep the flints dry.

Ryan posted one man in the far front and one in the rear. By noon the squad had covered around twenty miles through the Spanish countryside and paused when they reached the safety of the woodland. They were relieved to have some cover, as they hadn't run into any of Cuesta's men. McGowan told the others the story of what had happened to the much-loved Colonel Réné and his family when the geurrillas captured them when they were retruning from France. Ryan listened intensely as McGowan told how the guerrillas brutally raped the general's wife and then killed their eight-year-old son, before the general himself was sawn in two between in two planks of wood.

'That's enough, McGowan,' said Ryan. He had seen with his own eyes what guerrillas did to captured Frenchmen. The others didn't need to hear this now.

Ryan remembered the story about the fate of a platoon of teenage French conscripts who were set upon by local inhabitants near Talavera after they had been cut off from the main army. When they entered a village asking for food and water the locals butchered the twenty-five-man squad, but the women were the cruellest. One lucky conscript was allowed to escape so he could tell the tale. Yes, Ryan feared the guerrillas and being captured by them. He had witnessed French soldiers buried alive up to their chests, unable to dig themselves out as their hands had been tied. He remembered Étienne Dubois, a lieutenant in the Horse Artillery, whom Ryan used to drink with in Burgos. The guerrillas had tortured him so much that he had gone mad.

The war in Spain had degenerated into a bitter war of attrition, a war to the knife without honor and without glory.

As they marched, Ryan took out his rosewood whistle and motioned his fingers over the whistle's holes without blowing.

'You think Cuesta and his men have gone far, sir?' McGowan asked.

Ryan shrugged. 'Hard to say. We've received intelligence that he's encamped on the far side of that mountain.' He pointed towards the barren double-camelback mountain in the distance, around thirty miles away. 'We need to be very careful of the villagers in this area. They'll of course alert Cuesta if they see us and then we're really in trouble.' He broke a corner off his hard flat cake and washed it down with a swig of mountain stream from his canteen. 'Our biggest advantage is surprise,' he mumbled with his mouth full.

Slow moving clouds, swollen with rain, hugged the mountain. They pressed onwards, wading through swishing streams, and fast running rivers, jumping over rivulets. When they approached one of the many mountainous villages, they took care to march wide around it.

As the squad were negotiating a zig-zag goat path in the mountains, Lieutenant McCarthy lost his footing and tumbled fifty feet down the mountain. Ryan was first to come to McCarthy's aid. He ripped open McCarthy's blood-blotted trouser leg with a knife. A milk-white bone jutted out below his knee. McCarthy gritted his teeth in agony.

A frown spread across Ryan's face. 'This is going to be painful, McCarthy, but we're going to have to hooch you back up the ridge.'

A greatcoat was laid out and muskets were inserted into the sleeves to make a litter, and the wounded lieutenant was lifted back up the path.

'I'm sorry, Séan, but we'll have to leave you.'

'It can't be helped, I understand,' croaked McCarthy feebly. 'I'll be alright—just make sure we get our Eagle returned. My father and my uncles, as you know, served in Dillon's Regiment. The Irish Brigade never lost a battle-standard in over one-hundred years of service to France.'

Ryan patted him firmly on the shoulder and smiled. 'Don't worry, we'll get it back, and hopefully we'll return in a few days and bring you back with us to Burgos.'

McCarthy nodded.

Ryan knew all too well that the wounded McCarthy's chances of survival with a broken leg in a hostile country were slim. They placed McCarthy under the shelter of a large tree with rations for four days. Each man broke off a portion of his biscuit, giving McCarthy an extra two days' food.

NAPOLEON'S BLACKGUARDS

The four-man squad filed on without him.

Night fell. They were wet, cold and tired when they made camp under a gnarled, leathery olive tree. It must have been several hundred years old and was as wide as the Irish oak trees Ryan knew back home. They removed their wet boots and bivouacked on the ground. They lit a small fire, drawing their great coats over their shoulders and took turns to keep watch every two hours. They slept little as they itched and scratched because of a colony of ants that scampered and crawled where they lay. It wasn't just the ants that they were worried about, as Ryan knew there were snakes, too, whose bites could prove fatal.

A strong breeze rustled through the trees, carrying the sounds of the great Iberian wolf howling at the moon further up the mountain. Wolves were widespread in the forests and plains of Iberia and the voltigeurs took these sounds as good omens. They respected the wolf as a noble hunter.

'Wolves seldom attack man,' Ryan reassured them, observing that McGowan's face was flushed with worry. 'Only when a man is wounded and lame would he be in danger.'

Ryan instantly thought of the wounded McCarthy and regretted what he'd said. He'd been so concentrated on the mission to get the Eagle back that he'd forgotten about the wounded lieutenant they'd left on the hillside. 'Don't worry about McCarthy, lads. He'll be fine, and we'll bring him back on our return.'

Ryan stared into the faltering flames as the rain dripped down through the leaves. He remembered the time he'd come across the partial body of a man torn asunder by wolves. Ryan grimaced, thinking again of McCarthy.

Ryan told the story of a wolf. It was a story he'd recounted around the campfires many times. A veteran had told him in the days following the French victory at the battle of Austerlitz that the Imperial Guard had encountered scores of dead Frenchmen, all of whom had had their eyes gouged out by vultures—except for one. This one body was in perfect condition.

The men listened intensely.

'They soon discovered,' Ryan went on, 'that this was because the dead soldier's pet wolf had stood guard and snarled at all and sundry who approached, protecting his master even in death. The Guardsman who made the discovery,' Ryan recounted, 'later regretted that he didn't take the young wolf for himself, as its loyalty to its master had struck a chord.

'What about Kami's wolf?' McGowan wanted to know. 'We could have him as our mascot!'

Ryan nodded agreement. 'Good idea, McGowan. I'll speak to Commander Lawless—if and when we make it back alive. Now try to sleep, lads. I know it's bloody cold. If we're lucky we'll make it to one of the secluded caves in the mountains tomorrow night.'

He took out his pocket watch. He'd forgotten that it had gotten soaked wading a stream and no longer worked. He tapped it and put it to his ear, but it wasn't ticking. He raised his eyes to the night sky and knew by the moon's position it wasn't long after mid-night.

The moon emerged partially behind dark clouds, only to disappear again as if playing an elaborate celestial game of hide and seek. Ryan wrapped a shawl around his face and neck and covered everything except his eyes and forehead. He removed his boots and placed his legs inside the sleeves of his greatcoat, put his boots back on and raised the tails of his coat towards his face.

Ryan pushed his shako down on his forehead and

thought about the she-wolf Kaminski had shot and killed when he was out hunting and discovered she was with litter. The story of the wolf reminded him of the Irish wolfhound owned by the Irish kings and nobles to hunt large game and to protect their master's possessions. The ancient Celts also went into battle with them. The wolf would indeed make a great mascot for the Irish battalion. He regretted he didn't have a half bottle of rough Spanish wine to help him sleep, but he didn't need it. A brief internal shudder took over his body and seconds later, he closed his eyes and was fast asleep.

Early the next morning, the winter sun sat low on the horizon and flashed a circle of white light through the clouds. A blanket of dry snow had fallen in the night. A black rat, drawn to the smell of dried horse meat in Ryan's haversack, was gnawing on the meat inside. Ryan awoke abruptly and the sudden jolt startled the rat. It hissed and scudded across his body before biting him on the cheek. Ryan snatched the rodent by the neck and hind legs and stretched it until its neck snapped. He chopped the rat's head and tail off with his *épée*, and skinned and disembowelled it to cook it.

The rats of the Peninsula, having fed so long on the wounded, no longer feared the living. They'd grown so fat gorging on human flesh that some grew as large as cats. Two or three rats could devour a defenceless badly wounded man. Ryan had recently passed a group of bloated bodies on patrol. The rats had hissed and scurried under the dead men's greatcoats and fed on the rotting cadavers. Teams of them, covered in blood and gore, had twitched their whiskers back and forth, Ryan recalled. They peeked out through eye sockets. Their bellies were full and they were now unable to pass through the eye sockets where they had once nimbly entered, but instead emerged by the dozen from yawning mouths before scurrying away.

James Ryan had hated rats since he was ten years-old, after hearing the story his mother told him of how his baby sister died. The family were out working in the fields late in the evening as the three-month old baby lay asleep in her crib, but a team of rats entered the room. The young child must have died a horrible death for she was found several hours later. Ryan shuddered at the thought and put some snow on the rat bite on his face to stop it swelling. He took out the half-eaten chunk of meat from his haversack, rubbed it against his trousers to clean it and began to slowly chew. His back hurt like hell from bedding down on the hard cold ground, while his feet and fingers felt numb from the cold.

Speaking in whispered tones, the men rolled up their greatcoats, lit a small fire, roasted the rat, boiled coffee, and were on the move again. They all agreed it was the best meat they'd tasted, for it was not unlike chicken or rabbit.

They continued into the mountains and had climbed for hours when they encountered a shepherd boy with a herd of goats. He was wearing the wide brim hat and a long brown cloak that most of the peasants of the region wore. The boy was rightly frightened.

Vandam grabbed the boy by the lapel, hissing at him in Spanish to tell them where General Cuesta's camp was.

The boy froze in wide-eyed terror. Vandam pushed him and he fell down. The soldier flicked out a knife and was about to cut the boy's throat.

'Hold on!' intervened Ryan. 'We'll bring him with us, for he'll show us the way. Ask him his name.' No sooner had he said this, than Ryan remembered the boy who had walked them into an ambush months back, which led to his capture by the guerrillas.

'He says his name is Miguel de la Cruz.'

'What village is he from?'

'Treviso!' he answered as Ryan consulted his map.

'The little village by the river just lower down,' pointed Vandam.

Ryan scoured the map. 'It's not here, blast it! Make it clear to him that if he shows us the way to Cuesta's camp no harm will come to him. If he tries to escape or leads us into a trap,' said Ryan,' we'll kill him, return to his village and burn it to the ground.'

'*Entiendes?* You understand?' Ryan gesticulated with clenched fist.

The shepherd boy nodded in fear.

They searched the shepherd's cotton holdall and it was brimming with food. McGowan shrieked with glee as he pulled out a pigeon.

'We'll eat well tonight.' he grinned, and couldn't contain his delight when he also bagged a sheep's bladder full of wine. Shepherds typically carried generous provisions, as they had to fend for themselves in the mountains for days. Ryan ordered McGowan to butcher one of the kid goats and couldn't resist making the boy cook a meal. It took a while, but there was enough light and they were so hungry. They watched eagerly as McGowan cut the young goat's throat and placing the unfortunate animal on the ground, let the blood drain. He scraped the goat's soft cashmere off with his knife, jabbed the knife in and cut a large piece of meat from the animal's lower ribs. This was the tenderest part of the animal. Vandam gamely cut the pigeon into small pieces together with the goat meat, along with tomatoes, garlic and pepper, and boiled it. They added stale bread and it became a thick, soaking broth.

The boy nervously rattled off some Spanish.

Ryan looked at Vandam, waiting for the translation.

Vandam sighed, disinterested. 'The lad says it's a local dish, called *los Gazpachos,* or something.'

This was their first good feed in days. They left behind the herd of goats, trudging along the narrow mountain passes, always keeping to the spurs of the mountains. They avoided the small cut-stone villages and followed the goat paths, as goats instinctively knew the shortest routes.

The heavens opened up with sad, melancholic rain. The lush green countryside of Asturias and Galicia along the Atlantic Ocean were known to be the wettest part of Spain and reminded Ryan again of Ireland. The landscape was dotted with Moorish castles, watchtowers and Roman amphitheatres. It was criss-crossed with rivers, olive groves, fruit trees and camellia blossom. He had read that the Celts had arrived in Galicia in the 8th or 9th century B.C. and were thought to have then settled in Ireland, for the dolmens and standing stones, Celtic place names, bagpipes and dances reminded him of home. How, thought Ryan, had he changed from fighting the English to fighting the Spanish in an unjust and inglorious war? He was an invader and the Spaniards had every right to stand and fight for their country. His mind turned to Carmen; he imagined that he could someday settle down with her and buy a farm here in the mountains after the war. Returning to Ireland was not an option with a price on his head.

The weather improved. Through the thick trees in the far distance, they could make out the chain of humpback mountains stretching for miles.

'Cuesta? Show me where Cuesta is,' said Ryan in English to the shepherd.

The boy raised his hand and pointed towards a stream perhaps twenty leagues away: *'Los guerrilleros! Allá!'* he spluttered in Spanish. 'There!'

Ryan's face gleamed with delight. 'A days march away, I reckon. We'll soon recover the Eagle and reclaim our honour. We'll bivouac here tonight, lads.'

It was getting dark. A pack of wolves appeared along the goat trail. They jogged in front in single file with their tails down, sniffing the air and the trail, stopping every so often to look behind. The leading wolf turned towards the men defiantly, bared his teeth under his curled lips and snarled. Vandam raised his loaded musket and prepared to shoot, before Ryan grabbed the muzzle.

'They're just curious!'

The wolves trotted alongside for several miles before finally disappearing into a wooded area.

Ryan decided to make camp, and to climb down the mountain and follow the stream to the guerrilla camp in the morning. They tied up the shepherd, bedded under a canopy of trees, unrolled their greatcoats and settled down for the night. They huddled around the meagre flames of a small fire with their knees held tight around their arms for warmth. Ryan removed some horse meat from his pack and chewed voraciously while the others also ate their meagre rations. They laughed heartily as McGowan acted the fool, putting a great coat around his waist and clicking two sticks together like castanets as if he was a bolero dancer.

Ryan inhaled the sweet pungent scent of petrichor rising from the ground following the rain. The great orange-sun again sank behind the Cantabrian Mountains, almost bowing to them. Wolves howled plaintively in the distance, like a banshee's lonely croon, and Ryan was alone with his thoughts as he peered into the captivating, dancing flames. He listened to the sound of warbling birds across the horizon and the gentle rattle of a waterfall in the distance as he bedded down on the wet rock with nothing more than a small fire for warmth. He reflected that this life of hardship was the stuff of great stories and tales he'd carry into old age with him, provided he made it back alive.

CHAPTER 16

A kingfisher chirped cheerfully in the cold dawn, making its shrill *chi-kee* call before it darted out like a bolt of turquoise blue above the sleeping men and perched in a nearby tree. Ryan pulled his great coat's collar tight up to his neck and turned to check on the shepherd. The boy lay slumped forward on his side. A trickle of blood issued from his mouth and his poncho was heavily stained with blood. He appeared to be stone dead.

'What the devil!' Ryan cried springing to his feet. 'Who did this?'

Vandam sat under a tree chewing tobacco, cutting chips off a tree branch with his stag-horned knife. All the other men were still asleep under their greatcoats. Vandam was talking to himself, laughing. There was madness in his eyes. He stood up, spat a stream of tobacco juice on the ground and glared at Ryan with the knife in his hand.

'You murdering bastard!'

Ryan lunged forward and kicked the knife out of Vandam's hand before he punched him in the jaw, which knocked the Belgian unconscious.

Vandam came to with a groan moments later.

'I gave orders that the lad wasn't to be harmed; I gave him my word.'

Vandam sat smirking. Then he felt his jaw with his hand and narrowed his eyes, glaring back at Ryan.

'A voice inside my head told me that he was the devil and in any case he couldn't be trusted,' said Vandam. 'You remember what happened the last time our captured guide led us into a trap.'

Ryan knew the shepherd had signed his own death warrant by pointing to where Cuesta was. They had no more use for him and couldn't let him go. He knew he'd have informed the peasants in one of the nearby villages of a French patrol in the mountains and word would soon have gotten back to Cuesta.

Ryan picked up the knife and, pointing the tip at Vandam's throat, hissed, 'you're not right in the head. The next time you disobey my orders you're a dead man! You're nothing short of a blood-thirsty, murdering psychopath.'

He turned to the others. 'Wrap up, we're heading off!' He knew he'd made another enemy in Vandam and would have to watch his back from here on in.

The men hungrily tore the last few bites from their chunks of horse meat, took slurps from their canteens and, picking up their muskets from the stack, were on the move again.

It took five hours for them to descend the mountain and reach the stream leading to the guerrilla camp. When they spied women and children hew water into giant wooden barrels as another scrubbed clothes against a rock, they ducked into the undergrowth and watched downstream

'Another village, sir,' McGowan offered.

Vandam licked his lips salaciously as he eyed the women keenly. Ryan gave him a hard look. 'Nobody move!' he warned.

They squatted down silently for nearly an hour, until the women and the children left. Dogs barked furiously and loudly behind them as they scurried to circle past the village unseen.

As the squad followed the stream, their forward scout doubled back from around the corner.

'Four armed men with two mules on the far river bank around the next bend, Cap'n,' said McGowan.

Ryan and Hoffman crept silently under the foliage to take a closer look. They saw the Spaniards filling their canteens at the stream's bank; one man cupped his hands and plunged them into the water to drink while another dipped his head into the stream, and lapped the water up before dousing his neck. The Spaniards looked a rough bunch; all of them sported long moustaches and wore dirty homespun short russet brown jackets with red ribbons tied around their broad brimmed hats. Ryan saw that one of them carried a short-barrelled blunderbuss. A machete hung from his belt and a pistol was wedged into a wide silken waistband. Another sported a battered, bell-shaped French officer's shako with the brass plate removed and a heavily stained French infantry waistcoat that had once been blue, the spoils of war. Ryan's eye was drawn towards a leather satchel hooked onto one of the pack saddles, for it was the kind of bag carried by French couriers.

'They're guerrillas, all right,' whispered Ryan to Hoffman, 'probably Cuesta's men. Wade the river, take McGowan with you and we'll hit them from both sides. We can use their clothes as cover when we break into the guerrilla's camp. Keep an eye out for my signal from the other side. I want no musket-fire, give them only cold steel!'

'*Jawohl*, Captain,' Hoffman whispered.

Ryan slowly unsheathed his brass-hilted curved *épée* from its scabbard and waited for Hoffman and McGowan to appear on the opposite river-bank.

Ryan raised his sword as they roared splashing mid-waist through the stream. The guerrillas, stunned, were taken by complete surprise. Hoffman plunged his bayonet deep into a guerrilla's abdomen despite his pleas for mercy. Ryan slashed the tip of his sword through another's neck, severing his jugular vein and causing blood to shoot out in a fountain. The man grasped his neck in panic but fell down writhing, making a horrible gurgling sound. The two others raised their arms to surrender. Vandam kicked one of them hard in the head and he spat out several teeth.

'That's enough!' Ryan said as he wiped his bloodied blade dry. 'We're soldiers, not murderers. I want these men killed quickly!'

Vandam grumbled before he forced the two men down by the shoulders, into the kneeling position. '*Misericordia, señor!*' they blubbered, pleading for mercy. Vandam grabbed a guerrilla by the hair and swiftly cut his throat. Ryan seized the other one, as his sword swished across the guerrilla' neck, Ryan felt a surge of warm blood drench his knife hand, before the guerrilla slumped down silently, lifeless.

Vandam protested to Ryan that he didn't let him torture them before killing them. He argued that the guerrillas tortured captured soldiers so they died slowly and painfully. Ryan ignored him as he rinsed his bloodied hand in the stream.

They rifled the Spaniards' pockets but the poor peasants had few valuables and no food or wine. Ryan approached the oblong, tanned leather satchel. Embossed in gold lettering on the front were the words, '*Sa Majesté Impériale.*'—'His Imperial Majesty'. Inside the bag were a dozen cigars neatly tied together in a cotton ribbon and a leather *portefeuille* with French papers, including one signed in the high copper-plate 'N,' indicating it had been signed by the Emperor himself.

He jammed the document deep into the front of his tunic. 'Probably orders from France, taken from an ambushed despatch rider.'

They dragged the bodies in the undergrowth, taking their hats and jackets.

Hoffman shouldered his musket. 'What will we do with the mules, Captain?'

'Let them loose—we have no use for them.'

Hoffman nodded in approval.

Ryan thought about the time when a French officer had ordered the haunches of fifty pack mules cut to render them unserviceable to the enemy. The animals had whimpered and hee-hawed in agony and this had evoked great sympathy in Ryan. He was happy he could now at least save these two poor beasts from a similar fate.

They slugged their way along the banks of the stream in silence, sometimes having to strip and wade through icy water in long rushes up to their waists, holding their clothes and muskets above their heads. Ryan's legs went red as a lobster from wading through the cold river.

The slog of the march was the misery they knew all too well. Nothing sapped a soldier's resolve more than constantly being cold, tired and hungry. The elation Ryan had experienced when he had bivouacked on the brow of the mountain and gasped at the beautiful flaming sunset was now but a distant memory. He tugged the collar of his great coat tight as cold rain trickled down onto the nape of his neck. He already knew they'd get little sleep if the rain didn't stop. It was not going to be a good night.

They trudged on for six more miles through a dense forest covered in conifers and holm oak, as the rain pounded down heavily. The cold north wind chilled their bones and made their eyes water. There was plenty of time to think and Ryan observed that the patter of the rain on their shakos was reminiscent of the staccato drumbeat of the march.

He wondered what Carmen was doing. He wasn't sure if he loved her yet, or if he was capable of loving someone after all that he had been through. He felt like an emotional wreck. She loved him, for she told him so. She wouldn't have risked her life to rescue him from the guerrillas' camp if she didn't, he supposed. He certainly admired her guts. He hoped he would live. Maybe one day he could rebuild a life, and have a new family, perhaps with Carmen. This was the first time, he realised, he'd had hopes for the future since his family were killed. He thought again about Darkford. He tried to chase these thoughts out of his head as he had to concentrate on his mission to get the Eagle back.

They made camp. It was too risky to light a fire. It would have been visible for miles. Besides, to look for firewood was the last thing they wanted to do after a hard day's marching. It mattered little, anyway, as there was no dry wood. Instead, they fashioned canopies from fallen tree branches for protection from the rain and bedded down on tufts of damp foliage, stuffing some of it in their tunics for warmth. Ryan shivered from the cold as he prepared to rest. Even the jovial McGowan was silent. They stared for hours into the cold rain and wondered what would await them when they came across General Cuesta, and would they return alive.

CHAPTER 17

The voltigeurs broke camp at first light, ate their meagre rations and continued their mission. A rainbow arched broadly across the sky and the sun appeared behind the grey clouds. Further up the mountains they could make out the guerrillas' fires as light grey plumes of smoke emerged from the treetops. The enemy was close; they felt they could even now smell him.

They had marched for hours when suddenly they heard the sharp staccato of horses' hooves coming from behind. They took cover and shielded behind heavy undergrowth. Ryan counted fifteen heavily armed horsemen dressed in black bicorn hats and blue-tailed coats, carrying their short *escopeta* muskets. They trotted past quite relaxed, as there were no French troops in this part of the country and it was still firmly under guerrilla control.

'Spanish heavy cavalry,' Hoffman whispered to Ryan after the blue-coated cavalry squadrons had lazily sauntered past.

'The same bastards who took our Eagle,' snorted Ryan.

Ryan displayed no emotion but his heart sank, '*Damn it! Heavy cavalry!*' he thought. This would be no easy task for his half-famished band of brothers. 'Cuesta's camp should be close by!' he whispered.

Ryan knew the men needed to rest if they were to succeed. 'We're close now. We'll go on reconnaissance tonight to survey Cuesta's camp.'

The squad clambered up the mountain for another four hours before stopping to rest for the night under a low, overhanging rock. Their perch provided a good view of the surrounding area and a means of escape if they were surprised.

A black raven squawked loudly above the men's heads, which Ryan saw as a bad omen.

The men gamely wolfed down their horse-meat. This was the last of the rations. If the men were to survive the attack on Cuesta's men they'd better be well fed. McGowan would accompany Ryan into Cuesta's camp. Ryan was worried. There was a good chance neither of them would make it back alive. He'd already left one man behind, no doubt to die. The responsibility for all their lives weighed heavily on his shoulders. He imagined what Cuesta's camp was like and it sent a shiver down his spine. It was probably similar to General Don Julián's camp that he's seen when he'd been captured several months back.

'Hoffman! If we're not back by noon tomorrow I want you and Vandam to go and follow us into the enemy's camp and recover the battalion's Eagle and our honour.' Ryan thought if they didn't make it back alive, there was little chance Hoffman and Vandam could steal into the camp after them to retrieve their Eagle.

'*Jawohl*, Captain.'

'And you can take that as an order.'

Hoffman nodded, touching the visor on his shako.

They put on the wide-brimmed hats and ponchos they had taken from the Spanish, leaving their muskets and shakos behind, not expecting to recover them or to return alive. They were only lightly armed with Ryan's cavalry pistol and McGowan's six-inch knife.

The two men tramped down the mountain. There was

still several hours' march downhill before they reached the stream. They tipped out their canteens, topped up with freshwater and continued along the bank, carefully threading the undergrowth as quietly as possible. Ryan saw by the full moon's position that it was some time after two in the morning and he hoped to reach Cuesta's camp before dawn. They made good progress as the moon provided some light in the darkness, and the intrepid duo stumbled across the guerrilla camp just three hours later. Cuesta hadn't posted sentries around the camp in contrast to what Ryan had expected. Ryan shielded behind a tree and took out his battered telescope. A score of guerrillas were crouched around the dying embers with their cloaks wrapped tightly up to their necks and appeared to be asleep. It was still uncertain if the Eagle was here, as for all he knew, could already have been sent back with General Blake's army to León.

'Any sign of the Eagle, sir?' whispered McGowan.

'I'm asking myself the same question,' Ryan answered quietly, handing him the spy-glass, 'but from what I heard, General Cuesta is a vain man and with a French trophy like an Imperial Eagle he'd tend to display it prominently in front of his people, show off as he is. We need to find out where their headquarters is as we may find our cuckoo there.'

'Touched by the very hand of Napoleon,' McGowan sniggered.

'Yes, the very Emperor himself,' Ryan added with a wry smile.

'If you are challenged just pretend you're one of the guerrillas a little worse for wear on account of the drink and answer, 'sí,' to everything. Understand?'

'Sure, that won't be a problem,' jested McGowan, 'for I've years of practise being out of me mind with the drink.'

Ryan put an unlit cigar in his mouth, pulled the brim of his hat down on his face and made his way past the sleeping men at the fire.

'Where to now?' McGowan whispered.

'Over there!' gestured Ryan, pointing towards a large dirty white tent in the corner.

Ryan stood watch outside as McGowan stole into the tent.

'Anything?' he whispered

McGowan shook his head.

'There are two more tents over here.'

McGowan crept inside, but, again, saw no Eagle, just several men asleep.

As Ryan entered the last tent, there it was! The gilded bronze-cast Eagle was perched proudly on its mount beside a Spanish battle standard, the flag of the heavy cavalry regiment that had taken the French trophy. Ryan was mesmerised by the glistening Eagle and kissed it before removing it from its mount, bundling the Spanish flag under his greatcoat. 'I have the cuckoo,' he whispered softly to McGowan, but he tripped over a tent peg and woke one of the guerrillas from his slumber.

'¿Quien anda ahi?' the guerrilla challenged. McGowan answered stupidly with a slow, deep guttural 'Sí!'

With their cover blown, Ryan scudded the guerrilla's face with the Eagle, cracking his skull, and a horizontal line of blood emerged from over his forehead. The commotion woke many of Cuesta's men and as Ryan and McGowan pelted out of the camp into the darkness, several musket balls whizzed past their ears. McGowan was laughing his head off.

'You crazy bastard, McGowan. It may be your last laugh,' hissed Ryan as yet another musket volley zipped by but the men were by now almost out of range. A bullet whacked Ryan on the back, but as he'd gained so much ground it had lost its velocity and merely bounced off like a stone. 'We've stirred the hornet's nest, alright, and they'll be even more furious when they discover I have their flag,' laughed Ryan as he waved it with both hands above his head in the early morning air as they ran.

'Up the rebels!' McGowan shouted. *'Erin go bragh!'*

Ryan turned his head back towards McGowan. 'You're a madman! A mad bastard!' McGowan looked at him, laughing loudly.

They were like two school boys running away after being rumbled stealing apples from an orchard. They heard the sound of heavy hooves and the jangle of horse's harnesses in the rear as they splashed through the stream and climbed into the mountains, which were inaccessible to cavalry. The two Irishmen, still laughing, disappeared into the murky gloom.

Several hours later they made it back safely to Hoffman and Vandam.

'Mein Gott!' exclaimed Hoffman. 'I don't believe you have the Eagle!'

'Yes, but we have no time to waste as we were discovered.'

'Yes, I know. We heard the musket fire in the distance and didn't expect you to make it back alive.'

'We'll keep to the high ground. If it takes a week to get back into French-held territory and back to the battalion, so be it.'

They hiked to the highest peaks, sometimes forced to scramble on all fours, always taking the least favourable mountain tracks, constantly on the move. It was exhausting and by the second day with only water and no food, they decided to forage in one of the nearby villages. This was fraught with danger as several hundred guerrillas were at their heels, but they had no choice.

Ryan looked down the valley—a trail of white smoke betrayed the presence of a village nestled between the trees.

'Let's find some food and make this quick,' said Ryan. 'It'll take us a couple of hours before we reach the village. We won't linger, and I don't want to see any brutality when we get there.' He shot a hard look at Vandam. 'Understand?'

After a long downhill hike, they came to the banks of a river. They waded across as two small girls played with a small dog. When they saw the unshaved and unwashed ragged voltigeurs, they fled in terror. *'Mamá, hombres malos están viniendo,'* the girls said in a quavering, feebly voice as the dog barked incessantly.

'What did they say? Ryan asked.

'That bad men are coming,' translated Vandam.

Ryan and his men stood in the middle of the village, flanked by simple cut-stone grey houses; an open sewer meandered slowly through the cobblestones. No one appeared.

The small dog continued to bark furiously. Vandam swiped out his stag-horned knife, pulled it back with his wrist and flung it. The dog yelped sharply before keeling over onto its side, panting heavily. Vandam stooped down, twisted the blade and pulled it from the dog's side before cutting the animal's throat. He grabbed the dog's rear legs and disembowelled it.

'There's not much meat here, but it's better than nothing,' Vandam said as he wiped the blood off the blade and left the bleeding carcass hanging to drain.

Ryan disapproved of killing the dog but he knew the animal's meat would sustain them for just a little longer. He stood in the middle of the village and looked around. It was deserted.

Hoffman shoved his unlit pipe into his mouth. 'The Frenchies have done terrible things and the villagers are probably hiding.'

'Yes, and we've just killed one of their dogs,' Ryan said.

The crack of broken branches sounded in the near distance. Ryan nodded to McGowan. The corporal raised his musket to his shoulder and ran to investigate. He saw women, old people and children furtively fleeing, making for the river.

'Sir, they're getting away!' exclaimed McGowan.

'Let them go!' said Ryan as he gestured towards a large house off the square. 'I want those buildings checked thoroughly for hidden food.'

In one of the cottages, an infirm old woman lay in bed. She pulled her blanket up to her eyes, shivered with fear, and prayed as the famished men walked past her towards a pot on the fire.

Hoffman plunged a mug into the boiling broth and poured it down his throat. He recoiled and cursed 'Deine mutter, my mouth is burned.'

The others laughed loudly.

The old woman shouted nervously, 'Comed! Comed! Es bueno el caldo gallego! Comer!' The others turned to Vandam who filled the doorway, holding the dead dog by the rear legs like a rabbit as it dripped blood onto the flagstones.

'She said it's good, some sort of Galician soup,' Vandam explained. The others laughed as they, too, keenly plunged mugs into the boiling hot pot. They cut the dog's heart, liver and belly into pieces and threw it into a cauldron. The bloodied meat was soon devoured even though it was half raw as they couldn't wait, they were so hungry.

'Ruff! Ruff!' added McGowan and the men laughed.

Ryan shot a look at McGowan. 'Tastes better than rat!'

The others nodded.

'The rat tasted like pork shoulder,' Ryan offered.

'I like rat,' admitted McGowan, with a broad smile.

As Ryan ate he remembered the time McGowan had cornered a rat and whacked it with his carbine's stock. He should have skinned it but they were so hungry and tired they simply docked the tail and skewered it with a bayonet over a fire. The fur singed away exposing the rat's grotesque face with protruding front teeth. They were famished and so bit into the flesh, including the roasted head, the shrunken cooked brain rattling in the skull. The head had crunched under their teeth like a roasted chestnut. It tasted good.

Ryan threw McGowan a dirty look. He would eat rat when he had to, when there was no other option to survive. He remembered the story told to him by his grandmother after the Great Frost of 1740 had caused the crops to fail back in Ireland. His grandmother had passed a humble cottage and, a number of children emerged, half-naked and starving. Their eyes were bright with fever and their bones protruded in their emaciated bodies. They were too weak to stand and so supported themselves against a fence. Their pale, fleshless limbs and ghastly wrinkled faces exposed in the sunshine showed that they were dying. His grandmother was told later that their parents trapped rats—the family dog had been long eaten—and cut them up into small pieces and threw them into a stew. The children survived as the parents told them the meat was chicken, and they were none the wiser as they sucked the bones dry.

McGowan reclined on his three-legged stool, patted himself on his stomach with both hands and grinned widely with satisfaction.

'I'm as full as an egg!' he declared.

Hoffman pushed tobacco into the bowl of his long

stemmed pipe with his thumb, lit it and drew heavily on the pipe. 'Don't you get too comfortable, McGowan! *Scheisser!'* He turned to leave the cabin, irritated and muttering *'Schweinhund!'* as he was still annoyed that the men had laughed when he'd burned his mouth.

McGowan mimicking Hoffman's accent, cried out, *'Mein Gott! Meine Mutter!'* Vandam, who sat picking his sore feet, guffawed and nearly fell off his stool in laughter. Even Ryan managed a thin smile.

Ryan overheard Hoffman walking away, still grumbling and cursing. He turned his head and through the open door saw the sergeant bend down and pluck vegetables from a nearby field. Hoffman whacked the green cabbage against his trouser leg to release some of the soil before placing it into his shako, which he carried like a bucket.

'I wonder if Lieutenant McCarthy made it,' McGowan said later, scratching his week old beard.

Ryan threw a pained glance towards McGowan. He felt a gut-wrenching guilt having left McCarthy behind. It was too painful to think what may have happened to him. *Did the bandits get him?* Ryan wondered. *Or maybe wolves? Could he have limped back to Burgos? Unlikely, with that leg.*

Ryan got up, scooped some of the meaty broth into a bowl, and handed it to the old woman. He carefully removed the battalion's Eagle from his backpack and surveyed the damage to the gilded trophy. The damaged wing could be repaired, he thought, as he polished it with his sleeve. He placed the trophy on the cabin table. Rays of sunlight beamed through the door frame and illuminated the bronze bird, dazzling the men as light filled the room. They looked on in awe and devotion, mesmerised by the gleaming trophy.

'She's beautiful!' whispered Vandam.

'Sweet Jesus!' exclaimed McGowan.

'Perhaps we should leave it without the wing! Lost honourably in battle,' Ryan suggested as he stood up. 'Now hurry up, as we need to move. No time for this lark—put your boots back on, Vandam. If the guerrillas catch up with us they may very well make you eat those toes of yours—or worse.'

Ryan kissed the Eagle's head before carefully putting it back in his backpack. With their bellies full, the squad prepared to move out.

CHAPTER 18

The squad had spent four days in the mountains since they'd escaped with their Eagle. They contracted diarrhoea from eating the raw vegetables that Hoffman had collected from the village two days back. McGowan caught pneumonia. Ryan looked on as Hoffman limped badly, using a tree branch for a crutch as his knees were giving him trouble. Ryan admired him for never complaining.

Ryan unfolded his map and took another compass bearing. 'We should be approaching Burgos in five leagues, so chin up, lads, and look sharp!'

They reached the spot where they'd left McCarthy with his broken leg. Ryan's heart thumped hard in his chest as he made his way to the large beech tree, expecting to see a carcass perhaps half eaten by wildlife.

'McCarthy's not here!' Ryan cried. 'Have a look around, lads. Maybe he crawled away and didn't get far.'

'If he's dead we would have smelt him by now,' Hoffman added grimly.

'He's not here, sir,' reported McGowan, 'but what happened to him? Was he dragged away by wolves, sir?'

'I have no idea and I don't want to think the worst. We'll rest here for half an hour and then continue. We've nearly made it now, lads!'

They heard noises in the distance. Sergeant Hoffman went up the ridge to look and peered through the telescope.

His face blanched and supporting his knee with his crutch, he climbed down from the ridge. 'Horsemen coming this way —perhaps a dozen, two leagues back, Captain.'

Ryan grimaced. 'We'll keep going towards Burgos!'

They debouched into open ground to cross a half—mile wide plain. Ryan swung Hoffman's arm around his shoulder while Vandam helped McGowan along, as he could hardly walk. Ryan thought to bury the Eagle to prevent its capture, but there wasn't time. He felt the ground rumble and heard the clatter of horses approaching from the rear.

He glanced back and saw what looked like a half-troop of cavalry bearing down. *Jesus Christ,* he said to himself. 'Come on, lads!' he yelled as they approached the edge of the woodland, which would be inaccessible to cavalry.

The horsemen halted and formed into a line as they prepared to charge, chanting the words heard all over Spain. *¡Muerte a los franceses! ¡Muerte a los franceses!*

The familiar heavy scraping sound followed as the horsemen unsheathed their sabres from their scabbards.

'Line up and prepare to fire, lads! Prepare to protect the Eagle for the glory and honour of Ireland!'

The horsemen whooped loudly as they first trotted and then raised their sabres into the engage position as they charged down. When they entered range, Ryan's men unleashed a volley. Two men fell.

'*Hell's bells!*' exclaimed McGowan.

Vandam took down another horseman.

'Form square!'

The four men stood back to back and hunched down. They held their muskets firmly, with the musket stock wedged in the dirt and the bayonets extended outwards, keeping their heads down. Ryan quickly loosed off a shot. A horse floundered at their feet, throwing muck into their faces. The rider's leg was trapped under the horse's side. Hoffman stepped forward, and plunged his bayonet up to the hilt into the rider's chest. Ryan's men remained hunched down to avoid the guerrillas' back-handed, downward-lashing sabres. Ryan prodded a horse in its chest with his bayonet. It reared, throwing its rider, and Ryan lunged forewards, and jabbed the rider through his neck. Hoffman parried several sabre swipes before he sustained a wound in his upper arm.

Ryan heard the rumbling of horse's hooves and the faint sound of a bugle a cannon-shot away. He turned to look as green-coated French light cavalry peeled out from the woods and bore down on the enemy.

Vandam's face shone with relief. 'Chasseurs! '

'Yahoo!' they cried as the Spanish fled.

A fresh-faced sous-lieutenant reined up his horse. 'Mon Dieu,' he exclaimed, 'who are you?'

'Captain James Ryan, 2nd battalion Irish Legion, and these are my men.'

The French officer saluted, adjusted his busby and looked down incongruously at the Eagle at Ryan's feet. 'You recovered your lost Eagle! The whole garrison gave you up for dead, Captain.'

'Yes, but I cannot explain now—my men require urgent medical attention.' Ryan said as he removed his belt and tied it to Hoffman's arm to help stop the bleeding.

'Yes, of course, Captain,' replied the officer.

The chasseurs hoisted Ryan and his men onto their horses and, soon after, the welcome sight of the elaborate cut-stone steeples of Burgos Cathedral came into view.

Ryan jumped off the back of his horse and turned to Hoffman. 'We're going to walk into Burgos. I don't want to give the garrison the impression we were rescued.'

The chasseurs helped McGowan to his feet and the four men limped the final five-hundred metres into Burgos. Ryan calculated they must have covered two-hundred miles through scrubby woodlands and thorny mountain paths in ten days.

The huge wooden gates of the city's walls creaked open as the silhouettes of the four men stood motionless against the leaden sky. Ryan shouldered Hoffman as Vandam helped McGowan hobble in, followed by the chasseurs who trotted patiently behind. The whole garrison stood in silence as they looked on at the men.

They resembled beggars. Their bedraggled faces flushed with fatigue and their ragged and frayed uniforms were caked in dried mud and blood. Their tunics had bleached in the elements, and their buttons and epaulettes were missing. One of McGowan's tunic sleeves was missing. Their breeches were open at the knees, covered with bloodied scratches, and their shakos were battered and bent. Only Ryan retained the canvas cover over his shako plate, but his officer's boots had lost their tassels and were missing a sole. Vandam had lost one boot altogether. Their muskets were still well oiled but the blades of their short épées were blunted from hacking down branches to make paths through the thick forests.

Commander Lawless was waiting to greet them outside headquarters.

Ryan's face wore a triumphant smile. 'We've restored the Irish battalion's honour and have brought back our Eagle, sir!'

Ryan's eyes had sunk into his cheeks and his bearded face had turned a reddish brown caused by exposure. He unslung his backpack and struggled to bend down as he carefully unfolded the cotton sheet and handed Lawless the trophy. 'Here is our lost Eagle, Commander.'

NAPOLEON'S BLACKGUARDS

The sight of the Eagle proved too much, even for the hardy veterans of countless campaigns. Some of them began to sob. Ryan, too, was overcome with emotion. He hadn't wept since the death of his wife and child. Lawless passed the trophy back to Ryan, who raised it above his head as the battalion whooshed and cheered: 'Vive l'Irlande!' they chanted, 'Vive l'Empereur!' over and over again.

'You're a man after me aul' heart, me boy, and we'll celebrate in style,' Lawless said with a quiver in his voice as he clapped Ryan hard on the shoulder and led him away. The capture of the Eagle has taken a heavy toll as I had write a detailed report to Napoleon on the trophie's loss. I knew that the Emperor would be furious. General Junot told me that he sincerely hoped that Napoleon wouldn't go so far as to draw lots from each of the Irish companies, and those were to be court-martialled and shot for cowardice. Junot had seen this happen to another regiment when they had lost their Eagle.'

'Damn his eyes!' replied Ryan coldly.

Carmen came running towards him, and fell into his arms.

Lawless nodded and slapped his shoulder again. 'A mass and *Te Deums* are to be sung in the cathedral, and I'm organising a dance for tomorrow evening—only if you are up to it, mind. There'll be plenty of drink! You and your men have done a marvellous thing!' he affirmed. 'And I have some news for you! But I'll tell you more about this later—now go on, me boy! Get cleaned up and get some rest.'

'Any news of Lieutenant McCarthy, sir?' asked Ryan feebly, barely able to talk.

'Oh, yes,' said Lawless with raised eyebrows, 'he was a lucky blade, a very lucky blade, indeed. A foraging patrol found him hobbling along the Camino and brought him back. Surgeon-Major O'Reilly is looking after him.' Lawless paused and frowned sadly. 'He wasn't able to save the leg, though. He's convalescing in the hospital and is being discharged from the army and returning to France.'

He'd have been better off dead, thought Ryan, *better dead than crippled, blinded or hit in the balls*. Ryan knew what McCarthy's future held—a life of poverty, begging for alms along with the thousands of other demobbed invalid soldiers, tramping the streets all over France, with only drink for warmth and comfort.

Ryan hobbled back to his quarters, helped by Carmen, and following some bread and soup he slumped back on his bunk. His back, arms, legs, even his feet and neck hurt like hell. He was so exhausted he fell asleep on the instant.

A day and a half later, Ryan awoke from his heavy slumber.

'Are you feeling a wee bit better, sir?' Ferguson asked.

Ryan nodded and yawned mightily. He sat up in bed as his orderly prepared to shave him. Ferguson flicked open his cut-throat razor and sharpened it by sweeping it back and forth on a leather strap.

Ferguson placed a hot towel on Ryan's face and began to lather up his cheeks. Ryan thought about what Lawless had told him earlier and wondered whether he was to be promoted or receive the Legion of Honour.

Ferguson pulled the skin back on Ryan's face and the sharp blade made a rasping sound as it travelled down his cheek.

'Any news in the camp when I was away?'

'No, sir, but we lost one-hundred men to the guerrillas while you were gone. The 14*ème Ligne* lost an entire company.'

'Hmm,' Ryan murmured. He glanced over to his bunk and surveyed the neatly folded clothes laid out on the bed.

His olive-green trousers and shirt were new, but his heavily worn tunic was only brushed down; the missing tin buttons and epaulettes had been replaced and the tears had been patched up with another material.

The orderly read the disappointment on Ryan's face. 'Sorry, sir, I did the best I could mending the jacket, but you know, sir, few of our supply lines are making it from France, on account of the guerrillas. The company quarter master offered his apologies and told me he could only issue breeches and a fresh shirt,' he said plaintively.

'No matter!' said Ryan with a sigh as he wiped his face with a towel. He felt his smooth jaw. *A shave after two weeks certainly does a man wonders*, he thought.

'Will that be all, sir?'

Ryan nodded and the orderly turned and left.

Commander Lawless passed the orderly at the doorway. 'Feeling better, Ryan? Are you sure you don't want to rest a little more?'

'No, I'm fine and am looking forward to the shindig tonight, sir.'

'That's the spirit, me boy,' replied Lawless, 'General Junot wants to see you. Meet me in ten minutes in my quarters?'

'Yes, sir.'

Ryan put on his tunic and glanced back at his reflection in the gilt-wood framed mirror. His new breeches contrasted sharply with the hues of his patched up green tunic. It was still stained with Kami's blood from when he'd lifted him back to the rear after he was wounded. He was glad to be back and couldn't wait to see Carmen. He looked better for the shave but could do with a haircut; he regretted not getting the battalion's barber to trim his locks. He didn't give a tinker's curse about Junot; after years of campaigning he was too sick of war and its brutality to worry about what impression he'd make on a French general, no matter how heavily decorated; but Carmen mattered.

The prospect of seeing Carmen again put a smile on his face and he quickly forgot about the dull ache in his ankle as he limped across the parade ground towards Lawless's quarters.

He stopped dead in his tracks as an animal chased a ball across the square. He hobbled closer and saw that it was a wolf.

'What the devil!' he exclaimed.

Kaminski was crouched down, praising the animal. He held the ball aloft, goading the wolf to jump for it. It looked to be three or four months old.

'That's not a bloody dog, Kami!'

'He's already eating out of my hand, sir. He's lovely, isn't he, Captain?' Kami patted the animal's head affectionately as it nuzzled up to him. 'He's a bottomless pit, sir—always hungry!'

The young wolf raised intelligent grey eyes and met Ryan's. The animal's velvet ears flipped back, his long tail hidden between his legs, as he first sniffed, then licked Ryan's outstretched hand.

'He likes you, sir!' Kami said, excitedly.

The wolf cub resembled an Alsatian hound and was indeed a handsome beast with his long narrow snout and brown-grey mottled pelt.

'What are you calling him?'

Kaminski scratched his own head, as he evidently hadn't thought about naming the wolf, and paused before he blurted out, 'Wolf!'

'Wolf?' queried Ryan, perplexed, with raised eyebrows.

'Yes, Wolf is his name,' reaffirmed Kaminski.

The wolf was sitting on his hunches with a laughing face

like a dog ready for play. Kami threw the ball further down the parade ground. Wolf ran after it and retrieved it, panting with his tongue out while Kami again lavishly praised his new pet.

Ryan turned to walk away. *The wolf would make a great mascot*, he thought, but he would run it by Lawless first.

CHAPTER 19

In the corner of the room, an old grandfather clock ticked loudly as it marked time. General Jean-Andoche Junot was staring into the fire when the clock whirred and struck five o'clock.

'General,' announced Lawless, 'you remember Captain Ryan.'

Junot turned sharply and studied Ryan for a moment. 'Yes, of course. I want to shake the hand that returned our Eagle. It's good to see you again, Ryan, and I was delighted to hear you returned safely through that brigand country.' Junot paused. 'I have orders to send you to Paris to present your cherished Eagle to the Emperor.' The general paused to gauge Ryan's reaction. 'Corporal McGowan is to accompany you.'

Ryan's mind's eye suddenly saw the two of them, himself and McGowan, dressed to the nines, walking through the crowds dressed in finery in the Tuileries Gardens in Paris.

'You're leaving at dawn. There are dispatch riders travelling to Paris, carrying news of a major French defeat in the mountains,' said Junot. 'The whole patrol was rendered *hors de combat,* I'm sorry to say. The war is not going well for us, Captain, and the Eagle's return is a great morale boost that will be celebrated in Paris. I want your adventure published in *Le Moniteur.*'

'Thank you, General, I just did my duty. Will that be all?'

'He hasn't seen his sweetheart in a while, and he's dying to meet her, General,' added Lawless carelessly.

Ryan blushed, embarrassed by Lawless's statement about Carmen to a practical stranger. Lawless was also wrong, as Ryan wanted to first check on Lieutenant McCarthy.

'Yes, very well,' said Junot, 'and Ryan, I will never forget how you saved the Eagle—and, of course, my son's life.'

'Yes, sir,' replied Ryan.

Junot turned and stared back into the flames.

Lawless motioned to Ryan to leave the room with him and, closing the door behind the two of them, he whispered to Ryan. 'I told you I had great news for you and I was dying to tell you,' patting Ryan on the back. 'You're an auld gem! You are, James, an auld gem!'

Lawless gestured with his head towards the door of the room where Junot sat. 'He's a strange fellow, but he hasn't been well. I fear his nerves are gone from the wounds he received when he single-handedly killed six men. No matter, the mayor has invited us to a dance at eight this evening to celebrate your return. Only senior officers and their wives are invited mind, but we'll have a sing song afterwards, and that's a promise.'

Ryan made his way to the infirmary. He approached McCarthy's bed but he saw by the light of the dim oil lamp that he was asleep. He looked down and saw the heavily blood-stained and bandaged stump, and felt guilty and partly responsible for the loss of his leg. Ryan didn't want to wake McCarthy and quietly left.

A little later, Ryan knocked heavily on Carmen's door and fell into her arms. Her long locks smothered him as he buried his face in her shoulder. She smelled pleasantly of lavender as Ryan carried her to bed.

Later that evening, Carmen sat in the large drawing room

of the mayor's house and played 'footsie' with him under the table. The mayor of Burgos came from old Castilian stock and was an *afrancesado,* a liberal Francophile, Carmen had told him, who supported the French Revolution and the French invasion of Iberia.

A servant placed a large cauldron of dried salted octopus onto the table.

'*Señor* Ryan, I hope you like our dried fish,' said the old mayor.

'Yes, very much,' replied Ryan, flatly. He hated fish, all types of fish, but what he found most repugnant of all was salted octopus. He offered up his plate with a fake smile and washed down the first awful bites with bread and copious amounts of wine. Carmen smiled as she looked on and saved him from embarrassment by clandestinely removing several tendrils onto her plate, crunching down on them through her perfect pearly-whites. The meal improved, however, as dessert was a sweet cake called *bica gallega,* which Ryan devoured. They drank unrefined liquor made from grape skins, called *Orujo,* and brandy punch. Following the meal, they knocked back cups of thick hot chocolate and danced the quadrille.

Lawless, already half cut, stood up and clinked the side of his glass with a spoon, urging silence. All eyes quickly turned in his direction. 'Ladies and gentlemen, I just want to say a few words to congratulate Captain Ryan on completing his dangerous mission and getting our Eagle back.' He raised his glass and turned to Ryan with a glint in his eye, as he ran off a few lines of an old Irish drinking toast. 'May your glass be ever full! May the roof over your head be always strong! And may you be in heaven a half hour before the devil knows you're dead!'

The room exploded in loud clapping and raucous

laughter. Ryan stood up, self-consciously smiled and raised his own glass in salute towards Lawless before sitting down.

Following a few rounds of blackjack, General Junot retired to his quarters with one of his mistresses. A number of the officers and their wives followed his example. Commander Lawless, the battalion's surgeon O'Reilly and the mayor remained. Lawless and the mayor argued about Napoleon and the invasion of Spain. Lawless, drinking heavily and drawing on a cigar, even claimed he wanted to join the guerrillas to chase the French out of the country! The old mayor, who was also equally the worse for wear from the drink, tried to follow in broken English.

Then Lawless struck up with *'Mo Ghile Mear'* a lament for Bonnie Prince Charlie, and all the Irishmen heartily joined in when Ryan sang *'The Croppy Boy'*, a ballad about a doomed rebel. *The victors write the history and those who suffer, write the songs,* Ryan thought to himself. Many sad songs were sung that night.

'Vámonos!' whispered Carmen quietly to Ryan a little later and the two lovers departed into the night air. In the plaza in front of the cathedral, a crowd of musicians were playing. A large group of locals mingled with a score of French infantrymen as they slouched around an open fire with pigskins of wine. The twang of the Spanish guitar rang out amid the drunken cohort's shouts and hoots.

Ryan spied McGowan seated around the fire with one arm thrown around a harlot, the other holding a quart of wine.

'Jaysus, sir,' slurred McGowan, 'what do you think of me lady friend? She's gat a head like a lump of wet turf on her, but still, she'll do nicely, she will!'

'Just make sure you get back to the barracks before the drummers beat curfew. You know we're leaving at dawn,'

Ryan said firmly.

'Aye aye, sir, wouldn't miss it for the world!' McGowan garbled, 'for I can't believe we're goin' to see Napoleon.'

At ten o'clock sharp, the battalion drum-major led a platoon of drummers to the parade ground to beat the signal for soldiers to return to quarters. One hour later, a lone drummer beat a final set of three drum rolls before the barrack gates finally closed for the night. McGowan made it back to barracks just in time.

CHAPTER 20

The air was cold and heavy as the convoy prepared to move out of Burgos. The guerrillas had intercepted many of Napoleon's dispatches to the extent that a large cavalry escort was needed to keep crucial communication lines open between France and Spain.

Two squadrons of cuirassiers, who'd ridden into Spain the previous week on escort duty, joined the two Irishmen, and around fifty wounded men in six open-topped wagons accompanied them. They also escorted a dozen or so covered wagons containing bounty stolen from churches and palaces right across northern Spain. This included gold and silver coin, silver busts of the saints, priceless sculptures and gems, and golden, jewel-encrusted crowns of the Virgin and Child. There were also scores of paintings by the Italian masters, and by the Spanish painters Velazquez and Murillo, cut from their frames and rolled. These stolen masterpieces would soon adorn the galleries of the Louvre in Paris or hang side by side in the homes of Napoleon's inner circle and marshalate.

Ryan turned to McGowan. 'You can at least sleep your hangover off, provided we don't run into the guerrillas.'

'They can do what they like, sir—I'm sleeping through it. I've enough of fighting and, besides, I have a pounding head on me that would wake the dead.'

'You're a bad seed, McGowan. I always knew that.'

Ryan stepped up into his waiting coach. He latched the door, pulled down the shutters, jammed his shako down over his eyes and tried to sleep. As an officer Ryan rode in one of the *berline* coaches with three artillery officers. As an enlisted man, McGowan made do by riding in one of the rough open wagons with solid wooden wheels, hauled by half a dozen mules. This was the main mode of transport in Spain.

The convoy rode past the rotting carcasses hanging from the trees outside Burgos. They were now reduced to bare skeletons. They looked grotesque, since the corpse's hair and fragments of clothing still clung to their light frames as they swung sharply in the wind.

The safety of the French frontier at Bayonne lay further on, and from there they'd be travelling through the Bordeaux region to Paris herself. As the wagons tumbled onwards, the local Spanish muleteers drove the mules hard. *'Arre! Arre!'* they shouted for them to giddy up as they struck the beasts with their whips. The muleteers themselves were strong as oxen. They dogtrotted alongside the mules for hours, pulling their reins and ensuring the wagons kept a steady pace.

Spain was a country at war. Ryan peered out of his window. The road to France was littered with broken carriages and bloated carcasses of men and beasts. Here and there lay an old boot, articles of clothing or a wooden chest flung open. In the distance, he made out abandoned farmhouses and barren brown fields with unharvested crops left rotting in the ridges.

The convoy halted at a deserted Spanish village and were met by a company of dishevelled gendarmes behind improvised fortifications. The weary horses and mules were exchanged for fresh ones, and after some bread and wine the convoy were on their way again.

They finally stopped for the night at the Basque town of Vitoria which was heavily protected by a large French garrison. The wounded, including the amputee Lieutenant Séan McCarthy, were lifted off their improvised carriages and placed onto straw bedding in a number of out buildings in the town.

'Is there something I can get you, Séan?' inquired Ryan.

'I'll be alright... I could do with a little wine to numb the pain and help me sleep.'

'Listen, Séan,' said Ryan, 'I'm sorry we had to leave you on the mountain.'

'No need, Captain, you had no choice.'

'Yes, but if you had received medical assistance earlier they might have been able to save the leg. I should have sent two of my men back with you.'

'You say that, Captain, but you couldn't have as you had already lost one man and couldn't have given up two more.'

'Well, thanks for that, Séan, and I suppose you're right.' Ryan felt partly relieved.

He sniffed the lieutenant's leg for gangrene, but it seemed fine. He removed McCarthy's jacket, fixed his bedding and promised to return shortly with some wine.

He walked through the town and saw that Vitoria was thronged with activity. Nervous, wide-eyed teenage conscripts sporting scraggly sideburns and sparsely grown velvet moustaches were still finding their footing in the hastily formed battalions, which had been reformed and refitted for Spain, having served in the Austrian campaign. *The older the war the younger the soldiers,* Ryan thought to himself. *They'd soon die in Spain.* The quote of the Greek historian Herodotus entered his head. *In peacetime, sons bury their fathers, while in war, fathers bury their sons.* He reflected that this was very true.

Their puny bodies were not yet strong enough or hardened by daily agricultural toil, and so they succumbed easily to disease. They also couldn't judge the trajectory of incoming artillery by its sound, and so didn't disperse fast enough, or they were caught in enfilade fire and got killed in heaps. Ryan had once seen a conscript toss sand over the burning fuse of a cannon ball that had plopped between the men; all the others had scarpered but he was blown to smithereens. He saw another youngster foolishly stop a rolling cannon ball with his foot as one would a ball, and as a result he had lost his leg.

He studied them closely now, decent well-brought-up lads from Provence or Brittany, the sons of small farmers and bakers who were conscripted by means of drawing lots, whose family didn't have the necessary means to purchase exemptions. He had seen the same young men afraid to look as they passed a rotting corpse; some even retched. They soon changed, for combat changes everything, and they became natural killers. Following close hand-to-hand fighting, the same men would excitedly boast to their friends of the brutal manner in which they had killed an enemy by strangling him or bashing his head in with a musket butt, or by some other violent means. Ryan turned to walk away and knew they would lose all pity or compassion, and would soon pass a rotting cadaver without even knowing it.

Ryan sat down on the wall of the Plaza Mayor and cursed his poorly crafted boots, glued rather than stitched, for they were already worn through. He removed them together with his woollen socks and massaged his sore feet. They felt tender. He burst a large blister on his foot's arch and he saw that he had lost two toenails. He remembered that Hoffman had told him that throwing an egg, shell and all, into each boot helps keeps your feet cool and prevents blisters. He would try it.

He raised his head and took in the scene around him. A handful of lounging chasseurs were eating salted meat and lemon ice cream outside a café with their legs stretched out, proud as punch of themselves in their dashing green uniforms. They jeered at a raddled old man in an old brown cape who came up to them begging for alms. The slow melodic strains of a Spanish guitar drifted and lingered. The fountain gushed water and the local women stood around it and looked fetching in black silken mantillas; others wore cloaks over their heads held tightly under their chins like the women in the west of Ireland did. They stood around talking loudly, warily taking in the sight of the Frenchmen. The local men stood apart from the women and brought the collars of their brown, coarse cloaks tight up to their necks towards their greasy, broad-beamed hats, chewing their cigars with subdued rage.

Ryan lit his cheroot as he watched a group of children march along with broomsticks for guns and pots for helmets. An old woman sat in the shade and roasted chestnuts over a fire and hawks peddled wine and lemonade in large pigskins on their backs to the French soldiery at grossly inflated prices. A beautiful girl walked gracefully towards the fountain carrying an earthenware jug. She filled it with water before placing it on her head, coyly glancing with a faint smile towards the chasseurs at the café.

'Hola, chica guapa!' they shouted, whistling and catcalling after her.

The older women looked on disapprovingly but quickly dispersed as several cuirassiers with rough, weather beaten faces trotted up to the fountain. Their heavy bay mares plunged their heads into the fountain and greedily lapped up water. Their riders laughed loudly at some lewd joke or other as they swigged from bottles of local liquor. The enraged locals looked on askance and scolded with raw hatred as the French turned their chapel into a stable. To them, the French were worse than the Moors.

'*¡Viva España! ¡Bandidos! ¡Diablos!*' a gravelly voice bravely shouted. Another screamed out the threat '*¡Muerte a los franceses!*'

Ryan took out a piece of paper handed to him by the garrison's quartermaster. He read the address of the place where he was assigned to sleep that night. He called a boy over. '*Chico!*' He took a silver coin from his pocket and showed the boy his billet's address. The child's face lit up as he grabbed the sou and eagerly led the voltigeur to his billet. Ryan knocked on the door and a sullen woman opened it, surrounded by a handful of dirty-faced, barefoot, children. He handed her the paper and she glared defiantly at him as he shouldered past her and entered one of the bedrooms, unbuckled his sword and closed the door behind him.

Later that evening, he entered one of the *tavernas*, which were doing a roaring trade, as the town was a major stop off point for the French going into Spain and Portugal. He pushed through the swinging batwing cantina doors and they squeaked loudly in his wake. A pretty girl with dark intelligent eyes was busily serving the soldiers. Ryan caught her eye, and she flashed a shy nervous smile back at him.

'*Un vino.*'

'Two sous,' she replied in good French.

This price was four times what they'd pay in France. In a corner of the room, he spied McGowan sitting with a local whore on his lap, getting blindly drunk. *Always drinking and carousing!* Ryan thought. *He'll have lost all his wages before he arrives in Paris, the bloody fool!* He made his way to leave and gulped down his wine. The men's shrill, raucous laughter and slurred voices thick with wine unsettled him. He brought the skin of wine back to McCarthy, but he was sleeping and so Ryan placed it beside him and went back outside into the cool night air. He lit a cheroot and thought about the servant girl in the tavern, and how her deep, dark eyes had captivated him. He yawned heavily, for he was tired, and returned to his billet. He propped up the handle of his bedroom door with the back of a chair so that no one could enter as he slept and cut his throat. He scrunched his rough pillow and planted his face on it and within seconds had drifted off to sleep.

Early next morning, a heavy pounding on his door awoke him. He opened it and was met by a young officer dressed in blue uniform and buff breeches, sporting a pointed moustache; under his arm, he carried a red-plumed curved silver helmet with a long black horse's mane. Ryan recognised him as a cuirassier.

'My name is Major Pierre Godon,' the aide-de-camp coughed uncomfortably, 'I have received orders from a dispatch rider saying that one of Marshal Jean de Dieu Soult's divisions has sustained a heavy defeat and requires reinforcements to be sent from France post-haste. I have come to advise you that I am bringing the two escort squadrons with me to Paris. I am to leave at once.'

'Wait a minute, Major, you mean to say that you're taking my escort?'

'That's correct, Captain. The guerrillas ambushed the messenger and his escort. The dispatch rider has sustained a bullet wound in his leg and cannot go on. I am to bring the orders directly in his place.'

'What about the wounded, not to mention the looted paintings and the gold we're escorting? For we'll never make it to the French frontier without our escort squadrons—the guerrillas will have our hides,' Ryan said angrily.

'The paintings and gold are to be secured in the *caserne*, to be brought to France when the next escort passes through,' continued the cuirassier major indifferently. 'The wounded can provide no further assistance to the war office; they are of little use and an embarrassment to the army.'

'An embarrassment to the army? You scoundrel! Those men risked their lives for France,' blasted Ryan, choked with rage. 'I have been accorded an audience with Emperor Napoleon in Paris and I'll be making a full report, Major Pierre Godon, of your actions here today.'

Ryan slapped him hard across the face. 'Are you going to do something or just stand there?'

The ADC froze in shock and gulped nervously. Ryan furiously pulled back the door and slammed it in his face.

Ryan approached his window and drawing back the curtains heard the orders of the cuirassiers to mount up outside. 'Bloody bastards' he muttered. He glared down angrily as the two squadrons of cuirassiers riding two-abreast wheeled their horses around and trotted out of Vitoria. *How are we going to make it back to the frontier without an escort?* The safety and well-being of fifty wounded men was now his responsibility. Would he ever make it back to France alive?

CHAPTER 21

'What is the meaning of this?' garbled Colonel Claude Dubois the peg-legged French governor of Vitoria. It was morning and the colonel already looked drunk. 'You mean to say your escort has left and abandoned the wounded?'

'Yes, sir, that is exactly what's happened, and I want to enquire when the next escort will be arriving so we can gain safe passage across the frontier.'

'The next escort may be in a week, maybe two... We never know when the—'

'The problem is, sir,' interrupted Ryan, 'I am the senior officer accompanying the convoy from Burgos and am responsible for the wounded. Many of the men have sustained terrible wounds and have lost arms and legs. These poor beggars need to be treated at the military hospital across the border at Bayonne, but they hardly have a sou between them and can't afford to remain here a couple of days, never mind a week.'

Colonel Dubois poured himself a glass of wine and offered one to Ryan who declined.

The colonel's mauled and distorted face looked on sympathetically as he waxed his moustache slowly and thought. Ryan's eyes were drawn to a two-inch raised and puckered scar under the governor's eye. It was something he had seen often, as a badly stitched facial wound caused scar tissue to contract, resulting in facial features being left twisted and disfigured.

The colonel's black stony eyes bulged out from his ruddy-cheeked face. He had a red nose, the nose of a heavy drinker. 'Do you know, Ryan,' he said, 'the guerrillas are getting stronger by the month in this part of the country. They ambush us by the hundreds and woe to he who is captured by them.' He stepped up to Ryan's face, and the smell of wine and stale tobacco wafted up Ryan's nose. Ryan stepped back with a spluttering cough. The battle-scarred colonel passed his index finger from one side of his throat to another in the well-known cutthroat gesture as he made a grating sound.

'Yes, I know only too well, Colonel, and those are the lucky ones, for I was captured by those bastards and escaped by the skin of my teeth. I know what the bandits are capable of, I could tell you stories, sir, but I wouldn't want to spoil your appetite...'

'Hmm,' the governor grunted as he placed a walnut between the jaws of a nutcracker. The colonel had a blank, unfocused sad look, the so-called 'thousand-yard stare' of a man who had been among the cannon. Ryan thought that he looked like a bitter, defeated man, worn down physically, probably, by years of alcoholism.

The governor poured another glass from a decanter, drew the glass to his lips and threw it down his throat in one gulp. His contorted face paled. 'It is difficult to lead men in battle whom you know will not survive,' he said soberly. 'I was captured by the Spanish early on in the war, but not before all my men were murdered. The local padre encouraged them to butcher us. The women were the worst. Their fanatical priest turned the war into a religious one, a crusade, and preached from the pulpit, that to kill a Frenchman was not a sin but was God's will! I was held in one of the notorious stinking prison hulks moored off Cádiz before I escaped. The Spanish called them 'the ships of the dead'. We were kept barely alive on bread and water, but the Spanish never gave them to us together. When we were thirsty they gave us food and when we were hungry they gave us water, so we had a thirst that could never be quenched and a hunger than could never be satisfied. We lost a dozen men every day. The sick and dying were hauled onto the quarter deck with a jumble of bodies to die alone. *Bah!* Napoleon expected the Spanish to bend the knee to him like the docile populace of northern Europe, but no! Spain is a horrible country to war with,' he said, despairingly.

'Indeed it is, sir,' replied Ryan resolutely.

In the corner of the room a white and brown, short-haired, hunting dog, of the breed called a *Pachón Navarro*, eyed his master's jerky movements fearfully as the colonel hobbled around the room. The colonel kicked the dog and it whimpered and scuttled away.

'With respect, Colonel, if you can't give me any men, sir, I'm not wasting any more time here as I can't wait for the next escort to pass through. I need to be on the road while we still have light. I can't risk bivouacking in the countryside with the guerrillas about.'

'Very well, Captain, and good luck!'

Ryan saluted and turned to leave.

Ryan went searching for McGowan in the tavern he had visited the previous night. He stepped over the drunks who were slumped across the floor or conked out on stairs. In a small room, three partially clothed grenadiers lay sprawled across a bed with two whores. There were bottles everywhere, but no sign of McGowan. As he entered the last room on the corridor, he found McGowan, snoring loudly and lying next to the same ugly woman he had been carousing with hours earlier.

'On your feet, McGowan!' bellowed Ryan. 'On your feet!'

The stunned McGowan came to. 'Ah, it's yourself, Captain. What do you think of my lady? She's as ugly as the Earl of Hell's arse, but she's a feisty little thing.'

'Enough of that idle talk, McGowan, ye blaggard. Get dressed and meet me downstairs. We've lost our bloody escort.'

McGowan mumbled some sailor's curse and scrambled into his trousers as he made his way downstairs, trying to dress himself.

'Where are we going, Captain?'

'I've no time to explain—the wounded are going to come with me.'

'What, without an escort?' McGowan asked in horror. 'And the murdering bandits in the hills?'

'No choice, man—we're leaving within the hour.'

'And the artillery officers who travelled with us, sir?'

'They're coming with us.'

Ryan checked on the wounded, McCarthy was stable, but he discovered that five men had died during the night. Adding the two they'd lost earlier, this left forty-three severely wounded and sick men.

'I want every man who is capable of carrying a musket to assemble in the town plaza.'

Ryan soon discovered that the Spanish muleteers weren't prepared to undertake such a dangerous journey without an adequate escort back to France and squabbled loudly amongst themselves.

Ryan was losing patience. 'Can anyone translate?'

'I can, sir!' said a young French conscript. His right leg was amputated below the knee, and the stump was swaddled in a dirty bandage, reddened with blood. Using the butt of a musket for support, he hobbled towards the mulateers, who were still arguing loudly between themselves.

The young conscript turned to Ryan. 'They're not happy to travel through bandit country unassisted, sir.'

'Very well! Tell them that I promise to double their pay when we reach the French frontier.'

This was relayed to the men, but they still looked dissatisfied.

'They're not going and have made up their minds. You have to understand, sir,' the conscript explained, 'as Spaniards their fate would be even worse than ours if captured.'

Ryan stared into the faces of the wounded. They were eager to return to loved ones in France, but they had no money, as their pay was three months in arrears. Even if some were well enough to stay, hawks were demanding exorbitant prices for the simplest provisions and as they didn't have the funds to remain here, returning to France was their only hope.

'Are there any farmers among you who could drive mules?'

Several hands shot up in the air. Ryan smiled and turned to the conscript. 'Let the muleteers know that their services will no longer be needed.'

CHAPTER 22

Colonel Dubois ordered the garrison quartermaster to release two dozen Charleville muskets and ammunition from the town's magazine. Shortly afterwards, a coach and six heavily laden wagons kicked up a terrible dust storm as they pulled out of Vitoria.

The men felt happy to be back on the road, although danger lay ahead.

'If those bandits attack us,' shouted Ryan over to McGowan, who was crouched on the wagon behind him, 'we'll give them a run for their money!'

Ryan sat back and lit his cheroot. He was happy to have come this far.

'*Anda-ya!*' the men shouted in Spanish, whipping the stubborn mules down the dirt roads as the beasts whinnied and *hee-hawed*. This, the sharp crack of the whip and the heavy clatter of the wagons were the only noises heard. They were in great humour as they were going home. A solitary voice broke out the strains of '*La Marseillaise*'. Others joined in and belted out the great marching anthem as McGowan chimed in with his fiddle. They were defiant. All of them had been through a huge ordeal in Spain and they didn't care if the guerrillas overheard them or not.

McGowan was popular, even with his poor French, and lifted the men's spirits as he banged out several Irish jigs with his fiddle. Ryan chimed in with his whistle. The countryside soon echoed with the lonely, melancholic strains of an Irish lament. McGowan recited an old sea shanty before he broke into his favourite rollicking tune, 'Whiskey in the Jar':

> 'For as I was goin' over the Cork and Kerry mountains,
> I met with Captain Farrell and it was money, he was countin',
> I first produced me pistol and then produced me rapier,
> Said 'Stand and deliver or the devil he may take ye...'

I don't give a damn about dying—here I am going to see Napoleon himself! Ryan thought to himself as he listened. *If the bastards get me now, at least I can say that I lived well, and died a brave man's death.*

As the convoy clattered on through the Spanish countryside, Ryan turned to McGowan. 'Where are you from in Dublin?'

'I wasn't born too far from you, sir, down in Ormonde Quay along the River Liffey,' he replied. 'I served as a ship's gunner on a Royal Navy frigate before she was taken as a prize by the French off the Isle of Wight. The bastards threw me into one of the prison hulks moored off the French port at Boulogne. I was six months there before the Irish Legion's recruiting sergeants talked me into joining the regiment.' McGowan sniffed deeply, spat hard on the ground and continued. 'I never wanted to serve with the colours as I was happy enough, being what you and others would call a corner boy, where I was well known to the peelers, so I was. Nobody forced me into a life of crime and I could have easily chosen an honest life. Me old ma was respectable enough and made a good enough living as a seamstress while me da worked on the docks and spent his time in and out of the local whiskey houses.'

Ryan passed McGowan some tobacco and they rolled their cheroots.

'Yes, I was happy, alright. One of me favourite ploys was to lie in wait outside some back street whiskey house. I'd pick out a well-dressed victim, and sneak behind and bludgeon 'im over the head. I later became a pimp as Dublin's the largest whorehouse in Europe, as you know, due to the large British garrison and I made rich pickings, so I did, from the skin trade.' McGowan smiled to himself. 'There are many fringe benefits from pimping the ladies of the night along Dublin's lonely back streets and alleys, I can tell ye, sir.'

McGowan paused as Ryan lit his cheroot. 'I'd always sneered at those who courted the finely dressed recruiting sergeants who filled their heads with strong liquor, tales of glory, and took the 'King's shilling'. That wasn't for me, no way! I enjoyed the local whores too much and I was only too game to fight anyone standing in my way.'

Ryan took a drag on his cheroot, and knew that McGowan, although he was small in stature, was a wily, strong fellow.

McGowan clenched his fists and raised them like a boxer, as the cheroot dangled in his mouth. 'I loved sorting out those who treated me girls badly, especially me favourite girl, Piano Mary. She was called that because of her habit of running her fingers along her lover's spine when in bed.' He laughed loudly. 'I knew that if I'd remained in Dublin, I'd have likely been hanged. My fate was sealed one night when I was press-ganged.

'I was negotiating the price of a girl with a cockney sailor in an old gin house around the 'Monto' when I was bludgeoned on the back of me head, the bastards. When I came to, I found meself bound, gagged, and locked in the hold of a frigate with other unfortunates, all of us nursing sore heads. We arrived in Liverpool, so we did, and I was frogmarched under the point of a Royal Marine's bayonet onto an old leaky man-of-war, HMS *Sheffield* she was called, and thrown into the brig.' McGowan sighed deeply. 'That's me story, sir, and here I am, for better or for worse.'

Ryan liked McGowan, but he was glad when he finally stopped talking. He looked at him hard. 'I thought you would never shut up, McGowan. I only asked you where you were from! I didn't want to hear your whole bloody life story.' Ryan flicked the butt of his cheroot away and checked his watch.

'Did I ever tell you how the bastards in the Royal Navy flogged me, sir? I never made a sound, that's the God's truth, sir.'

Ryan turned to him and raised his eyebrows in disbelief.

'Well, sir,' began McGowan, 'I was found sleeping on watch, and for a punishment the captain, a right aul' bastard he was, placed me in leg irons on the upper deck, he did, and told me to make me own cat o' nine tails. I was placed on the ship's gangway, and brought forward to the sound of hollow drum-beats and lashed to a metal punishment triangle. They concocted this from a number of Royal Marine's halberds. I barely gave out a whimper as the boatswain swung the three-foot cat keenly over his head. Sure I'd been forced to witness other floggin's and knew that an experienced flogger aimed the whip between the shoulder blades. They weren't supposed to break the skin, mind! The boatswain bent his body around to give the cat its full force. I felt the noise of the whip snap sharply onto me back and it quickly swelled as the muscles tore and the skin broke and bled. I remember how the drumbeats tapped out the strokes of the cat as ship's captain and the whole crew looked on.'

'The bastards gave me one-hundred and fifty lashes, and I knew that two-hundred and fifty could kill a man. I counted each one, I did. Me poor auld back began to bleed after the twentieth lash and I lost count. I must have passed out soon after, but the pain caused me to come to. After the fiftieth, the boatswain stopped to rest and gave the dreaded cat to his mate. I knew then I was a third of the way through me punishment, but yer man was a less experienced flogger and I painfully felt the tip of the whip on the nape of me neck. I never let out any sound, no I didn't, before the last crack of the whip. After a half an hour, I was dragged off the whipping post and brine was thrown onto me open back, for good measure.'

'You never made a sound, McGowan? I don't believe it, ye lying blaggard.'

McGowan made the sign of the cross. 'May the Lord in all his mercy strike me down this very minute, if any word of it is a lie, sir.'

Ryan took a swig of water from his cantina and turned his head away in mild disgust. He looked towards the horizon and knew that the safety of the French frontier wasn't too far away.

Later on, they stopped to water the horses in one of the French outposts located in a desolated village, manned only by a platoon of weary gendarmes and continued onwards.

The guerrillas ambushed them as dusk was falling. They had planned it well. As the convoy traversed through a deep valley, the guerrillas charged down the mountain gorge.

Ryan looked up and thought there must be well over a hundred of them. He shouted, 'Here they come! Load your weapons!'

'*Anda-ya!*' the wagon drivers yelled nervously. '*Anda-ya!*

Anda-ya!' cracking the whip as the mules gathered speed.

The men held on for dear life as the open wagons, without any suspension, cut through at a gallop and pounded down the road before one of them hit a bump and two wounded men fell out. The guerrillas fired at them, and two balls lodged deeply into the back of Ryan's wooden seat but they were soon beyond range. Ryan climbed on top of his coach and saw that the guerrillas were gaining ground, but it was impossible to get a good steady shot because the coach was bumping heavily. It was only when two guerrillas rode up and tried to grab the reins of Ryan's coach that he was able to shoot two out of their saddles. Further ahead, Ryan saw that the guerrillas had blocked their path with large stones.

'What'll we do, Captain? One of the wounded lieutenants asked.

'We're not going to stop! We're going to ram our way through, just hold on tight.'

Ryan grabbed the reins and whipped the horses into a frenzy. 'Come on! Come on!' he shouted as they ploughed through at breakneck speed.

Ryan saw one of the wheels of the wagon behind him leap into the air and smash after hitting a large stone, throwing off a handful of men. 'Come on, lads! We've nearly outrun the bastards!' cried Ryan.

Ryan's coach and four wagons managed to break free, but only just.

'¡*Muerte a los franceses!*' Ryan sneered in Spanish repeatedly, flushed with adrenalin.

He glanced back. The guerrillas were encircling the broken wagons, and he shuddered to think what the men's fate would be. The artillery officer who had been sitting beside him was now gone. *He must have fallen off the coach or being hit,* Ryan thought, *the poor bastard!*

Ryan reined the horses to a trot and continued for what must have been a further four miles before he raised his hand and called for a halt. A middle-aged man stepped off one of the wagons and limped towards him. His right arm was missing below the elbow and the stump was heavily bandaged. Ryan recognised him as a sergeant of the Old Guard by the two gold chevrons above the cuff of his navy tunic, while chevrons on his upper arm marked long service, and he also wore the *Légion d'honneur.* His tunic had seen better days but it was set off beautifully against his once-white breeches and waistcoat.

He saluted sharply. 'Sergeant Bourgogne, Premier Grenadiers, Imperial Guard, sir.'

Ryan was surprised to see one of Napoleon's *Vieille Garde* among the wounded, as the Emperor only sent his personal bodyguard into battle at the last resort, to save the day, but Ryan could not recall them having been deployed in the Peninsula.'

'At ease, Sergeant'

The sergeant removed his shako and scratched his tanned leathery forehead. His hairline was receding and he sported an enormous heavy moustache, the type of moustache many of the younger conscripts aspired to. 'I want a report on the dead, missing and wounded, Sergeant.'

'Yes, sir,' came the prompt reply, and the sergeant went off.

Ryan climbed down from the wagon and followed him with his gaze. There was always jealousy in the army concerning the Emperor's bodyguard. They famously never retreated and only fought with the bayonet. The Imperial Guard enjoyed extra privileges and higher pay than regular soldiers and were drafted from among those who had distinguished themselves in battle and had at least ten years' service. Even privates of the Guard were paid as much as sergeants in the regiments of the line. They also enjoyed better quality uniforms such as their highly prized bear-skin hats, worn only on parade.

The sergeant reported back quickly to Ryan. 'Twenty men missing, four dead and six wounded, and two of the mules are lame, sir.'

'We won't have time to bury the dead and can't afford to carry excess baggage at this stage as the mules are exhausted. Put the lamed mules out of their misery and see that the wounded are bandaged as quickly as possible, Sergeant. We have another four leagues to travel before we reach the safety of the next French outpost. By the way, Sergeant, I wasn't aware that the Emperor's Old Guard were engaged in battle, so how did you lose your arm?'

'I accompanied the Emperor on his recent visit to Spain, but I remained convalescing from a wound I received in a duel with a gendarme. I killed him but the bullet lodged in my upper arm and the surgeon-major thought it best to remove the shattered limb.'

Ryan nodded sagely. As he went to check the wounded he remembered when he himself had been shot in the arm. He was relieved to see that McCarthy was unscathed. The lame mules had been humanely pierced through the heart with bayonets, the wounded were bandaged, and the dead had been lifted off the wagons and placed face down on their stomach.

'I've seen too many dead men's faces mauled by vultures and don't want these to share the same fate,' explained Ryan to Sergeant Bourgogne.

The sergeant nodded knowingly.

The convoy moved on again.

When they reached the last French fortified outpost before the frontier, Ryan sighed in relief as four dishevelled gendarmes pushed open the heavy wooden doors and the wagons trundled inside. The wounded were treated and the mules rested for the night.

After a meal of stale bread, watered soup and rough Spanish wine, Ryan bedded down alone on a truss of straw in an old grain barn. It smelled as old as the world, he thought, and it teemed with mice. A solitary brown owl stood sentry and perched high up in the rafters, its wide eyes scanning the barn floor for prey. Ryan recalled that McCarthy had told him that in Irish folklore owls were viewed as harbingers of death. An owl's screeches resembled the banshee's shrill keening as the ghost adopted the owl's form, warning of impending death. He took out his amulet and rubbed it between his thumb and forefinger. He recalled how all the soldiers said your fate was sealed and no matter what you did, somewhere, there was a bullet with your name on it. Ryan, too, was superstitious, but knew this to be false. It was luck, and luck alone, which kept men alive. It all came down to being in the wrong place at the wrong time.

He felt responsible, as the senior officer, for the dead and the wounded. This weighed heavily on him. This is what he had feared when he'd lost his escort. He felt lonely, perhaps the loneliest person in the world. He brooded again about his life before the rebellion and the forced exile that had sealed his fate. He wondered about what Carmen was doing and the thought of her consoled him and put a smile on his face. His mind then turned again to Darkford, as it did so often before he fell asleep.

The flat-faced owl clacked its bills together loudly and made eerie, low-pitched trilling, hissing and snoring sounds all night, but he was so exhausted it didn't stop him from falling asleep.

He was awake well before the drummer beat reveille and checked on the wounded. 'Sergeant Bourgogne,' he rasped, 'assemble the men and have them ready to break camp.'

Three more had died during the night and two wounded men were too sick to travel and would be left behind for the following escort. He surveyed the repairs on the wagons.

Soon afterwards, the convoy pulled away. If only they could reach the safety of the French town of Bayonne, just over the Franco-Spanish border, they would be home free. The scenery changed as they traversed through the Basque country, becoming lusher and greener.

A ragged cheer rose up from the men when the great citadel of Bayonne came into view. They crossed the border and brought the wounded, including McCarthy, to hospital. So many thousands of severely wounded men had now passed through the doors of the great military hospital there due to the war in Spain, that it was now reduced to a hospice for the dying. McCarthy had been a good friend over the years, and Ryan had always valued his wise advice. He would miss him, but he couldn't tell him this. He wished McCarthy luck, handed him some money and shook his hand firmly as he left him in the hospital, knowing that they would likely never meet again.

Shortly after they pulled out, Ryan's coach broke its axle and was jettisoned six leagues outside Bayonne. Ryan, McGowan, and Bourgogne had to continue onto Paris in their rough Spanish open-wagon pulled by a team of tired mules.

'Where in Paris are we heading for?' McGowan asked.

Ryan searched in his pocket for General Junot's letter.

'It says, blah, blah, blah, report to Adjutant-commandant Duchamp at the Caserne Babylone.'

Ryan turned to Bourgogne. 'Do you know where that is, Sergeant?'

'Yes, I do, as I have lived all my life in Paris. Wait until you see the girls there—they are the most beautiful creatures in the whole world!' he exclaimed enthusiastically, bringing his fingers to his mouth and kissing them as Frenchmen are well known to do.

'Where are you heading to, Sergeant?'

'To the Imperial Guard's own military hospital at *Gros-Caillou*. The treatment there is first-class, and as I have served in the army for twenty years I intend to enter the old soldiers' home of *Les Invalides*.'

'You *grognards* are bloody well spoilt!' Ryan sneered.

'Why do you call them *grognards?*' asked McGowan in English.

'Because,' explained Ryan, 'grenadiers of the Old Guard gained a reputation for complaining to Emperor Napoleon himself about the rigours of military life. They commanded so much respect with him that they were permitted to openly criticise, whereas other units would've been severely punished for doing so. Consequently they're known as *les grognards*, meaning "the grumblers".'

McGowan laughed while Ryan turned to Sergeant Bourgogne and began to translate, but the old sergeant nodded and smiled, explaining that he understood well enough.

Onwards into the French interior they travelled—through the vast vineyards of Bordeaux, past corn fields, groves of magnificent cork, fruit and oak trees, ancient forests and elegant chateaux, always moving onwards, to Paris.

They travelled slowly and Ryan reckoned that they only

covered ten leagues a day. They stopped off at towns en route and rested and exchanged their mules for fresh ones.

It took them nearly two weeks to reach the city walls of the great metropolis. The convoy proceeded down the great *Champs Élysées*. The mules whinnied and farted loudly and the genteel Parisians turned in horror at the sight of the weather-beaten soldiers of Napoleon's once-elegant *Grande Armée*. Their shakos were battered, dulled and discoloured, and their tattered uniforms and short-tailed tunics had epaulettes and buttons missing. Their rough wagon with primitive solid wooden wheels squealed loudly and bumped noisily on its wooden axles as it jolted along, drawn by a yoke of mules.

'Good heavens!' the Parisians exclaimed. Some young ladies turned their heads away; others smiled demurely at them.

McGowan stood up on the wagon. 'Come over here for a kiss, me beauties!' he shouted in English and blew wolf whistles.

'You should really improve your command of French,' said Ryan. 'You're going to get into trouble someday.'

'Arah, blast them to hell and bad cess on them, the Frenchies. Sure I don't care—I'm going to live it up tonight and that's a promise, for ye only live once.' McGowan laughed. Even old Sergeant Bourgogne managed a smile.

'*Les Irlandais sont fous!*'—'Crazy Irishmen!' he cried, laughing loudly, delighted to be back home.

'Turn down this street!' Bourgogne pointed as their wagon turned down the *Rue de Babylone*. 'I'll hop off here.'

The men shook hands and parted. '*Au revoir, mes amis!*' cried the sergeant as he flourished his hat in the air. 'Give my best wishes to Bonaparte!' he laughed.

Ryan and McGowan waved goodbye before they entered the four-storey Babylone Barracks.

Adjutant-Commander Duchamps was seated at his desk writing when the two dishevelled men entered. He looked up and both men saluted sharply.

'Ah, gentlemen, we were expecting you. I have prepared new tunics, boots, shakos and greatcoats for you both, as you cannot see the Emperor—let alone walk around Paris—dressed as you are. Now go and get some food, as I'm sure you're starving after your long trip.' He opened a drawer under his desk, took out some paper, dipped his goose quill into the inkwell and began to write. 'Here are two-day passes. Report back tomorrow and I'll provide you with letters to see Emperor Napoleon.'

'Thank you, sir,' replied Ryan, and the two men saluted and went out.

CHAPTER 23

The two men were given a warm bath and a hearty meal and hadn't felt better in weeks. Ryan firmly shook McGowan's hand. 'We're going to part ways, he said. 'I can't keep pace with your carousing and whoring! I want you back here in twenty-four hours, and don't forget the generous bounty of one-hundred gold Napoléons you're due, along with the Legion of Honour!'

'Arah, don't you be worryin', Cap'n. Of course I'll be here.' The green-coated voltigeur picked up his knapsack, pulled his shako down over one eye, shoved an unlit cheroot into his mouth, and headed into the sprawling metropolis.

Ryan swung his bag over his shoulder and wondered which dens of debauchery and vice McGowan would end up. 'You alright for money?' he called after him.

'I'm canny enough, Cap'n!' he shouted back. 'I've six months' back pay, although I've spent half of it already,' he retorted with a shrill, nervous laugh. 'And I spent it wisely, too: on women and drink while I squandered the rest!'

Ryan tutted and shook his head as he watched him walk away singing: '*As I was goin' over the Cork and Kerry mountains...*'

Ryan had also received six months' captain's back pay, seven-hundred and fifty francs, and to celebrate his arrival in Paris he checked into one of the finest hotels in Paris, the magnificent *Hotel des Étrangers* on the *Rue de Vivienne*. He felt that he deserved it after his ordeal, and, besides, he rationalised, there was little worth spending his money on in war-torn Spain. As he maundered along the wide boulevards and took in the sights of Paris, it seemed that every third man he came across was in uniform. He passed many mutilated invalided soldiers, medals proudly pinned to their chests. Some were missing arms and legs and were begging for alms. He worried that his friend, the wounded Lieutenant McCarthy, would also end up begging on the streets.

His attention was drawn to a horse race on the *Champs de Mars,* and he jostled through the crowds to get a glimpse of the jockeys on fine Arab thoroughbreds as they galloped at breakneck speed along the makeshift track.

He continued down the *Champs Élysées* and marvelled as a man lit the gas lanterns by a system of pulleys suspended between two buildings. He paused to take in his reflection in one of the fancy boutiques and was pleased with himself. He looked like a seasoned soldier. His green tunic and breeches offset the parchment yellow facings of his collar and cuffs, exposing a crisp white waistcoat. His *épée* and the waxed brown leather scabbard were the only pieces of his original kit. He tilted his shako over one eye and cursed as a passing cart threw up muck from the road, spoiling his boots. He stooped down to wipe them and continued on his journey. He stopped to take off his knapsack and removed his tobacco pouch. He crumbled the tobacco leaves between his thumb and forefinger, placed them on a sheet of paper and rolled it tight, twisting the ends. He raised many eyebrows as he smoked, as cheroots were rarely seen outside the Peninsula.

Many stared and whispered, wondering to what regiment the dashing voltigeur captain belonged.

'*Mademoiselle,*' he said, tipping his hat as another pretty girl stared at him with a glint in her eye as she passed. *A bloody uniform certainly helps,* he thought.

An old man, bent forward nearly double with a hunchback, stopped and asked him what regiment he belonged to and where he had served. Ryan told him how the campaign was going in the Peninsula, and that it was tough going as the Spanish had put up stiff resistance, but he spared the old man some of the grimmer details.

'I served under General Lafayette,' the old man explained, 'a long time ago, during the American War in the 1770's; I fought alongside your countrymen in the Regiment of Dillon at the Siege of Savannah.'

Ryan smiled and bowed. The old man tipped his hat, adding that he hoped it would not be long before the French would strike again for the cause of Irish freedom, before continuing on his way.

He strutted past the partly built buttresses of the *Arc de Triomphe,* commissioned by Napoleon to celebrate his victory at Austerlitz two years earlier. He visited the neo classic Pantheon in the Latin Quarter and climbed up to the top of the monument, gazing and marvelling at the surrounding countryside and the great city of Paris laid out before him. It was the most magnificent spectacle he had ever seen in his life. He even went to visit the Catacombs and was passing the *Palais de Justice* when a troop of mounted Imperial Gendarmes trotted past followed by a caged cart carrying women clipped in leg-irons. The gendarmes jostled the prisoners out of the cages and tied them to a stake where a paper was stuck over their heads indicating their particular crimes. Ryan stood and watched as the Parisians hurled obscenities and rotten fruit at them before they were hauled away. Ryan observed that some of the fettered prisoners were but children, branded for life on the check with the letters 'TP', which he understood to mean: '*Travail Perpétuel*', imprisonment for life with hard labour. It was indeed a tough, unrelenting world, he mused.

He went to see the popular comedy '*La Rosière de Hartwell*' at the Théatre Feydeau and entered the opulent *Restaurant de Beauvilliers*, as Commander Lawless had recommended. He dined alone there, and ordered the tiny ortolan songbird, which was considered a great delicacy. The unfortunate bird was trapped, drowned in Armagac and roasted. It was then eaten whole—bones and all. Ryan covered his head with a white handkerchief while he downed the single mouthful—as tradition dictated—shielding the act from the eyes of God, for such a shameful act.

Departing the restaurant, his mind's eye vividly recalled the waitress and how she'd played with her hair and smiled at him seductively.

He meandered down the *Rue Jacob* heading to the London Coffee House where he and the former United Irishmen had met when they'd first come to Paris. He had spent much time there, where he and the others plotted, drank, caroused and fought. They had lobbied Irish generals in the French army to persuade Napoleon to form them into a new Irish corps to spearhead another invasion. This had led to the creation of *La Légion Irlandaise*.

Ryan pushed open the door and looked around, but he couldn't find any familiar faces. He turned to leave and heard a voice bellowing behind him 'Ah, *M'sieu* Ryan, is it you?' It was the distinctive low bellow of the café's owner. 'I heard you were serving in that dreadful war in Spain. You have to stay a while and tell me all about your adventures.'

Ryan shared a bottle of wine with old Jean. They spoke about old times and forgotten friends, and before leaving he promised to return the next time he was in Paris.

NAPOLEON'S BLACKGUARDS

A sudden shower forced him into a café and, following several glasses of cognac, he doused his cheroot, paid his three sous and left. The sudden rush to the head of the wine and brandy, the excitement of being in Paris and his meeting with old Jean caused him to lose his bearings and he roamed off the beaten track to the seedier underbelly of Paris.

The noxious smell of the city struck him when he crossed over the Seine, and he felt nauseous as he passed several tanneries which used a combination of dog excrement and urine in the process of tanning leather. Not once, but twice, he had to dodge the contents of a bidet being thrown out of an upstairs window. He also had to be careful dodging the open sewers, which flowed down many of the smaller streets. A rat with a long greasy tail scurried along the side of a building beside him before it dived head first into a crack in a wall. Ryan reckoned that the rat must have been eight inches long, not taking into account its tail. He shuddered as images of the devastation the rodents had left behind in Spain flashed before his eyes.

The area around the *Palais Royale* was the part of the city where prostitutes plied their trade. This was no place for a man to venture alone, not even for a sword-carrying veteran of Napoleon's Imperial Army. He had to use his full strength to prevent being dragged indoors by two toothless prostitutes who accosted him at a doorway. He saw that one of them had syphilis boils around her nose and mouth. He'd managed to wrangle himself free when he felt an unwelcome hand searching inside his tunic pocket. He was trying to make his escape when two men snuck up behind him and bludgeoned him on the head. A trickle of blood travelled down his face, dazed, he fell backwards as one of the attackers produced a knife. Ryan kicked him in the stomach before he was clasped tightly in a headlock. He grabbed the attacker in the groin and squeezed as hard as he could. The man unleashed a groan and loosened his grip. Ryan turned to the other attacker, drew his sword and with a swift upward motion of his left hand, brought the sword's pummel under the man's chin. He recoiled backwards as Ryan ran the attacker through the heart. His eyes bulged with terror and his face paled as he made a long-drawn, hissing sound through his teeth and fell dead. The prostitutes screamed in terror and fled indoors.

He passed the other man, who was on his knees soothing his groin, and kicked him squarely in the face as he passed. The man spat out teeth and passed out cold. Ryan brushed himself down as he returned to the safety of the main boulevard. He felt his bloodied head wound with his fingers. It was only a slight wound and he hadn't spoilt his uniform. The palm of his hands anxiously felt his pockets for his *portefeuille*. He was relieved when he made it back to the *Rue de Vivienne* and spotted his hotel. When he lay down on the bed his heart was still racing, he felt dizzy and his hands and legs trembled. A heavy feeling of dread and fear came over him. He took hold of his amulet again. He slept little that night. It was a pity because the bed was the most comfortable he had ever lain on.

The following day, he paid a visit to Monsieur Begot, an officer in the Imperial Guard who ran a fencing academy in the *Rue du Cadran*. He knew only too well that proficiency with the blade could mean life or death, in the event of being called out in a duel. Every regiment in the army, including Napoleon's Irish Legion, possessed a regimental *maître d'armes*. General Junot had kindly provided him with a letter of introduction, as to receive instruction from the renowned fencing master. Monsieur Begot was indeed a great honour.

'Now here, *m'sieur,*' Begot began, while he swished his sword lavishly through the air, 'the whole art of fencing consists of two rules—giving and not receiving.'

Ryan couldn't stop staring at Begot's face, for it was criss-crossed and seamed with fencing scars. This had caused his mouth to droop and atrophy. Razor sharp *épées* sliced through flesh without bruising, enabling wounds to close cleanly. Some men packed their wounds with horsehair and left them agape to irritate the wound so as to form prominent scars. These wounds were seen as badges of honour.

Begot demonstrated a fencing movement to Ryan. 'Now turn the blade of your adversary from the line of your body with a sharp flick of the wrist, either inward or outward. You see, the art of fencing combines athleticism, swiftness and the ability to anticipate an opponent's next move. It is an elaborate game, and one part of this game is politeness, or the pretence of courtesy, that ordinarily precedes a fencing contest. Open your eyes, Captain!' he demanded. 'More!' continued Begot. 'When you salute you must open your eyes, sir, like the crystals of a watch. Show your presence and antagonise your opponent, not, of course, by hurling unruly retorts, but as gentlemen we can, for example, praise the fencing masters of other regiments, and disparage the fencing master of our opponent's.'

Begot stood with his legs bent, his right leg forward and his left leg extended behind. He drew all his weight down, and his left hand was placed behind his back for balance, as he cleaved the air with the *épée* in his outstretched hand. 'I assure you, your opponent soon loses composure *and his* temper and foolishly goes straight in for the lunge, which I parry, following through with a riposte. Before he regains his composure, I lunge forward in a *flèche* attack with a quick, nimble step, transferring all my weight onto my leading foot while extending my arm. I then run him through the heart for his trouble,' he explained, laughing to himself, as he curled his enormous moustache between his fingers.

Ryan then went through the various moves—lunges, parries, ripostes—with the blades clattering off each other at dazzling speeds. He was exhausted when the lesson ended, but he was delighted to have improved his fencing techniques, particularly his counter-attack riposte manoeuvre. Moreover, he wanted to hone these skills for use against Darkford! He shared a couple of glasses of claret with Begot and thanked him.

He departed into the street with a spring in his step, while mentally going through the fencing movements. He received some odd looks from passers-by, as he resembled a music conductor when he flicked his wrists, recalling the various thrusts and parries he had just learned.

Ryan returned to the Babylone Barracks later that afternoon and there was McGowan, leaning against the barrack's wall. He was glad to see that McGowan had shaved.

'Always a corner boy, McGowan!'

'Always!' McGowan retorted.

'How did you get on?'

'Ah, you know, just drinking and whoring, the usual bill of fare—and you?'

'Proceeded on more gentlemanly cultural pursuits. I dined in one of the best restaurants, went to the theatre, took in the sights, and climbed the Pantheon.'

'Climbed the wha...?'

'Oh, never mind! I was nearly violated by two whores. I killed a man who tried to rob me, and severely crippled the other.'

McGowan's face lit up and he stood up straight. 'Now that's more like it, Cap'n!' he cried wondrously, wringing his hands together.

Ryan reached forward and knocked McGowan's shako off his head with the back of his hand.

'Ah, sir!' he protested as he bent down to pick it up. 'I'm tryin' to look me best for Boney.'

'Come along, now, can't be late now for the Emperor!'

'Bloody Emperor, me arse. Thinks he's the bloody Pope, he does,' McGowan grumbled as he brushed his hat down with the back of his sleeve. 'He can kiss the back of Hell's arse for all I care.'

They made their way to the barracks and arrived at the commander's' office.

'There you are, now, Captain,' said Commander Duchamp as he handed Ryan the invitation. 'You can go and see the Emperor at six o'clock this evening. We can't have you arriving on foot, so I have arranged for you to use my personal carriage. You should leave at once.'

The two Irishmen climbed into the richly adorned coach and set off like royalty to see Napoleon.

'If me poor auld ma could see me now,' McGowan said proudly. The two chocolate-coloured mares kicked up a trail of dust as they sped away towards the Tuileries Palace. Ryan said nothing as he was deep in thought as he peered out of the window.

CHAPTER 24

A little later, McGowan and Ryan pulled up to the gates of the Tuileries Palace. They handed over their letters and were told to wait outside until summoned. Ryan watched as a dozen or so coaches, escorted by a dashing troop of cavalry in full military regalia, entered the palace gates. Napoleon alighted with the ladies of the household.

'*Vive l'Empereur!*' the crowds shouted when they caught sight of Napoleon. '*Vive l'Empereur!*'

Napoleon was wearing his heavy grey greatcoat and distinctive bearskin bicorn, worn sideways. He raised his arm in salute, his other arm folded behind him. Ryan stood and watched as a sergeant of the Imperial Guard came out and gave newly minted gold Napoléons to the children in the cheering crowds.

An hour passed. Two *gendarmes d'élite* of the Imperial Guard finally escorted the two Irishmen through the gates and down the long mirrored hall adorned with gold-painted walls. The noise of boots on the polished parquet floors reverberated loudly. Ryan's heart pounded heavily at the prospect of meeting the Emperor.

They stopped in front of an elaborate double door where a man dressed in an enormous white turban and baggy trousers stood guard. A curved ivory-handled dagger was hooked to a leather belt around his waist. Ryan thought he must be Napoleon's famous bodyguard, Roustam. He had read in *Le Moniteur* that the sheik of Cairo had presented the Egyptian Mameluke to Napoleon following his Egyptian Campaign.

The two Irishmen entered Napoleon's lavishly adorned study. It was filled with carved furniture copiously inlaid with gold in the French Empire style. The Emperor was lying on his belly peering over charts sprawled over the floor. Ryan recognised a man wearing the uniform of a marshal of France writing at his rosewood bureau. Napoleon rolled up one of the maps, raised himself up from his knees with difficulty and straightened. He was about five foot six inches tall but stooped considerably, and in his early forties he was at the height of his genius. He was dressed simply in the green tunic and red facings of the Chasseurs of the Imperial Guard with the Cross and Grand Eagle of the *Légion d'honneur*. His kerseymere waistcoat stretched out to reveal a round stomach. His knee breeches were stained heavily with ink from his habit, Ryan presumed, of wiping the tip of his quill on them.

'Did you fart, McGowan?' Ryan whispered out of the side of his mouth. McGowan was going to say something but Ryan elbowed him sharply in the ribs to remain quiet.

Ryan stood swiftly to attention and saluted. He introduced himself and McGowan and handed Napoleon the letter from General Junot. Napoleon stared at the two men closely with a pair of blue-grey, beady eyes. He screwed his monocle into his eye socket, cracked open the wax seal between his thumbs and began to read. '*Bravo!* I have heard that you have recovered my Eagle?' the Emperor said in a low and hollow voice as he raised his head.

'Yes, sire,' answered Ryan. 'We recovered it from Spanish guerrillas who had taken it in battle.'

'*Bravo, les Irlandais!* Thank you for saving my Eagle.'

Napoleon shook Ryan and McGowan firmly by the hand.

'Where did you learn to speak French?' Napoleon asked. 'For you speak it well for an Irishman.'

'Thank you. I learned it from my uncle. He was cleric to the Irish college in Lille and served as chaplain to Lord Clare's Regiment of the Irish Brigade.'

The Marshall of France placed his quill pen back in the pot, removed his spectacles, and turned his head in interest. He approached the two men and extended his hand. Ryan shook it firmly.

'I am General Clarke, the Minister of War. I may have known your uncle, Captain Ryan. I served in Clare's Regiment. Was your uncle Father Charles Ryan?'

'Yes, *Monsieur le Maréchal.*'

'Both my parents are Irish, and I visited Ireland several years ago,' added Clarke. 'Your French is indeed impeccable, Ryan.'

'Thank you,' replied Ryan. 'My uncle taught me well.'

Clarke said something to McGowan, and he replied that he was sorry but he didn't understand.

'You are a deserter!' exclaimed Napoleon.

'I was a prisoner of war,' answered McGowan in English, 'and volunteered to serve your Majesty.'

Ryan translated with trepidation for Napoleon.

The Emperor nodded, and waved his hand to his *valet de chambre*. A bottle of wine was poured into four fluted crystal glasses. 'This is my favourite wine, a Chambertin 1805.' Napoleon swirled the glass and sniffed deeply. *'Salut!'*

They all drank.

Clarke turned to Ryan. 'Did you ever meet Wolfe Tone?'

'No, General, I never did, but he was a brave man and a patriot.'

'Yes, he was!' agreed Clarke, and he paused in thought.

'Tone was tireless in his efforts to procure our help in Ireland. He spent years drafting memorials and holding endless meetings with myself, other Irish generals and the Directory to persuade them that Ireland was ripe for invasion, and was ready to embrace the French revolutionary ideals of *liberté, égalité, fraternité.* We gave him a fleet and 15,000 troops, but, as you know, our fleet was battered by storms and returned to France.' Clarke added sadly, 'Poor Tone, the rebellion was a fiasco.'

'You may recall he was later intercepted by the Royal Navy,' said Ryan. 'He was brought to Dublin, found guilty of treason and he cheated the hangman's noose by cutting his own throat.'

'Yes,' Napoleon said slowly. 'I pitied his widow, a charming lady called Mathilde, if my memory serves me well. She came to visit me last year. I gave her a pension and obtained naturalisation and a position in the cavalry school for her son.'

'Permit me, sire,' added General Clarke. 'I tried to persuade her to send her son into Ryan's Irish Legion, but she refused. She wanted to send him into a respectable cavalry regiment of the line. She'd no wish to send him to Spain, into the plodding infantry and into your low-life, rough corps of foreigners, Ryan. She'd grand plans for her son and protested that as her husband gave his blood for France, she wanted her son to enter Saint Cyr to serve, perhaps, as an aide-de-camp to one of our marshals in the Austrian campaign.'

Clarke paused in thought. 'Did you join the rebel army, Ryan?'

'Yes. I escaped from Dublin and made it safely to France.'

Napoleon's brow furrowed. 'I had no confidence in the other Irishmen in Paris, as they constantly quarrelled among themselves.' He picked his nose before flicking his find away with his fingers, for the Emperor was a prolific nose-picker. '*Basta!*'—'Enough,' he spat.

Ryan also observed that Napoleon spoke French with a heavy Italian accent interspersed with Italian nuances and expressions.

'If General Hoche had not been placed on-board a frigate instead of a man-of-war and hadn't been blown off course by storms I am sure he'd have landed in Ireland and been successful!' Napoleon boomed, punching down hard on the table with his fist. 'With Ireland gone, England would have been on her knees. The 'wooden walls' of the Royal Navy continue to stall my plans for invasion of that cursed nation of shopkeepers,' he snorted, adding disdainfully. '*Perfide Albion!*'

Ryan pursed his lips and nodded soberly.

Napoleon paced the room with his hands folded and paused under a huge wall painting. 'I am a great admirer of Celtic mythology, especially those of the legendary Gaelic poet Oisín—the Homer of the North—I always carry a copy of his poems into battle for strength and inspiration.'

He pointed to the painting. 'I commissioned Girodet to paint Oisín receiving the ghosts of the French heroes...'—he paused before adding sadly—'one of whom is Hoche.'

Ryan walked up to the painting and took in the mythological scene. The blind poet Oisín was featured as an old man, surrounded by naked redheaded nymphs playing lyres in the clouds, together with Oisín's father, Finn McCool and Cuchulainn, warmly receiving, as in a biblical scene, French soldiers into paradise. One of these, Ryan observed, was, indeed, General Lazare Hoche.

'I hope to have the Spanish on their knees soon, and it will take more than 50,000 English soldiers to remove us from the Peninsula,' the Emperor said stoutly. He turned to Clarke and flicked his fingers several times impatiently. 'What is the name of the general who is leading the English, Clarke?'

'General Sir John Moore. I understand that he's a very capable general, sire.'

Napoleon removed a small silver casket from his hip pocket and placed a pinch of snuff on to the back of his hand. 'Yes, but is he lucky? I sincerely hope that he isn't. I would rather have a lucky general than one who was good. The war in Spain is my Spanish ulcer,' he uttered ruefully as he deeply sniffed the tobacco through each nostril in turn, 'and it is draining my resources. I have 325,000 French troops in the Peninsula when I desperately need them to fight the Austrians.' His eyes suddenly flashed. 'Once I have Spain subdued, I am going to focus on Ireland. I have great plans for you, Ryan. You strike me as an intelligent man. As with your experience of leading rebellion in Ireland, not to mention your perfect French and your military training in the best army in the world, you should go far. My spies have advised me that the British have finished building a string of fortifications around the Irish coast, to scupper my plans to invade Ireland. I am most concerned about a new type of fortification, which they call Martello Towers, which had proved to be impenetrable in Corsica. I need to know a lot more about these fortifications, how many guns they carry, and what calibre they hold, and more importantly where their weak points are.' He pinched more snuff onto the back of his hand and sniffed it through each nostril. 'When I have Spain under control, I would like to send you to Ireland on an information gathering mission, for a proposed invasion.'

Ryan's eyes lit up and he raised his eyebrows. 'You mean spying!'

'I am a great admirer of Frederick the Great. The former King of Prussia used spies extensively and to great effect. You would be paid well for your trouble, for a man who risks being hanged in my service needs to be well rewarded,' added Napoleon.

Ryan knew that military personnel found in disguise were customary hanged without trial.

'I am a patriot, and to help liberate my country is payment enough for me, sire,' answered Ryan.

Clarke looked on with approval.

'Hmm,' grunted Napoleon as he stared squarely at Ryan. '*Bravo,* Ryan! I am pleased to hear that. We would have to smuggle you across, perhaps in a fishing vessel. Would you be interested?'

'I may assure you, Emperor, that whatever interests you and *Monsieur le Maréchal* concerning the liberation of Ireland also interests me entirely,' replied Ryan.

Napoleon and Clarke laughed heartily. Ryan laughed, too, and even McGowan—although not getting the joke due to his poor French—managed a wide, toothless grin.

The Emperor placed his hands firmly on Ryan's shoulder. 'I like you, Ryan, and I see you are a man of honour.' He turned again to Clarke. 'I completely forgot your reward! Forgive me. Clarke, do you have medals for these brave men?'

General Clarke rummaged through the papers on his desk.

'I will check the other desk, sire.' He pulled out two silk purses containing gold coins and a handful of brightly adorned *Légion d'honneur* medals.

'It never ceases to amaze me, how men will sacrifice their lives for a piece of enamel and coloured ribbon,' Napoleon said as he examined the medals before pinning them onto

Ryan and McGowan's chests, amicably pulling on the lobe of each man's ear. 'Here are one-hundred gold Napoléons,' he added as an afterthought while tossing Ryan the leather pouches. 'I will give you two more medals and two-hundred gold Napoléons and will leave it up to the discretion of your *Chef de Battalion* to present them to the bravest men in the Irish battalion.'

'C*hef de Battalion* William Lawless, sire,' interjected Clarke.

Napoleon nodded his head. 'Yes, Lawless, indeed.'

Ryan was a little taken aback, as he had had visions of receiving his medal on the parade ground in front of a Guard of Honour of Napoleon's bear-skinned Imperial Guard, complete with drum-rolls and the Emperor perhaps making a small speech before pinning his medal. But Ryan didn't care for pageantry anyway. He didn't even care about the medals or the money. He only cared about avenging his family's murder.

Napoleon turned and stared into the fire and began dictating as General Clarke hurriedly returned to his bureau, quill pen in hand, diligently scribbling down the Emperor's words as he spoke. The noise of the quill's tip scratching the paper reverberated through the room.

'That will be all!' said Napoleon.

Ryan and McGowan saluted and went out.

The heavy boots of the two Irishmen clapped down through the mirrored halls and highly polished inlaid parquet floors of the *Palais de Tuileries*.

McGowan's voice echoed through the long corridor.

'*Jaysus!* One-hundred bloody gold Napoléons! Forget about the bleedin' Legion of Honour and its pension! I'm a bloody war-hero! What'd me auld ma think about that! And me meeting Napoleon! One-hundred bloody gold

Napoléons!' he repeated gleefully.

Heads turned and eyes squinted angrily on hearing the language of Perfidious Albion spoken in the Emperor's palace.

'*Mon Dieu!*' bystanders tutted and grumbled disapprovingly, but Ryan didn't care. He grasped McGowan by the arm. 'Just you make sure you don't blow it all on wine, women and song.'

'Can't guarantee that, Cap'n,' replied McGowan as he skipped out the main door.

'Although the song I can get anywhere, even in bloody Spain,' he laughed. 'You can keep the song, I'll just have women and the wine.'

The two friends linked arms and sang a bawdy song as they danced out of the palace in bouts of laughter.

CHAPTER 25

Ryan and McGowan travelled in style back to Spain, accompanied by two aide-de-camps in a comfortable *berline* carriage, escorted by two squadrons of light cavalry. They returned safely to Burgos without encountering any guerrillas.

Ryan was dying to see Carmen again but he had to report first to Commander Lawless.

'How did your trip go in Paris?' asked Lawless.

'Very well,' Ryan said and went on to explain how the guerrillas had attacked them, of his adventures in Paris and, of course, their meeting with Napoleon and General Clarke. He rummaged through his pockets, pulled out the two medals and polished them across his sleeve before handing them to Lawless. 'Napoleon also gave me two extra medals with two -hundred gold Napoléons and, to tell you the truth, I was more afraid of losing the gold as we travelled than of anything else. Napoleon said that he would leave it up to you who you would give the extra medals to.'

Lawless smiled. 'It's good to have you back, and, by Jove, you were sorely missed. We lost another fifty men to a guerrilla attack two days ago.' Lawless paused, adding grimly, 'there were no survivors!'

Lawless breathed in deeply and grimaced as if he was in pain. 'General John Moore's Expeditionary Force has landed in Lisbon and is advancing through the Spanish interior, but thank God we've been chosen to lead the advance on him!

Napoleon is to march to Madrid with a large army. The British have no chance!' Lawless said. 'You recall Moore, don't you Ryan?'

Ryan nodded, remembering. 'I was "out" with the boys in Wexford. We took Enniscorthy by stampeding herds of cattle through the town's defences—behind the animals came the rebel army. Wexford town fell afterwards, but we couldn't take nearby New Ross or Arklow, which led to our 15,000 men falling back to the stronghold at Vinegar Hill. Twenty thousand redcoats arrived with an artillery train. We ran out of ammunition and their artillery massacred us, but many escaped to wage a guerrilla campaign. Terrible atrocities followed.'

Lawless considered him closely. 'Well it'll be a more equal contest if and when we meet again; he won't be fighting farmers armed with pikes and hurley sticks. Although, to his credit, Moore was a humane commander and prevented the sacking of Wexford town afterwards, not like that butcher General Lake, the bloody bastard! In any case we'll give him a proper thrashing.'

'He'll meet his match alright,' added Ryan pensively while his mind again fixated on Darkford. He walked solemnly towards the window and stared outside.

'Ryan, you were miles away.'

'I was just thinking of the atrocities committed by the British.'

Ryan followed Lawless with his gaze. 'And it's not much different to what the French are doing in Spain today.'

'Yes, I know, but we are soldiers and we can only do our duty and stop atrocities when and where we can. War is cruel,' Lawless declared sagely.

'Indeed it is savage, sir.'

Ryan left the room. The words of Lawless were still

ringing in his ears. His heart was beating fiercely from the prospect of catching up with Darkford. His daughter's face flashed before his eyes. Ryan read this as a good omen. It was as if she was urging him towards Darkford, her ghost demanding revenge. He made his way towards Carmen, and knocked loudly on her door. She opened it and he fell into her arms. He spent a very pleasant evening with her before he returned to his quarters.

The bugler blared reveille the next morning and shortly afterwards the Irish battalion formed up in light marching order, ready to move out. They were to force march to Carrion to re-enforce Marshal Soult's II Corps to attack the British who were just two days away. The black uniformed Death Hussars led the march, followed by the Irish battalion and two regiments of the line. The artillery caissons and a detachment of gendarmes formed in the rear.

'En avant, Au trot!' the hussars' command came, low and guttural, as they led their horses out. Ryan waited for Hoffman. The big sergeant about-faced the battalion and blared out the command, 'En avant, Marche!' and the column stepped out again through the narrow medieval streets of Burgos, past the cathedral and the bullring, through the city's gate and across the river. Ryan looked on as the company's much loved wolf cub mascot happily scuttered alongside Kaminski's ankles like a pet dog. They passed the skeletons hanging from trees. Ryan winced at the sight of them and thought they now resembled ghastly scarecrows. Ryan wished they were taken down

The column debouched into the open countryside; the drummers beating time as they trundled through the Spanish interior. Ryan listened to the shuffling and pounding of boots, the jingle of arms and kit hitting off each other. He heard the horses in the rear grunting and making shrill skittish sounds through their nostrils as the artillery caissons rumbled on noisily. His mind drifted.

Several miles into the march, the column finally found their natural rhythm as they curled their way on the Camino, with perhaps the odd cough or odd curse from the rear. The smells of sweat and stale tobacco, poor wine and cheap cologne, garlic and flatulence wafted up Ryan's nose. He didn't mind the obnoxious smells. He even liked them. They were familiar and welcome. The march was where Ryan could let his thoughts run and no other demands were made but to keep pace with the *rat-tat-tat* of the drums. The *45ème Ligne* initially provided the entertainment, springing up with the oft-played song extolling the virtues of the onion called 'L*e Chant de l'Oignon*'. Ryan laughed; he was happy again and forgot all about Captain Darkford.

A string of lewd jokes followed several more marching songs.

Night fell.

Ryan missed his comfortable quarters now. As he marched deep into the night, twisted ropes of lit straw dimly illuminated the gloom. When marching in daylight, there was always something in the landscape for him to look at, to grab his interest and keep his mind focussed—but there was nothing to see when marching in darkness. The monotonous hum of horses' hooves, the jingle of equipment, of cavalrymen snoring in the saddle, made him drowsy, and to be exhausted and to be unable to sleep was torture.

The men were happy when they could made camp for a few hours, and they began to chop and haul firewood to light the field kitchen ovens. The familiar distant shuffling of sentries' boots, and the noises of the tethered horses, was the only noise Ryan heard. He bedded down and tried to keep himself warm, and huddled so close to the burning braziers that the flames scorched his face. He hated sleeping beside the camp fires, because one side of your body always froze on the cold ground while the heat broiled you on the other. Although he was so tired and soon drifted off to sleep.

He was woken by the thud of horses' hooves reverberating through the ground, followed shortly afterwards by hoots, cheers and the staccato rattle of musket fire.

'Wake up, damn you!' he bellowed at the others. 'Attack!'

A dozen horsemen burst screaming through the French pickets and stampeded through the camp. Ryan reached for his carbine and shot two of the guerrillas out of their saddles before the others quickly dispersed and disappeared into the cold darkness.

The guerrillas had made a brave and foolhardy run through their bivouac, for their attack had been more a brazen show of strength, than anything else. It had cost them dearly. Ryan saw several horses dashing away riderless in the chaos when the guerrillas drew off. The French suffered no casualties. Ryan walked towards a dead guerrilla who had fallen face first into one of the campfires. His hair was burning and the smell was terrible. Ryan dragged him off the fire by his ankle and, turning him over, saw the face of a boy, although it was partially charred. He mustn't have been a day older than sixteen years-old. His eyes were open and raised to the heavens as if in shock. Ryan had seen this look often and he felt sorry for him.

He questioned again what he was doing in Spain. The French called them bandits, but he considered them freedom fighters because they were fighting for their country just as he had in Ireland. He tried to sleep but he couldn't settle. He lay in front of the crackling fire and turned as a spark from the fire flew up on his greatcoat. He smothered the burning ember with his hand and he stared back into the flames before finally falling into a light sleep.

They broke camp when the sun rose. That evening, the convoy approached a village. The locals spotted them in the distance and rang the church bells as a signal. The villagers abandoned their homes, taking their valuables and all the food they could carry with them before the French arrived.

Ryan kicked in the door of one of the cabins. Inside there was an old man, sitting on a chair with a blanket wrapped over him. '¡No tenemos nada!' he shrieked nervously and repeatedly.

'Nada!' You have nothing, you say?' Ryan shouted as he grabbed the man's blanket to find a large bread tucked under his arms. Ryan tugged heavily at the bread as the old man struggled and cried loudly. His tears evoked pathos in Ryan and he paused at the doorway, tore a corner of the bread, and handed it back to the man.

Ryan heard a noise outside and went out to see what it was. The men were shouting because Vandam was coming up the lane with a goat hung around his neck. He held the animal's legs securely with his hands.

'We'll eat well tonight!' declared McGowan, rubbing his hands furiously.

Vandam began to cut the goat's hindquarters before Ryan ordered him to bring it to the field kitchen to share with the rest of the company. 'Get some deadwood and straw, Kami, and start a fire to roast the goat,' he instructed as Wolf whined at his heels, as he was also anticipating a hearty meal.

The sky turned red at sunset. They were happy as they ate. Kami tossed a goat's hoof to Wolf to gnaw on as Ryan took out his telescope. In the distance, several miles away, he saw the town of Carrion and he could make out hundreds of cotton tents pitched outside the town.

'Soult's II Corps,' he told McGowan. 'We've finally caught up with them.'

'Wonder if there are any pretty fillies left...' McGowan said, but with 16,000 Frenchmen quartered nearby, Ryan knew there would be slim pickings, if any at all. He walked down to report to Commander Lawless and then made camp for the night.

Shortly after noon the following day, a platoon of drummers beat a series of short drum rolls as the convoy entered Carrion to join up with Soult's Corps. Ryan easily picked out Marshal Jean de Dieu Soult, the 1st Duke of Dalmatia, in the company of several high-ranking officers. The staff officers and ADCs wore heavily garlanded navy uniforms and jackboots, which contrasted sharply with the appearance of Ryan's rag-tag voltigeurs. Ryan saw Marshal Soult standing next to Commander Lawless and he was pointing at him. Lawless had gone on ahead on horseback.

'Ryan!' shouted Soult, waving his enormous bicorn through the mass of high-ranking officers. '*Capitaine Ryan!*'

Ryan was surprised to hear his name being called from the circle of the high-ranking cohort.

'Take over, Lieutenant,' Ryan instructed as he stepped out of the marching ranks and walked slowly towards the general.

Soult addressed his officers as Ryan approached, '*Messieurs,* I would very much like to introduce you to one of our most gallant Irish allies, Captain James Ryan. He saved one of our Eagles at Medina de Rioseco.'

Ryan saluted, slightly embarrassed. 'Thank you,

Monsieur le Maréchal, I am always happy to serve the Emperor and France,' he said in his best French.

The other officers ringed around and looked on approvingly; keenly taking the *Légion d'Honneur* pinned to Ryan's chest.

'Are you looking forward to catching up on the British, Ryan?' asked Soult.

'Yes, *Monsieur le Maréchal,* for I fought against General Moore in Ireland. We were only armed with a few firearms and had no artillery, but we still gave the British more than a little trouble.'

The other high-ranking officers nodded. '*Bravo! Bravo!* Ryan, we need more men like you in the army,' said one of Soult's generals.

'Come drink with me,' offered Soult as he left his entourage, and the two men walked away and entered his tent. 'The Emperor has done some checks on your background with his spies in Ireland and both he and General Clarke are very impressed with you.'

Soult called his valet. 'Bring me a bottle of champagne—a *Moët!*'

Taking the bottle, Soult drew his sword, and holding the bottle out with his left-hand he knocked the neck off with the back of the blade *à la bataille,* before toasting the Emperor. 'I do not know much about your country, Ryan. Tell me about Ireland.'

'The British rule the country and the Irish people with a cruel, iron hand, but the ideals of the American and the French Revolutions, especially those of Liberty, Equality and Fraternity, have inspired many. General Humbert landed with one-hundred veterans in County Mayo on the west coast and joined up with the Irish rebel army. They defeated a British army in Castlebar but, faced with overwhelming odds, they were forced to surrender.'

'Perfide Albion!' Soult snorted.

'I narrowly escaped certain death,' continued Ryan, 'by slitting the throat of a militiaman, and donning his redcoat after Wexford town fell to Crown Forces.'

Marshal Soult drank and listened attentively.

'I spent four years on the run, much of it holed up in the Wicklow Mountains, following the Rebellion, maintaining contacts with the rebel leader Robert Emmet to organise another rising, which failed again with heart-breaking familiarity.'

The bottle of champagne was soon empty and quickly replaced by a corked bottle of *Courvoisier* cognac.

'I again evaded capture by hiding in a wooden barrel at the quayside, intending to stow away on a ship. I was nearly discovered by the authorities when they pulled the top of the barrel off, but it had a false top with a few inches of corn covering it, which helped my concealment, and I sailed from Dublin. A privateer then brought me to France, and here I am.'

As the cognac continued to loosen Ryan's tongue, he even told Soult about the despicable Darkford.

'You are indeed a *beau sabreur*.' The general paused. 'I have also heard that you have an ongoing quarrel with an officer of hussars which has led to a number of duels.'

Ryan looked into Soult's face with a mixture of surprise and contempt. 'Well, with respect, that is something I would rather not discuss openly and, yes, I do have a feud, but the cause is not mine and it is between two gentlemen, *Monsieur le Maréchal.*'

'Forgive me, Ryan. I only received a dispatch two days ago from Napoleon. He told me to speak with you. He wants me to learn more about you, as we have great plans for you.'

'I am flattered, but I'm just doing my duty here in Spain for the glory of France.'

Soult threw back his drink. 'Although I have a title, I am a simple man from a humble background. My father was a cooper and died while I was young. He'd always wanted me to become a lawyer, but he left many debts, so I joined the army as a private when I was fourteen years old and used my pay to buy back the family's seized furniture. I left the army shortly afterwards and became an apprentice baker, but I re-enlisted and climbed the ranks. I am a duke only because Napoleon rewarded me with the title of Duc of Dalmatio following the battle of Austerlitz.'

'Do you know what my men call you?' asked Ryan in English. 'The Duke of Damnation!'

Soult looked closely at Ryan for several seconds, then howled with laughter. He repeated in broken English. *'Putain!'* he cursed, 'I was aware that my nickname in the army was 'iron' due to my strict discipline, but I know now that I am no longer the Duke of Dalmatia, but the Duke of Damnation!' He pounded his arm on the table in convulsive drunken laughter. When their second quart of cognac was half drank, Soult yawned loudly and stood up to leave. 'Of all the regiments in my army corps, the Irish cause me the most trouble.'

'The enemy make the same complaint, *Monsieur le Maréchal.*'

Soult smiled. 'We will have to drink together again, Ryan, and you can teach me more English, but I will have to leave as I have a prior engagement with my mistresses, two Andalusian girls.'

Ryan remained, emptied the quart of cognac, took out his wooden whistle, and played a melancholic melody before falling into a heavy slumber. Hoffman and McGowan came looking for him. Ryan's two friends swung his arms over their shoulders and carried him to his bunk, where he slept like a lord.

CHAPTER 26

Ryan woke up with a horrible hangover, one of the worst he'd ever had. He swore blindly that he'd never touch a drop of brandy again. His head hurt like hell and he knew that a tough day lay ahead. The Irish battalion were ordered to form part of Soult's advance guard, along with two squadrons of *chasseurs á cheval*. As he made his way towards his company, he was relieved to see that Hoffman and McGowan had already prepared the men and they were soon ready to move out of Carrion.

They force marched for the best part of a day and a night before they made camp in the small village of Sahagún. They still hadn't run into any of the British rear guard, although they'd seen British patrols in the distance and knew that they weren't far away. Ryan came across a jumble of bones strewn in a vineyard. He saw that they belonged to Frenchmen, as he recognised fragments of their uniforms. Vandam grabbed hold of a local Spanish boy and, under pain of death, forced him to tell what had happened.

The boy rattled off in Spanish while Vandam translated. 'They were a French patrol, sir, captured by the guerrillas,' he says. 'A pack of dogs came and fed on the corpses. They were then dumped in a pit and wild pigs came from the forest at night and dug up the bodies and ate the rotting corpses until only bones were left.'

Ryan told Vandam to let the boy go. Vandam roughly

pushed the boy to the ground. Ryan twitched up his nose as he turned away from the ghastly sight. *There was no rest even in death,* he thought. *It was a pitiful demise for once brave and honourable men.*

It was quiet that night, save for the sentry's shuffling feet as they tried to keep themselves warm by stamping their feet and flapping their hands under their arms; they nearly plunged their hands into the fire to get some relief, it was so cold. Ryan was exhausted as he chewed down the last morsel of food beside the fire. He thought again of Darkford. He couldn't keep his eyes open and, bringing his great coat over his shoulder, keeled over and was soon fast asleep.

The enemy attacked swiftly and silently before dawn. A *vedette* heard a muffled sound in the distance, followed by the jingle of harnesses and a heavy, dull rumble of horse's hoofs. *'Alarme!'* the sentry cried as he fired a shot into the air as a warning.

Ryan sprang to his feet and began to rally the others. The enemy horsemen stormed towards the town. Wielding their heavy sabres in back-hand strokes, they easily overpowered the French sentries.

It was still dark and so it was unclear to Ryan what was happening. He thought at first the enemy horsemen, who began huzzahing and cat-calling, were the same guerrillas who had attacked them several days before. Then he heard English being spoken. He peered closer and saw from their uniforms that they were British! He wasn't the only one. A voice, alarmed, came behind him. *'Les Anglais!'* he heard a *chef d'escadron* shout. The last thing Ryan and his men had expected was that the British would attack them first.

Trumpets were sounded as a troop of hastily mounted chasseurs scrambled for their mounts. It took time for them to saddle their horses and form up to meet the attack. They had rushed to their mounts so quickly that many troopers were missing boots and gloves. It was so cold that they could now hardly hold the reins of their seasoned chargers.

From the tail of his left eye, Ryan spied enemy cavalry dashing around towards the rear; he knew that the English were trying to block off their escape from the village.

The French cavalry hurriedly formed into line. Ryan heard a pistol shot beside him and turned as a chasseur fell from his horse. He concluded that he must have been killed but he heard loud bursts of laughter from the other chasseurs exclaiming that the fool had shot his own horse. Ryan laughed, too.

When the enemy's order of battle was formed, the French cavalry unleashed a loud cheer. The British dragoons wheeled their horses into line. They clasped spurs into their horse's sides as they began to walk, and, as the spurs were pushed in harder, they trotted towards the French. Ryan heard a British officer; his voice was crisp, loud and cold. '*Blood and slaughter!*' he shouted. This was repeated down the line of British horsemen.

The chasseurs raised their carbines and loosed off a volley into the British dragoons before they clashed. The sharp clatter of metal on metal rang out as the snorting horses slipped on the frozen flagstones. A cacophony of shouts, oaths and roars chimed in with the heavy exertions of the horses as they entered the fray.

Ryan's voltigeurs spurred up to join the action, while the Irish battalion were forming themselves into line.

'Come on!' Ryan croaked loudly still in his shirt, 'Now is your chance, lads. Shoot these bastards out of their saddles!'

A thunderous massed volley followed and a dozen horsemen fell. A British dragoon officer yelled and pounded down towards Ryan with his sabre raised. Ryan kept to the horseman's left, away from his sword arm. He'd perfected this manoeuvre. He ducked as the horseman passed and smashed the stock of his musket into the rider's back. Ryan pulled him down and clubbed him on the head.

'That was an easy kill!' affirmed McGowan, impressed. He had suddenly appeared beside Ryan, taking a moment to plunder a gold watch and chain from the dead dragoon.

'Thieving bastard,' Ryan spat at him, before shouting through the din, 'Come on!'

The British dragoons massed and formed up for another charge, but the heavily outnumbered chasseurs broke ranks and fled, leaving Ryan's voltigeurs exposed.

Ryan made a speaking trumpet of his hands. 'Come back, you cowardly bastards!' he shouted.

The Irish battalion, with their mounted support gone, got scattered in the chaos and were ordered to withdraw from the town. Some of Ryan's voltigeurs, who had taken up a skirmish line in front of the Irish battalion, also tried to scurry to safety, but couldn't. They were trapped. A dozen French infantry were cut down by a series of back-handed sabre blows, while others were trampled upon. The dragoons shrieked with wild laughter as they gained ground on Ryan's men, who turned into a dark twisting lane—but it was a poor choice.

'It's no good, Cap'n, it's a dead end,' cried McGowan. '*Hells bells!*' he gasped, 'we're gonna be cut to smithereens!'

The fear in his voice was plain to all who heard.

Ryan looked up towards a wrought iron balcony. 'We're going to climb out! Now get on top of that roof! *Move!*'

Hoffman hooched Vandam up as he clutched hold of the balcony's iron bars and shimmied himself up.

'Hurry up!' yelled Ryan as Vandam climbed to the top,

followed by McGowan.

'Watch out, Captain!' warned McGowan as an enemy horseman sped up behind him. Ryan turned and kneeled to take a well-aimed shot. He could clearly make out the rider's features—a furious look of determination was drilled on his face. His eyes were wild. *'Victory!' Victory!'* he screamed. Streams of steam panted out through his horse's nostrils.

The fourth horseman of the apocalypse! Ryan said to himself as he raised his carbine, He pulled the trigger and the flint fell. *Bang!*

The shot hit the horse and it skidded on its haunches, throwing its rider and causing him to crash headlong onto the ground. Ryan pounded the butt of his carbine into the horseman's head, splattering Ryan's white shirt with slick, warm blood.

Ryan threw his musket up to the others in the balcony.

'Take my hands, Cap'n,' McGowan said, and he and Vandam hauled Ryan up as he scrambled over the balcony.

'Now we'll repay them! This'll be like shooting fish in a barrel.'

They sent several well-aimed shots down onto the dragoons, caught in the dead end. The remaining troopers realising they were caught exposed, and hearing a fresh fracas behind them, reigned in their horses and galloped away.

Ryan was worried. 'We're cut off from our own lines and cannot linger here too long,' he said.

Through the murky moonlight, he took out his telescope and saw the dark silhouettes of the French light cavalry, followed by the Irish battalion, as they disappeared over the horizon. He knew that they were heading back to the safety of Soult's main army who were bivouacked at Carrion, ten miles away.

Ryan sighed deeply.

'Our only hope is making our way out of this town,' Ryan said, pointing towards the fleeing chasseurs. 'It'll be daylight in a couple of hours and we need to make it back to Soult. The whole place will be swarming with British patrols and we won't stand a chance.'

'Sure, we'll never make it back travelling in the dark, will we, sir?' McGowan asked.

Ryan looked around. 'We'll use the moon as our guide.'

Hoffman nodded agreement.

The four men carefully hunched over the red rooftops, eased themselves down on the far side of the town's walls and disappeared into the dank darkness.

CHAPTER 27

A luminous blue moon gleamed through shrouded veils of cloud. The temperature dipped as Ryan and the others trundled over hedgerows, through wheat fields and across small streams. A white mist descended and clung to the fields, so thick that the four men could hardly see the man in front. Only Vandam wore his tunic—with the rush to leave their billets, Ryan, McGowan and Hoffman were dressed only in trousers and light cotton shirts.

'Captain!' called McGowan. 'You remember seeing that monastery when we arrived?'

'Yes, I'd forgotten about that—it's worth the risk. We may not survive the night out here in this cold and, besides, we'll never make it back to Soult in this weather. Do you still remember where it is, McGowan?'

'Not in this fog, but it was somewhere to the right of a small forest.'

The four men slogged along through the marshy fields. Luckily, the ubiquitous fog lifted and they could miraculously make out the monastery's bell tower nestled in a pine forest, a short distance way.

Vandam breathed a sigh of relief. 'Well, there it is!'

The wind carried the noise of horses' hooves and harnesses; they dropped behind a small rise to let them pass.

'British cavalry! Must be a reconnaissance patrol!' whispered Ryan. 'It won't be long before Moore's main force will be passing. We must be quick, for we'll soon be left exposed in the dawn.'

A short time later they approached the monastery. Ryan pounded heavily on the ancient heavy oak door. An elderly Benedictine nun, dressed in a black habit and veil with an enormous silver cross hanging around her neck peered out suspiciously through the wrought iron grilled peephole.

Ryan whispered to Vandam, 'Now explain that we're British, not the hated French!'

'*Qué deseais*? The nun asked, nervously—'What do you want?'

She held up a candle, which battered in the cold night air. The nuns had heard the commotion of the attack at Sahagún, several miles away.

Vandam lied, saying that they were Irishmen in the British army who were running from the French and had lost contact with their regiment, and that they just needed quarters until the morning. The four men were shivering violently as the abbess considered whether she'd let them in or not, before reluctantly pulling the three iron locks open.

'She's buying our story,' whispered Vandam as their heavy boots reverberated loudly on the flagstone floors.

'Come, I will give you something to eat,' the old nun said solemnly, as she led them through a long corridor to an enormous kitchen where several elderly nuns appeared.

McGowan whispered, 'I'm sure they're hiding the prettier, younger nuns away somewhere for their own safety.'

They sat down as a pitcher of warm milk was poured into earthenware bowls and bread was placed before them. They greedily wolfed it all down.

McGowan smiled happily as he patted his stomach with satisfaction.

The old abbess lighted the way with her candle as she led them to the convent's chapel. Two other nuns brought clothing and bed linen as the men prepared to lie down on the chapel's benches. Ryan raised the black habits up to eye level and stared at the white starched veils with surprise.

'I'm sorry, but we have nothing else,' the nun told them softly as she lit an oil lamp for them. 'You understand that we, of course, would have no men's clothing here,' she added solemnly before she left the chapel.

The voltigeurs laughed loudly at their sudden change of fortune, their laughter reverberating loudly through the vast emptiness of the chapel's high ceilings.

'We're on the pig's back now, lads!' McGowan said as he lay snuggled up under his blanket. 'I wonder what nuns wear under their habits,' he said cheerfully. 'Sure, maybe they're naked underneath.'

'I know,' answered Ryan with a wistful frown. 'The French raped and butchered many nuns in Madrid when the Madrileños rose up and, no, McGowan, they don't go naked but wear modest cotton undergarments!'

'Well, you just blew my dream as I was very much looking forward to those thoughts before heading off to sleep.'

Vandam smirked as he prepared his bedding. The Belgian sat down on his bed and took out a crucifix from the inside of his shako. He kissed it and laughed sinisterly.

Ryan glared at him disdainfully as he prepared his own bedding. 'What are ye laughing about, Vandam?' He stared angrily at the crucifix in Vandam's hand. 'And where did you get that, ye scoundrel?'

Just then, the door squeaked closed and the heavy muffled snick of metal grating into the socket echoed as a key turned in the lock, followed by the sound of soft receding footsteps.

'Hold on! We're not out of the woods yet,' Ryan affirmed.

McGowan ran to the door and tried to open it but it was locked from the other side. He began to pound it with his fists. *'Hells bells!'* he uttered nervously.

Ryan shook his head and scrunched his pillow hard as he lay down. 'Leave it, McGowan, either mother superior didn't believe our story and will keep us here until a British reconnaissance patrol passes or, hopefully, she'll let us out in the morning. In any case, our fate is in her hands, so try and get some sleep.'

When Ryan woke the next morning, he recoiled hysterically as McGowan looked ridiculous wearing a nun's habit and veil. His bearded face peeked out through the white veil as he smiled stupidly through a mouthful of discoloured teeth.

Even Hoffman smiled.

'Laugh all ye want, lads. Sure, I'm warm as toast in here,' he retorted happily.

'I'll wear the black habit, as I've nothing else to wear, but damn it if I'll wear the veil,' added Ryan.

A key turned in the lock and the abbess entered the chapel. She looked at McGowan with a severe expression on her face. Her arms were folded solemnly in her habit's sleeves. McGowan whisked off his veil and excused himself to the abbess.

'I'm sorry, as I locked you in for our own safety. I could not take the risk that you would come looking for and violate some of our younger daughters of Christ.'

She led them to the door and handed them some food wrapped in cotton. 'I knew very well by your friend's tunic that you were not British, but *French!*' she said.

'We're Irishmen,' affirmed Ryan.

The abbess smiled and pointed. 'If you follow the little stream on the right this will bring you to Carrion. The road has been teaming with passing soldiers all night.'

The men thanked the old abbess and were on their way.

The intrepid four were careful to keep ahead of the British reconnaissance patrols, and waited for the main column of British troops to pass. Ryan knew that if they were captured in the green uniform of the Irish Legion they'd be hanged. McGowan's tattoos identified him as a deserter as he'd served with the British fleet.

'You're a dead man, McGowan, if they get you,' sniggered Vandam as he grasped an invisible rope and tilted his head sideways with his tongue protruding in a hanging gesture.

'Arah, don't be worrying,' replied McGowan. 'Bastards won't get me! And if they do, sure, I'll tell them how many of their gallant Spanish allies you butchered, including that shepherd boy, and sure enough you'll dance on the end of a rope with me!' McGowan laughed giddily.

Vandam momentarily froze and swallowed hard.

Ryan listened as he had a price on his head, and he would share a similar fate, with perhaps a show trial in London, followed by a public hanging.

Two hours passed before the British column had trundled by. Ryan surveyed the bopping knapsacks and heads of lines of red-coated infantry and could easily make out their white cross belts and grey trousers as they marched along. Between the red jackets, there were green-uniformed riflemen, with blue-cloaked cavalry in the rear. The column must have been two miles long. He wondered if Darkford was among them. Ryan adjusted his telescope's focus and nervously zoned in on the horsemen but he couldn't get a proper look at them.

He turned his telescope towards the distinctive British general in front. Sir John Moore looked tall and dignified in his grey cloak and braided bicorn and although he had aged since Ryan had fought him back in '98, he still recognised Moore with his long nose and penetrating eyes.

The noise of horses' hooves pounding the ground in a gallop came racing from his left. Ryan jolted his telescope and trained it towards a lone rider who brought his horse to a crashing halt at the top of the British column. He looked like a guerrilla as he was dressed in a homespun brown jacket and wore a wide, broad-brimmed hat; a rifle was sheathed in a leather scabbard on his horse's saddle. He heard the order given for the column to halt and watched as the rider dismounted. The bearded man reached into his saddle bag and handed the British general what looked like a letter. Sir John put on his spectacles and began to read. A number of staff officers walked their horses up to the British commander and a conversation followed. Ryan then heard orders repeated down the British lines of infantry to turn about, and shortly afterwards the cavalry in the vanguard reined their horses sideways and doubled-back.

'Jaysus, I don't believe it—they're turning 'round,' said Ryan as he handed the telescope to Hoffman.

'Does that really mean they're retreating?' Hoffman asked incredulously.

'Perhaps Moore knows the Emperor's on his tail! Whoever would have thought it?' said Ryan.

'They may have the best navy in the world, but, by God, the French have the best field army,' added McGowan, vigorously wringing his hands.

'Yes, indeed,' said Ryan as he snapped his telescope shut. 'They've met their match against Boney. We gave Moore a run for his money when the boys were "out", but he's no longer facing pikemen and rusty old muskets now. We need to get word to Soult that the British are trying to make a run for it.'

He turned to McGowan and broke out in muffled laughter. 'Ye big eejit! Sure, look at the cut of ye, McGowan!' He looked on as McGowan's dirty and tawny-gold bearded face presented a ridiculous picture through the nun's white veil.

'Sure, didn't me poor old mother, God have mercy on her,'—McGowan crossed himself—'always want me to join the religious orders.'

'I'm tired listening to ye!' Ryan said disdainfully. 'Ye dirty fool!'

Even the sullen Vandam joined in on the fun. 'And she'd be right proud of you now,' he added, and the men laughed as they made their way to get word to Soult.

Two hours later they arrived safely back at the French camp.

'Qui vive?'—'Who goes there?' the sentries challenged with levelled muskets before they recognised McGowan dressed as a bearded and toothless Benedictine nun. They laughed loudly as they lowered their weapons to let the men through.

Ryan was happy that he and Vandam had sensibly tossed their black habits aside before approaching the camp, but McGowan had refused to discard his robes for sheer devilment. 'But I don't want to, for its warm and rather comfy,' he had protested, scratching his itchy beard.

Ryan, in the end, had given in and told him he could do as he liked.

McGowan walked sedately, his arms folded in his habit's wide sleeves and his head bowed as if in prayer. When the garrison came to see what the commotion was, they, too, wailed in laughter and became hysterical when McGowan raised his hand to make the sign of the cross and blessed them as he passed. The French were on high alert, preparing for a British attack, and McGowan's antics lifted the tension.

'Just ignore him, lads! He's just looking for attention!' Ryan shouted. 'You're only encouraging the fool!' he cried as he kicked McGowan with the side of his foot on his behind. 'Get up there!' he snarled as he made his way towards French headquarters.

'Bloody hell, there's Kaminski and Wolf!' McGowan exclaimed as Wolf walked up to them and sniffed McGowan's extended open hand.

Kaminski looked shocked to see them. 'We gave you up for dead, sir!'

'How the hell did you get here?' Ryan wanted to know.

'Wolf bolted from me back in Sahagún when the British cavalry attacked and I had to follow him. I just made it back today,' Kaminski explained. 'The poor pup was terrified from the noise of the muskets. I chased after him and lost contact with the battalion. I laid low in the town until the coast was clear before making my way here.'

'Hmm!' Ryan grunted unconvinced. 'You weren't skulking, Kaminski?'

'No, sir! Upon my honour,' he replied plaintively.

'You shouldn't have left the battalion when we were engaging the enemy.'

'Couldn't help it, sir—had to get Wolf back.'

'I'll speak to you about this later, Kaminski,' Ryan said as he hunched down.

The young wolf sniffed Ryan's blood-stained shirt, then snuggled up to him and suddenly he felt a warm wet tongue lick his face. 'Yuck!' spat Ryan, wiping his face with the back of his hand.

'Have you not heard, sir?' asked Kaminski

'Heard what?'

Kaminski searched Ryan's face.

'The Irish battalion's gone, sir! They pulled out yesterday. They were ordered back to Burgos with the wounded.'

'Blast it!' Ryan cursed, again and again, as he walked away towards Marshal Soult's headquarters.

The French general's headquarters was a hive of activity as staff officers stood dictating reports and scoured over numerous maps sprawled out over campaign desks. Soult removed his spectacles from his nose and peered up at Ryan, who was still dressed in his bloodied shirt and green breeches.

Ryan saluted. 'Captain Ryan, Voltigeur Company, 2nd Irish battalion, *Monsieur le Maréchal.*'

'Ah, Ryan! Stand at ease!'

'I have come to report that General Sir John Moore's army has turned back, ten leagues beyond Sahagún.'

Soult froze as a hushed silence reverberated through the tent. All eyes turned towards the Irishman.

Ryan looked around. 'Ah-hmm,' he began, coughing nervously into his hand and clearing his throat. 'I escaped from Sahagún after our advance guard were overrun by British light cavalry. We followed the British on the road to Carrion before they halted and turned around.'

'Turned around?' Soult asked with astonishment.

'Yes, sir! I was surprised myself. Moore appears to be retreating without a fight.'

'*Sacre Coeur!*' exclaimed Soult as he hurriedly consulted a map. 'Turning back? Turning back?' he repeated. 'He must have gotten word that our glorious Emperor has marched out from Madrid and is catching up with him. If the British are falling back then we've no time to lose. There's still time for us to cut off his retreat.'

He planted his hand heavily on Ryan's shoulder. '*Chapeau!*'—'Well done!' Turning to his staff officers, he said, '*Messieurs*, you have just heard that the British are in full flight without as much as a fight. Give your orders! We're moving out immediately.'

He faced Ryan. 'Put a coat on. We don't want you catching your death. Your information may spell the demise of the British army in the Peninsula and may win the war in Spain!'

Within hours, the respective commanders had received their hastily drawn up *feuilles de route*. A French advance guard of 3,000 light troops, followed shortly by Soult's army corps, made their way on the ancient road of the Camino to catch up with Moore. It was a slow and cumbersome journey, for the snowstorms and blizzards had turned the Camino de Santiago into a muddy quagmire.

CHAPTER 28

The British had indeed received messages from their Spanish allies saying that Napoleon was moving up from Madrid at the head of a large army to join up with Soult. Sir John Moore knew that his only escape was to march his British army back two-hundred and fifty miles to the Spanish coast where a fleet was to evacuate his army to England. His retreat in the depths of winter through a poor and barren country was not going to be an easy one.

As the British army marched back to Sahagún, Rifleman Tom O'Hara could hear the heavy snick of metal on metal, as the mens' equipment hit off each other and it chimed in with a chorus of angry murmurings. The men weren't happy at retreating. Their cavalry had just bested Soult's light troops in a major rear-guard action and now they were pulling back!

They had marched 500 miles from Lisbon and had built themselves up for a fight. They had pulled out of Sahagún hours earlier to make battle with the French, without the women, children and their regimental baggage, only to return there exhausted without a fight the next day.

They continued their retreat. It rained heavily and this only added to the dark gloom and resentment.

As the days passed, the officers found the men difficult to manage on the forced march and discipline soon broke down. It didn't help, either, that the men weren't told the reason they were retreating. The British soldiers went on the rampage. The officers were powerless to stop them. Although the Spanish welcomed the British troops as allies in ousting the French, the local people, being Catholics, treated the heretics with suspicion for the Protestant British were from the wrong faith.

In turn, the anti-papists British began to detest the priest-ridden country, full of prowling wild wolves and violent bandits, and indeed considered themselves, by all accounts, to be in a hostile country. They began to detest Spain.

The redcoats passed through a village and ravaged it in search of loot and wine. The men scrounged for any swag they could get hold of and brawled amongst themselves, harassing and beating up the local villagers. The local peasants looked on and even shouted insolently, '¡Viva Francia! Vivan los franceses!'—'Long live France! Long live the French!' When the British finally passed through, the Spanish rang the church bells in gratitude to God the Almighty that such heathen heretics were removed from their midst.

The British trudged onwards.

Rifleman O'Hara formed part of the Reserve Division, under the command of General Paget. They were tasked with covering the rear of Moore's retreating army. He knew that the French were gaining ground as the sharp ring of musket fire echoing loudly in the wind was getting closer.

A red-faced lieutenant of dragoons in a sky-blue tunic galloped up and brought his horse to a skidding halt. He saluted General Sir Edward Paget, and the lieutenant appeared visibly nervous. 'Sir, the French are trying to cross the river. They are engaging our pickets, who are retiring!' he announced breathlessly.

'Take your time, Lieutenant,' said Paget coolly. 'You

mean to say that our pickets are retiring?'

'Yes, sir, I'm afraid so, sir.'

'Well, don't be bloody afraid, Lieutenant,' Paget replied angrily, 'and, my God, return to your fighting pickets and ensure they do their duty, sir, or heads will roll...'

The abashed lieutenant saluted, jabbed spurs into his bay mare and sped away.

The French *were* coming. The British needed to blow the bridge at Castro Gonzalo over the River Elsa before the French could cross it. Within hours, the French light cavalry stood on the opposite river bank and keenly watched the enemy's rear guard. Their horses nickered and neighed loudly through their nostrils, their undocked tails swishing in irritation, hooves scratching the frozen earth as they waited for the order to charge.

General Black Bob Craufurd, commander of the Light Brigade, was drenched to the skin and wrapped his light cloak tightly around himself as he dismounted from his dappled charger, his bicorn hat and cloak providing scant protection from the pouring rain. He passed a metal canteen of rum to O'Hara.

'Thank you kindly, your honour,' said O'Hara, touching his peak.

Black Bob snorted loudly. 'Where are you from, Rifleman?'

'Tipperary—there are many Irishmen serving in the 95th Rifles, sir.'

Black Bob nodded thoughtfully. 'There isn't much time! When you hear the order, Rifleman, cross the bridge quickly, and mind what you are about and no slacking! The Royal Engineers have planted explosive charges to blow the two-arched bridge to kingdom come.' Black Bob surveyed the mined bridge. He took out some paper and a pencil from his saddle and began to sketch it. He tilted his head towards O'Hara. 'It's a shame to blow it. It's a masterpiece of ancient bridge building, solidly built by the Romans with cut-stone and concrete under Emperor Augustus's reign.' He went on as he drew. 'Two thousand years ago, in their quest to subdue Hispania, the bronze-armoured and red-caped Roman centurions marched over it in their open hobnailed *caligae*. It's a damn pity, Rifleman, by Jove, but the bridge has to go.'

Moments later, three squadrons of French light cavalry charged the British picket post guarding the bridge, but crippling rifle fire from O'Hara's men who sallied forth to meet them, repelled their attack and they drew off.

Black Bob watched intensely as French infantry now prepared to rush across the bridge.

'Fall back!' a Rifles' officer bellowed.

Rifleman Tom O'Hara was the last to run across while under enfilade fire as a company of French light infantry dashed across.

'Blow up the bloody bridge!' O'Hara heard Black Bob shout. His ears buzzed in panic as he glimpsed from the corner of his eye an engineering officer promptly light the fuse. The fuse sparkled furiously as O'Hara ran faster—he had scarcely run this fast in his life.

A loud boom rumbled as barrels of gunpowder sent both arches high into the air and into the swollen river, pulverising at least thirty French infantrymen amid wild cheering and hooting from the British lines. O'Hara was thrown twenty feet in the air by the blast's impact and fell flat on his face. Stones and dirt rained down on him. He was blown out of his boots, covered in dirt, and his ears rang like hell, but he hobbled away unhurt and bent down to retrieve his badly worn boots.

Black Bob passed O'Hara, who was still dazed from the blast, with his company of riflemen. 'Keep on moving! Spanish guerrillas will hold the line from the opposite river bank and prevent the French infantry fording the river. We may only have a couple of hours.'

This action by the guerrillas enabled the British rear guard to escape, as it pulled back to the nearby town of Benavente. Destroying the bridge had won the British time.

Later that night, the French led a sortie across the river and the guerrillas fell back and dispersed into the mountains.

CHAPTER 29

A company of French engineers spent two days repairing the damaged bridge. The *pontonniers* and sappers hurriedly rebuilt it using spikes, anchors, bull hooks and beams. Within hours all the hammering had ceased and heavy wooden planks were shot across it. The distinct crack of muskets, and the sharp snap of rifles echoing in the distance broke the fragile silence. First to cross the rickety pontoon bridge were the *chasseurs á cheval,* walking their horses across, followed by the light infantry.

Ryan saw a thick column of black smoke rising a few miles away at Benavente. 'The British!' he muttered to Hoffman in a low tone. 'We've caught up with them.'

The old sergeant nodded. 'We have them on the run, Captain!'

Ryan mopped the sweat off his brow with his forearm. 'We'll soon see what their rear guard is made of.'

'There are rumours that the Emperor is here!' said the old sergeant. 'He came up with a large cavalry escort, as he was eager to face the British.'

They marched for an hour when the French light troops approached the town of Benavente, and faced the British rear guard.

The rumours were true. As Ryan and the other voltigeurs jogged up to form a skirmish line, he saw General Charles Lefebvre-Desnouettes's three chasseur squadrons of the

Imperial Guard trot up from the rear, followed by a detachment of Mameluke cavalry.

'Have your men form up,' Ryan head General Lefebvre-Desnouettes instruct his officers. 'I want to attack before darkness. Have them ready, for today will be a day for glory!' The French general turned towards his men to rally them and raised his plumed bicorn high. *'Vive l'Empereur!'* he shouted. *'En avant! L'Empereur regarde!'*—'The Emperor is watching!'

The chasseurs repeated the salute as they cautiously advanced; the horses began to walk and broke into a trot towards the line of British cavalry. They formed into line and halted.

Ryan watched as the British cavalry waited. The French cavalry ploughed a volley from their carbines into the British horsemen. Several men slumped out of their saddles and lay wincing in agony on the ground.

Ryan watched eagerly as a Frenchman sporting an enormous moustache, long black curls and sideburns, raced halfway between the opposing horsemen and reared his horse up. 'Gentlemen,' he began in good English as he raised his curved sabre high above his head, 'are there any men brave enough to come and face me alone?'

A British dragoon answered the challenge, unsheathing his sabre and digging in his spurs. His horse reared as he raced towards his opponent. The Frenchman parried the dragoon's first blow, but another one cut the Frenchman's shoulder. But he managed to pull the dragoon off his horse and lunged at him in a backward swipe. The dragoon instinctively raised his arm for protection and the heavy swipe sliced his lower arm off. The Englishman's arm spurted a fountain of bright red blood. The chasseur followed through with a lunge to the dragoon's neck and the

Englishman thumped to the ground. His beautiful chestnut Arab lowered her head compassionately to the dying dragoon.

The French cavalry raised their muskets and unleashed a loud chorus of whoops and cheers. The British were incensed at the loss of the fallen rider, for the young cornet was a popular officer and a favourite of the men.

A dragoon officer unsheathed his sabre. 'No quarter, lads! *Charge!*' The British dragoons jabbed spurs in and galloped towards the French cavalry. The chasseurs closed ranks and took potshots at the dragoons.

General Lefebvre's chasseurs managed to push the British back before the British counter-attacked. Ryan stopped to reload his musket as the dragoons galloped around the outskirts of Benavente and, concealed from the enemy's view, fell heavily on the French left flank.

The heavy clank of crashing steel accompanied the desperate hand-to-hand fight that ensued as arms were hacked off and well-delivered *coups de sabre* divided heads down to chins. A chasseur fell backwards as a sabre cleaved his shoulder—the heavy blow had travelled past his rib cage. Carbines and pistols also took their toll in the melee. The troopers' sword arms were getting tired now; some were wounded and drenched with blood, but the adrenalin surging through the blood gave them enormous strength.

Ryan saw a number of riflemen run up. 'Pull back!' he implored. A good run was better than a bad stand, he reckoned, as he pushed his shako back and shouted again, motioning his men to withdraw.

Trumpeters sounded the recall as the French cavalry recoiled, helter skelter, back towards the River Elsa. They galloped back towards the rickety pontoon bridge but couldn't cross it in time and waded through the raging current. A French horse ran dragging its dead rider behind it. The young chasseur's foot was caught in his stirrup, and his head repeatedly thumped hard on the ground behind the terrified horse, before it submerged into the River Elsa.

A British dragoon bounded down towards Ryan through the water. Ryan saw he'd a large scar on his right cheek, and as he stood up high on his stirrups, he was waving his sword around his head to gain momentum for a fatal blow. Ryan kept himself on the horseman's left, away from his sword arm. He ducked and wielded his carbine's stock into the rider's midriff. The dragoon leaned forward with a groan; Ryan lunged and stabbed him with his sword and ran, relieved when he made it back to the safety of the opposite riverbank.

General Lefebvre-Desnouettes was hurriedly led away, escorted by two trumpeters of the Imperial Guard, but he was being pursued by the British horsemen. The French general's escort were cut down, and when his horse reared he fell into the water. A dragoon saw his chance, splashed through the mud-coloured river after the general, and took him captive.

Meanwhile, Ryan limped back across the bridge and saw the French general being captured but he could do nothing to help because more enemy horsemen had waded up to him. Lefebvre-Desnouettes threw his own sword away as a token of surrender. *'Je me rends!'* Ryan heard the general say as he raised his hands. Ryan snapped open his telescope and watched how the dragoon seized the general's pistol, sash and leather *sabretouche* pouch emblazoned with a golden Eagle, as trophies. He looked up to the ridge and saw the distinctive silhouette of Napoleon, who reined his horse away in disgust.

The French remained in position on the opposite river

bank, as they were not strong enough to attack. The British dragoons held their ground and enabled their Reserve Division to fall back.

The French had lost several dozen men in the action; the British rearguard was not to be underestimated, Ryan realised. The French army rested and moved out at dawn. The dead were left unburied, and the wounded were left behind, to be picked up by Soult's main army when it passed through.

CHAPTER 30

Over the next two weeks the French continued to pursue the retreating British in two forced marches, bivouacking under light cotton tents, while being subjected to guerrilla attack. As the French made their way across the flatlands, there was no escape from the biting elements when the snow turned to sleet, followed by hailstorms the size of hens' eggs. They marched over the goat trails and through icy streams and the heavy rain reduced the track to mud. They pushed themselves and their horses to the limits. The French had always lived off the land, and had scrounged, bought or stolen whatever they needed. However, the Spanish had removed their livestock, had let their crops rot in the ground and had hidden their food stores or had fled with them into the mountains. The British, who'd marched through before them, had taken whatever else had remained. The French were hungry and low on rations, and could only issue a half ration of dried biscuit to their men.

As Ryan passed through a village, McGowan caught a peasant hiding in one of the hovels. 'God damn yer soul to hell, tell me where ye have 'idden it!' bawled McGowan as he held the peasant by the throat against the wall. The man could scarcely breathe, let alone understand Hiberno-English.

The peasant, released from McGowan's grip, fell down, and coughed and sputtered his way towards the corner of a wall. He removed a stone brick and revealed, hidden in a cavity, several goat bladders of wine and salted fish.

'*Bloody hell!*' McGowan's voice exclaimed with delight, but his delight was short-lived as the chasseurs fought him over the bounty and in the fray most of the wine spilled onto the flagstone floor.

The French horses, caked in dried mud, and reduced to eating straw, as they had long run out of oats, were also hungry. The horses' stomachs were bloated with gas. The chasseurs began to recognise the telltale signs of exhaustion early on. Some horses foundered and stomped the ground looking for a place to lie down or rolled on their sides refusing to move. Their nostrils flared pink as they sweated heavily and lowered their heads or stood with their front legs stretched out, indicating they wanted to lie down.

A chasseur was brought to tears before he shot his lame horse, and he then turned the pistol on himself. Ryan heard the commotion and walked up to see what was happening. The handsome four-year old dark brown gelding, who Ryan reckoned was over fourteen-hands high, lay wounded on the ground, unable to raise himself up. His loss was another man's gain. A hungry chasseur bent over him with a small knife and began hacking through his neck. The horse groaned as the chasseur made another clumsy incision. The horse's legs scrambled wildly for footing and it started flailing as it thrashed its head, trying to escape. The chasseur kept hacking into the tendon but he was nowhere near the jugular vein. The animal's nose bled and it vomited as the severed main artery drenched the chasseur in warm blood. The horse finally dropped its head. The chasseur threw the gelding's heart into a cauldron, while a metal breastplate was used to boil the horse's blood into what they euphemistically called soup.

'I swear,' the swarthy chasseur from the slums of Vieux Marseille declared after chopping the horse's liver into a pot, 'this was the best meal I've ever tasted.' He belched loudly after eagerly lapping up the lukewarm, bloodied gunge.

The British had abandoned the heavy wagons of the Royal Artillery, they had ploughed deep furrows into the road, and had become bogged down in the mud. Ryan was dumbfounded at the loot—if that is the word for it—taken by the redcoats. Items squabbled and killed over days before, Ryan supposed, now lay discarded. He came across brass saucepans, old metal spoons and forks, gilt crucifixes, chalices, silver plate, and broken candlesticks, in short, anything that could fit into a British infantryman's knapsack. When the items became too heavy and cumbersome to carry they were simply tossed aside.

Ryan stood on a ridge, took out his telescope, and saw smoke rising above a town in the distance. A scout party cantered back to Ryan. The chasseurs brought news that there were still British soldiers in the town but they were out of control and most, if not all, of them were drunk. Their Reserve Division had abandoned them, left them for dead, and continued their march.

As Ryan pulled into the outskirts of the town, he saw how the redcoats had ransacked a castle. He learned later that the castle's owner was a prominent Spanish aristocrat and Grandee of Spain. The rabble had bayoneted all who stood in their way, fired wildly at windows, kicked down doors, and plundered. They had even lifted the castle's beautiful inlay parquet floor with their bayonets, and thrown it into the burning pyres, including elaborate gilt furniture and panelling. Shutters and doors were ripped off, oil paintings and hangings were slashed, priceless seventeenth-century

Flemish wall tapestries were torn down and used for blankets before they, too, were tossed into the flames. Here and there, a dozen or so redcoats lay drunk. Ryan ensured they were rounded up before the chasseurs came and put them to the sword.

Ryan passed a monastery. The sacristy, tabernacles and tombs had been smashed in the search for gold. The drink-fuelled mob had tossed the mummified bodies of monks, some dating from the Middle Ages, out of their coffins in the monastery catacombs and destroyed them. Bookcases were stripped of medieval illuminated manuscripts of the saints. Rare works of philosophy and science, including books by the Greek historian Herodotus and the Roman poet Virgil, were tossed into the flames.

As the French entered the town's plaza, the drunken redcoats were oblivious to their arrival. Ryan looked around, aghast. A nun sat crying in the town plaza in front of jeering crowds of drunken soldiers. Ryan thought that she'd been raped.

Ryan stood and watched as the redcoats took out their muskets and fired wildly at a stash of wine, expecting to knock the necks off the bottles, but instead the glass shattered, sending pools of wine cascading into the street. The soldiers scrabbled on all fours on the cobblestones, lapping the wine up like water as the terrified Spanish peasantry looked. The redcoats then turned their attention to a young girl they'd found hiding under a bed. She screamed loudly as a burly private carried her into the plaza and several men approached as if in a trance, licking their lips salaciously.

Ryan fired his pistol in the air and the drunken mob turned in the direction of the noise, to stand face to face with the French. The British mob fired at them, drunkenly and blindly. The French returned fire, and in less than a minute all the redcoats lay dead.

The French moved on.

'Well, I know what the Emperor's tactics are,' McGowan said as he shivered and pulled his collar up to his cheeks. 'He's going to freeze our bloody balls off and walk us to our deaths. If I knew I'd be walkin' the distance from Dublin to Galway in the middle o' winter, I'd have deserted long ago! The faster Moore marches, the faster we're forced to pursue him. This doesn't bode well, Cap'n.'

'Don't you worry about that, McGowan,' cut in Hoffman, 'for nobody can march like the *Grande Armée*. We should catch up with Moore in a day or two.'

Ryan threw a glance at Hoffman and continued walking in silence.

'Napoleon is returning to Paris!' Hoffman announced. 'An old comrade in the Imperial Guard told me yesterday. He overheard this when he was posted sentinel to the Emperor's headquarters. They say Napoleon is leaving the pursuit of the British to Marshal Soult as he has more pressing matters to attend to, namely the war with the Austrians.'

'Yes, a more important war, no doubt,' sneered Ryan grimly. 'That's why he's removing his fittest troops from the Peninsula and bringing them to fight east.'

'Yes, including his beloved heavies,' added Hoffman.

'The heavies?' queried McGowan.

'The heavies are the nickname for our armoured cuirassiers,' explained Ryan.

'I can't wait to get a crack at old Moore,' McGowan said a little later.

'I just wonder when we can finally join up with the Irish battalion,' said Hoffman.

Ryan hoped he and the others wouldn't be ordered back

to Burgos to rejoin the Irish battalion, as then he wouldn't be able to catch up with Darkford.

They stopped to make camp for the night.

The next morning, buglers flatly sounded reveille and the great sleeping mass of humanity huddling around the dying campfire embers slowly came to life. Two men who had been sleeping around Ryan's brazier had died of hypothermia during the night. It was so cold that Ryan's hair froze to the cold ground and he tugged at it until it finally gave way.

He prepared to face the day and knew he'd be tired and hungry. A long hard march in atrocious weather still lay ahead.

Arriving in a small Galician mountain village, the poverty there struck Ryan hard as it reminded him of home. The local peasants with dirty faces, dressed in strange gypsy clothing, glared out at him from the doorways of their windowless hovels. Some of them made the sign of the cross as the army passed. One deranged old woman with her rosary beads entwined around her hands chanted in Spanish, pointing her long, gnarled finger at them.

'I've no idea what the hell she's saying,' said Ryan, 'but she sure as hell isn't wishing us God speed.'

'Some tinker's curse more like,' replied McGowan as he spat heavily at her feet.

Ryan was relieved when he saw that the road to Astorga was well sanded, as it was easier to march on. He passed a number of Spanish refugees who were caught on the open road; they were mostly elderly and children. Fear was etched on their faces. They carried their few miserable possessions on their backs or pulled small hand-carts behind them, clogging up the road. Ryan pitied them. Those who were ill with typhus hid and huddled for comfort in dirty hovels and muttered oaths and curses at the French as they passed.

After three days of sleet, there was a welcome break in the weather.

They halted again.

'There you go, Cap'n,' McGowan said with his mouth full, as he handed Ryan a metal beaker.

'Hot coffee is welcome, but what I wouldn't do for a strong quart of tea, like back home!' Ryan cupped his hands and blew heavily on his fingers to generate warmth.

'I second that, sir,' McGowan said. 'I searched a clodhopper two days ago.'

'A clodhopper?'

'We call redcoats clodhoppers. They carry loose tea leaves in their pockets, but I didn't come away empty handed,' McGowan explained with a toothless grin, 'for I found two Spanish silver dollars, together with a small locket from an officer who I copped with a bullet in the head.'

He fumbled in his inside pockets. 'Aha, here it is! I thought I lost the bloomin' thing,' He handed it to Ryan. 'Dead officers have richer pickings!'

Ryan opened the finely made silver clasp. Two enamel portrait engravings were inside.

'Some beauty, sir, isn't she!'

There was a miniature of a young woman, with fair hair piled up and curls at her temples. She peered out at him with a pair of blue eyes and ruby lips. She was wearing a white dress and a gold tiara. The other miniature was of two young girls, probably five or six years old, Ryan thought, pretty like their mother. He clasped the locket shut and flipping it over in his hand, read the inscription on the back: *To dear Charles, with all my love, Fanny.*

Ryan's heart sank as he anticipated the grief the girls would suffer knowing their father would never return. He cursed the war and his pity turned to righteous anger when he thought about his own family.

He raised his head and tossed the silver locket back to McGowan, who kissed it and put it back in his pocket. 'I have bad news for you, Cap'n!' he said. 'That bastard Carpentier you duelled with rode in with his troop from Burgos and joined our column during the night.'

Ryan sighed heavily. 'Blast him! I nearly forgot that bastard.'

The last thing he wanted was his vendetta with bloody Carpentier, especially as Darkford was in his sights. 'I'll try and avoid him as long as I can; I've fought that bastard twice now and have no wish to duel with him again.'

They heard the order to break camp. Ryan pulled his great coat over, sloped his musket and wearily re-joined the column.

The misery of the forced march continued on the long and winding mountainous road through the desolate Cantabrian Mountains and onto the barren plains

Ryan had already walked for four long days until late into the night with just a few hours rest. He had marched eleven hours per day through heavy snow, carrying a heavy pack—before he'd discarded much of it—and covered up to 30 miles daily. It was taking its toll. He and the others were now exhausted. The drowsy monotonous sounds of arms, accoutrements and of boots on hard soil made him want to stop and sleep. Those who stopped to sleep never woke up.

Ryan halted and bivouacked for the night, but the lonely howls of mountain wolves kept him awake as he contemplated the frozen carcasses of his fallen comrades that had been torn and gnawed by wolves. Musket shots echoed in the distance, from marauding British stragglers who would soon run carelessly into the French.

STEPHEN MCGARRY

The French advance guard caught sight of the British again along a steep mountainous pass. Ryan opened his telescope and scoured the fleeing army. He reckoned that they formed a straggling line two and a half miles long and now resembled an undisciplined rabble rather than regular troops. He saw through his lens that some men had mounted mules or asses without bridles or saddles, and he thought they looked ridiculous, their legs trailing the ground as they goaded the beasts with their bayonets. He laughed to himself at the sight.

Ryan knew the British were lame and hungry but they could still find their strength somewhere and they earned their reputation amongst the French who respectfully called them *'les squelettes féroces'*—'the ferocious skeletons'.

Later on that day, Ryan watched closely through his telescope as the British abandoned their heavy supply wagons, probably, he thought, because they were too slow and were unable to keep up with the infantry through the steep passes. Teams of horses drawing four-wheeled fully laden wagons were unlimbered as men shouldered the wagons and heaved them over the mountain. With an almighty series of deafening crashes they fell into smithereens below.

He wasn't sure, but boxes containing what looked like glittering coins were chucked over and shattered loudly against the rocks into the snow. Some soldiers, Ryan saw, shimmied down the precipice to fill their pockets before climbing back up the precipice to re-join the march.

A French advance guard of mounted chasseurs, seeing the opportunity, flashed past him.

Ryan watched the stragglers bravely form up as the French light cavalry approached, and although they put up a

261

stout defence, they were overwhelmed and killed. He heard their unheeded cries for mercy carried by the whistling wind as the chasseurs slashed downwards with their sabres onto their backs and shoulders. The chasseurs then wheeled about and returned to the safety of their advance guard.

CHAPTER 31

The British stopped to make a stand in the small hamlet of Cacabelos, close to Villafranca. To enable Sir John Moore's main army to escape, the Reserve Division were ordered to protect the bridge over the river Cúa to stop the French. An advance picket of the 95th Rifles had taken up position behind some overhanging rocks.

'Rifleman O'Hara!' bellowed the sergeant. 'O'Hara!' Sergeant Wilson was a round-faced, bald, pot-bellied man, and he was furious. 'O'Hara! What the devil are you doing, man?' he screamed in a strong Birmingham accent.

The rifleman emerged from behind a boulder and turned to the sergeant with a look of disgust on his face.

'Have you been sleeping on post?' the sergeant snarled. 'You were bloody snoring, you bloody bog plodder—I can have you flogged!'

O'Hara had been sleeping with his stovepipe tipped low over his eyes. He was far too experienced a soldier to worry, as he knew the French pickets were several miles back, so he'd taken the opportunity to take forty winks.

Sergeant Wilson, red-faced, stood over the rifleman as he continued shouting. 'I'll have you flogged! I'll talk to the officer on watch! You'll be flogged, man!'

O'Hara stood up and eye-balled Wilson. A smirk spread across his face as he turned towards the other riflemen. 'Keep your hair on, Sergeant. Sure wasn't I just pretending to be asleep to fool the froggies? And sure enough, wouldn't I spring out from behind the rock and shoot them.' He raised his rifle muzzle and pointed it at the sergeant's middle.

The other riflemen laughed loudly as they sat and lapped up their cold stirabout of oatmeal and water. O' Hara roughly shouldered past the sergeant and sauntered away. It was always a pleasure to get one past Sergeant Wilson, who was left speechless and humiliated.

'I'll have you flogged, Paddy!' he could only retort after the rifleman. 'Just you wait, you bloody bog plodder.'

'Go ahead, for all I care!' O'Hara muttered loudly, cradling his rifle.

'You'll care alright!' Wilson shouted after him. 'When you're lashed to the triangle getting fifty lashes!' He rubbed his hands together in a circular motion, laughing in anticipation of O'Hara's comeuppance.

Moments later, the French launched an attack. The rifle battalion were caught unawares. O'Hara raced towards the pot-bellied sergeant. 'French cavalry and voltigeurs approaching!'

'Very well,' Sergeant Wilson replied, calmly, 'retire and make for the village.'

The 15th Dragoons and a number of wide-eyed, panic-stricken staff officers who had run into the French advance posts while out on reconnaissance stampeded through the riflemen. 'Make way for the cavalry!' they shouted, and the rifles opened their lines and let them pass before facing about.

Swarms of voltigeurs formed a skirmish line and pounded into them with their smooth bore muskets. A squadron of French light cavalry formed up and prepared to charge.

'The *moustaches* are coming, but show no hurry!' shouted Sergeant Wilson. 'Aim for the horses, lads!'

'*Company!*'

'*Prepare!*' He breathed in and held his breath.

'*Fire!*' He bawled in his best baritone.

The hail of bullets broke the chasseurs' charge, leading to several maddened, riderless mounts, trailing their reigns, crashing into the muddled ranks of riflemen.

'Fire at will!' Wilson said calmly.

O'Hara watched as the chasseurs, exposed to such a furious volley, pulled back. They reformed and charged again towards the British-held line with swords drawn, yelling at the top of their lungs.

'Fire and retire!' cried the pot-bellied sergeant. 'Make for the bridge! Double-quick time!'

O'Hara dashed pell-mell over the bridge, chased by the chasseurs. The British formed five-hundred paces from the bridge. The riflemen took up position behind the rocks and surveyed the enemy's movements. The chasseurs drew off and prepared to charge again.

Rifleman O'Hara, sweating profusely, turned to his lieutenant. 'Be Jaysus, your Honour, sure I never ran so fast in me life!' He straightened his belt, for the 23-inch sword bayonet had become twisted and caught between his legs and nearly tripped him up.

'We're not out of the woods yet!' replied the officer. O'Hara removed his black stove-pipe, wiped the greasy sheen of sweat from his brow and watched scores of voltigeurs fanning out.

The officer extended his brass telescope to take a closer look. There were hundreds of infantrymen, supported by a large body of cavalry, preparing to ford the river. A magnificently dressed French officer sat on a grey horse.

'Must be a bloody general,' the officer muttered.

'You're the best shot in the regiment, O'Hara. Could you

shoot that bastard?' The officer handed O'Hara the telescope. 'There'd be a guinea in it for you!'

O'Hara gazed through the lens. He'd never seen anything like it, because few British officers wore such flamboyant finery. O'Hara surveyed the officer's aristocratic face. *He is young and classically handsome, with a face that could adorn an old Roman coin,* he thought. The Frenchman's navy tunic was trimmed with braided gold. On his head he wore an immense black bicorn, pointed outwards in the fore and aft position. A circular tri-colour adorned its front, white ostrich plumes stuck out of it and blew hither and thither in the light breeze. A broad red sash and silver-starred Grand Eagle, the size of his fist, hung over his breast. *He looks like a bloody peacock. I'd bet a hundred gold guineas to sixpence he's a right bloody bastard,* thought O'Hara. *Not unlike our own toffee-nosed General 'Black Bob' Craufurd. The flogging bastard!* O'Hara resolved to kill the French general. He looked down the telescope and saw that there was a flurry of activity among the French officers on the other side of the river. He saw what looked to be the general's staff officers saluting as they scuttled off to their respective commanders.

'I think I can do it, sir,' said O'Hara as he handed the telescope back. He removed a paper cartridge from his pouch, bit and spat out the top and loaded his rifle.

For two-hundred yards, O'Hara made his way around the crest of the rocky mountain, slithering on his stomach for much of the way and careering through undergrowth. His olive-green uniform provided ample camouflage from the French troops below. He peered down from behind a granite boulder and could see the French were forming for another attack. He watched as officers dashed from sector to sector, rallying their tired troops.

'Nobody's seen me,' he whispered with relief. He could

see the French sentries posted along the riverbank. *If I could just get one shot at that bastard,* he thought as he felt his heart momentarily rise onto his mouth. *Shoot a bloody French general! Wait 'til the lads hear of this.*

The problem facing him was that the general was still some three-hundred yards away. O'Hara had hit a target at a comparable distance before with his Baker rifle. He was a crack shot and had once felled a stag at three hundred yards, but a bloody general! O'Hara couldn't risk being exposed and revealing his position.

The French had lost hundreds of officers to the marksmanship of the green-clad riflemen, whom they disdainfully called 'Les Sauterelles'—'The grasshoppers'.

O'Hara spat on the dull steel rifle barrel, rubbed it with his sleeve, and kissed it. His heart sank as he recalled the incident with Sergeant Wilson. There was a good chance he'd receive the lash. He remembered the last time he was flogged. He'd been recently promoted to sergeant and was drunk on duty when he brought the whole parade into chaos. Captain Stewart gave him a hundred lashes, which he'd bravely suffered, bit his lip hard for the pain was excruciating.

It had been humiliating but his wounds healed, although he was unable to sleep flat on his back for a month. O'Hara was furious, and the next day he barricaded himself in his quarters with a dozen loaded rifles and a quart of whiskey and swore he'd shoot Captain Stewart dead. An officer who was popular with the men finally persuaded him to give himself up, and as a punishment he was busted to private and received another flogging.

As O'Hara lay hidden beneath the undergrowth in the wilds of northern Spain, beads of sweat ran down his forehead and into his eyes. He was thirsty. A fresh blanket of snow had fallen through the night and much of it had now turned to a semi-frost. He grated up a handful and slurped it into his mouth, letting the cold snow melt before swallowing. His toes and fingers were freezing and he shivered violently. He cupped his fingers and blew into them hard—rubbing them vigorously to generate heat—and looked to check that the enemy hadn't skirted around and sneaked up behind him. Over the hill he could just make out the distinctive stovepipe of the other riflemen. They knew he was up to something and were eagerly following his progress. He put a round into his mouth, turned it around several times with his tongue and felt the cold steel intensely. He spat it out into his hand, kissed it and loaded his rifle. He flipped up the rifle's leaf sight. 'I hope the powder's good,' he prayed, as it wouldn't have been the first time poor quality gunpowder fizzled out when a rifle was discharged. He licked his finger and held it up. 'Good, there's no wind,' he whispered to himself.

He slithered on his stomach towards the open ground and turned around in the undergrowth, sliding the frog of his bayonet scabbard along his belt. He turned and lay flat on his back in the supine position, his rifle pressed hard into his body, the mussel tip nearly hitting his nose. He looped the rifle's leather strap around his right foot, crossed it over his left leg, and looking down towards his feet, took aim. 'Bless me, Father, for I have sinned.' He always murmured this before making a kill. For although he received general absolution from Father McCann, which forgave him for taking someone's life in times of war, he knew deep down it was wrong to kill. He regulated his breathing by inhaling and exhaling deeply for several moments. He looked down, aligned the rifle's sight with the top of the barrel and aimed a little left of his target, as he was firing well above the rifle's recommended 200-yard range. He held his breath for several seconds, and lay motionless until he pulled the trigger. The flint fell.

Bang!

The sound of the bullet echoed loudly and the rifle recoiled hard into his shoulder. O'Hara had hit his target. The French general slumped out of his saddle and fell quietly onto the ground. O'Hara had already reloaded when the French general's trumpet-major rushed and bent down to attend to him. Another shot rang out and the aide's lifeless body keeled forward over the dead general's chest.

O'Hara stood up, proud as punch. He could hear the cheers of the other riflemen. *'Hurrah!'* they shouted as they covered his dash back to British lines, taking shots at the furious chasseurs who pursued him across the bridge.

Ryan saw the rifleman emerge from his lair and resolved to cut off his retreat; he led his men around the flanks of the French cavalry in front of the British. Scurrying in the undergrowth, he cupped his hand over his ear and listened, and heard the riflemen shout to one another. One of the accents was Irish. A rifle shot whooshed past Ryan's ear, displacing the air against his face as his heart skipped a beat. 'Good shot, Rifleman!' he shouted.

Rifleman Tom O'Hara was astounded to hear English spoken from the enemy's lines.

'Where are you from, Rifleman?' Ryan shouted.

There was no reply.

He repeated his question, and a voice was heard. 'What's it to you, Frenchie?'

'I'm not a Frenchie,' replied Ryan.

'You don't sound like a froggy!' The rifleman roared.

'That's because I'm not a bloody Froggy,' replied Ryan as

he darted towards a tree and, again, a shot ploughed past him. It thumped into the wood, narrowly missing him. 'I'm an Irishman myself, laddie! Born and bred in Dublin, the best city in the world. My name's Ryan, Irish Legion.'

'We've heard of you lot,' the rifleman replied. 'Your bloody regiment is known to us. Your recruiting sergeants harp on endlessly for prisoners to join Boney's Irish regiment.'

Ryan smiled. 'Then why don't you come over and join us? We're the best regiment in the French army. Your small army will dissolve in the face of Marshal Soult's mighty columns. Join us while you still have a chance.'

Another shot whirred past Ryan.

'No fear of that, ye dirty blackguard!' O'Hara shouted, and he stood up and broke cover to fire a shot, which ricocheted and missed. The bullet smacked into granite and a chip hit Ryan on the cheek.

Ryan laughed loudly and shouted back in the direction the shot had come from. 'That was a terrible shot. I thought you riflemen were sharpshooters.'

Another shot followed, this time whizzing past his shoulder. Ryan made a speaking trumpet with his hands and shouted. 'Now that was a lot better, son!'

Ryan removed his shako, snaked his way through British lines, and, dressed in his green uniform, was mistaken for a British rifleman. O'Hara heard the ratcheting click of a cocked musket behind his right ear. He whirled around and saw Ryan.

'Captain James Ryan of Napoleon's Irish Legion at your service, and you are in luck,' Ryan said with a wry smile as he touched his peak. 'We're recruiting! Will you join us?'

Rifleman Tom O'Hara swallowed deeply and stuttered, 'Y-yes!'

Ryan took O'Hara's rifle and led him back to French lines, amid cheers and hoots by the other voltigeurs at Ryan's daring feat.

CHAPTER 32

A pervading silence permeated the French camp that evening. The loss of the thirty-one year-old General Auguste-Marie Francois Colbert was felt deeply. He had been a good officer who always had the best interests of his men at heart. The French pitched their tents not far from the river and lit braziers, and the soldiers huddled around the burning embers for warmth. The captured rifleman cut a sullen figure as he was led back to French lines.

A group of chasseurs leered with hatred and shouted obscenities at O'Hara. He was jumped on and received a tirade of fist blows and kicks to his body and head. Ryan finally pulled him from their clutches, as otherwise he'd have been beaten to death. In the fray, they knocked off O'Hara's stovepipe shako and everyone stood and stared. His head was shaved except for a three-inch long narrow strip of hair, which ran down the middle of his head from the nape of the neck to his forehead.

Ryan seized him and escorted him through the French camp, and he stayed in Ryan's tent for his own safety. The tent consisted of a blanket held up with three sticks, bedded down with tufts of damp straw. Ryan watched O'Hara as he sat with his arms crossed over his knees.

'Where did you get such a strange haircut?' Ryan asked.

'The warriors of the Mohawk tribes in the Great Lakes of Canada shave their heads, so they do, leaving a narrow strip in the middle before going to war,' O'Hara explained as he checked his badly swollen lip for blood with the back of his hand. 'It gives them a fearsome appearance to frighten their enemies.'

Ryan was unimpressed. 'You're Irish? Yet you fight for the British?'

O'Hara clenched his fists angrily. 'Don't take me for a fool! Sure there was no work back home, not even for good farm hands like meself, so when a recruiting party passed through Kilfeacle Fair in Tipperary, I thought I'd take a gawk, I would. A finely dressed sergeant told me stories of adventure and glory. I was promised a shilling and a tot o' rum a day and a chance to see the world, with a penny pension a day and lodgings in the Kilmainham old soldiers' home in Dublin, and, of course, I took me chances and ran!'

He paused as he spat out blood from his cut lip.

'I've spent five years as a chosen man with the Rifle regiment. We wear the olive green uniform instead of the red coat worn by infantry.

'Chosen men?' queried Ryan.

'Chosen men is the name given to rifleman, in recognition of their marksmanship, intelligence and bravery. And it also gave other privileges, so it does, like excusing them from latrine digging and the like,' he replied proudly.

O'Hara rubbed the stubble of his three-day old beard and gazed around. A number of heavily moustachioed faces emerged through the shadows as the men sat curled up in their capotes and glared with hatred at him. They were eager for retribution because a rifleman had killed their beloved General Colbert.

'Small fellows, these Frenchies!' declared O'Hara.

Ryan glowered at him. 'I can't leave you alone for a second. They want nothing more than to kill you slowly.

'Have you heard about the torture called death by a thousand cuts?'

The rifleman shook his head.

'Well, let me explain...' Ryan paused as he took a plug of perique tobacco from his pocket and shaved it with his *épée*. He pressed it into the bowl of his long clay pipe with his thumb, removed a strand of straw from his bedding, placed it in the fire and lit his pipe. His bottom lips made the familiar popping sound as he puffed, drawing a long draught of tobacco smoke as he slowly exhaled. The sweet and fruity tobacco aroma filled O'Hara's nostrils and the swirly smoke lingered pleasantly under the tent.

'As I was saying, they learned this torture from the guerrillas. Spanish missionaries in China suffered this horrible fate.' Ryan paused, smoking his pipe thoughtfully for a while. 'The torture called "death by a thousand cuts" was used in China for thousands of years and involved small cuts being made on the body which were designed, not to kill, but to prolong suffering. The torturers began with a blade on a non-vital part of the body, perhaps a leg. They may next slice off flesh from an upper arm, or an ear or the nose, perhaps. A cut to a cheek may follow, until finally they cut the poor devil's throat or perform some other violent act. This involved up to a thousand cuts being carved on a victim, with a painful death usually by the third day.'

The young rifleman sat mesmerised at the news of such blood-curdling cruelty. 'That's not Christian!' he replied aghast.

'Why, no! Indeed it's not,' agreed Ryan.

'I've seen cruelty among Indian tribes when I was posted to Canada, so I have. The Indians scalped the top of their enemies' heads as trophies, but I've never heard of such a horrible death.'

The two men could have been two friends chatting over the hearth at home.

O'Hara snorted and cleared his throat. 'The savages valued bravery above all other things and had no respect for those who surrendered or let themselves get captured. I saw a tribe of Pequot Indians tie a white fur trader to a stake and flay him alive before he finally died of his wounds.' He snorted loudly. 'The British got their own back and retaliated in kind.'

Ryan continued puffing on his pipe. 'But don't underestimate the cruelty of the French horsemen. There are cuirassiers who have learnt other torture techniques from the guerrillas. I have to tell you what happens to the body after the cuirassiers cut off some body part. They throw it into the fire or perhaps boil the meat in their metal breastplates, and as their blocks of salt were long consumed, they added saltpetre from their cartridges for seasoning and fed on the human flesh. They say it tastes like beef only sweeter and softer in texture.' Ryan searched into his eyes. 'They believe it gives them special powers.'

'Cannibalism!' exclaimed O'Hara with open mouth. 'I don't believe it!'

'It's true, for I've seen it with my very eyes,' Ryan affirmed. 'The men go into a frenzy, like demons possessed, and it's quite impossible for the officers to stop them, and in any case I've seen officers, respectable, honourable men from good families, also take part in this practise.'

Ryan stood up to stretch. He reached down, picked up the unloaded Baker, and handed it to O'Hara. 'You're going to train us on how to use it,' Ryan again looked at O'Hara's strange Mohawk haircut, 'and, by the way, welcome to Napoleon's blaggards,' he said wryly, before he took his mug and scooped some coffee from a pot on the fire.

Rifleman O'Hara gazed around. The French looked tired, hungry and dirty, and their horses also looked weak and forlorn in their long, dirty winter coats. Many of the officers were dressed in various non-regulation garments and they, too, resembled a tribe of travelling beggars. Tom O'Hara dejectedly buried his face in his hands. The veteran soldier— the best shot in the regiment—suddenly looked like a frightened little boy as his keen eyes stared into the dancing flames and he weighed up his fate. Snow began to fall. It looked beautiful as the light flakes sizzled into the flames. He'd already decided not to escape. It mattered little that he'd shot the French general now. Discipline in the army had deteriorated so much that the officers meted out punishment without mercy and he knew that if he hadn't killed the French general, Sergeant Wilson would've followed through with his threat, for sleeping on picket duty was a serious offense; and so, too, was showing open hostility to a superior. He might have avoided the lash this time but would have faced it again. It was only a matter of time. He decided then that he'd try his luck under the Irish Legion's green flag. He was still hungry. He pulled his collar towards his neck, turned on his side, shivered uncontrollably as he peered into the fire's dying embers, and tried to sleep.

Further up the hillside, dozens of flickering red and golden lights sparkled brightly on the mountainside. The British had lit fires on the hilltops as a *ruse de guerre* to give the impression that they had made camp, but silently the Reserve Division moved out that night, escaping the clutches of the French, for now.

CHAPTER 33

Ryan kicked O'Hara in his side, rudely awakening him. 'Get up and come with me!'

The two men walked over to a huge red-and-white striped canvas tent. Colonel Marchand sat behind a desk as he cradled a chicken leg and read a dispatch. 'Go and get some rest,' he told the sodden dispatch rider who was standing at attention. He'd ridden all night for ten hours, and had covered forty miles, to bring news that the British had split their forces and had sent a contingent of their army west on the road to Vigo, while the main army continued onto Corunna.

'*Ser-geant!*' shouted the colonel. 'Organise a fresh horse for this man and ensure he is fed well. I'll reply post-haste.'

The order was addressed to the dead General Colbert, but as Colonel Marchand was the most senior officer, he was now in charge. The colonel looked up from above his pince-nez and stared at the two men.

Ryan saluted. 'Sir, I have a captured British rifleman.'

'Was he the fellow who shot and killed General Colbert?'

'No, sir!' Ryan lied.

The colonel walked up to the rifleman and eyed him up sharply. O'Hara met his gaze defiantly.

'You look like a savage!' the colonel hissed as he took in O'Hara's strange Mohawk. 'I do not like this new type of war waged by these riflemen. It is without honour and glory. You lie in wait for hours and sneak around on your bellies. It is not befitting a man of honour. Our soldiers call you grasshoppers but I prefer to call you snakes!' He ripped off some meat from his chicken and shouted at O'Hara with his mouth full. 'I served in the Americas during their revolutionary war. When the British General Cornwallis was reconnoitring the ground before the battle of Yorktown, one of the American rebels, armed with a hunting rifle, had him in his sights. My superior told him not to shoot as it was not proper—now what do you think of that?' The red-faced French colonel flushed with anger and he threw his chicken leg at O'Hara, hitting him in the face. 'However, your boys go and shoot our beloved General Colbert!'

Ryan sensed trouble and quickly intervened. 'He's an Irishman, Colonel, and is volunteering to join our Irish Legion. He has also agreed to provide details on the enemy.' Ryan lied again for he knew well that the colonel was at the point of ordering O'Hara outside to be shot. He'd seen this many times before.

'Very well,' replied the colonel. 'But he's your responsibility, Captain,' he added waving his arms dismissively.

Ryan saluted and the two men went outside.

'What did he say?' asked O'Hara nervously, wiping the spit from his face.

Ryan acted as if he hadn't heard him. He stood and watched as a message was rolled inside a tiny brass barrel and secured to a homing pigeon's leg. An orderly raised it to his shoulder and let it go. The bird fluttered its wings vigorously as it took flight.

'What did he say?' repeated O'Hara plaintively.

'Oh, I forgot—you don't speak the froggy language, do you?' replied Ryan. His eyes followed the bird's trajectory as it, no doubt, brought more bad news of the war in Spain back to France.

'No, and you know damn well that I don't,' replied O'Hara.

'He said you'd be shot in the morning!'

O'Hara's face blanched and he swallowed hard.

Ryan laughed loudly. 'I'm only joking. I told him you were an Irishman pressed into the British army and would join the Irish battalion.'

'And where is this Irish battalion? I've only seen three or four of you in this green uniform,' he said, pointing to Ryan's green tunic.

'We got separated from our battalion after a scrap with British cavalry at Sahagún,' Ryan explained. 'The battalion returned with the wounded back to Burgos without us, but hopefully we'll join them soon. We've no green legion uniforms, but we'll get you out of that bloody rifleman's uniform or you won't live to see the end of the day.'

Later that morning, Voltigeur Tom O'Hara, attired in a French infantryman's blue uniform, demonstrated the Baker rifle to Ryan's men.

'I don't want to blow my own trumpet lads,' O'Hara said, as he passed the rifle to Sergeant Hoffman, 'but I am—I mean—I was the best shot in the regiment.'

Hoffman held the rifle in the crook of his arm. 'Nice weapon!' he said as he rubbed the barrel in admiration and looked down the rifle's gun sights. He nodded in approval as he passed it to McGowan.

'The Rifle Corps was formed back in 1800,' explained O'Hara, 'and the Baker is well known for its accuracy and effectiveness at long ranges. Its effective range is two-hundred yards, but I've hit targets above that!'

'You mean targets like French generals, O'Hara?' said Ryan.

The others chortled.

O'Hara ignored him.

'The difference with the musket, as you know, is not just that the musket's range is only 100 yards, but that it's much slower to load.' O'Hara took out a lead ball and presented it at eye level. 'We routinely fire two balls per minute, but better riflemen, like meself, can manage three per minute,' he declared proudly.

'In battlefield conditions, we sometimes load the rifle without the paper packing, but keep in mind that this can affect the ball's accuracy.'

He raised the rifle and put it at half cock. 'Riflemen carry a number of cartridges made of beeswax paper containing gunpowder.' O'Hara bit the cartridge, spat the end out, poured the powder into the muzzle's barrel, and put a pinch into the priming pan. He placed a bullet into the muzzle, followed by the cartridge paper, which he pressed down with his thumb while standing the rifle on it butt. He then used his ramrod to push it into the rifle's stock.

He replaced the ramrod, poured a small amount of gunpowder to prime the pan and raised the weapon. He took aim, pulled back the cocked trigger and fired. The rifle slammed into his shoulder as a bloom of white smoke rose and a flock of birds in the tops of the trees overhead scattered.

'We need to keep the rifle clean,' he explained as he removed a pick and rush from his belt and cleaned the touch hole and priming pan.

Ryan was impressed. They took turns loading the rifle when sitting, kneeling and lying down in the prone position. These were the different postures used to make the best use of cover. The four men spent the whole day practising this routine. They were experienced soldiers and so adapted well to using the new weapon, firing it with increasing accuracy. Ryan was already experienced using the Versailles rifle and even Hoffman could fire three shots per minute before the day came to a close.

Early the next morning, the French advance guard, together with Napoleon's blaggards, or what remained of them, broke camp and moved out.

CHAPTER 34

As the French advance guard trekked through Galicia, the province erupted into a kaleidoscope of winter colours. Muted greens, browns, and copper-tans, shrouded in mist, covered the valleys below.

The men dreaded the windy mountain passes the most. In these steep gorges the guerrillas waited to ambush them. The French had been ambushed a handful of times already in vicious hit-and-run attacks. The guerrillas melted away into the mountain ranges to launch yet another ambush further down the passes, maybe a day or two later. It took two able-bodied men to attend to each wounded man, which stymied their progress. In the end the wounded, with scant medical attention, often succumbed to their wounds.

The French took out their revenge on a young boy taken in a punitive raid in the last village they'd passed. Ryan heard the lad's screams from the rear and ran up as a yellow-toothed chasseur with a heavy moustache tortured him. Ryan landed a hard kick into the chasseur's back. 'Lay one more hand on the lad...' Ryan hissed and unsheathed his sword. The chasseur grumbled, but put up no resistance and shrugged his shoulders, as Frenchmen characteristically do, then walked away.

The boy's horribly disfigured face resembled a grotesque, blood-stained, bruised mess. Ryan cut off the boy's short jacket and pressed it into his face to help stop the bleeding and let him go. The youth ran down a ravine and within seconds had disappeared into the low-lying mist.

They trudged on the snow-covered mountain path and stopped. Ryan took out his telescope, and saw the vague silhouettes of the red-coated infantry and blue-coated light cavalry slowly snaking their way ahead through the lonely trails.

The French later pulled into a village at the foot of the Cantabrian mountain ranges. The village was a mess, for the British had passed through earlier. Ryan saw a number of lame, mangy and emaciated horses, which had been shot so as not to aid the enemy. As he walked, his boots scrunched on broken glass—there were shards of glass scattered everywhere. All around him, houses and shops lay plundered, every window and door was broken and every lock had been forced. Rivers of wine ran along the flagged floor of the deserted local bodega. A number of drunken redcoats lay slumped against the bodega's wall oblivious to the arrival of the French troops. He came across a number of dead Spaniards, bayoneted by the out-of-control troops. The chasseurs put all the drunken redcoats to the sword.

A shot rang out, and one of the chasseurs tumbled dead from his saddle. Ryan saw a girl drop a pistol and run. The chasseurs galloped up and quickly apprehended her. The Spanish girl's simple, yet elegant cream dress was torn. Ryan presumed she had been raped earlier by the redcoats. She was to be hanged. The girl stood tall and erect, she had a clear, peaches and cream complexion, full lips and luscious jet black hair. Ryan looked on sadly, for she was young and pretty but prepared to meet her death with dignity and pride.

A noose was swiftly placed around the girl's neck and the ends of the rope were thrown over the bough of a tree. She shuddered as her hands were tied behind her as she stood on a wooden tripod stool. She shouted nervously, '*¡Muerte a los franceses! ¡Viva Esp!...*' but she was cut short when the stool was kicked from under her feet.

The rope creaked loudly. '*Viva España,*' Ryan muttered solemnly to himself as he looked on.

The girl had been purposely dropped from a short height so that the fall didn't break her neck. Her feet twitched violently mid-air. She gasped and struggled for air as the arteries and veins that carry blood to her brain were blocked.

Ryan had to stop himself running to the girl's assistance and cutting the rope, for his child had died the same way. He felt sick and wanted to flee, to run, to disappear, to crawl into the dirt, to desert the army, to leave Spain. She made a wailing, sobbing sound. He stood horrified as the girl continued to gasp for air while her feet and legs kicked violently, and she struggled for footing. Her face turned purple and the veins in her neck and eyes bulged due to the pressure on her trachea. Urine trickled down her legs and she defecated, turning her cream dress a dirty brown. The smell of this alone was awful. This was the ultimate disrespect and humiliation.

Ryan wondered if his child had suffered in the same way when she was hanged over Darkford's back. He told himself this was untrue but he knew deep down that she probably had. He couldn't bear to think about it. He closed his eyes and felt he was going mad. He wouldn't look, but the smell and the sounds of the swaying, creaking rope and the girl's gurgling were too much to bear. He tried to say a prayer but he couldn't think straight. He felt his right hand shake rhythmically, uncontrollably; he breathed heavily and bit his lip so hard that he drew blood. Finally, after ten minutes, the girl's heart gave out, her arms and legs became limp, her eyes went dead and her face turned grey. She was just another dead Spaniard. A stony silence followed.

The girl was left hanging there as the convoy resumed its march.

As he marched he hoped the other men hadn't noticed his unease at the girl's hanging. *He could have saved the girl*, he thought, *maybe he could have talked to one of the officers to let her go. He had a knife. He should have cut her down, taken a horse and escaped with her. He rationalised that this wasn't possible.* He spat out the name of the man who murdered his daughter. 'Darkford! Darkford! Darkford!'

A little later, when they crested a ridge, Ryan encountered scores of deserters crouched together, sheltering in hovels from the sleet and snow. The chasseurs put them to the sword and left them. Ryan was powerless to intervene. A silhouette of a lone cavalryman stood black against the sun. Ryan thought perhaps he wanted to parley to negotiate his surrender and cautiously approached with his raised musket, but still the trooper didn't stir. As Ryan walked closer he noticed that the man and horse were frozen, resembling a white marble statue. The cavalryman's moustache and eyebrows were covered in snow, but the man's eyes remained open as if he was still alive.

A few steps further, a kilted and bonneted Highlander lay at the side of the road. These hardy soldiers were accustomed to the harsh, inhospitable Scottish Highlands, but they, too, fell in their hundreds that winter. The Highlander's piercing, pale blue eyes emerged from a thick tuft of heavily overgrown ginger eyebrows. He held a shawl wrapped around his face, exposing only his eyes and mouth. His feet and knees were cut, bloodied and bruised. When Ryan passed and glanced back, his heart jumped because he was sure the deadman also turned his head to meet his gaze. Ryan was spooked and he nervously took out his bog oak amulet and kissed it.

There were hundreds of small mounds of snow scattered everywhere. Ryan didn't know what they were at first until he discovered that they were bodies covered in snow. There were women and children among them. As he drew nearer, he observed that one of the mounds was partially covered. He walked closer and spied a swaddled baby snuggled up to his mother's breast and he bent down to pick it up.

'Sergeant!' he called.

Hoffman dog trotted up. Ryan pulled back the blanket protecting the baby and saw the infant was frantically sucking on its dead mother's frozen breast. He removed the heavy blanket from its mother's shoulders. 'I want you to bring it to one of the *cantinières,* and ensure no harm comes to him.' He pulled the mother's blond hair away from her blue-lipped face and saw the pale, translucent complexion and aquiline nose of a handsome young woman. He removed her shawl and wrapped it tightly around the freezing infant, who began crying incessantly.

He gently handed the baby into the sergeant's waiting arms. 'Why the bloody hell did they bring so many women and children with them into Spain? I don't understand it.'

The bones of the fallen—fibulae, tibiae, ribs and skulls— would snap and crack under the weight of the advancing French caissons, for the road to Corunna would be soon paved with the bones of those left behind.

Ryan jumped on top of a granite boulder, took out his telescope, and scoured the terrain ahead. The British were slowly snaking their way through the snow-covered passes. He saw a number of figures, including young children, limping towards a barn, to seek shelter, a half-mile away.

'Stragglers!' muttered Ryan, 'more bloody British stragglers!' He'd hardly spoken when a half-troop of French light cavalry dug in their spurs, peeled off to his right and bore down on them.

'Hussars of Death! Those bastards have seen them, too,' McGowan said. 'They'll be slaughtered!'

They watched as the hussars galloped towards the barn where the stragglers were hiding.

Ryan adjusted the focus of his telescope and saw the scene unfold. The hussars were shouting and laughing and had surrounded the barn.

Ryan looked on as a redcoat nursing a blood-stained bandage wrapped around his knee limped out of the barn, sword in hand, to bravely meet his attackers. A drunken hussar lifted his carbine to his midriff and fired a charge into the man's belly. The redcoat was jerked back two feet by the power of the blast, and fell back dead.

Others, armed with muskets and swords rushed out, only to be met by a heavy discharge of carbines from the drunken Frenchmen. A redcoat pulled one of the hussars from his mount. He plunged his bayonet into the Frenchman's chest, before receiving a backhand slash to his neck and falling, his frontage spurting a sea of blood.

Ryan's telescope zoomed onto a hussar and he watched as the man removed a bottle from inside his pelisse, he uncorked it with his teeth and took a long draught. He then pulled the barn door's lever across and locked it. He crouched down, removed a flint and some dry tinder from his saddle and rasped the flint with the edge of a knife until the sparks caused the kindle to catch fire.

'They're trying to burn those in the barn!' said Ryan.

It stopped snowing but the thatched roof structure was too wet to burn. Leather straps were secured to the wooden beams of the barn and attached to their saddle pommels, and spurred forward by a sharp slap on the horse's rear thighs.

The two horses bolted forward and part of the structure came tumbling down. Ryan could make out the faint muffled cries from those inside.

'What can we do, Cap'n?' McGowan asked him.

'We must do *something!*' Ryan replied as he snapped his telescope shut. 'Follow me!' he said as he started to run.

Ryan and his men sprinted the half-mile and stood panting heavily at the barn. 'Move that horse any further and you're a dead man!'

McGowan and O'Hara levelled their loaded muskets on either side of the hussars.

A toothless hussar, with a sinister and dirty face, snarled insolently. 'We know of you Irishman and your antics in Madrid—I'm not afraid of you!'

Ryan then heaved the hussar's leg out of his stirrups and he fell off his horse onto the hard ground. Ryan's boot stood on the Frenchman's chest as he pointed the tip of his *épée* to his neck. 'These people are prisoners of war, and there are women and children inside. I'll kill the first man who enters.'

The toothless hussar sheepishly remounted as the other hussars laughed drunkenly and cursed, before they galloped away.

Ryan entered the barn where the sick and infirm lay. 'Don't worry, I'll ensure no harm comes to you. I'm an Irishmen in Napoleon's army. You'll be brought to the rear to receive medical attention and food.' Ryan cleared his throat. 'Does anyone here speak French?'

A lieutenant dressed in a navy uniform meekly raised his hand. 'Yes, I d-d-do,' he stuttered nervously in a crisp Home Counties accent.

Ryan saw on his shoulder the insignia of a cannon on a plinth and assumed he was from the Royal Artillery.

'Good!' replied Ryan. 'Just keep away from the French

light cavalrymen. Make yourself known to an officer and no harm will come to you. Stay as you are here until the French advance guard passes and wait for the main army to come.

'Tell me,' he added, as he grasped the young lieutenant's arm, 'is there an albino captain called Darkford here with the British army?'

'There is an albino called Captain Darkford, alright,' the artillery lieutenant answered. 'I've no qualms about telling you about that scoundrel for he's a conniving, bloody heathen...' The lieutenant paused. 'He's marching back to Corunna with General Sir John Moore. The brute stole twenty silver dollars from me. He's a murderer but his rank saves him from suspicion. Even his superiors fear him. He's a clever, cunning, evil swine.'

Ryan smiled, relieved that he had Darkford in his sights. His legs were shaking as he walked back to rejoin the column. The closer he was getting to his nemesis, the more intense his feelings were becoming. The anger was welling up inside him. He felt he could hardly breathe. He wanted to grab a horse and chase after Darkford right then. He'd get revenge. This was the only thing that was getting him through the war. He hadn't slept properly in weeks, for the night sweats and nightmares wouldn't stop. His mind's eye went through the episode of his family's horrific death. The killings in Madrid, and the murder of the Spanish girl haunted him too, even more then the atrocities of the guerrillas that he had witnessed. His hands and limbs were starting to shake. It was only his nerves, he told himself, but he knew the nightmares were getting worse. That night he'd dreamt vividly that his daughter was still alive and he was carrying her home on his shoulder on a summer's evening. They were both laughing together and were happy. He had then woken up suddenly with the bitter realisation that she was dead and he was inconsolable with grief.

CHAPTER 35

The British had nearly reached Corunna and they could smell the sea-washed air. Sir John Moore had already spotted flocks of circling seagulls swooping through the mist before he finally caught sight of the sea from the hills overlooking Corunna. His elation was short-lived, however, because the Royal Navy were not in the bay!

He knew that his army had suffered terribly during the two-hundred and fifty-mile harrowing march over the snow-capped Galician mountains. It was only now that the ramshackle army tramped into town that its deplorable condition became clear. Sir John curbed his horse to watch the men pass. Their once-fine bright scarlet tunics were now brick red, ragged and torn; many were lame, shoeless and ridden with lice. A number of battalions had lost over a hundred men—dead or missing—for the 6th and 9th Foot had lost several hundred men between them.

Sir John's sullen face lit up and broadened into a smile as two battalions of the 1st Foot Guards filed past, for they alone had kept their numbers and fared well on the march. The Guard's regimental drum major held a blood-soaked bandage around his head and limped heavily as he led his men in. He gamely twirled his staff and his drummers played proudly, as if they were home on their regimental parade ground at Aldershot.

Shortly afterwards, General Sir Edward Paget's Reserve

Division trundled into Corunna, four infantry battalions, two regiments of dragoons and a battalion of the 95th Rifles.

'¡Viva los ingleses!' the local inhabitants shouted as the first British soldiers toiled into Corunna. 'Que Dios esté con vosotros'—'May God be with you!' The inhabitants looked on, but their elation turned to pity as the army limped slowly past.

Sir John and a half dozen heavily cloaked staff officers walked their tired horses into the city's Plaza Mayor.

A small, plump, middle-aged man, sporting an enormous drooping black moustache, sat on a beautiful white Andalusian horse, waiting for them. 'My name is Juan Rodriguez Sánchez and I am the mayor of Corunna. Forgive me for I speak only a little English.'

Sir John doffed his hat. 'I am delighted to make your acquaintance, señor. I am Lieutenant General Sir John Moore, Commander-in-chief of his Britannic Majesty's' forces here in Spain.'

The plump mayor touched his hat and smiled. 'I want to assure you that we are prepared for the French.' He spat heavily on the ground at the mere mention of the hated invader. 'We will not give up our city without a fight.' Resting his fist on his hip, the mayor followed the rag-tag infantry battalions with his gaze, concerned and shocked at the men's condition.

If the Spanish were unimpressed by the British, Sir John *was* impressed with the resolve of the local people. He turned and looked around. He watched as the local inhabitants hurriedly constructed street barricades from shop counters, church benches and tables. Men, women and children were frantically scraping loop-holes and making embrasures in walls and buildings to shoot from. They furtively distributed amongst themselves muskets, old fowling pieces, axes, blunderbusses, hatchets, machetes, and even sticks and scissors. If only he'd seen such a hotbed of resistance in other areas of Spain he might not have retreated, he reasoned.

'Gracias, señor,' replied Sir John to the mayor, 'but I regret that a far greater army under Marshal Soult is approaching and I intend to save my army by shipping them back to England.'

The mayor's face dropped in horror. 'You mean you plan to leave before the French arrive? Then why did you come to Spain at all, if you do not fight?' he asked incredulously.

'I am sorry, señor,' added Sir John gravely, as he wrapped his cape before gently spurring his mare forward towards his staff officers. He needed to plan the embarkation of the wreck of the army. There was not a moment to lose.

Later that day, the tall masts and wide, swollen canvas of a dozen Royal Navy frigates and one-hundred troop transports slowly emerged over the horizon to evacuate the army back to England. The men threw their hats in the air and hooted and cheered loudly when they saw the ships to bring them home.

A break in the weather gave the British hope, for at least it was getting warmer. Sir John established his headquarters in a grand old house close to the harbour. He furtively paced up and down the great drawing room in front of his staff officers, his arms folded firmly behind him.

'General, you must conclude an armistice with Marshal Soult, for there's not enough time to load up the army,' implored one of his officers.

'I will not,' Sir John replied sternly, pursing his lips. 'If the army is not loaded up in time, I intend to stand and fight! And I want all of the cavalry horses slaughtered.'

'Sir?' exclaimed a senior staff officer.

'Yes, all of them!' he repeated. 'Including the mules and draught cattle.'

An eerie silence descended on the room.

'Our beloved horses!' someone exclaimed.

'It hurts me to issue this order, gentlemen,' Sir John continued as his staff groaned, contemplating the terrible command.

'Is there any way we can bring them with us, sir? One officer asked. 'The poor beasts deserve it. It was the 7th who broke Napoleon's elite chasseurs at Benavente and captured their general, while the horses of the 10th and 15th Dragoons left the French running at Sahagún—'

Sir John cut him short. 'Yes, I know, and it pains me, too.'

'But, sir,' a grey-haired officer began as he fiddled nervously with his bicorn, 'our horses saved our army and also endured the horrors of the march here, and without them we'd never have made it.'

Sir John sighed sadly as he walked up to the window of the grand dining room and watched his own bay mare tethered outside. The well-trained horses of the Cavalry Division had indeed saved the British army and many were fine animals brought over from Ireland. He stood there motionless in his red tunic for around a minute—nobody spoke—before he solemnly turned his grey head towards his staff. 'I know it's a dreadful order, but I have no choice. We'll be lucky if we manage to load any of our men aboard the ships.' He turned again to the window and surveyed the fleet moored in the harbour, shrouded in fog. 'I cannot and *will not* make Napoleon a gift of our cavalry!' he said with determination. 'That is why we are loading up the cavalry regiments first, without horses! At this stage, we may have to face Marshal Soult in battle. I'm sorry, gentlemen, but that will be all.'

As the staff officers glumly left the room to relay the orders to their respective commanders, a voice exclaimed, 'Destroy our beloved horses?' while others grumbled collectively in disbelief as they filed out.

Thousands of horses soon clogged up Corunna's cobbled streets when the shooting started. The troopers, many of whom were brave and hardened veterans of many difficult campaigns, were exhausted and distraught. When pulling their triggers, some troopers faced away, resulting in the animal falling down badly wounded in the neck or body, requiring a second shot or a bayonet being thrust through the heart to deliver the *coup de grâce*.

As this was happening, longboats continued to ferry the cavalry troopers, many of whom were in tears, onto the transport ships in the harbour.

The situation quickly escalated out of control and became chaotic.

'There must be already five hundred wretched dead horses in the market square,' a loud Cockney voice shouted.

Teams of horses fled in terror, slipping and stumbling on the bloodied cobblestones as they galloped through the blood-stained streets of Corunna making low, long snorting sounds through their nostrils. Their mouths were open and their manes were erect in fear as farriers frantically formed lines in front of them with outstretched arms, trying fruitlessly to stop them, but hundreds stampeded out of Corunna and escaped into the hills. The whinnying screams of the terrified horses and mules and the sharp discharge of pistols reverberated through Corunna as over 3,000 horses were destroyed.

By evening, the carnage was nearly over; save for the

occasional report of a pistol, all was quiet. The carcasses were already putrefying and bloating in the rising temperature, and a terrible stench soon emanated from Corunna. The air filled with the smell of death. Lime from the city's stores was shovelled over the carcasses to ward off disease and mask the odours, but it wasn't enough.

The town's mayor and the local Spaniards were shocked at the destruction and grimly wondered what havoc the British heathens had brought to their once beautiful town, now strewn with bloodied carcasses.

The regimental farriers spent the night putting the remaining wounded equines out of their misery. The destruction of the horses had been performed with breath-taking clumsiness, which had led to much unnecessary suffering. The farriers completed the deadly task, using a combination of pistols, hammers and knives, to give the final death blow as humanly as possible.

The cavalry was now loaded up and many of the transport ships were ready to clear port. There wasn't enough time to load up the infantry. They remained to take up key defensive positions in and around the town.

CHAPTER 36

The French advance guard stood on the heights of the Palavea Mountains that towered over Corunna and waited for Soult's main army corps to come up from the rear. Suddenly a panic came over Ryan. What if Darkford escaped? He was so close to his nemesis and had him nearly in his sights. Darkford had ruined everything for him. He *must* have his revenge! Ryan watched eagerly as a despatch rider galloped back to inform Marshal Soult that the British had arrived safely in Corunna and the Royal Navy had docked in the harbour, waiting to bring the army safely back to England.

Ryan took out his battered telescope and saw Soult's main army corps marching in the distance. Soult must hurry! He turned his gaze towards the town as the heavy sea fog dissipated and the coastal city of Corunna slowly came into view. A brilliant panorama unfolded before him. Ryan could now make out the lines of British troops in their ragged brick-red tunics as they formed a chain around Corunna. They formed up, two lines deep and a half a mile wide. He counted what looked like four squadrons of dragoons supported by several infantry battalions posted to the south of the town. He trained his glass down on several British Foot regiments as they took up position on the flank to protect the harbour.

Beyond the harbour the remaining transport ships lay

anchored to ferry the infantry home. On a high point further away stood a magnificent ancient lighthouse—the Tower of Hercules—built around 1000 A.D. by the Romans during Emperor Trajan's reign to guide their oar-driven galleys safely through Corunna's bay. Ryan was relieved when Soult's army corps, comprising three cavalry and two infantry divisions, followed by the artillery train, finally joined up with his advance guard.

The French staff officers stood on the mountain range above the bay and trained their lenses down on the British positions. Ryan approached the staff officers before Soult recognised him.

'Captain Ryan, good to see you again. You have followed the enemy since they arrived. What's your estimation on the enemy's strength?'

Ryan took out his note-book and read it. 'General, I have counted around fifteen-thousand men, together with eight or nine artillery guns arrayed in two batteries.'

'We have finally cornered the British!' Marshal Soult announced gleefully. 'They are stuck with their backs to the sea!' He perched his one metre-long nautical brass telescope across the back of an officer's shoulder. 'We must not underestimate these men, for they fought well on the march. There's fire in British hearts yet.'

Staff officers, who were also looking through their telescopes, glanced over at Soult and nodded.

'I will hold off in attacking until General Delaborde's division comes up from the rear.'

Ryan couldn't bear the prospect of Darkford escaping. 'If we don't attack soon, the British will escape, General,' he advised hurriedly. Ryan hoped that he hadn't given himself away and he tried to keep his composure

Soult made no reply as he continued to train his telescope

down on the harbour and gazed at the teams of sailors in longboats as they ferried men across the quayside to the ships. He clicked his tongue before he snapped the brass tube shut.

A despatch rider climbed the heights of Palavea, gasping for breath as he furtively handed Soult a message. The French general smiled as he recognised the rider. 'It's one of Delaborde's aides!' he announced as he eagerly cracked open the wax seal and read the high, forward-sloping copperplate handwriting of General Henri Francois Delaborde. 'Well done, Delaborde!' he beamed. 'Gentlemen, Delaborde's division is just three leagues away.'

Soult called for some paper and quickly scribbled a note instructing Delaborde to force-march his men to Corunna as fast as he could as the British were cornered but trying to escape. He turned to the messenger. 'Take a good horse—do not stop for food, just make off as fast as you can,' he ordered. 'I'll speak to the Emperor myself about rewarding you with a *Légion d'honneur* if you're successful.'

Ryan looked on nervously as the aide saluted and jogged down to the French position where a fresh stallion, all black, lay saddled. He hurriedly gulped down a canteen of water, and adjusted the stirrups before he swung himself up, gathered the reins and dug spurs into the animal's sides. The stallion reared mid-air before he sprang forward and galloped away.

'Come on, Delaborde!' Soult urged through clenched teeth and turned to his staff. 'If Delaborde arrives on time, I intend to send three infantry divisions through the British left and centre, while the cavalry under La Houssaye and Franceschi will punch through their right.' He paused, pointing towards Penasquedo Mountain overlooking the bay. 'I want ten guns brought up onto the heights over there; we'll pound the British infantry lines at the foot of the slope with hot cannon.' He clicked his fingers and an officer ran towards him with a vellum map of the town and harbour and hurriedly unfolded it. Soult's finger eagerly hovered over the map, finding his bearings; then tapped sharply on it, pointing to a small village outside Corunna called Elvina. 'We'll concentrate our attack *here!*'

One of Soult's aides-de-camp, dressed in a yellow uniform with blue shako, sprang to attention. Within an hour the French gunners, stripped to the waist, using ropes and tackles, brute force and brawn, had winched and hauled their 8-pounders up the mountain, and ranged them into position. They waited.

General Delaborde's division finally arrived and an order of battle was hastily drawn up.

Ryan and the four other voltigeurs of his company waited in front of the columns of French infantry for the order to advance. A thundering first salvo from the French 8-pounder perched high on the ridge shattered the silence.

The roof tiles of many of Corunna's fine buildings made a deafening '*cor-ro-ump*' sound as they crashed to the ground, not unlike the noise crockery makes when falling off a tray. The artillerymen adjusted their trajectories. The barrages of round shot plunged into the British lines of infantry. The French assault columns with a frontage of twenty-four ranks nervously stood and waited. The order to advance was sounded. A loud roar rose from the front as swarms of skirmishing voltigeurs, followed by the assault columns stalked out and came pouring down the mountain, platoons of drummers vigorously beating out the *pas de charge*.

Ryan listened as the men waited for the pause between the drum rolls to unleash their war cry, *'Vive l'Empereur!'* He smiled as he chimed in with them.

Then the familiar strain of 'La Marseillaise' was sounded with great *élan* as drummers fervently beat the refrain. The hair stood up on the back of Ryan's neck as thousands of raucous voices hoarsely roared out the revolutionary anthem. He knew that from three or four-hundred yards away, the British could now make out the French blue uniforms, the outlines of the men's shakos and the battle-standards of their glistening golden Eagles hoisted high in the sun.

'*En avant! En avant!*' the French officers yelled. '*Tuez! Tuez!*'—'Forward! Forward! Kill! Kill!'

Ryan was skirmishing in pairs alongside Corporal McGowan. He heard McGowan singing 'Whiskey in the Jar' beside him. Ryan joined in with him. They had killed four officers between them and were in their element. This was the buzz of combat, when a cocktail of adrenaline, fear, vengeance and hatred created a strange, enraged euphoria, when men felt they were invincible, and sometimes they were! The prospect of sudden death only increased the rush.

Ryan ducked as a shell exploded just over his head and sprayed the area with the latest British weapon -shrapnel. A Frenchman wasn't so lucky, however. A shell took his head clean off and as he'd raised his arms up instinctively, it had appeared to Ryan, from behind, that his arms went up as if to catch it. 'Poor bugger!' Ryan muttered, but he felt guilty as he couldn't stop laughing at the comical sight.

Ryan shouted out to rally the men. 'Keep firing! Remember, knock out the officers first, then the NCOs!' The voltigeurs gamely darted from one rock to another, hitting the deck when they heard the British officers' order to volley fire.

Ryan ran for cover to reload. As he reached for a cartridge

from his hip bag, he cursed as his clay pipe fell and snapped. He looked around, paused, and listened. The heavy guns boomed as they delivered their thunderous roars, showering all and sundry with soil and gore. The thick smoke generated by thousands of muskets, cannon and howitzers spread out and covered Corunna in a heavy fog of war. He squinted his eyes upwards and saw the French battery perched high above the Heights of Penasquedo continued to pound the town.'

Ryan heard that the *canonniers* were still firing deadly canister shot. They cupped water from wooden buckets to sponge the guns to keep them cool, loading the metal cylinders with various chugs of metal packed with sawdust to spread out the projectiles. He knew they fired blindly at this distance, for even at three-hundred yards they could not distinguish their own from enemy troops. He needed to heed not only the enemy's fire, but also that of his own army.

He shouted to the voltigeurs. 'Watch out for our own guns!'

Boom! one of the guns sounded loudly as it slammed back.

Charred chugs of metal rained heavily on the redcoats, the steel bits plunging mercilessly into soft flesh and lodging deep in skulls.

Ryan followed the trajectory of a shell as it plopped unexploded, next to a column of French infantry behind him. A private breathed a sigh of relief, but it was short-lived. He screamed in agony when a bullet instead entered his thigh and lodged painfully in his groin.

Ryan cursed and shook his head in horror as an ammunition caisson pulled by four terrified horses bolted at great speed, narrowly missing Hoffman. The wagon was ablaze after being hit by a cannonball. Seconds later the ammunition exploded, spattering the horse's entails and drenching the area with blood and gore. Ryan took out his lens, and saw the big sergeant was still on his feet.

The French light cavalry were lurking behind the columns of infantry when the order for the artillery to stop firing sounded, enabling them to advance. The green-coated chasseurs spurred their mounts to a brisk trot before racing towards the slopes of San Cristobal, just beyond the town. They intended to skirt around the British flank to cut off their retreat to the harbour. Ryan saw that the British Foot were struggling, and that without the support of their riflemen they were nearly overrun. The redcoats took post behind stone walls and staggered the enemy's advance with steady fire. The French cavalry withdrew, re-grouped and counter-attacked.

A team of *canonniers* dragged their heavy guns forward, changed their shot, and hammered a deadly mass of metal slugs and musket balls deep into the British position, inflicting horrendous casualties. A *cannonier* loaded and sponged the hot muzzles of the guns. He had just rammed down a shot and was stepping back when his foot caught in the mud. He raised his hands up as he fell, catching the cannon ball as it spun out of the muzzle. His arms were blown off. He looked down in horror at his bloodied stumps and into the face of the artillery captain commanding the battery. The gun was re-loaded without him. The wounded man tried to make it back to the rear on his own, but he quickly bled to death.

Ryan had to pull O'Hara out of the path of a British officer on a cream horse as he dashed through the smoke like a bat out of hell to reconnoitre enemy lines. The horse and rider rounded a corner at such a ferocious pace that the horse slid on its haunches. The British rider, nearly thrown over the animal's head, held fast onto the mare's neck.

Pressing the horse firmly with his knees, he remained mounted and stared face to face into Ryan's eyes, which were mesmerised by this strange sight. The officer smiled and doffed his hat before he galloped away.

Ryan and his voltigeurs fanned out in open order towards the British centre at Elvina and continued picking off the officers and NCOs. A British officer, sword in hand, shouted, urging his men to rally before a ball hit him squarely in the forehead just above the eyes. Ryan had fired the fatal shot and cursed as he reloaded his carbine. He saw that the felled officer was but a teenager. He quickly tore open another cartridge paper with his teeth, poured the powder down the barrel and spat down a musket ball, thumping it hard on the ground, ramming it home. He could taste the saltpetre cool on his tongue as he swallowed which made him thirsty.

A screen of riflemen emerged from Corunna to counter the French attack, 'Les Sauterelles!—'The grasshoppers!' The voltigeurs called out to their comrades as a warning, 'Riflemen!'

The riflemen with their longer rifle range easily out ranged the voltigeurs' Charleville muskets. Ryan turned and saw that the French columns had now reached Elvina. The musicians were playing the strains of 'Veillons au Salut de l'Empire', the great unofficial anthem of the French Republic. The men were fervently shouting 'Liberté, liberté!' and they chimed in with the last line at the top of their lungs —'Les hommes libres sont Francais!'—'Frenchmen are free!'

Cannon balls landed into the packed mass while riflemen whacked their rounds into the French column to weaken their advance.

Dozens fell.

The French officers shouted hoarsely for the men to close ranks. 'Fermer! Fermer!' they bellowed, and those behind instantly filled the gaps, and the blood-splattered columns stepped over the dead and dying and continued forwards, the officers shouting at the men to avenge their fallen comrades.

Ryan paused to reload, shouting the refrain, over and over. *'Liberté, liberté! Les hommes libres sont Francais!'* He took a sip of water from his canteen and looked aghast at the destruction. Enemy artillery was hammering them. Where were the French guns? he asked himself. He looked around for his men and pressed on.

The British held their ground at Elvina. Colour Sergeants uncased their six-foot square colours. The heavy silken Union Jack and a sky-blue Regimental Colour, with royal crest and a jack in the upper left canton, fluttered proudly in the stiff wind to inspire the men. Ryan heard a British officer shout the order to form up. The red coats nervously lined up two deep, while the low roars of the French soldiers were coming closer.

The French infantry had covered a lot of ground now; they were out of breath, and tired. *'En avant! Marche!'* the officers bawled to rally them while their drummers continued to beat the attack charge through the repeated chant *'Vive la France!'*

They marched straight into the thin line of redcoats, now just fifty paces away. The French column hadn't time to form into line.

A British captain cleared his throat. 'Present!' He shouted as hedges of cocked muskets were raised to eye level.

The Frenchmen's faces flushed with fear as they stalled in the face of the impending British volley.

The captain paused, held his breath, and shouted. *'Fire!'*

A tremendous volley punched into the front of the French column. The British reloaded and the Frenchmen nervously stood to receive it. The men in the front of the column moaned and wavered, and reeled left and right before the second volley came. The front face of the column fell as men dropped and staggered from the force of the shock and the officers and NCOs shouted abuse for the men to continue on. A French officer, happy to cover himself in glory, ran impetuously towards a British officer and discharged his blunderbuss at point blank range into the astonished officer's face. He reached over and ripped an epaulette off his shoulder as a prize.

A loud French roar rose up. *'Huzza! Huzza!'* The war cry buzzed and rang in Ryan's ear

Ryan whirled around and saw more French infantry behind him. It was a reserve battalion coming up from the rear. Buoyed by reinforcements coming up and by their officer's dazzling bravery, the column bolted forward into a charge. *'En avant! À la baïonnette!'* The French officer shouted in a thunderous voice.

'Fall back!' shouted the British sergeant. 'For God's sake, fall back!' he screamed through cupped hands.

Ryan had just shot another officer when he spotted a highland regiment advancing. He recognised their uniforms and their tam o' shanters as the Black Watch regiment. He had fought against them in Ireland

The Scottish Highlanders streamed out with bagpipes skirling.

'Fix bayonets!' Ryan heard the Highland officers shout as they prepared to overrun the screen of voltigeurs. The Highlanders' blood pumped with patriotism and adrenaline as the loud skirl of the bagpipes gave them fresh courage. The sergeants thumped the men forwards, cursing in Gaelic, as pipers strained out the Jacobite lament; *'Johnny Cope, are ye waking yet?'*

The voltigeurs, exploiting their advantage as the regiment was still in column, seized their chance and surged forward in their hundreds to pick off the officers. A flame-haired Highlander hadn't even seen Ryan when a ball lodged into his chest and an ensign spun around violently from the force of Ryan's musket ball hitting him in the shoulder. The wounded ensign cursed back loudly in Gaelic *'Mac diolain!'* which Ryan knew to mean 'son of a bastard.'

The Black Watch deployed into line formation without halting, and by doing so, forced the voltigeurs to disperse. Ryan felt fruitlessly in his cartridge box but his ammunition was empty. 'Damn it!' he cursed and called to O'Hara behind him for extra rounds. He took out his canteen, but it was dry.

'These are the last I have,' replied O'Hara as he opened the palm of his hand to reveal five leaden musket balls.

Ryan sighed, removed his hat and took out two cartridges he kept for emergencies in the lining of his shako.

Through the din and black smoke, they heard the order of a crisp voiced British officer. *'Let them loose!'*

A British infantry regiment hoisted their silken colours and, reinforced by the Black Watch, charged the French shouting oaths, threats and obscenities. Ryan thought that the flags looked beautiful fluttering in the sun as he aimed for the colour bearers.

The blue-coated French infantry gave out a tremendous withering volley at twenty-five paces, which stalled the British charge, but only temporarily.

Ryan grasped the shoulder of a young voltigeur. 'Come on!' he cried. A dark patch appeared over the youth's crotch. He was so scared that he had wet himself. The voltigeur looked at Ryan shamefaced.

'Hell's bells!' cried McGowan.

'Quick!' Ryan told McGowan when he observed the

French pulling back, 'Let's get out of here while we still can!' He cupped his hands around his mouth. *'Retirer!'* he shouted in French to the hundred or so voltigeurs skirmishing in the village.

The British Foot lined up two-deep and continued to pour volley fire into the French formations. The French broke and tried to run but as they were still in column, they could not get away easily and ran straight into the tight line of men in the column behind. The French officers thumped and whacked them hard on the backs with the flats of their swords for them to go on. It was to no avail.

'The French are running!' Ryan heard a British officer yell as they pulled back from Elvina. 'Press forward! Kill as many of these *crapauds* as you can!' The British officer leapt forward at the head of his regiment, but he charged too far and ran into the voltigeurs supporting the column. A Frenchman clubbed him with the stock of his musket as another stabbed him in the back and ripped his fringed epaulettes off. He fell to his knees and just when a voltigeur was about to plunge a bayonet into his neck, Ryan pushed the bayonet aside and saved the man's life.

Ryan ran forward and took cover behind a granite boulder. He paused for breath and saw with his naked eye the blue-coated 31*ème Ligne* split into two as it prepared to counter-attack.

The 31*ème* advanced and then it halted to deploy into line. The British Foot closed ranks as they unleashed their muskets, together with a number of forgotten ramrods that whizzed out. The British followed up and charged with fixed bayonets.

The French batteries were still keenly aiming for the British colours as grape shot pounded the badly damaged silken flags. The flags fell as two ensigns carrying them were killed instantly but a burly sergeant swept them up. One flag was on fire and he fanned the flames out and hoisted the flags high through the smoke as a rallying point. Ryan shot at him twice but missed. Ryan's gaze followed the trajectory of a cannon ball as it struck the British commander and he slumped from his saddle, hitting the ground with a groan. He could see that Sir John Moore lay mortally wounded as his shoulder was shattered and hanging on by a sliver of skin.

The French sensed victory, their columns were still pushing ahead, determined to punch through and take the village of Elvina. The men again rose up with the strain of 'La Marseillaise.' British grapeshot poured in. The deadly steel balls smashed gaping holes in the French infantry but the gap closers filled the gaps and continued their forward momentum.

To the right of the British position, Ryan watched the scene unfold as a score of riflemen supported by two infantry battalions came forward. Facing the British were several squadrons of French light cavalry.

'The ground is too rough for the horses,' exclaimed Ryan as he turned to McGowan. 'There are small stone walls blocking their cavalry advance but I don't think their commander has seen them.'

Ryan was right. The two voltigeurs looked on with dismay as *Chef d'Escadron* Lacroix dug in his spurs, giving the order for his chasseurs to advance at a trot and then to a gallop when they heard the trumpets sound the charge. The chasseurs bounded across before stalling on the rough ground. They were trapped and were racked by a point-blank barrage of ferocious rolling fire. They dug in their spurs and fell back. The French cavalry officer could see that a score of his men had made it over the stone walls and, fired up with patriotic revolutionary fervour, he rallied his men for a fresh charge. They were received by the British who, faced with so few horsemen, had no need to form square and fired freely into their ranks.

Another French squadron of cavalry came from behind to reinforce Lacroix's squadron. They prepared to charge. Through the din and the thick, acrid smoke, Ryan heard the British officer shouting. *'Bat-t-a-lion form square!'* and the redcoats furtively began to change from line to square.

'En avant! Au trot!' shouted the *Chef d'Escadron* as he spurred his horse forward. *'Au galop, En avant!'*

'Vive la France! Vive la France!' the chasseurs chanted as they unsheathed their swords and pointed them in the engage position.

'Chargez!'

A trumpeter, distinctive in the reverse uniform of the *9ème Chasseurs*, to make him recognisable in the field, repeated the command as two-hundred French cavalry raced down towards them. They skirted the British square but couldn't get close enough to use their sabres as the fire was too heavy. A score of men fell from their saddles. They bravely returned two more charges before they were forced to withdraw.

'Bloody hell!' cried Ryan. He dived for cover back towards the French lines. Dropping on one knee in some grass, he levelled his carbine and fired, another redcoat fell face down.

Ryan twirled around and then, through the smoke, Wolf emerged and was running towards him. The smoke cleared and Ryan's gaze met a mounted figure wearing a blue uniform of the 4th Light Dragoons. His heart raced as he made out the distinctive pale complexion of the albino. Ryan momentarily froze and trembled uncontrollably. Every nerve and sinew of his body was tightly tensed. He furtively rubbed his amulet before regaining his composure. 'Colonel Dartford!' he shouted hoarsely. The dragoon turned his pink eyes in astonishment in the direction of the voltigeur captain.

'I am Captain Darkford!' he spat disdainfully as he raised his loaded carbine to Ryan and fired but missed.

Ryan lunged at him and pulled him off his horse. 'Get on your feet!' Ryan demanded, as Darkford picked up his sabre and swung it, just missing Ryan's face.

Wolfe came out of nowhere, sprung from behind, and leapt at Darkford, who swiped his sabre through the animal's mid-riff, leaving the wolf whimpering in pain at his feet.

'You bloody deserter!' the albino bellowed. He wrongly assumed that Ryan had deserted from the British.

'I'm no bloody deserter!' retorted Ryan angrily, as he parried the albino's sabre blow. 'You killed my wife and daughter back home in Ireland.' Ryan kicked Darkford hard in the groin and he keeled over double.

The albino coughed and spluttered in agony clutching his hands between his legs, trying to sooth his badly bruised groin. 'I've killed many women and children there. Why should I remember *them*?' he sneered pitilessly.

It was as if in slow motion. Ryan took out his loaded cavalry pistol from his belt, aimed it and pulled the trigger, but at the same time a cannon ball landed nearby, causing Ryan to lose his footing, and he fired wide.

A trail of blood dripped down from Ryan's forehead and entered his eyes. Through the billowing smoke he searched frantically for Darkford and from the tail of his eye he could just about make out the blue-coated figure slinking away, glancing nervously over his shoulder, back to British lines. Ryan chased after him, shouting and cursing, but, faced with a number of volleys from a thick screen of riflemen, he was forced back.

The French frantically sent in their reserves. The British pulled back and abandoned their positions around Elvina. Ryan heard loud shouts of joy coming from the French behind him.

Ryan picked up the wounded wolf and crouched down behind a rock, catching his breath. His legs and hands were shaking violently. He watched as the British infantry were being loaded onto their ships as two Spanish regiments held the citadel until the British sailed safely out of the harbour. He pulled out his lucky pig amulet and vigorously rubbed the piece of bog oak between his thumb and forefinger. He wept, not from fear, but on finally coming face to face with his nemesis, and he vowed again on the soul of his wife and child that he'd avenge their murder.

THE END

HISTORICAL NOTE

Napoleon's Blackguards is the first novel written on Napoleon's Irish Legion and it is based on real events. In 1803 Napoleon created an Irish light-infantry battalion—grandly called *La Légion Irlandaise*—to spearhead an anticipated invasion of Ireland. They initially comprised Irish revolutionaries who had fled to France following recent rebellions against British rule, together with former Irish Brigade officers under the *ancien régime*. The Irish Legion was later renamed the 3rd Foreign Regiment (Irish) and its strength was raised to a four-battalion regiment with headquarters, all told, 2,000 men. It was regarded as one of the best foreign units in the French army (of more than a hundred!), and although its ranks later filled with different nationalities, including many Poles, it maintained a tough, hard fighting, Irish core.

The unit received one of Napoleon's bronze-cast Eagles on the *Field of Mars* much as I have described. The Imperial Eagle symbolised the soul of the regiment as its loss brought dishonour and it would become a battlefield trophy. The Irish narrowly prevented their Eagle from being captured, once by the British in the Low Countries in 1810 and two years later by the Russians while they were campaigning in Poland. Many strived to receive the coveted *Légion d'honneur*, France's highest military decoration. It was awarded for valour on the battlefield, and it was also highly sought after because it came with a generous pension.

For a number of years, the Irish garrisoned the French ports in Brittany, but following the defeat of the combined Spanish-French fleet by Admiral Lord Nelson in the Battle of Trafalgar in 1805, Napoleon cancelled his plan to invade the British Isles and pulled his Irish troops and his other divisions from the French coast. The Irish went on to serve in Germany, the Low Countries and in the Iberian Peninsula. The regiment was disbanded after Napoleon went into exile following Waterloo.

In 1807, Napoleon sent his *Grand Armée*—the finest in all of Europe—into Spain, on the pretext of invading Portugal. However, the Spanish soon realised that Napoleon's invasion of Portugal was a ruse to conquer Spain herself. This led to the Spanish War of Independence, or, as the English called it, The Peninsular War. Two Irish battalions in the French army served two and four-year tours of duty during the war.

Early on in the war in, 1808, the Spanish army, although poorly trained and equipped, achieved some successes, notably with their crushing defeat of a French flying column at the Battle of Bailén. This sent shock waves throughout Europe, provoking the Spanish to proclaim themselves 'the conquerors of the conquerors of Austerlitz.' This victory lifted Spanish morale, for it was a great propaganda coup and undermined French control in Spain. It was one of the few Spanish victories but it was marred due to the subsequent treatment of the French soldiers.

The Spanish army, however, after suffering a string of defeats, were unable to challenge French troops in open battle, but instead took to the hills and adopted a guerrilla campaign against the hated invaders. The *guerrilleros* quickly gained a notorious reputation for vicious hit-and-run attacks and atrocities against the invading French.

For seven long years, hell was let loose onto the once fair

plains of Spain.

England entered the war as allies of Spain against Napoleon. In late 1808, General Sir John Moore's British Expeditionary Force landed in Lisbon, and marched through the Iberian interior to assist their Spanish allies in ousting the French. Sir John's army not only included women and children but also many men drawn from the gutter who came from the wrong side of the law and were difficult to control. They were often farmhands and labourers drawn from many of the impoverished villages across Ireland and Scotland— blackguards, alcoholics and ne'er do wells—happy to receive their shilling a day. Discipline soon broke down.

As detailed in the book, Sir John had planned to fight Marshal Soult but was forced to retreat when he learned that a far larger army led by Napoleon himself was advancing against him, and he feared being enveloped in a pincer movement. The Light Brigade under the harsh disciplinarian General Craufurd's command, was ordered to march west to Vigo, leaving General Paget's Reserve Division, including the 1/95th Rifles to cover Moore's retreat to Corunna. They bore the brunt of the action.

In the end the British escaped, but only just, by means of a harrowing three-week-long forced march through difficult mountainous terrain in atrocious winter weather. They suffered greatly. Napoleon was not the commander of the best land army in the world for nothing and had orchestrated his army's movements with precision and skill, and without Spanish spies and their reliable intelligence; Moore's small British Army would surely have been destroyed.

I have adjusted some sequences and various battles and skirmishes to fit into the story but hope that I have captured the difficulties encountered by both armies during the war. The British lost four thousand men, women and children, captured, frozen to death or cut down by the French during the retreat to Corunna. The focus has always been on British losses, but the French also suffered terribly in the pursuit of Moore, and were almost as exhausted. Some sources estimate Soult's losses alone to be anywhere from 7,000 to 10,000 men, before he even made battle at Corunna.

I have drawn many of the episodes in the book from real events. The 2nd Irish Battalion were one of the first troops to arrive in Madrid, and they subsequently put down the Spanish rising on the 'Second of May', which ignited the struggle for independence from the invading French. They later garrisoned the northern Spanish city of Pamplona when they were ordered to advance on the British as part of a larger French force, but Moore's rapid retreat to Corunna, Dunkirk-style, led to the Irish being ordered to halt at Burgos. One could almost taste Irish disappointment at not having a chance to engage the old enemy, especially as many had fought Moore during the 1798 Irish Rebellion.

Later on in the war, elite companies of the Irish battalion engaged an Anglo-Portuguese army under General Arthur Wellesley, the Duke of Wellington at the Battle of Busaco. Wellington was forced to retreat to Portugal, and the Irish, being light troops, formed the advance posts of VIII Corps that pursued him to the fortified Lines of the Torres Vedras outside Lisbon. They later formed the rear-guard of the French army in daily skirmishes with the British when it pulled back to Spain.

Most of the characters in the book are based on real people, although Voltigeur Kaminski, Corporal McGowan, Sergeant Hoffman and Lieutenant McCarthy are fictional characters, but I have tried to have their back stories and their national characteristics and personalities reflect the men who would have served in the Irish Legion during the period. *Chef de battalion* Lawless, Marshal Soult, Generals Junot, Lefebvre and Colbert, Marshal Clarke, the Spanish rebel leader Don Julián Sánchez, Sir John Moore, and Generals Paget and Craufurd are lifted from the pages of history.

'Any hussar not dead by the age of thirty was a blackguard,' according to the French hussar, General Antoine Lasalle. He was probably right. The black-garbed Hussars of Death with skull and crossbones insignia were modelled on a Prussian regiment called the Black Brunswicker in the British Service who, incidentally, also served in The Peninsular War.

An Irish rifleman, Thomas Plunkett from the 95th Rifles, formed the rearguard with the rest of Paget's Reserve Division and did shoot General Auguste-Marie Francois Colbert with his Baker rifle on the retreat—at a distance of 600 yards according to the legend—much as I have described. However, it is more likely that the distance was 300 yards or so, and this has been a matter of discussion for some time. In any case, no matter the distance, it remained a great shot! I've based the character of Rifleman Tom O'Hara on him.

The book's protagonist, James Ryan, is loosely based on John Allen from Dublin, a key figure in Robert Emmett's 1803 Irish Rebellion, who with a £300 bounty on his head (an enormous sum at the time) escaped to France and joined the Irish Legion. Allen, a real life war hero, famously led his Irish voltigeurs through the breach in the 'forlorn hope,' which lifted the Siege of Astorga in 1810. He was decorated with the *Légion d'honneur* for his actions there and rose to *Chef de Battalion*. Later in the war, Spanish guerrillas captured him and he was badly wounded. A ransom secured his release before he was handed over to the British. Upon Napoleon's removal from power, Allen was arrested, as he was still a wanted man, but he escaped while being taken to England to face a hangman's noose, no doubt. He lived the rest of his days peacefully in Normandy.

There must have been over two-hundred memoirs, of varying qualities written by soldiers who served during the Napoleonic Wars, over one-hundred accounts were written during The Peninsular War alone. I found a number of French publications invaluable in the course of researching this novel, chief among them are Hussar Rocca's *Memoir of the war of the French in Spain*, *The exploits of Baron de Marbot* and *The Diary of a Napoleonic Foot Soldier* by Jakob Walter. I should also mention Captain Coignet's *A Soldier of Napoleon's Imperial Guard* and Von Brandt's *Memoirs of a Polish Officer in Spain and Russia,1808-1813* as well as Bourgogne's *Memoirs of Sergeant Bourgogne*. Also worthy of mention are T.E. Crowdy's *Napoleon's Infantry Handbook* and Stephen Talty's *The Illustrious Dead,* while Byrne's well-written *Memoirs of Miles Byrne* was particularly indispensable in researching the Irish Legion's travails in Spain.

The inspiration for the book's title, *Napoleon's Blackguards* came from the nickname of the 18th (Irish) Regiment of Foot in the British Army—'Paddy's Blackguards.' The 18th Foot stationed the Channel Islands during the Napoleonic Wars and a number of 'Paddy's Blackguards' were reported as having rowed across the Channel and deserted to join the Irish Legion. Joseph Conrad's story *The Duel* inspired Ryan's on-going duels with Captain Carpentier and it, in turn, is based on the real life series of duels spanning decades fought between two French hussar officers during the Napoleonic Wars. The description of Ryan's wanderings in Paris was taken from the Irish Revolutionary leader Wolfe Tone's account of his time in the city.

The Irish were not present at the battle of Medina de Rioseco. Ryan's dash through enemy lines on horseback to get word to the surrounded Irish battalion, who waved their

Eagle up high indicating they were standing firm but needed help, was taken from the French memoirist, General Marbot. The occasion when the Irish Eagle escort fought with their fists to protect their Eagle when their weapons were broken, came from a French report describing the 87th (Royal Irish Fusiliers) Regiment of Foot in the British Army fighting at the Battle of Barrosa, 1811.

When the French landed in Ireland in 1798, some of the French soldiers cut off the tin buttons from their tunics with their bayonets to give to the local children as souvenirs. In the novel, Ryan does the same for the local Spanish children to show he means them no harm. Some descriptions I included in the book simply because they stick in one's mind. An account of the atrocities of 1798 mentions Crown Forces going on the rampage in the Rising's aftermath, bayoneting all those they found. An eyewitness described blubbering, distraught children running to a neighbouring house, telling them to come as their parent's lay dead and the family's pigs were lapping up their blood from the flagstone floor.

I hope that I have portrayed Ryan's post-traumatic stress disorder believably. This frightful condition wasn't recognised as such until later in the nineteenth century.

First-hand accounts of the war in Spain often mention that it was common to see men walking around with a pet rat or mouse, or perhaps with a wolf pup on a leash. The poignant account of how the wolf protected his master's body from the vultures, as all the other bodies had their eyes pecked out, I took from Subaltern Gleig's *Chronicle of the Peninsular War*.

Mark Twain wrote 'truth is stranger than fiction,' and many of the grisly accounts in *Napoleon's Blackguards* were so horrific that I could not possibly have made them up. I hope I have captured the mood of the war in Spain as the book drips with the horrors of war, and contains perhaps some the most vivid and gruesome accounts of its bloody effects written during the Napoleonic Wars. The grim descriptions of medical procedures, of the *cannonier* that tripped as he sponged the guns and blew his arms off, of guerrilla and French atrocities, were sadly true, derived from memoirs. As was the story of the wild pigs that dug up and devoured the bodies of the fallen, in the weeks and months following the battle of Medina de Rioseco, until there was nothing left! What a sad, inglorious end to once brave lives.

Men *were* sawn in two between planks; letters home tell of body parts placed into soldier's mouths when they were left to die, and rats springing in their dozens from yawning mouths. The French did hang bodies outside Burgos's city walls, and left them rotting for many months to serve as a warning to the local Spaniards, but this only incited hatred against them. Indeed, I haven't included it in the novel, but I read that the French governor of Burgos reputedly always kept three guerrillas nailed to a door in the town. When a family member took down one of the bodies at night, another prisoner was nailed there in his place! One supposes that the relatives then left the bodies there to rot.

There are two stories about the fate of the French Colonel Réné—was he sawn in two or boiled alive? In any case, it matters little. The guerrilla's cauldrons *did* glint with severed ears and fingers complete with golden rings. The account of decomposing bodies and body parts left hanging from trees was taken from Francisco de Goya's graphic 'Disasters of War' sketches and other eye-witness accounts. (Indeed, the French firing squad poised to shoot the Spanish resistance fighters in Goya's graphic *Tres de Mayo* painting could just as easily have been, ironically enough, the green-coated Irish Legion, as they suppressed the Madrid rising.) I also took the suffering endured by both armies on the road to Corunna from contemporary accounts, lest we forget the poor horses and mules! To this day, the descendants of those horses who escaped the slaughter in Corunna still roam wild in the forests and plains of Galicia. One would hope that the baby Ryan found at his dead mother's breast on the road to Corunna (again taken from a memoir) survived long into adulthood. But we shall never know.

Ryan and his company of blackguards still have a difficult three-year tour of duty ahead of them in the Peninsula and the dogged pursuit of the evil albino Darkford continues.

THE ORGANIZATION OF NAPOLEON'S GRAND ARMÉE

Napoleon's *Grande Armée* was the finest and largest army ever raised at the time. At its zenith, it comprised 650,000 men organised into self-contained Army Corps, commanded by a Marshal of France, complete with artillery, cavalry and support services, numbering anywhere from 10,000 to 40,000 troops. A division of infantry or cavalry comprised two or more regiments (ca.5,000 men). The regiment was the administrative unit, made up of battalions (typically 500 men) commanded by a *chef de battalion* and comprising a number of tactical units called companies (ca. 80 men). They were led by a captain, assisted by *sous-lieutenants* and NCOs (Non-commissioned officers). *Aides-de-camp* (ADC's) were officers assigned to assist high-ranking officers.

A soldier's training in Napoleon's army was limited. Following two weeks at the regiment's depot, recruits would practise firing only several musket shots a year. Very often firearm training consisted of recruits going through the motions and being given orders for the twelve drill movements, but without powder and ball. In many cases, the recruit learned the trade of soldiering from the hard school of the long grinding march from France through the vast plains of Russia or the arid Iberian Peninsula.

Napoleon was the master of artillery; his favourite was the heavy 12-pounder Gribeauval cannon—which he affectionately referred to as '*Les belles Filles*' (the beautiful girls)—which he used to full effect. In 1812 for example, the French army deployed 600 guns against the Russian army during the Battle of Borodino, firing, on average, 8,000 rounds *per hour* over the day's fighting.

Traditionally, elite voltigeur companies were formed from the most agile men. Light regiments (like Napoleon's Irish Legion), supported by light cavalry on fine, swift horses, formed the advance guard ahead of the main Army Corps, which comprised the Regiments of the Line, the heavy cavalry, the artillery and support units.

Along with the reliance on artillery and light and heavy cavalry, the *Grand Armée's* battle tactics were characterised by closely packed infantry formations marching in column towards the enemy. Nimble pairs of voltigeurs broke away from the main marching column and formed skirmish chains to weaken an enemy's line by picking off officers and NCOs. When they had advanced to within around 60 paces from the enemy, the leading battalion deployed from column and spread out into line to pummel the enemy with a volley. A bayonet charge followed, but if the enemy was too strong, the leading column withdrew and the column behind would form into line and unleash *their* volleys; they would then bayonet charge the weakened enemy to, hopefully, overwhelm them.

This tactic worked well against the Austrians and the Spanish, but less so against the British because they used companies of olive-green uniformed riflemen in loose skirmish lines to weaken the French column as it advanced. Then, when the French column was within range, well-drilled red-coated British infantry were 'told off' by platoons, and they unleashed tremendous 'rolling' volleys down their lines, battering the column, leaving it stunned and stalled. The British would then follow through their wavering ranks with cold steel, which in many cases led to a French withdrawal or rout.

About The Author

Stephen McGarry

Stephen McGarry is an author from Dublin, Ireland. He has spent many years in Belgium where he explored the Continent's links to Ireland. This led to his fascination with the story of the 'forgotten' Irish diaspora—fondly known as the 'Wild Geese'—who fought in most of the defining battles in the 18th century and also under Napoleon. He is the author of *Irish Brigades Abroad*, chosen as one of *The Irish Times'* Best Books of 2014, and has contributed widely on the subject in a variety of magazines, journals and newspapers.

For many years, he aspired to write a novel set during the Napoleonic Wars, drawing inspiration from the likes of Bernard Cornwell's, C.S. Forester's and Patrick O'Brian's Napoleonic novels, but with key differences. The book was to be written not from the British but from the French point of view, and he also wanted to vividly portray the fragility of the novel's protagonist. This culminated in *Napoleon's Blackguards*, his first foray into historical fiction.

He lives with his Belgian wife, three teenage children and a dog, at the foot of the Dublin Mountains, where he writes and enjoys long walks.

If You Enjoyed This Book
Visit

PENMORE PRESS

www.penmorepress.com

HOUSE OF
ROCAMORA

DONALD MICHAEL PLATT

A new life and a new name ...

House of Rocamora, a novel of the 17th century, continues the exceptional life of roguish Vicente de Rocamora, a former Dominican friar, confessor to the Infanta of Spain, and almost Inquisitor General. After Rocamora arrives in Amsterdam at age forty-two, asserts he is a Jew, and takes the name, "Isaac," he revels in the freedom to become whatever he chooses for the first time in his life. Rocamora makes new friends, both Christian and Jew, including scholars, men of power and, typically, the disreputable. He also acquires enemies in the Sephardic community who believe he is a spy for the Inquisition or resent him for having been a Dominican.

Praise for Rocamora, 2012 Finalist International Book Awards:

PENMORE PRESS
www.penmorepress.com

Midshipman Graham and the Battle of Abukir

BY

James Boschert

It is midsummer of 1799 and the British Navy in the Mediterranean Theater of operations. Napoleon has brought the best soldiers and scientists from France to claim Egypt and replace the Turkish empire with one of his own making, but the debacle at Acre has caused the brilliant general to retreat to Cairo.

Commodore Sir Sidney Smith and the Turkish army land at the strategically critical fortress of Abukir, on the northern coast of Egypt. Here Smith plans to further the reversal of Napoleon's fortunes. Unfortunately, the Turks badly underestimate the speed, strength, and resolve of the French Army, and the ensuing battle becomes one of the worst defeats in Arab history.

Young Midshipman Duncan Graham is anxious to get ahead in the British Navy, but has many hurdles to overcome. Without any familial privileges to smooth his way, he can only advance through merit. The fires of war prove his mettle, but during an expedition to obtain desperately needed fresh water – and an illegal duel – a French patrol drives off the boats, and Graham is left stranded on shore. It now becomes a question of evasion and survival with the help of a British spy. Graham has to become very adaptable in order to avoid detection by the French police, and he must help the spy facilitate a daring escape by sea in order to get back to the British squadron.

"Midshipman Graham and The Battle of Abukir is both a rousing Napoleonic naval yarn and a convincing coming of age story. The battle scenes are riveting and powerful, the exotic Egyptian locales colorfully rendered." – John Danielski, author of *Capital's Punishment*

PENMORE PRESS
www.penmorepress.com

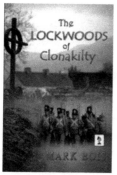

The Lockwoods

of Clonakilty

by

Mark Bois

Lieutenant James Lockwood of the Inniskilling Regiment has returned to family, home and hearth after being wounded, almost fatally, at the Battle of Waterloo, where his regiment was decisive in securing Wellington's victory and bringing the Napoleonic Wars to an end. But home is not the refuge and haven he hoped to find. Irish uprisings polarize the citizens, and violence against English landholders – including James' father and brother – is bringing down wrath and retribution from England. More than one member of the household sympathizes with the desire for Irish independence, and Cassie, the Lockwood's spirited daughter, plays an active part in the rebellion.

Estranged from his English family for the "crime" of marrying a Irish Catholic woman, James Lockwood must take difficult and desperate steps to preserve his family. If his injuries don't kill him, or his addiction to laudanum, he just might live long enough to confront his nemesis. For Captain Charles Barr, maddened by syphilis and no longer restrained by the bounds of honor, sets out to utterly destroy the Lockwood family, from James' patriarchal father to the youngest child, and nothing but death with stop him – his own, or James Lockwood's.

PENMORE PRESS
www.penmorepress.com

A Sloop of War

by

Philip K.Allan

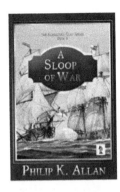

This second novel in the series of Lieutenant Alexander Clay novels takes us to the island of Barbados, where the temperature of the politics, prejudices and amorous ambitions within society are only matched by the sweltering heat of the climate.   After limping into the harbor of Barbados with his crippled frigate *Agrius* and accompanied by his French prize, Clay meets with Admiral Caldwell, the Commander in Chief of the island. The admiral is impressed enough by Clay's engagement with the French man of war to give him his own command.

The *Rush* is sent first to blockade the French island of St Lucia, then to support a landing by British troops in an attempt to take the island from the French garrison. The crew and officers of the *Rush* are repeatedly threatened along the way by a singular Spanish ship, in a contest that can only end with destruction or capture. And all this time, hanging over Clay is an accusation of murder leveled against him by the nephew of his previous captain.

Philip K Allan has all the ingredients here for a gripping tale of danger, heroism, greed, and sea battles, in a story that is well researched and full of excitement from beginning to end.

PENMORE PRESS
www.penmorepress.com

Penmore Press

Challenging, Intriguing, Adventurous, Historical and Imaginative

www.penmorepress.com